COLD DEAD
CASH

LOOK FOR THESE EXCITING WESTERN SERIES
FROM BESTSELLING AUTHORS
WILLIAM W. JOHNSTONE AND J.A. JOHNSTONE

The Mountain Man

Luke Jensen: Bounty Hunter

Brannigan's Land

The Jensen Brand

Smoke Jensen: The Early Years

Preacher and MacCallister

Fort Misery

The Fighting O'Neils

Perley Gates

MacCoole and Boone

Guns of the Vigilantes

Shotgun Johnny

The Chuckwagon Trail

The Jackals

The Slash and Pecos Westerns

The Texas Moonshiners

Stoneface Finnegan Westerns

Ben Savage: Saloon Ranger

The Buck Trammel Westerns

The Death and Texas Westerns

The Hunter Buchanon Westerns

Will Tanner: U.S. Deputy Marshal

Old Cowboys Never Die

Go West, Young Man

Published by Kensington Publishing Corp.

A SHOTGUN JOHNNY WESTERN

COLD DEAD CASH

WILLIAM W. JOHNSTONE
JOHNSTONE
and J. A. JOHNSTONE

PINNACLE BOOKS
Kensington Publishing Corp.
kensingtonbooks.com

PINNACLE BOOKS are published by

Kensington Publishing Corp.
900 Third Avenue
New York, NY 10022

All Kensington titles, imprints, and distributed lines are available at special quantity discounts for bulk purchases for sales promotion, premiums, fund-raising, and educational or institutional use.

Special book excerpts or customized printings can also be created to fit specific needs. For details, write or phone the office of the Kensington Sales Manager: Kensington Publishing Corp. 900 Third Avenue, New York, NY 10022. Attn. Sales Department. Phone: 1-800-221-2647.

PINNACLE BOOKS, the Pinnacle logo, and the WWJ steer head logo Reg. U.S. Pat. & TM Off.

First Printing: June 2020

ISBN-13: 978-0-7860-5110-6
ISBN-13: 978-0-7860-5240-0 (eBook)

11 10 9 8 7 6 5 4 3 2

Printed in the United States of America

The authorized representative in the EU for product safety and compliance is eucomply OU, Parnu mnt 139b-14, Apt 123
Tallinn, Berlin 11317, hello@eucompliancepartner.com

CHAPTER 1

Jake Teale lined up his Winchester's sights on the broad back of the man riding horseback on the trail below Teale's rocky perch. Teale grinned, his heart quickening. He had the old bounty hunter, Weldon Parsons, dead to rights.

Teale drew a breath, held it, keeping the sights steady on his quarry's back, and slowly squeezed the trigger. The rifle belched, spitting flames, the butt plate slamming back against Teale's right shoulder.

Jake smiled again as he watched through his own wafting powder smoke Parsons slump forward in his saddle then drop down over his left stirrup. The bounty hunter hit the ground with a grunt so loud that Teale could hear it from his position a hundred feet up the rocky escarpment. Parsons's horse, startled by the echoing rifle report, put its head down, laid its ears back, and kicked its rear legs straight out behind it, like an angry jackass.

The horse galloped straight up the trail, buck-kicking, reins bouncing along the ground, bouncing higher after a hoof came down on them. The mount followed a curve in the trail and was soon gone from

Teale's sight, hoof thuds quickly fading. Parsons lay in the horse's sifting dust, unmoving on the narrow, two-track mining trail. The beefy man clad in a blanket coat lay on his side, one arm thrust above his head, the other hanging slack over the Colt revolver holstered on his right leg. He'd lost his curl-brimmed hat in the fall.

Jake Teale laughed. "There you go, Weldon. That's what you get for comin' after Jake Teale, you lowly headhunter." He rose from his kneeling position and shouted at the top of his lungs. "Feel good? That bullet in your back—*feel good, does it, Weldon?*"

Jake wasn't worried anyone would hear him. He was high up in the remote Sierra Nevadas west of the Avalanche River and the mountain boomtown of Hallelujah Junction. Oh, maybe a few bighorn sheep, even one or two *human* sheep, sparsely populated the area, the human sheep panning for gold in one of the bitterly cold snowmelt streams that drained this craggy, pine-stippled, up-and-down country. Otherwise, all that inhabited this remote, rocky promontory were eagles, condors, grizzlies, mountain lions, and wolves.

They didn't give a rip about Jake Teale nor about the old bounty hunter he'd just killed—Weldon Parsons. The prospectors, too. They kept to themselves; they betrayed no secrets.

And now Jake Teale had one less scavenger dogging his heels.

"Feel . . . real . . . gooooood?" he shouted again, even louder than before.

As his shout echoed off the craggy spires around him, Teale made his way down the rocky finger he'd perched on. He followed a deer trail down the steep declivity—the same one he'd followed up from the trail after tying his horse in a ravine off the trail's opposite side, well out of sight.

Teale stepped onto the trail and walked toward where Parsons lay, still as a statue. Dead as stone. Jake grinned.

His heart warmed to see the notorious bounty man lying dead like that, sprawled upon a trail in some nowhere neck of the high-and-rocky. Never to be seen or heard from again. Jake would drag the man off the trail and dump him into the same deep ravine in which Jake had tethered his dapple-gray gelding. No one would know. He'd just be gone. As though Parsons had never even lived.

Likely, no one would miss him. Who could miss a man like that—a man who'd hunted men for the bounty on their heads for the past twenty, thirty years? A foulmouthed, old ex-Confederate who'd dragged his raggedy ass west after losing the War of Southern Rebellion and made a living hunting other men . . .

Damn fool.

That was Parsons. A drunken lout and a braggart not above cutting the head off a man to bring back for bounty so he didn't have to haul back the entire heavy, smelly carcass.

Damn savage! That was Weldon Parsons.

Teale continued walking up to the dead bounty hunter, barely able to contain his joy, repressing the urge to break out in song. Nothing stood between Teale and Dixie Wade now. God, how he loved that woman! Imagine that. Jake Teale having tumbled for a girl. Have fallen in love, no less. With a percentage girl, no less.

Hah!

Oh, but Dixie Wade was not your ordinary percentage girl. No, no, no. Dixie had turned to servicing lonely Lyles as a last option. Her good, upstanding family had died in a boardinghouse fire down in Reno, and she'd had no way to make a living for herself. No other way but to practice the world's oldest trade, that was.

Dixie was a charmer. A real charmer. She had depth and intelligence. She had a big warm heart, and that heart and spirit were reflected in her soft blue eyes and in her heart-shaped face with that cute little pug nose of hers. Her warmth and kindness fairly shone like gold in her long, straight blond hair. It radiated like a halo in those satiny tresses.

Jake had never tumbled for a girl before. Not in all his twenty-three years. He'd never really even had a crush on a girl. Oh, he'd enjoyed their bodies, sure enough. He'd *loved* their bodies. But real love for the whole dang package?

Nah.

Not Jake Teale. His heart had been as hard and cold as the stones lining one of these snowmelt streams.

He'd tumbled for Dixie the moment he'd laid eyes on her in the Grizzly Ridge Inn, ten or so miles from the Reverend's Temptation Gold Mine. She'd been singing a church hymn while the old pimp and whiskey-slinger, Heck Torrance, had played the piano. "The Old Rugged Cross," if Jake remembered right. Imagine singing a church hymn in a brothel. Hah! Only Dixie Wade could pull that off and not get struck by lightning. Only Dixie could have all the customers—right down to the last jaded man jack of 'em—holding his hat over his heart and showing the glitter of emotion in his eyes.

He envisioned her now—her sweet little face, long pale neck, cool arms and legs and dancing eyes, her little nose that wrinkled so beautifully when she laughed. All that long blond hair curling around her head when she wore it up or down over her shoulders when she let it tumble where it may. He imagined her taking off her clothes in her second-story room lit by candles, sitting on the bed before him, looking up in that special secret way of hers, a look she reserved only for Jake, as she removed her camisole, making it look so darn sexy and—*whoa, hold on, now, boyo!*

Jake laughed at himself.

He couldn't think about that. He couldn't think about sweet Dixie under the sheets. He still had a few miles to ride, and he didn't want to get bogged down in lusty thoughts. That would only make the ride up to the Reverend's Temptation seem that much longer and more painful on his nether regions.

Teale laughed again, tamping down the heat of lust in his blood.

Soon, he'd have Dixie in his arms. They'd spend one more night in the Grizzly Ridge Inn, which was where she was working now, only a few miles farther up the mountain. Jake didn't mind that she was still working. It didn't mean anything to him because it didn't mean anything to Dixie. It was just a job to her. At least, lying with other men was a job. Jake had known from their very first time together that lying with him was far more than a job to Dixie, though he'd paid her that first time and even for the second and third times.

After that, she was free.

And Dixie had Jake for free, too—his entire being, including his heart.

All right, stop thinking about that stuff now, you cork-headed polecat, or you're gonna get yourself all worked up!

Tomorrow morning, packing the money he'd taken from the last two banks and one stagecoach he'd robbed across the border in California, he and Dixie would light out together. They were going to celebrate their newfound freedom in San Francisco. They were going to get hitched by a real Presbyterian preacher, because that's how Dixie wanted it. She wanted their union to be sanctioned by God. Later, they'd head to Mexico, where the loot Jake had hauled in—almost fifty thousand dollars—would take them so much farther than it would here in their home country.

If they played their cards right, neither Jake nor Dixie would ever have to work another day in their lives.

Teale stopped and looked down again at Weldon Parsons. He frowned, his heart lurching a little in his chest. He could have sworn Parsons's Colt had been in the man's holster just a minute ago.

It wasn't there now, however. The holster was empty. In fact, glancing around quickly, Jake didn't see Parsons's Colt anywhere . . .

In a blur of sudden motion, Parsons lifted and turned his head quickly toward Jake. He raised his right hand. That's where the Colt was.

In Parsons's consarned hand!

"Whoa!" Jake said, stumbling back one half step and throwing his free hand and rifle forward, as though to shield himself from the bullet he knew was coming—and knew he couldn't stop.

Parsons grimaced, flaring his broad, pitted nostrils in pain and anger. The gun in the bounty hunter's hand thundered, flames lapping from the barrel.

The bullet was like a punch from a burning hot fist.

Jake looked down to see red blossoming from his checked flannel shirt, maybe six inches above his cartridge belt. Parsons raked out a curse from taut jaws, and again the .45 barked.

"Oh!" Jake said. *"Mercy!"*

He took one step back and twisted to his right a little. More blood blossomed from his shirt. The second blossom was a little above the first one. Even as he watched, the twin blossoms became one.

CHAPTER 2

Jake returned his gaze to Parsons.

The bullets had come so quickly that only now did Jake realize what had happened. Jake had let his guard down. He'd been so certain-sure that Parsons had been dead that Jake had gotten careless. He'd started thinking about Dixie, and he'd thrown caution to the wind.

Distracted by those lusty dang thoughts.

Meanwhile, the bounty hunter had been playing possum.

Rage filled Jake. Cursing loudly, he raised the Winchester in both hands and levered a fresh round into the action. As he did, Parsons slumped backward, rolling onto his back, his gun hand dropping to the ground at his side. The light had left his still-open eyes, but Jake pumped two more rounds into the man, anyway.

"Damn you!" he said, firing yet another shot into the man's inert body. "Damn you, Parsons!" He fired one more shot before the rifle became too heavy for him to hold anymore.

Jake's hands opened. The rifle clattered onto the

ground at his boots. He took another couple of stumbling steps backward before his knees buckled and he sat down hard on his butt.

"Damn!" he said, staring down at his shirt. "Oh, dammit all, anyways!"

His dipped his right index finger into the blood soaking the right side of his shirt—nearly the entire right side now. Jake raised the finger, looked at the dark red blood. For some reason, he found the sight of his own blood amusing, and he let out a bewildered chuckle.

He'd been robbing banks and stagecoaches for several years now—since he was fifteen years old, in fact, after leaving a bad situation at home—and he'd never once been shot. He'd been shot *at* several times, but never actually shot.

Lead had never pierced his youthful body.

Until now. And here he sat in the middle of the trail, ten feet from the dead bounty hunter who'd shot him, looking at his own blood and chuckling incredulously. Suddenly, the full force of the pain hit him. It was like a giant rabid rat tearing into him. He must have been in shock before, because the wounds hadn't felt this bad.

But they felt bad now.

What's more, he was in real trouble. He was losing blood fast. He needed a sawbones. If a medico didn't dig the bullets out and sew him up, he was going to die.

That thought was like an extra bullet. It left him reeling in terror, his heart racing and skipping beats. *Dixie.*

He had to reach Dixie. She'd know where to find a

sawbones out here, if one existed. He had to believe that one did, or he was a dead man. And he and Dixie would never get that chance they'd been hoping and planning for, of a free life together.

Christ almighty—he had fifty thousand dollars in stolen loot. He couldn't die!

He had to get to his horse.

He heaved himself to his feet. It wasn't easy. He seemed to suddenly weigh three hundred pounds. The maneuver caused more blood to gush out of him. He could feel it leave him, such a terrifying feeling. His very life oozing out of him by the cup, by the pint. He was leaking like a sieve, his shirt growing more and more soaked with the thick, oily stuff.

Weak. Oh God—he was so weak!

He couldn't do anything with Parsons. The bounty hunter would have to lie right where he was. That was all right. The predators would take care of him. A grizzly or a wildcat would likely drag him off during the night and feed on him. Probably by tomorrow or the next day there would be no sign of him. No one would find the body. This was a seldom-used trail, a shortcut to the saloon at the northeast end of Grizzly Ridge.

Jake looked around, got his bearings, then slogged off the south side of the trail and into the high grass and brush. He was so weak that he was almost literally dragging his boot toes. Somehow, he remembered the way down into the ravine, and he made the descent without stumbling and falling and ending it all right there.

He finally reached his horse, Lucky. He'd named the dapple-gray after what had up to now seemed his own boundless luck. Eight years of outlawry including a couple of killings, and, until now, not a single bullet. The law had been after him. Bounty hunters, too. More than just Parsons. Better men than Parsons, in fact. Younger men.

Teale had eluded them all.

Damn Parsons. He'd finally gotten him. Jake had lost his head, thinking of Dixie, sweet Dixie, a vixen under the bedcovers. And Parsons had drilled him twice through his consarned liver!

Oh well, maybe this was a good lesson. He wouldn't make the same mistake again.

Yeah, that's what this was. A good lesson. He'd find Dixie and a sawbones and he'd live to learn from this lesson.

He untied the reins from the aspen branch and crawled heavily onto Lucky's back. The gray sniffed him, whickered edgily. The horse didn't like the smell of blood. Wasn't used to it. He'd probably never smelled it before because he and his rider had been, well, *lucky!*

As Jake turned Lucky away from the aspen growing out of a crack along the ravine's base, he glanced at the saddlebags draped over the gray's hindquarters, behind him. He pulled back on Lucky's reins, stopping the horse. He stared at the bags.

In his condition, should he ride up to the Grizzly Ridge Inn with fifty thousand dollars bulging those bags? He was wounded, vulnerable. Someone would likely lighten his load by fifty thousand dollars and maybe finish him off for his stupidity.

He thought for a time, sucking back the rusty bayonet blades of pain lancing his side.

Maybe he should hide the bags around here some-where. Once he was in better condition, all healed up, he and Dixie would return for the loot and head on over to San Francisco on the other side of the moun-tains and get married.

Once he was feeling better.

Oh God—the pain!

Breathless, vision sparking with the pain of his wounds, and growing weaker from blood loss, Jake nixed the idea of hiding the bags. That would be a recipe for losing them. He likely wouldn't remember where he'd hidden them, and he probably wouldn't be able to give Dixie clear enough directions to the cached loot. No, he'd keep the bags close. Real close.

Groaning and cursing, he twisted around in the saddle. Sobbing with pain, he grabbed the bags off the dapple-gray's rear end and pulled them around in front of him. He draped them over his saddle pommel, half sitting on them.

He'd keep them close. Damn close. Anyone trying to separate him from the bags would get a gut full of lead for his trouble.

He nudged the horse forward with his spurs. He crouched low in the saddle, holding the reins in his left hand, clamping his right hand over the wound, trying desperately to hold his life-sustaining fluids inside.

He put Lucky up the game trail and leaned ever farther forward, trying to keep his seat, to not be hurled back over the horse's tail. Once back on the trail where Parsons lay, already looking pale and yellow, his lips turning blue, Jake swung the horse northeast, meandering between the stony spires and

pine-peppered pinnacles like that from which he'd
back-shot Parsons.

Damn bit of lousy luck.

He had love to blame, he supposed.

Dixie. Oh God, he couldn't wait to see Dixie again!

Chapter 3

"Who in thunder *are* you, anyway, hombre?"

"Deputy U.S. Marshal Johnny Greenway."

"Ah hell!"

"That a problem for you, feller?"

"Yeah, I reckon it is," the dying man said as he dropped to his knees on the ground still wet from a recent rain, the mud and grass around his knees turning pink from the man's blood and viscera. "I was just killed by Shotgun Johnny!"

He dropped facedown and lay quivering as he died. His straw sombrero slid down from his head to lie against his back, fluttering in the strong wind that had blown up after a recent storm had passed.

Running footsteps sounded behind Johnny, beneath the wind, making squeaking sounds in the wet grass. Johnny whipped around, raising both of his signature sawed-off, double-bore shotguns. The right shotgun's left barrel, which he'd discharged into the dead man, was still smoking though the wind was tearing it quickly from the large, round maw.

"Don't shoot, Johnny," the raspy voice urged. "It's Mike!"

"Mean Mike," that was. No moniker had ever been better suited to man or beast.

Johnny lowered the shotguns. "Did you take out the other guard?"

"Of course!" Mike crowed, grinning. He was a little birdlike man with an owl-like face and a lunatic's glittering eyes. He'd tugged his battered, curl-brimmed hat down tight on his head so the wind wouldn't take it.

Dryly, Johnny said, "You must have performed the task a little more quietly than I did."

Again, Mike grinned and drew his gloved right index finger across his throat then glanced down at the big Arkansas toothpick sheathed on his skinny waist.

"You'll do, Mike," Johnny said, chuckling and placing an affectionate hand on the smaller man's shoulder. "You'll do just fine."

"In a pinch," Mean Mike quipped.

Johnny looked down at the dead man and grimaced. He'd intended to take down "his" guard quietly, as well, but the Mexican must have winded him, for he'd turned around suddenly when Johnny had stolen up to within five feet of him. Or maybe he'd heard the soft squawk of Johnny's boots in the wet grass. "I hope none of those other jaspers down at the road ranch heard my Twin."

That's what Johnny called his sawed-off, double-bore, ten-gauge shotguns, each housed in a custom-made leather holster tied down on each thigh—the Twins. He preferred the savage little gut-shredders over revolvers in close quarters, for they were far more efficient than six-shooters, if rather messy.

They were also more intimidating.

That said, he often carried a Winchester in his saddle boot as a backup to the gut-shredders. He'd left the rifle in its scabbard today, however. Since the robbers had taken two bank tellers hostage when they'd robbed the bank in Hallelujah Junction, he'd likely need to steal in close and go to work with the Twins.

"Hell, I can hardly hear myself think up here," Mean Mike said, loudly enough to be heard above the near-constant roar of the wind. "I doubt them tough-nuts heard a thing. They're prob'ly all snug as bugs in rugs down there. What with the rain covering their tracks, they're likely cocksure they done got out of Hallelujah Junction with twenty thousand dollars of Miss Bonner's money. Little do they know what a fine tracker I am!"

The little crow of a man grinned delightedly and bounced up and down on the toes of his mule-eared cavalry boots.

Johnny gave him a blank look.

"All right, all right," Mike said with boyish chagrin. "What fine trackers *we* are."

Johnny broke open the ten-gauge and replaced the spent wad in its left tube with fresh from his cartridge belt. He snapped the Twin closed and looked around, narrowing his dark brown, raptorial eyes as he scrutinized the pines towering around him. His thick, dark brown hair curled down over his ears to touch his neck-knotted red bandanna, the long ends of which flapped around his thick, ruddy neck in the wind.

He started walking through the cedars and spruces

peppering the ridge, holding the ten-gauge in both gloved hands before him. "Keep your eyes skinned, Mike."

Mean Mike hurried to keep up with the taller man. "Hell, I was born with my eyes skinned, Johnny. I came outen my mother's belly so mean I knew right away I was liable to get back-shot even before I left rubber pants!" He laughed through his tobacco-rimed teeth and brushed his bony fist across his nose.

As Johnny approached the lip of the ridge, he dropped to his hands and knees. Mike followed suit. Both men doffed their hats to avoid being seen from below. Johnny gazed down at the road ranch nestled in the canyon directly below his and Mike's position.

The ranch consisted of a two-story, mud-brick saloon with a barn, corral, and privy flanking it. The place had been established here at the junction of two mining trails a few years ago, after gold had been dis-covered in this neck of the Sierra Nevadas, and when the Washoe Indians had been driven out.

The canyon was filled with cool blue shadows now in the early evening. It wasn't as windy down there as up here on the ridge. Woodsmoke rose from the large stone chimney jutting up from the roof at the build-ing's east end. The smoke was pushed down by fierce, errant drafts of wind hurling their way down from the ridge that Shotgun Johnny and Mean Mike were on, shoving the smoke down low to the ground.

A long-haired young man was out in the corral behind the main building, lazily setting feed buckets down for the horses milling there—a good dozen or so mounts still silvered with sweat lather from their recent hard ride out from town. The horses belonged to the men who'd robbed the Hallelujah Bank & Trust in Hallelujah Junction earlier that day, making off with twenty-six thousand dollars in greenbacks and coins as well as two of Sheila Bonner's pretty young bank tellers—Camilla Rodrigues and Rachel Harper.

The robbery had occurred around ten in the morning. Johnny hadn't been in town at the time. He'd ridden out to arrest a couple of moonshiners in a neighboring village for selling whiskey at a nearby Indian agency. Serving federal warrants was in Johnny's purview now, since he'd accepted the job not only of Hallelujah Junction town marshal but a commission as deputy U.S. marshal for Nevada and California's northern district, as well.

He liked having the old moon-and-star pinned to his shirt again, though it weighed heavy at times. Especially when he thought about what he'd given up to get it—namely, the woman he loved.

Aside from the hostler feeding the horses, Johnny couldn't see anyone outside the road ranch's main building. The small, square windows shone with wan lamplight from within. Brother Tobias, the defrocked priest who ran the place, had lit the lamps against the canyon's early night though the flour-sack curtains further muted their glow.

The curtains would make it harder for anyone inside to see out.

"What're we gonna do, Johnny?" Mike asked softly, kneeling to Johnny's right. "How you think we should play it? Wait till good dark? That's likely only about a half hour away."

"I don't see how we have much time to shilly-shally," Johnny said, keeping an eye on the main building. "They have the two young women down there. Probably putting them both through seven kinds of hell while we hunker out here, palavering. Brother Tobias doesn't run whores down there any-more."

Mike was surprised. "He don't?"

Johnny shook his head. "The last three ran out on him. Couldn't take the abuse, I reckon."

"That wicked old gospel grinder!"

Johnny spat to one side in frustration. "If they didn't have the young ladies, I'd say we wait and take them after sundown when they'll likely be good and drunk. As it is . . ."

"We best not shilly-shally," Mike finished the thought for him.

When the gang, which Johnny knew was led by a local toughnut named Red Murphy, had struck the bank, they'd done so lightning-fast. They'd exploded out the front door, holding the two young tellers before them like shields while the rest of the gang had formed a human, rifle-wielding barricade in the street before them. Red Murphy had warned Johnny's two deputies, Mean Mike and Mike's big, taciturn sidekick and former bare-knuckle fighter, Silent Thursday, that if they moved on the gang, Murphy would kill the girls.

The bulldoglike, stony-eyed outlaw leader had said that if in two days he was sure his men hadn't been followed, they'd turn the girls loose unharmed. He warned that if he even just *suspected* he was being shadowed, he'd blow both girls' brains out.

Mean Mike and Silent Thursday knew Red Murphy was not a man to issue idle threats. They'd sat tight in Hallelujah Junction waiting for Johnny. He'd re-turned ninety minutes after the robbery and made the decision to go after the gang despite Murphy's threat. Johnny knew that if he caved to Murphy's orders, he'd only encourage the man and his gang of cutthroats to make the same play again. Maybe even on the same bank.

Maybe next time, Sheila Bonner, the Bank & Trust's beautiful owner and president—the woman Johnny loved but knew he couldn't have—would be one of the gang's hostages. She likely would have been one now if she hadn't been attending a meeting with a local cattleman's association when Murphy's bunch had stormed into town and effected their savage assault.

Johnny was damn glad she wasn't down there in Brother Tobias's perdition. He couldn't have her, but he still loved her more than she could ever know.

Sheila wasn't down there, but it was likely a horrific situation for Camilla Rodrigues and Rachel Harper. One or both could be dead by now. Or wanting to be. When both girls had separately wandered into Hallelujah Junction alone, Sheila had hired and trained them in teller work to keep them out of prostitution. That was the sort of thing Sheila was known for— taking in society's castaways and making room for them in her life.

Johnny knew that from personal experience.

Without Sheila, prostitution likely would have been the girls' only way to make a living, since society frowned upon women who worked outside the home, unless at some domestic chore like housecleaning or sewing or some such. Of course, society frowned on prostitution, too, but that's where most women who didn't have a man to support them ended up out of desperation. Not Sheila, of course. She'd been tough enough to thumb her nose at the norms. When her father had died, she'd taken over the bank as well as the mine he owned—the Reverend's Temptation up near Grizzly Ridge.

"Damn peculiar—society."

"What's that, Johnny?"

Johnny hadn't realized he'd spoken aloud, much less been heard above the wind. "Never mind." He was staring at the building below all but concealed in smoke from the chimney and deep purple shadows, wondering how they were going to get the girls out of there alive.

Finally deciding there was really only one way, he said, "Mike, you take the back door. I'll take the front. Take it slow and easy-like, but once you get inside—"

Johnny stopped. Beneath the wind, his keen ears had picked up the squawk of a door opening. It was followed by a hard, desperate thumping sound.

A girl screamed, *"Nooo!"*

CHAPTER 4

A silhouetted figure just then leaped off the saloon's back porch and into the yard.

The girl's silhouette quickly separated from the building's shadow. A shimmer of copper-salmon light glinted off the girl's bare back as she ran.

Fled.

She wasn't wearing a stitch of clothing. At least, none that Johnny could see from this distance of a hundred yards or so.

Johnny lurched to his feet. "Change of plans, Mike! You take the front. I'm taking the back!"

He bounded down the hill in a leaping run, taking both Twins in his gloved hands.

"Be glad to," Mike wheezed behind him, breaking into his own run down the hill. "I'm a front-door sorta fella, don't ya know!"

Johnny stopped when two men ran out the saloon's rear door and onto the porch. They laughed as, slowing their pace, they dropped slowly, casually down the porch steps and into the yard. One held a rifle. They stopped about six feet out from the steps. The man who was not holding a rifle raised his right hand straight out from his shoulder.

Vagrant light flickered off the cold steel of the revolver in his hand.

The pistol's hollow bark reached Johnny's ears two heartbeats after flames flashed from the barrel. The girl stumbled and dropped to her hands and knees.

"Noooo!" she screamed, her shrill, brittle voice rife with terror echoing around the canyon.

She scrambled back to her feet and continued running.

"Damn," said the man wielding the revolver to the man beside him. "I think I missed her clean!"

"You're drunk," the other man said, and laughed, raising his rifle. "Don't worry—I got her!"

Johnny cursed and ran, heading toward the dark ravine twisting at the bottom of the slope.

The rifle barked.

The girl gave a startled cry but kept running.

The man with the rifle cursed and ejected the spent round before pumping a fresh one into the chamber.

Johnny ran hard along the ravine's floor. The channel's course would take him nearly directly to the girl, who was running toward the ravine about fifty feet ahead of him now. The two bank robbers trailed her with drunken ease and confidence, knowing she couldn't get far.

Then Johnny could no longer see the pair nor the girl as the ravine bank rose sharply on his right.

He could hear the girl running, breathing hard and sobbing. He heard her two amused stalkers talking and laughing.

The rifle barked again.

Again, the girl gave another startled cry.

"Keep running, girl!" Johnny grunted out as he dug his boots in, scissoring his arms and legs, grasping both Twins in his hands. He ran as fast as his long legs, unaccustomed to walking much less running, could carry him.

Running footsteps sounded on his right. The girl was close. Damn close.

Johnny swung to the right and ran three feet up the bank, his head rising above the crest. The girl ran nearly straight toward him, a slender, cinnamon body in the gloaming of the canyon, dark hair flying out behind her. She ran sort of shamble-footed, awkwardly, the rocks and gravel likely tearing at her bare feet.

Johnny crested the bank and ran toward the girl. He could see the anguished expression on her face a quarter second before the rifle blasted behind her. Johnny felt something wet splash against him.

The girl gave a strangled cry as she flew forward into his outstretched arms—her trembling, sweat-soaked body crumpling against him as he lost his traction on the steep bank. He fell backward, clutching the girl to his body, feeling her slacken as they tumbled together down off the bank and into the ravine.

Johnny struck the ravine floor on his back. The girl's body slammed on top of his, for a few seconds knocking the wind out of him. He lay back against the ravine floor, head reeling, grunting against the pain of the violent fall. He lifted his head to stare at the girl lying on top of him, her head on his chest.

"Girl?" Johnny nudged her. "Camilla . . . ?"

She lay unmoving, a dead weight on top of him. Still, he thought he could feel the soft but frenetic beating of her heart against his chest.

He had held on to both Twins during the fall. Now he released the left one and reached down and gently lifted the girl's chin from his chest, tilting her face up toward his own. Her wide brown eyes, at once startled and forlorn, bewildered by this harsh and undeserved fate she'd met, stared back at him. For two or three seconds, those eyes begged, pleaded with him to help her . . . to keep the cold-blooded killers from taking the only thing she had left—her life.

Those two or three seconds passed with savage speed, and when they were gone, her eyes, still locked on his, glazed over in death. They were like lamp wicks turned down to darkness in side-by-side windows.

Voices sounded as the two killers approached the ravine, their boots crunching weeds and gravel. One of them said, "Did you see that?"

"I don't know—I thought I saw *somethin'*."

"Looked like someone comin' up out of the ravine just as the girl . . ."

The man with the rifle let his voice trail off as he and the other killer stopped on the lip of the ravine and stared down at Johnny. Johnny had just rolled the girl off him and raised his right-side Twin. He grinned coldly, fury a wildfire raging inside him, as he raised the savage, short-barreled cannon up toward the two killers gaping down at him.

He rocked both rabbit-ear hammers back with his thumb.

The man with the rifle leaped with a start. "Oh, jumpin' Jehosha—"

The ten-gauge roared like a keg of dynamite. The double-ought buck ripped a big, round hole through the man's middle, picking him up off the ground and throwing him straight back out of sight.

The second man just stared down at Johnny, frozen in place. His lower jaw hung nearly to his chest. His knees quivered. He dropped the pistol he'd been holding in his right hand; it thumped to the ground. He raised both hands, palm out, and shook his head slowly to each side. "Wait, now . . . just you wait!"

"You wait for this, you low-down dirty scum-suckin' devil."

Again, the shotgun thundered, and the second killer went the way of the first.

Johnny thrust up onto his knees. Quickly, with the easy adeptness of long practice, he broke open the shotgun and replaced the spent wads with two fresh ones from his cartridge belt. Snapping the gun closed with a one-handed upward jerk, he gained his feet, leaped onto the bank, and strode toward the saloon humping up darkly against the green sky arching over the canyon. The wind on the ridge was howling like a dozen crazy demons.

Johnny had both Twins in his hands now, each thumb on a hammer.

The saloon's back door opened with a squawk of rusty hinges. Figures jostled out onto the porch, one man saying in a deep, gravelly voice, "What in hell was *that*?"

"Sounded like a damn Napoleon cannon!" exclaimed the shorter man standing next to him.

Johnny kept walking, holding the shotguns down low against each long-striding leg. A red curtain of pure, unadulterated rage had dropped down over his eyes. His heart beat slowly, heavily, pumping boiling blood through his veins. He kept seeing the girl's eyes.

Those pleading eyes . . .

The bigger of the two men on the porch stepped forward. Johnny couldn't see him clearly. He could see only that he was big. Neither was wearing a hat. They were blurred, vaguely man-shaped silhouettes against the pale mud bricks of the building. The bigger man shucked a gun from a holster on his right hip. Johnny heard the click of the hammer being cocked.

"Boone!" the man called in his gravelly voice. "Charlie!"

He stared at Johnny, canting his head to one side, slowly raising his six-shooter. He couldn't see Johnny clearly in the near-darkness of the canyon. He wasn't sure whom he was looking at.

"Boone an' Charlie are in hell by now," Johnny said in a voice taut as piano wire as he drew within fifteen feet of the big man on the porch. "You'll be seein' 'em again in one second, partner."

The big man's eyes widened.

He raised the Colt in his hand more quickly but he did not get it leveled before Johnny's right-hand Twin spoke, flames rolling from the left barrel. The blast picked the big man up and threw him savagely back against the building's rear wall with a heavy *thunk* of fat flesh against adobe. The Colt cracked in his right hand, flames stabbing at the floor a quarter second before the big man's body dropped and he rolled to one side, giving a heavy sigh.

"Oh, oh—whoa now!" the other, shorter man said, trying desperately to unsheathe his own six-shooter. The gun got caught in the holster, or maybe he was too drunk to remember he hadn't unsnapped the thong from over the hammer. Whatever the case, he died still trying to jerk iron, the buckshot turning him to bloody bits and throwing him back into the open doorway behind him.

Inside the saloon, men were scuffling around in a frenzy, yelling.

Shotgun Johnny reloaded his right-hand Twin as he walked forward, snapped it closed, and took the porch steps two at a time. He stepped around and over the dead men on the porch and went inside to join the festivities.

Time to let his hair down a little.

CHAPTER 5

The sawed-off ten-gauge in Johnny's left hand bucked and thundered.

The two men who'd been running toward him, toward the rear door, Winchesters in their hands, were blown back in the direction they'd come from.

Johnny strode forward, stepping over the two dead or dying men, as pistols and rifles roared in the room before him. The bullets sliced the air around his head to slam into the adobe behind him.

Johnny took a quick look around as he passed the crude bar on his left, which ran along the inside of the saloon's rear wall. On both knees behind the bar, the fat and aproned Brother Tobias glanced up at Johnny warily, poking two fingers into his ears against the din of the fusillade. Spread out in the room before the bar, on the cracked stone tiles, were a dozen or so scarred wooden tables. Several of these tables had been overturned, and the ten or so remaining killers crouched behind the tables, throwing lead at Johnny.

He couldn't see much because of the smoke—only parts of a few heads poking up from behind the tables and the flashes of the roaring guns.

That was all right. He didn't have to see much. It was testament to the Twins' effectiveness, spitting broad gobs of double-ought, flesh-rending buckshot charged powerfully enough to pulverize two-by-fours, that he needed only a general target. Still striding into the room, the rage boiling inside him turning his heart to stone, making no room for fear but only a wild vengeance fury, he fired one barrel into the face of an overturned table on his left.

He fired another tube into a table on his right and then triggered the last load at a man who'd risen, howling and clutching his bloody face with both hands, from the table he'd shot into first.

That load of buckshot picked the man up and hurled him into the shadows, knocking over another man who'd gotten up from his kneeling position behind a chair to run toward Johnny, cocking a rifle.

Fresh out of wads, Johnny ran to his left, threw himself over a table, and slammed to the floor on the other side of it. His three blasts had caused the gang a brief hesitation. They no doubt were a little rattled from the ten-gauge's ear-numbing thunder and the howling of one of their fallen, a man who'd taken a blast of buckshot from behind the second table Johnny had fired at, near the building's right wall.

They hadn't figured on being followed here. They'd been arrogant enough to assume their threat had been taken seriously and/or they'd assumed the rainstorm had covered their trail well enough to confound would-be stalkers.

Even Deputy U.S. Marshal "Shotgun" Johnny Greenway.

The problem was this wasn't Johnny's first rodeo.

He'd taken down Red Murphy before. He knew Red's ways, Johnny did. Of course, Red would head east of Hallelujah Junction instead of into the desert to the south or the higher mountains to the west, like most self-respecting outlaws would. Johnny knew Red well enough to know Red would not do what his less-imaginative albeit more self-respecting brethren would do, because that's what Red would think Johnny would *think* he'd do.

And Johnny and Mike had found just enough sign—a few soggy horse apples and a cigarette butt—to confirm his suspicion.

"Damn!" a man yelled in the smoky shadows beyond Johnny. His voice was thick with drink and shock. "What in holy blazes . . . ?"

Johnny pulled a table down in front of him and went to work reloading the Twins.

The wounded man was still howling to his right.

"It's Johnny!" yelled another killer. "Johnny an' his damn gut-shredders!"

Yet another man said, "He's up there—near the bar. Storm him, boys, before he reloads them nasty Twins!"

Johnny could reload each twin in five seconds. It wasn't fast enough.

As he shoved the second shell into his right-hand gun, boots thundered toward him. He looked up and even started to bring up the Twin, but he knew he wasn't going to make it. A big, bearded man in a sheepskin vest and brown slouch hat stopped six feet away and grinned down at him as he snugged a Spencer repeater to his shoulder, aimed down the barrel, and started to pull his right index finger back against the trigger.

Johnny felt a cold spot on his forehead, right between his eyes. That's where the bullet would strike him in less than a single heartbeat.

At least, it would be fast . . .

Still, he continued to raise the ten-gauge but held fire at the last eighth of a heartbeat when a different gun thundered near the front of the room. At the same time, the forehead of the big, bearded man towering over Johnny blew across the upper edge of Johnny's shielding table. Blood, brains, one blue eye, and bits of bone as well as blood dribbled down the face of the table toward the floor.

The big man dropped his rifle and staggered forward, kicking the table then dropping like a windmill toppled by a cyclone, dust wafting up around him from the cracked stone floor.

"Sorry I'm late, Johnny," rose a crackling cry at the front of the church. "I fell and hurt myself comin' down that hill, but I'm here now and ready to dance!"

Mean Mike loosed a coyote-like whoop as he pumped a fresh round into his Spencer's breech.

Johnny picked out another target—a shorter man who'd been coming up on the now-dead bearded man's left flank, and blew the shorter man's head clean off his shoulders. It bounced along the floor— *plunk, plunk, plunk*—like a child's ball. Meanwhile, Mike's rifle barked like a baritone banshee. Johnny could see the little human sidewinder, long gray hair curling onto the collar of his leather vest, standing just inside the church's front door.

Flames jetted from his rifle's barrel as he fired quickly, cackling and picking out targets and dropping the startled outlaws as they turned toward him. When he'd emptied his Spencer .54, he went to work with his .44 Remington, whooping and hollering, face lit up like that of a kid seeing his first elephant.

Staying low so Mike didn't inadvertently blow his head off, Johnny triggered his right-hand Twin's second barrel, blowing a gourd-sized hole in a man bolting toward the saloon's rear door, trying desperately to flee the massacre. As the echo of Johnny's last thundering report hammered around the cavelike room, Mike's Remy stopped barking.

Johnny peered through the smoke webbing through the shadowy room that reeked of whiskey, beer, and the rotten-egg smell of cordite. At the front of the room, Mike tossed his apparently empty Remy onto a table and produced the hideout Colt .41 Thunderer he kept in his boot.

Raising the stubby pistol, he clicked the hammer back but did not fire. He looked around, swinging his craggy-faced head with his little, pale blue eyes from side to side, apparently not finding another target. Johnny couldn't find one, either.

Dead outlaws lay everywhere in pools of dark red blood. They lay twisted on the floor or slumped over fallen tables or, in one case, sitting in a chair with his head tipped back as though the man were only sleeping.

Only one side of his head was missing, blown out by Mean Mike's Spencer .54.

None of the outlaws moved.

All that moved was the wafting powder smoke.

Johnny reloaded both Twins then rose and, flicking a hammer back on each gut-shredder, walked slowly around the room, kicking dead men onto their backs.

Mean Mike stood at the front of the room, covering Johnny with his Remington.

When Johnny had kicked the last dead outlaw onto his back, he turned to Mike and said, "Red Murphy."

"What about him?" Mike croaked.

"Not here."

Johnny swung his head right and left, sweeping the room with his anxious, suspicious gaze. He turned toward the bar. Brother Tobias stood behind it, his long gray hair strewn across the nearly bald crown of his liver-spotted skull. The former priest's eyes were characteristically grim as well as glassy from drink.

"Where's Murphy?" Johnny asked him.

The ex-priest's brown eyes lifted. Johnny swung around to follow the man's gaze to the saloon's left wall. The former sky pilot had strung a curtain of mismatched Indian blankets across that side of the room. Behind the blankets were several squalid whores' cribs in which his former calico queens had plied their trade before they'd gotten tired of the old drunk's abuse and lit a shuck out of the place.

One of those blankets had been flung aside. A man and a young woman with long, thin blond hair and pale green eyes stood in the opening. The girl was trembling. The man was lean of limb and tall with a bulging paunch and red-brown hair that matched his curly beard. Close-set, dark brown eyes stared with a lunatic ruthlessness across the carnage-strewn room at Johnny. The man's square, bearded jaws were hard, and set with a bold determination.

The man wore only a pair of wash-worn long-handles and a dirty green bandanna knotted around his neck.

Red Murphy held the girl taut against him, pressing

the barrel of a Colt revolver against her right temple. He held her before him, shielding a good portion of his body with hers.

He clicked the hammer back and spat through gritted teeth, "Long time, no see, Johnny. Lose the Twins or I'll blow this girl's head clean off her shoulders!" He glanced at Mike, who flanked Johnny and stared at Red Murphy and the girl in hang-jawed surprise. "You, too, you little buzzard. Toss the hogleg onto the table!"

"Who you callin' a buzzard?" Mean Mike snarled, flaring his nostrils indignantly.

"Easy, Mike," Johnny said.

"You heard me, boys!" Red Murphy barked, pressing his Colt's barrel more firmly against the girl's right temple.

Rachel Harper sobbed as she gazed across the room at Johnny. She wore only a grimy man's undershirt that hung low on her legs, like a short skirt. Her blond hair, usually pinned into a neat roll atop her pretty head, hung down across her shoulders. Tears streamed down her cheeks. Her lips trembled.

"Please, Marshal Greenway!" she cried. "Don't let him kill me. I don't want to die, Marshal Greenway!"

"You'll be all right, honey," Johnny said. "I promise you."

"You can't promise a damn thing, Johnny—till you and that snaky little jasper put down your smoke wagons. I mean *now*!"

The girl yelped as the big outlaw pressed his Colt still harder against her head.

"I don't want to die, Marshal Greenway!" the girl sobbed, shifting her weight from one tender bare foot to the other. "Please don't let him kill me!"

"Put 'em down!" Murphy raged.

Johnny looked at Mike, who looked back at him. Mike always looked as though he'd just bit into a lemon. He looked even more so now.

"Put down the hogleg, Mike," Johnny said.

"You sure, Johnny?"

"No." Johnny reached forward and set both of the Twins on a table in front of him. "But put it down."

"All right . . . if you say so," Mike snarled, keeping his eyes on Murphy. He uncocked the Thunderer and set it on a table to his left.

Johnny stared at Murphy. "Let her go, Red."

Murphy stared back at him. A slow smile arranged itself on the man's savage, bearded face. He removed his Colt from the girl's head. But she'd already stopped sobbing. She remained standing before the outlaw, gazing at Johnny. On her face, too, a smile gradually took shape.

"I don't want to die, Marshal Greenway!" she cried. "Please don't let him kill me!"

This time, her pleas were pitched with biting mockery. Her eyes danced with jeering.

Mike turned to Johnny again, his craggy features dark with befuddlement. "What the . . . ?"

The burn of chagrin followed closely by his previous rage swept through Johnny. Murphy's smile broadened as he turned his big Colt on Johnny, keeping one eye on Mike. With his other hand, Murphy squeezed Rachel's shoulder then fondled her lewdly. Her own smile grew on her lips, danced in her drink-bright eyes. Murphy pecked her cheek then turned to Johnny again and laughed.

Rachel laughed, too. She lifted her right hand and poked her finger in open mockery at the dumbstruck

Shotgun Johnny Greenway, who'd tumbled for her and Murphy's ruse. She slid the hand toward Murphy and opened it, palm up. "Red, can I have the honors?"

She had a high-pitched little girl's voice.

Red smiled again, keeping his gaze on Johnny. "Sure, Jane dear. Why not?"

He set the big pistol in Jane's little hand and turned to Johnny. "As savage as she is beautiful. As smart as she is cunning. Why, she's been working for me—or I should say *with* me—for nigh on a year now." He fondled her again lewdly, nuzzled her neck. "I must say I do enjoy her company!"

Jane didn't seem to mind the fondling or nuzzling. Keeping her eyes on Johnny, she wrapped both of her small hands around Murphy's big Colt. She aimed it at Johnny and clicked the hammer back. She narrowed one eye in an almost-seductive stare as she aimed down the long barrel, tucking her plump bottom lip under her upper lip in concentration.

Johnny stood frozen, still trying to work his mind around the masquerade the girl had obviously been performing in town, learning the workings of the bank so she could inform Murphy in preparation for the robbery. Johnny glanced over his shoulder at Mike, who wore much the same expression that must have been on his own face.

"So long, Marshal Greenway," Jane said. "Thanks for coming to my rescue." She tittered a girlish laugh. "No hard feelings, I hope!"

Johnny lurched forward toward the Twins on the table before him. He'd taken only one step before the gun bucked in the girl's hands. The bullet slammed into Johnny's upper-right chest. It was like a savage thrust of a red-hot branding iron, stopping him dead in his tracks and sending him stumbling back and to one side.

An enormous concentration of will as well as fury kept him on his feet. As he staggered to one side, using a chair back to help him regain his balance, he saw Jane swing the Colt toward Mean Mike, standing roughly twenty feet behind Johnny and near the saloon's front door.

The little sidewinder cursed and hurled himself sideways over a table.

Jane triggered the Colt again. The bullet ripped into the table Mike had just thrown himself over, missing the deputy by less than three inches. Jane cursed, hardening her jaws and narrowing one eye as she cocked the Colt again, tracking Mike to the floor.

Johnny stumbled forward.

"Jane, darlin'—Johnny!" Red cried.

In the periphery of his vision, Johnny saw Jane swing the Colt back toward him.

Johnny pulled both Twins off the table and threw himself sideways, rolling over another table to his right.

Jane threw another round at him.

The slug slammed into the table as Johnny hit the floor beside it, almost passing out from the pain grinding inside his chest. Desperately, he raised both shotguns, thumbing all four hammers back with a single swipe of each thumb.

Jane screamed and lowered the heavy Colt to cock it.

"Give it here, Jane!" Red yelled, wrapping his hands around the Colt in the girl's hands.

For half a second they appeared to be fighting over the revolver but then, as though both sensed the jaws of hell opening for them at the same time, they froze and flicked a dark, terrified glance toward Johnny.

He grinned coldly as he tripped all four eyelash triggers.

Jane screamed. Red wailed.

The scream and the wail echoed around the room on the heels of the thundering shotgun blasts as the buckshot-shredded outlaw and his lover disappeared into the crib behind them. Johnny slumped back against the saloon floor, lowering both Twins that suddenly seemed to weigh twenty pounds apiece.

Throbbing, burning pain engulfed him. He looked down to see blood oozing out of the ragged hole in his upper-right breast. When he looked up, Mean Mike was standing over him, staring down at him grimly. The raisin-faced little man clucked and shook his head regretfully.

"Women," he croaked. "I never met one I could trust as far as I could throw her drippin' wet uphill against a Texas twister!" He dropped to a knee and placed a hand on the wounded lawman's shoulder. Concern shone in his washed-out eyes. "Don't die on me now, Johnny boy, or you're gonna make Mean Mike madder'n an old wet hen!"

CHAPTER 6

"Ed, you have to leave. When you're done, you leave. Those are the rules, Ed. You can't sleep here. This is a whorehouse, not a hotel." Dixie Wade looked at the bearded old gent snoring in her bed upstairs in the Grizzly Ridge Inn. He looked quite content, even smiling. Dead asleep and in no hurry to leave.

Dixie swatted his shoulder. "Ed—did you hear me, Ed?"

The old man, lying naked on his back and with skin as white as a baby's behind, grunted, brushed a hand in the air before his face, as though swatting a pesky fly, and resumed snoring. He had a long, hooked nose as red as a railroad signal lantern. A large wart grew out of the side of it, sprouting one long, curly gray hair.

Ed Taylor had fallen asleep after Dixie had gone out to the backyard to clean herself with a sponge and a bucket of water kept out there for that very purpose. She'd returned only a minute ago to find her customer—far-too-*regular* customer, by her estimation—asleep in her bed when he should have lit a shuck by now.

Those were the rules.

Besides, Dixie found Ed revolting. He was old, ugly, and sour-smelling even after the rare bath he took in the creek that meandered near his prospector's shack on the side of Bucket Butte. He always reeked of whiskey, as though his blood was nearly one hundred proof. He even had little insects tangled up dead in his curly, gray-brown beard.

The man who ran the brothel, Heck Torrance, turned no one away as long as they were flush with cash and not shooting up the place. Heck was bedridden now after a stroke he'd suffered last winter, but Dixie and the other two doxies, Clementine and Henrietta, continued to follow Heck's rules. They still had to eat, after all. Dixie and the other two girls in the Grizzly Ridge Inn serviced the undesirable men who toiled in these mountains, but Dixie wanted them out of her room when their business was done.

She didn't think that was too much to ask.

That meant they had to leave when the time they'd paid for was up so she could get her room aired out in time for the next customer.

Dixie gritted her teeth in growing anger. "Ed! Wake up, Ed! You have to leave! Wake up now, dammit!"

Ed's eyes sprang open, startled. He lifted his grizzled head from the pillow. "Huh? Wha . . . ? Wha . . . what's goin' on, Dixie? *Fire?*"

He looked around fearfully, sniffing the air like a dog.

"No, there ain't no fire!" Dixie gave Ed a hard shove. "You have to get out of here. This ain't no hotel, Ed. I keep tellin' you that. You had your fun an' now you have to go. You paid for a half hour. You been here nearly an hour now, so you go or I'll charge you double!"

"Oh hell, Dixie!"

"Don't 'oh hell, Dixie' me!" Again, she shoved him toward the bed's far edge. "Get up and get out of here, Ed! It ain't like I don't appreciate your business," she was quick to add, being nearly as business-minded as Heck was, and sweetening her voice accordingly, "but I've got more customers than you today, Ed . . . honey," she added with a smile she knew did not reach beyond her mouth.

"Oh hell, Dixie!" Ed rose from the bed with a feeble grunt and a curse, his old bones crackling inside the pale, wrinkled skin sagging on his frame like a wet animal hide scraped of hair. "I thought . . . I thought . . . well . . ." Grumpily, clumsy from all the whiskey still coursing through him, he gathered his rancid-smelling longhandles and raised a bony knee as he stepped into them. "I thought we was special . . . you an' me . . ."

Dixie stood at the end of the bed, staring at the man, her faced crumpled with befuddlement. She'd donned her usual corset and silk wrap. That, excepting a few faded feathers in her hair, was about all she had on. That was about all she ever wore except in the bowels of a cold, howling mountain winter. She had a nice body still at twenty-three, and since it was for sale, she was compelled to show it off.

She'd seen in the cracked mirror hanging over the washtub that her face paint was badly mussed. She hadn't bothered to reapply it after her earlier tussle with the always boisterous Melvin Hopkins, a middle-aged game hunter from Reno who stopped here to "frolic" with Dixie from time to time.

She'd known that Ed wouldn't mind the smudged rouge and lipstick. Rather, she wouldn't have cared if he had.

"'You an' me,' Ed?" she said in exasperation. "What're you talkin' about?"

He picked up his worn, knee-patched duck trousers and looked down at them as if considering the torn back pocket. "You always treat me so nice." He looked up at her and smiled from beneath his bulging, gray-brown brows, spreading his lips back from a devil's mouth of twisted brown teeth. "An' you're sooo pretty, Dixie. Why, I declare . . ."

"That's sweet of you, Ed," she said, shaping her own manufactured smile again now, canting her head a little to one side. "But it's . . . well, it's my job to be nice to you. I'm sorry, honey, if you got the wrong idea."

"You don't . . . think . . . we'd ever . . . well . . . marry one day?"

Marry?! she wanted to scream. *You actually believe that I—a girl in her midtwenties who still has her looks despite all the whiskey I drink to get through the day and all the wild, savage men I take to my crib over the course of twenty-four hours—would be so desperate in life and low in my fortunes that I would stoop to the likes of hitching my star to* your *lowly wagon, Ed Taylor???*

The very thought of it made her physically ill.

"No." Dixie shook her head. She could no longer look at the man. She could only stare at the floor and continue to shake her head, keeping her wolf on its leash, her anger at bay. Ed was a paying customer, after all, and business was not what it once had been before the gold had started growing scarce on this end of the ridge and all the men had gone off to work in the Reverend's Temptation Gold Mine on the other end of Grizzly Ridge. They patronized the parlor houses that had grown up around the mine, like wildflowers sprouting around a seep.

Dixie had to keep every customer she had. Even old, softheaded Ed Taylor with his rotten teeth and death odor.

"That's not likely, Ed. I'm sorry."

"You got another fella?" Ed asked, resuming the strenuous task of gathering his worn-out rags, and dressing.

"N-no," Dixie said, halting a little on the word.

She crossed to the room's lone window and opened it to let some of Ed's stink out, to welcome some of the crisp autumn air into the room. "No . . . there's no . . ." She couldn't finish the sentence without her voice cracking, so she stopped and gazed out across the glaringly bright beaver meadow, beyond the creek and the evergreen-forested ridge climbing beyond it. The otherwise dark green forest was dappled with the lemon yellow of the changing aspens.

Pulling herself together, Dixie drew a breath and forced herself to finish the thought. "No, there's no one."

There was not. She'd thought there was, but she'd been wrong. She'd been duped. She didn't think of herself as the type of gal who would let herself get hoodwinked by a handsome face and a trim pair of Levi's, but she had, all right. She tried not to let it bother her.

But it did.

In fact, for a couple of months now she'd woken

every morning with what felt like a dull knife in her heart. She'd gone to bed—to sleep at the end of another long day—with that dull knife still firmly embedded.

"There's no one, Ed." Dixie drew another breath, calming her heavy, anxious heart, and regarded the feeble old drunk sitting on the bed now, tying the laces of his cork-soled miner's boots. "There likely never will be. You see, I'm an independent girl. I'm right set in my ways. High-strung. Some might even say hot-tempered." She tried another smile. "You're lucky not to have me around, Ed. Truly you are."

"I doubt that, Dixie." Ed glowered his disappointment then rose heavily from the bed. He walked over to the wall by the door and removed his ragged hat from a peg. Holding the weather-stained topper in his large, age-gnarled hands, he turned to Dixie and stood pinching the hat's brim for a time, thoughtfully, as though looking for flaws in the felt.

Finally, he looked up at the pretty, blue-eyed blonde. With a sad smile on his ugly face, he said, "Gets lonely, you know, Dixie. Over at the cabin. Just me an' my muskrat, ole Duke. Iffen you ever change your mind . . . hell, I'll try to make you happy. I know I ain't much, but I'd never overwork ya or hit ya. I can promise you that. Not even when I'm drinkin'. No, sir."

Oh, thank you for that, Ed! I could come live in your filthy, falling-down cabin and wash your rags and scrub your floors, but at least you wouldn't sucker punch me when you're stumbling around drunk! Maybe I could even feed your vile-smelling muskrat . . .

Again, she smiled. She tried to make it tender. She knew the man was as lonely as she was. Maybe even lonelier. She canted her head to one side again and blinked slowly. "Thank you, Ed. Good day to you, and hurry on back, now, hear?"

Her own feigned good cheer seemed to cheer him up a little. He smiled, nodded, set his hat on his head, pinched the brim to her, turned to the door, and left.

Dixie let her breath out with a long, windy sigh.

She leaned back against the wall beside the window, crossed her arms on her corset, and stared at the heavy-beamed ceiling of this barracklike log building. Spiderwebs clung to the beams. There was even a bird's nest up there. Earlier this spring, when she'd opened the window to the warm spring breeze, to freshen the stale winter air tainted with the fetor of the many men who'd come and gone over the long frigid months, a robin had built a nest up there.

The bird, realizing its mistake, had soon abandoned the nest, leaving the eggs unhatched. The crib had been far too busy a place for a bird to raise a family in, what with the interruptions of Dixie and her "gentlemen" callers, some who sang and howled at the moon.

Still, the eggs remained. Lying in bed at rare, peaceful moments, alone, looking up at the beam, Dixie could catch a glimpse of the fragile eggs inside the nest of woven sticks; they were the turquoise color of the mountain sky. Pretty little coffins for the tiny would-be robins that would never know life nor the sky that should be their home but would not be.

Dixie felt a large bubble of inconsolable emotion rise in her chest and make its way up into her throat and mouth. She convulsed, head jerking forward, as the sob exploded from her lips.

Another sob followed the first. Tears oozed out of

her eyes to dribble down her cheeks, and soon she was in the full grip of her sorrow. She hung her head and bawled. She raised her hands to her face, splayed her fingers across her cheeks, soaking them with her tears.

"Jake!" she cried softly so no one else could hear her embarrassing display of emotion. "Oh, Jake, why didn't you come back to me, Jake?"

Sobbing, she staggered forward and slumped down on the bed. Instantly revolted by Ed Taylor's deathlike stench, she bounded off the bed, sobbing even louder.

She ran across the room to the wall opposite the bed where an old ambrotype of her and her parents hung from the whitewashed logs. It was the room's only decoration—three dour faces staring dark-eyed into the camera, posed so phonily in the photographer's small studio just as phonily furnished with the lush Victorian furniture of a rich family's drawing room. The kind of drawing room furnishings Dixie Wade's family could never have afforded, her parents having both died paupers when their boardinghouse had burned.

Oh, Jake—why did you lie to me? Why did you let me fall in love with you? Why did you allow me to believe your empty promises?

"Dixie?" a young woman called from somewhere in the Grizzly Ridge Inn.

When Dixie didn't respond, one of the other doxies, the girl who called herself Clementine but whose real name was Alice Munro, called again.

Dixie stifled her sobs, swabbed tears from her cheeks with her hands. "What?" she yelled, her voice pitched with annoyance, anger. "I'm busy!"

"I think you better come down here," Clementine called from the first floor. "I think you better come down here right now!"

"Oh, what the hell is it?" Dixie yelled, her anger building. Couldn't she have two minutes to herself?

"Take a look out your window!"

Dixie swabbed more tears from her cheeks, cursed under her breath. She pushed herself to her feet and wearily strode toward the window on her right. It looked out on the brothel's front yard and Cavalry Creek, which bisected the meadow and along which several prospectors' shacks hunched, sheathed in green grass, sage, shrubs, and a few scattered pine trees.

In addition to the Grizzly Ridge Inn, which sat off by itself, there were enough shacks and stables and even three shops—a saloon, a small mercantile, and a meat market—to make a town of a fashion, albeit an unofficial town. Folks just referred to it as "that raggedy-assed little settlement on Cavalry Creek, near the Grizzly Ridge Inn."

Dixie stepped up to the window and peered through the warped, flyspecked glass.

A rider was crossing the meadow at which she'd stared so piningly only a few minutes before. A lone rider on a dapple-gray horse.

CHAPTER 7

Dixie stared at the lone rider approaching the raggedy-assed little settlement on Cavalry Creek.

He was coming along the trail from the southeast. Dixie couldn't see him well from this distance of a hundred yards. Mostly, she saw only his silhouette. But the horse was a dapple-gray. She was sure of it.

Like a fledgling robin learning to fly, hope rose in Dixie's chest. She placed a calming hand over her heart.

"No," she whispered. "It can't be . . ."

"Dixie!" Clementine yelled again from below.

Dixie turned and hurried toward the door. "Coming!"

As she left the room, she glanced into the room on the opposite side of the dingy hall. The door of Heck Torrance's room was open enough that she could see the big, fat man lying in bed under the heavy white bedcovers, his gaunt, hollow-eyed face framed by his long, greasy hair. Henrietta was spooning gruel into the old pimp's mouth, which he opened only an inch or so. He ate the gruel by rote and without relish, staring out over the end of his wood-framed bed.

Henrietta wiped the cracked wheat and cream from the man's thick mustache with a napkin then glanced over her shoulder at Dixie.

"What's all the fuss, Dixie?" Henrietta was a plump, round-faced girl with light brown hair and rarely any expression, least of all joy, on her face or in her eyes. She usually went to the men who liked their women *with a little tallow on their bones*, and such men were not always gentle. She was sporting a shiner this morning, one that she'd sported for a couple of days. The man, contrite after he'd sobered, had compensated her well the next day.

"I don't know," was all Dixie could say as she hurried on down the hall.

She fairly ran down the creaky, halved-log steps that served as a stairway. As she reached the first floor, she saw Clementine standing silhouetted by the brothel's open front door. She crossed the parlor part of the house in which a small fire snapped and crackled, warding off the night's lingering chill.

As Dixie approached the open doorway, Clementine turned her molasses-black face and amber eyes to her, vaguely puzzled, curious, then wrinkled her peppered forehead and stepped to one side.

"It ain't him, is it?" Clementine asked in her heavy Southern accent.

Her family had been plantation slaves before the Emancipation Proclamation had freed them and they'd drifted west to a new beginning. Illness from tainted beef had taken her family not long after they'd arrived in Nevada to pan for gold, and Clementine's new beginning had been to seek refuge here at the Grizzly Ridge Inn. She'd worked here—mostly on her back but as a housekeeper, as well—since she was twelve years old.

Dixie didn't know how old she was now. They didn't talk much, feeling as though they were in competition with each other for patrons. Dixie was friendly with Henrietta and vice versa, but not with Clementine.

Clementine drew a half-smoked cigarette to her blue-black lips, took a deep puff, and blew the smoke out at Dixie, regarding the pretty blond doxie with the question lingering in her eyes.

Dixie responded neither to the spoken nor unspoken question. She stepped through the doorway and onto the timbered front porch, squinting her eyes at the approaching rider. The man was just then reaching the line of tamaracks and spruces clustered along the creek and which shaded several low-slung, mossy-roofed shacks.

He followed the trail through the trees, the heavy shade of the woods all but concealing him for a few seconds. A few prospectors stood outside their shacks in their traditional dungarees, suspenders, and stout-heeled, round-toed boots, smoking their pipes and regarding the stranger suspiciously.

The man emerged from the shade and into the sunshine as the dapple-gray clomped onto the log bridge that spanned the narrow stream.

Dixie stared, hopeful but also hesitant, troubled. The man was Jake Teale. At least, she was 80 percent certain it was Jake. He rode with a pair of saddlebags draped over the saddle in front of him. They'd slid down the side of the horse so that one bulging pouch was nearly dragging along the ground.

Dixie recognized the man's brown slouch hat as well as the horse. Judging by the way he rode slumped low in his saddle, so that she could see only the crown of his hat, something was wrong with him.

Horse and rider clomped across the bridge. The dapple-gray took a couple of steps along the dirt trail, heading for the Grizzly Ridge Inn and the other shacks beyond it, to the west. A pica streaked across the trail in front of the horse, peeping.

Startled by the rodent, the horse whickered and lurched to one side. As it did, the rider jerked to the opposite side and tumbled out of the saddle. He struck the ground with a heavy grunt and a groan, the saddlebags thumping onto the trail beside him.

"Jake!"

Dixie ran down the porch steps and across the brothel's grassy yard. She ran down the hill toward the bridge, following the secondary trail down to the main trace on which her lover, Jake Teale, now lay unmoving.

She dropped to her knees beside him. "Jake!"

He lay on his side. He wasn't moving. Gently, Dixie placed her hand on his shoulder and turned him onto his back. As she did, Jake grimaced and groaned, opening his eyes halfway. They were bright with pain. His checked shirt was soaked with fresh, dark red blood.

"Oh, Jake!" Dixie cried, cradling his head in her arms, wedging one knee under it for a pillow of sorts. "What happened?"

Jake sucked a phlegmy breath. "Close. So . . . close . . . my Dixie girl." He smiled up at her though it was partly a grimace of miserable pain. "I was . . . damn close, then . . . Weldon-damn-Parsons c-caught . . . up to me . . ." He smiled, blinked slowly, then looked up at Dixie again. "I got . . . a stake . . . for you an' me . . . Dixie." He glanced at the saddlebags that had fallen from the horse. "A good-size stake. It took me a while. I'm sorry I wasn't back wpicahen I said, D-Dixie, but . . . I wanted a good stake . . . you know . . . to . . . to take us to Frisco . . . Mexico . . . live high on the hog . . . just like we talked about."

"Oh, Jake . . ."

Quick footsteps rose behind Dixie. She turned to see Clementine walking toward her, gray skirt swirling around her long legs. The tall, slender young woman still held the quirley as she stopped and gazed down at Jake Teale uncertainly, maybe with a little disgust, even disappointment, in her expression.

"He's been shot," Dixie said, her voice cracking on *shot*. How quickly her delight had turned to sorrow. Her lover had returned to her with money to fund their future together. Only, he'd come bearing a bad case of lead poisoning, as well. "Clementine, saddle up Minnie and fetch Maud Horton. She'll know what to do."

Maud was the stubby, full-hipped prospector's widow who served as a sawbones in these parts, setting bones and delivering babies not because she'd had any formal training but merely because she'd proven to be good at it. She also got a lot of practice, there being no bona fide doctor within a hundred square miles of Grizzly Ridge.

At least, none that Dixie knew about.

"I'm cookin' your dinner," Clementine barked. "Besides, it'd be a wasted trip. He's dyin', Dixie. Can't you see that?"

Dixie had spied movement behind Clementine.

Now she looked toward the saloon/brothel and saw Henrietta standing atop the porch steps, shading her eyes with one pudgy hand as she stared toward the bridge. Raising her voice, Dixie said, "Henrietta, saddle Minnie and fetch Maud Horton. We have an injured man here!"

Minnie didn't hesitate. Dixie saw the plump doxie widen her eyes in instant acknowledgment of the direness of the situation. Hitching up her skirts with her hands, Henrietta hurried down the porch steps and into the yard, swinging to her right and running toward the log barn and corral. Not the sour, contrary creature Clementine was, Henrietta wasn't above taking orders from Dixie, who was several years her senior.

"You're wastin' that girl's time," Clementine told Dixie.

Dixie was about to respond but then she saw that Clementine's attention had strayed to something on the trail near Jake Teale. Dixie followed the black girl's gaze to the saddlebags. One flap had come open during the bags' tumble from the gray. A couple of paper-banded wads of greenbacks had spilled out of the pouch and onto the ground beside it.

The face of Abraham Lincoln stared up from one of the notes, above the bold numerals forming the number 100.

Dixie eased Jake's head down to the ground then hurried over to the saddlebags. She shoved the spilled packets back into the pouch from which they'd fallen and secured the flap. With a grunt, she drew the bags up over her shoulder.

They were heavy. Well over ten pounds. Her mind

flashed again on the face of Abraham Lincoln staring up from that one-hundred-dollar bill, and she felt a little woozy.

He'd returned for her, after all. He'd returned a rich man. But likely a dying man, as well. Her head spun with mixed emotions.

Dixie walked back over to where Clementine stood, exhaling a plume of cigarette smoke, a wry smile causing fine, shallow lines to spoke out away from the young woman's dark amber eyes. "How much he got in there?"

"None of your business." Dixie knelt beside Jake then looked up at Clementine again. "Help me get him inside."

Clementine flicked the quirley stub into the dirt and shook her head. "Oh, he's none of my business!" She turned and started walking back toward the road ranch.

"Clementine! He'll die!"

Clementine threw up a dismissive hand and kept walking.

"How much do you want?" Dixie called, her voice cracking again with emotion.

Clementine stopped and turned back around to face the blond doxie and the half-dead outlaw in her arms. "Half," she said with a shrewd smile.

Rage burned through Dixie. "You go to hell!"

Late that night, Dixie stood in the Grizzly Ridge Inn's second-story hall watching candlelight dance shadows across the door of her room. Beyond the door, she could hear Maud Horton chuffing and clucking and grunting with the effort of her toil. She was a big woman, Maud was, and even simple movements tired her.

Maud spoke in low tones to Henrietta, whom she'd chosen to have assist her in her tending of Jake Teale. Dixie had tried helping Maud, but the blond doxie had kept tearing up at the thought of Jake riding all this way with all that money to retrieve her and to take her to Mexico, as he'd promised he'd do. The weeping had gotten on Maud's nerves until she'd finally kicked Dixie out of the room and called for Henrietta.

They'd been working in there for over an hour. Dixie was beside herself with worry.

She couldn't believe he'd actually returned, just like he'd promised. She'd given him up for a lying cad . . . or dead. He was neither. At least, he wasn't dead yet. He loved her. That was the most amazing part of all. She'd lost hope that he did, but he did truly love her!

No one had ever loved her before. Her mother used to say she did but Dixie had never seen much evidence of it. Her father, a cardsharp who took odd jobs from time to time and who'd been a part-time bartender when their flea-bit boardinghouse had caught fire, killing him and Dixie's mother, had never even bothered pretending he'd loved his only daughter.

He'd been too busy scrambling to feed himself, Dixie, and Dixie's mother. When he wasn't drinking up his earnings, that was.

No one had ever loved Dixie until Jake Teale had sauntered into her life. As though to prove how much he loved her, he'd brought her a pair of saddlebags bulging with money. Stolen money, of course. But money, nevertheless. She'd never had any delusions about who Jake Teale was. She just knew that despite him being a hardened and somewhat notorious outlaw who'd been preying on stagecoaches, saloons, and banks throughout the Sierra Nevadas for several years, he'd fallen in love with her. And she, him.

She didn't know how she'd ever gotten the wounded man not only back to the saloon but upstairs to her room. He'd had enough strength that he'd been able to walk, albeit with a lot of her help. He'd been nearly a dead weight at times but had rallied and gotten his feet moving again just before they'd both been about to fall.

It had taken a good half hour, Clementine having disappeared into the kitchen, where Dixie, cursing the doxie under her breath, had heard her angrily knocking pans around. Dixie knew she was only jealous of Dixie for having found a man, jealous of the saddlebags bulging with money. Dixie would have to keep an eye on the bags. Clementine wasn't above stealing the loot and running away with it herself.

The bags were in Dixie's room, squirreled away in her closet. Soon, after Maud and Henrietta were done tending Jake, she'd find a safer hiding place for them.

Oh God, she hoped Jake lived so they could spend that money together in Mexico!

Dixie took another drag off the cigarette she was smoking and was about to indulge in a fantasy about her and Jake living high on the hog down in Sonora, when the door of her room opened. Henrietta stepped out carrying two porcelain washbasins filled with crimson water and bloody rags. Dixie dropped the cigarette, mashed it out with her well-callused bare foot, and stepped forward, breathless with anxiety.

"How is he, Henrietta?"

Henrietta only sighed and shook her head as she headed for the stairway at the far end of the hall. She'd left the door partway open behind her. Dixie shoved it farther open and stepped tentatively into her room, steeling herself for possibly finding that Jake had died.

She stared at the man in her bed, sheets and blankets drawn up midway on his broad chest. Feeble lantern light danced around the room, illuminating Jake's ruddy, sweat-beaded, unshaven cheeks and thick, sweat-damp chestnut hair as he lay his head back against two or three pillows.

Jake's eyes were closed, but she was relieved to see the sheets and quilts rising and falling. He was breathing, still alive. She could hear him raking air in and out of his lungs. He sounded like an old man with pneumonia or consumption.

Dixie turned to Maud Horton standing at the dresser to Dixie's left. Maud was shoving instruments into a couple of accordion bags she'd arrived with a little over an hour ago, when she'd ridden up to the Grizzly Ridge Inn with Henrietta, Maud steering her single-seater buggy behind a beefy cream mare.

"Maud," Dixie said, moving slowly up to the bed. "H-how is he?"

Maud, a large barrel-shaped woman clad in men's bib-front overalls and with twin jowls, a doughy little nose, and tiny ears, cast Dixie an admonishing scowl. "You wasted my time, Dixie. I dug one bullet out but there's another one still inside him. It bounced off a rib and tore itself to hell. It's in pieces. There's no way to get all those pieces out of him. Even if I went to the work of trying, he'd still die. Both bullets hit his liver. It's shredded. Rarely have I witnessed wounds so severe and the man still alive!"

She closed one of the bags and swung toward Dixie, holding out one small, fat hand, palm up. The hand was stained with Jake's blood. "That will be five dollars. I'm charging you two extra dollars for the long ride out here and the danger involved in traveling these mountain roads at night. There are more men just like *him*"—she tossed her brown-haired head toward Jake—"stalking those trails!"

Suppressing her sorrow, Dixie went to the wardrobe standing near the dresser. She stowed her meager savings in there, in an old cigar box. She opened the box, counted out five dollars' worth of coins, then walked over to Maud and dropped the gold and silver into the woman's open palm. Tears dribbled down her cheeks. She didn't want to cry in front of Maud, but she was having trouble keeping the dam of her sorrow from breaking.

The only man who'd ever loved her had returned to her only to die!

Maud closed her hand around the coins and shook her head reprovingly. "I swear, Dixie—*Jake Teale?* What on earth has gotten into you?"

Dixie turned back to Jake. She entwined her hands together tightly, staring through a blur of tears toward her lover on the bed. "He loves me."

"Hah! The man's a damn killer. He don't know what love is!"

"He does," Dixie insisted, her voice quavering. "He really does love me. I know it's hard to believe, but he came all the way back here to take me away with him."

When Maud did not respond, Dixie turned to see that the woman had gone. She'd left the door standing open behind her.

CHAPTER 8

Three weeks after Johnny Greenway had been hauled back to Hallelujah Junction half-dead, Sheila Bonner reined her sorrel filly off the main trail leading west out of town and onto a narrow right fork.

She rode over a mountain shoulder, the crisp mid-autumn air rife with the refreshing tang of pine and the smell of the sun-soaked pine needles, moldering aspen leaves, and the heavy black dirt of the forest floor. She pulled her tan felt hat down against the sun angling through the pines and the aspens fluttering their autumn gold leaves in the high-country sunlight, then dropped down the slope and into the open.

By way of a wooden bridge, she crossed a creek nearly hidden in deep grass, purple mountain sage, and willows also touched with the colors of autumn, the sorrel's shod hooves clomping over the worn gray half logs.

On the far side of the bridge Sheila passed through more trees offering ink black shade contrasting sharply with the bright, early-afternoon sunlight, then entered a sun-splashed clearing gleaming like jade.

Here she reined the sorrel to a stop, and the horse tossed its head, chomping its bit.

Sheila leaned forward to pat the mount's right withers as she inspected the humble log cabin set in the forest in front of her and swallowed down a knot of emotion in her throat.

She'd been out here before.

In fact, the small cabin before her, with a covered front stoop and a corrugated tin washtub and a pair of snowshoes hanging from nails in its front log wall, right of the door, housed many memories for her. Fairly recent memories. Good memories.

Not all that long ago she'd ridden out here to offer Johnny Greenway the job of hauling gold bullion down from her Reverend's Temptation Gold Mine to her bank in Hallelujah Junction. He'd been the town drunk, literally crawling through the muck and the mud of the town's back alleys, so drunk he could barely stand. But he'd pitched his true colors unexpectedly one day when he'd cut down a gang of desperadoes trying to rob the bank.

That's when she'd realized he was so much more than a drunk. She'd ridden out here that day to offer him the job as well as a new start in life. Her condition had been that he give up the bottle. Then the job would be his. She hadn't expected to fall in love with him. That hadn't been part of the plan.

But she had.

She'd fallen hard.

She still was in love with him, of course. A love like her love for Johnny didn't fade overnight. She was *too* much in love with him. In fact, that's why she'd called off her marriage to the man.

Now as she sat staring at the cabin, remembering, trying not to cry for what could have been if he'd only not accepted the deputy marshal's commission, a liver-colored cat moved out from the shade beneath a hammock hanging from hooks in the porch roof. The cat, as large and ratty as a bobcat, arched its back and curled its tail in cautious curiosity at Sheila's sudden presence.

"Hello, Louie," Sheila said with a smile. "Anyone here besides you?"

She switched her gaze to the cabin's partly open door. It was propped open with an old boot. The same boot she remembered from previous, happier rides out here to visit Johnny and the cat he'd adopted after Louie's previous master, Bear Musgrave, died working with Johnny on a job for Sheila.

The door's being open didn't necessarily mean Johnny was in the cabin. She remembered that he kept the door propped open so Louie could come and go as he pleased. Louie would make sure no rodents got in, or, if they did get in, Louie would make sure they didn't wear out their welcome.

Sheila smiled. A darn good mouser, Louie.

The cat sat atop the steps and blinked his green eyes at her slowly. She could hear him purring. He remembered her . . . from those happier times.

Shelia cleared her throat and called, "Johnny, are you here? It's Sheila."

The only response was the soughing of the breeze in the forest behind her.

Sheila dismounted and tied the sorrel at the worn hitchrack fronting the cabin. She moved up onto the steps, paused to give Louie a few strokes, then crossed the porch to the door. She poked her head into the cabin.

"Johnny?"

He wasn't inside. The cabin was a mess, as it usually was. The bed at the rear of the single-room shack had been slept in recently. Two pillows were piled up against the log wall behind it, and the covers were thrown back. Sheila hadn't seen Johnny since the night Mean Mike O'Sullivan had brought him back to Hallelujah Junction, nearly dead from the bullet wound in his chest.

She'd distanced herself from him, trying to pull back her emotions. Her love for the man. In case he died. She'd told him she wouldn't marry him if he pinned the badge back on his shirt, because she loved him too much to lose him to a badman's bullet, which was likely to happen in these savage mountains. She hadn't wanted him to make any more bullion runs for her, either. If they'd married, she'd wanted him to come work with her in the bank.

"For you, you mean," Johnny had said in an accusing tone.

"*With* me," she'd insisted, taking his hand in hers and squeezing. "Why can't we just be husband and wife, like normal people?"

"Because I'm not normal," Johnny had said.

And he'd taken the job.

Then he'd taken a bullet while retrieving the money stolen from her bank. She supposed she should feel more grateful, but all she'd felt was a deep sickening dread that he would die. After seeing him upstairs in the hotel where he'd kept a room, when Dr. Albright and the doctor's pretty assistant, Glyneen MacFarland, had been working on him to extract the bullet and get his fever down, she'd vowed not to see him again and to put him out of her mind.

She'd ridden out here today, on a rare day off from her work at the bank, to . . .

What?

She herself wasn't sure. She'd told herself she was riding out here merely to thank him for retrieving the bank's money. She'd have thanked any lawman for that. It was common courtesy. Maybe she'd also wanted to tell him that she understood why he'd taken the job as town marshal as well as accepted the deputy U.S. marshal's commission—because that was the man he was.

Being a lawman was Johnny Greenway's identity. He'd been raised in a Basque family as Juan Beristain. When his family had been murdered by ranchers, he'd been adopted by Joe Greenway and raised by Greenway and the rancher's old Basque foreman, Marcel, on Greenway's prosperous Maggie Creek Ranch. Sheila believed that such a splintered history as well as the tragedy that had befallen his wife and young son had rendered his identity murky.

The badge gave him a nonnegotiable one. Neither she nor any other woman could offer anything equivalent to that. He could not simply be a husband or a father; he could not simply work in a bank. That would be like trying to train a wild bear for the circus.

She understood that now. She did not resent him for it anymore. Maybe that's what she'd ridden out here to tell him, too.

Or . . . was there something more?

Why was her heart beating so quickly? Why were her hands sweating? Why did she feel dizzy?

Why, deep down, did she feel so desperate to see him if only one more time?

She turned to sweep the shack's front yard with her gaze. Not seeing Johnny, she stepped off the porch and looked around toward the back of the place, toward the privy.

She called his name again.

Again, no response.

Shading her eyes with her hand, she looked around once more. A footpath led off through the grass and brush to the west. Sheila knew the path climbed a hill on the other side of which was a fishing hole in the creek that Bear Musgrave had, with characteristic immodesty, named Bear Creek since it had had no other name the old mountain man had known about.

Johnny might be out there, taking some sun on his sutured shoulder.

Sheila headed for the path. She'd walked about fifty feet beyond the yard when she stopped suddenly, pondering.

Should she do this? Should she see him?

Why not leave him alone? She hadn't seen him for nearly a month. By now, he'd gotten the message that she wanted nothing more to do with him, that she wanted them both to go their own separate ways.

Wasn't coming out here today only complicating matters?

She tried to turn and walk back to her horse but her feet weren't having it. As though of their own accord, they continued ahead along the narrow, winding path that traced a pale ribbon through the sunlit meadow, birds piping in the scattered clumps of dogwoods and pussy willows, mountain bluebirds flitting about the branches—lovely wisps of vibrant blue even bluer than the mountain sky.

It was beautiful out here, and quiet. She saw why Johnny had returned to Bear's old cabin to finish healing, which he'd started at the hotel in town. He was essentially a loner, Johnny was. A quiet, thoughtful man who needed time to himself beyond the hustle and bustle of Hallelujah Junction.

She'd heard that the Basque people in general were that way. That's why so many had taken to herding sheep in the remotest parts of the Nevada and California mountains after immigrating from France and Spain in the Old World. They felt at home in the Sierra Nevadas because most of them had come from the Pyrenees mountains separating Spain and France.

She followed the path up the hill, lifting the hem of her split riding skirt so she wouldn't trip on it. She crested the hill and, a little breathless and feeling sweat bubbling up on her brow, she stopped suddenly. Below and to her right, maybe fifty yards away, Johnny sat on the grassy slope overlooking the stream. He mostly faced away from Sheila, who could see him clearly from his left flank.

Clearly enough, anyway, to see that he wasn't wearing a stitch of clothing.

He sat with his knees raised nearly to his chest, leaning over them, arms around them. Obviously, he'd been swimming in the creek. His long, dark brown hair hung thickly down his broad back, which was tanned to a deep summer bronze.

He must have been lying out naked in the sun for the past several weeks, taking advantage of the sun's healing rays, for every inch of him that Sheila could see—his back, his left arm and shoulder, and his upraised left leg—were the same deep gold color. In profile, his long, raptorial nose looked especially long and severe. She thought his nose—a Roman nose, some might call it—was the most handsome thing about him.

He was smoking a cigarette and staring pensively down at the creek. He appeared to be smiling. He was happy, sitting there in the sun after his swim in the creek. He didn't look one bit wasted from his injury. A tall, broad-shouldered man, he looked as hearty and hale as he ever had.

When he blew out the cigarette smoke, it was torn away on the breeze. Sheila could smell the smoke even from here. She let it linger in her nostrils, savoring it along with a remembered smell of Johnny himself.

She didn't know why, but seeing Johnny so content annoyed her. Shouldn't he be longing for her at least a little? He had professed his love for her, after all.

She found herself staring at his broad back, his large brown hand lifting the cigarette to his lips. She felt a warmth in her belly, remembering their nights together in the mountains . . . swimming together in a remote mountain lake . . .

Something moved on the other side of Johnny. At first, Sheila thought it was him moving but it wasn't him. It was someone else sitting beside him, previously blocked from her view by Johnny's large body. Sheila heard herself make a small gasping sound when the second person, a woman, leaned forward, sitting up straight, then turned her blond, blue-eyed head toward Johnny.

Glyneen MacFarland, Dr. Albright's pretty, young

assistant, said something, her laughing words ringing like chimes on the cool fall air, carried by the breeze. She wrapped her arms around Johnny's neck, and her lips moved as she spoke to him, her lips only inches from his.

She was smiling, her blue eyes narrowed. They owned an intimate, loving glow, her cheeks flushed like those of a woman whose desires had been more than adequately satisfied.

Glyneen was naked, as well. Her blond hair, a couple of shades darker than usual now, being wet, was pasted with an otterlike sleekness to her head and shoulders. She slid her head closer to Johnny's, and then she was kissing him, mashing her mouth against his.

Johnny wrapped his long, muscular arms around her, drawing her naked body taut against his, returning the kiss . . .

"Oh!"

Sheila hadn't realized she'd exclaimed aloud until both heads turned toward her.

Instantly, her cheeks burned. She lowered her eyes, trembling with embarrassment, humiliation. She raised one hand in a wave of sorts, or of appeasement—she didn't know what the hell it was—muttering, "Sorry . . . sorry, I . . . didn't mean to intrude."

She swung around and started walking back toward the cabin. "I'm very sorry!" she said, louder, keeping her eyes aimed forward, not wanting to see them together again, fearing even now that the last thing she would see on her deathbed was the very two of them as she'd just seen them a second ago.

She heard Johnny's muffled voice on the breeze behind her: "Sheila!"

She picked up her skirts and she ran as fast as she could without falling and killing herself. She ran into the yard and glanced back over her shoulder. Johnny stood on the hill behind her, where she'd been standing a minute ago. He held a wad of clothing in front of him, against his nakedness.

Sheila turned forward again. Her heart thundered in her ears, emotions roiling inside her—shame, mortification . . . regret.

Jealousy as deep as the deepest sea on earth.

She ripped the filly's reins from the hitchrack. *My God, why wouldn't the ground just open up beneath her feet and swallow her?!*

She did not turn back toward the hill again. She didn't want to see him again. Neither of them.

Never again.

She clambered into the saddle. She'd been insane to ride out here! What had she expected? She'd known months ago that Glyneen MacFarland was in love with Johnny. She'd gotten to know him when he'd previously been wounded and she'd taken very good care of him even back then, when she'd known good and well that he and Sheila were growing closer. When they were falling in love with each other.

Obviously, Glyneen had been waiting for Sheila to bow out of his life so she could move in and get what she wanted. Opportunity had struck in spades when he was wounded again a month ago.

Lowly Southern slattern!

Sobbing, Sheila heeled the sorrel back in the direction of Hallelujah Junction.

CHAPTER 9

"What was she doing out here?" Glyneen asked Johnny. She knelt on the grassy slope, holding her fitted shirtwaist against her naked breasts. She still looked startled.

Johnny walked toward her at an angle from the crest of the slope. "I have no idea."

Glyneen continued to frown at him as he sat down again beside her, dropping his balled-up pants on the ground between his legs. He could feel her eyes on him, studying him closely.

"Are you still seeing her, Johnny?"

"No."

"Please, tell me if you are . . ."

Johnny turned to her with a reassuring smile. He slid a lock of damp blond hair back from her cheek with his thumb. "If I was still seeing her, I wouldn't be out here with you."

She smiled. He could tell she wanted to believe him but something was holding her back from completely trusting him. Maybe she knew how much he'd loved Sheila. And still did. Johnny knew Sheila loved him, too—just as much as he loved her.

But she'd made her decision. She would not be married to a lawman.

While he loved her, he'd separated himself from her in his mind. And now he felt himself being drawn toward love for Glyneen MacFarland, the pretty young blonde with a direct, intelligent, blue-eyed gaze, delicious mouth, and a petal-soft Southern accent as pleasing to the ear as a slow mountain rain.

Glyneen also had a heart of gold as high-grade as any in the Sierra Nevadas. She'd assisted Doc Albright in digging the bullet out of Johnny's chest and then had patiently, tenderly, and purposefully nursed him back to full health.

At least, damn close to full health. He'd recovered nearly all of his former strength. While the pain still bit him from time to time, that was growing less severe by the day.

He didn't think he'd have healed nearly as quickly as he had—in just over a month—without Glyneen by his side, distracting him from the pain and keeping him from drinking more whiskey than was necessary to subdue the pain. And then, of course, when he'd finally coaxed her into his bed—which had been no easy task since she was a girl with a strong moral upbringing behind her as well as a sense of professionalism—there was the soothing and restorative properties of the nights they'd spent in each other's arms, as well.

He would lie neither to himself nor to Glyneen—he was not yet *in* love with her, at least not deeply—but he did very much care for her. He enjoyed her company and delighted in her youthful winsomeness and, under the covers, found her beguilingly mature beyond her years. He wanted her, needed her in his life. He had little else beyond his job. He was not ashamed to admit that he was a man with a man's needs.

He'd tried to assure her he would not betray her. He'd done that before—to his wife, Lisa. His betrayal of Lisa with another woman was what he and Lisa had been arguing about the night the men had invaded their home in Carson City . . .

The front door explodes inward, several armed men rush through it, one after another . . .

"*No!*"

Lisa screams and her blond hair flies as she swings around from the dishes she's returning to their shelves in the kitchen . . .

"*No!*"

Johnny tosses away the newspaper he's been reading in his elk-horn rocker and reaches for the shotgun leaning against the wall behind him. Too late. Three men rush him, grab him, bull him back against the wall by the fireplace . . .

"*No! No, dammit!*"

"*Daddy!*" *David screams. He's been lying on the floor in front of the fireplace, reading and penciling away on his schoolwork. As the boy leaps to his feet, a shotgun explodes and Johnny watches in horror as his son is blown back onto the kitchen table, howling.*

"*Nooooo! Oh God—noooooooooooo!*"

Johnny doesn't feel the fists hammering his face, the boots being rammed into his belly and ribs and hips and legs. Instead, he's trying in vain to get to Lisa, who's being ravaged on the kitchen floor by four men. She screams as she's beaten, her clothes ripped off her body and tossed aside like newspapers being swept away in the wind . . .

"Johnny!" Lisa reached out and placed her hands on his face, stared deeply into his eyes, lines of grave concern carved deeply across her forehead. David hovered behind her, a shadow made of dusky vapors, appearing as Johnny had last seen him, turning toward the door in wide-eyed shock a half second before the shotgun had blasted him out of this world.

"Johnny, what's wrong? Come back to me, Johnny!"

Johnny blinked, and then it was no longer his wife—a pretty blonde, as well—gazing into his eyes from only inches away, but Glyneen MacFarland. Johnny's cheeks warmed with embarrassment.

He blinked, cleared his throat, tried a smile but his face felt as though it were carved of wood. Sometimes the scene replayed itself in his mind, catching him unawares. Sometimes he'd be standing on a street corner or sitting in a barber's chair, and he'd be back there in his house in Carson City . . . amidst the chaos . . . the gun blasts . . . the screams.

It had happened to him again now, when he'd been trying to find the words to reassure Glyneen that he would never, ever betray her. Not like he'd betrayed his wife and would spend the rest of his life regretting it, paying for it with a razor-edged guilt that dogged him like a hungry cur.

"I'm sorry . . ." Johnny shook his head, chuckled again unconsciously. He wrapped his arms around the startled girl before him and drew her against him, hugging her tightly.

Still, the uneasy sensation that he was holding his wife, Lisa, was slow to fade.

"I can feel your heart racing," Glyneen said, pressing her cheek against his. She pulled her face away and stared into his eyes again. "Where did you go just now, Johnny? Where were you? What was happening?"

"Not now," Johnny said. "Some other time."

Her brows rose and she caressed his cheek gently with her open hand. "Promise?"

He tried another smile and felt that it came off a little more genuine this time. "You bet. Until then, just know I won't hurt you." He kissed her ripe lips then gazed into her eyes again frankly. "I promise."

"Really?"

"Really."

"It wouldn't be very nice, letting a girl fall in love with you, Shotgun Johnny Greenway, and pulling a dirty trick like that on her."

He covered a wince of guilt with a lopsided smile. "It wouldn't, would it?"

"You still love her, don't you?"

"Sure."

"Do you love me?"

"You bet I do." Inwardly this time, he felt himself wince with guilt. But, then, there was no point hurting her when it wasn't necessary. He may not have been in love with her now, but he was falling in that direction.

At least, he was sure he was. But, then, no one really knew Johnny Greenway, formerly Juan Beristain, least of all himself.

Could it be that he only loved sleeping with her? Could it be that he was only replacing Sheila's body with Glyneen's while his heart very much remained with Sheila?

"Damn, I'm hungry," he said, quickly changing the

subject and shooing the sudden attack of unpleasant thoughts from his mind. "What do you say we go back to the cabin, and . . ."

Glyneen's heart-shaped face blossomed into one of her playful, coquettish smiles, and she leaned toward him, placing two fingers on his lips. "I'd love to, but I have another patient to check on in town. And then my mother will be expecting me home for supper."

At twenty-two, she still lived with her folks in a little cabin along the Paiute River. They'd migrated here from their home in the South, her father having been struck, like so many others after the war, with gold fever.

Unfortunately, Liam MacFarland suffered from the chilblains from too many cold springs and late falls panning for color in knee-deep mountain streams, and rarely left his cabin anymore. Glyneen's mother took in sewing and laundry and raised chickens, and Glyneen helped Doc Albright. In fact, her skills had advanced to the point that many folks around Hallelujah Junction saw her as nearly Albright's equal at almost everything—save the most complicated surgeries—including delivering babies.

So far, Glyneen had kept her and Johnny's burgeoning romance a secret. She might have felt ashamed, he suspected, of having slept with a man she was not married to, which of course flew in the face of her Christian upbringing. And sleeping with a patient was downright unprofessional.

Not that Johnny thought she had any intention of stopping. He knew the way a man can know such things that she was as intrigued by what was happening between him and her as he was.

She kissed him playfully three times then turned to gather her clothes. She gave a sharp, startled gasp. Johnny, who'd started to pull on his longhandles. looked at her sharply then followed her awestruck gaze to where a big man sat a beefy horse on the ridge where Sheila had been standing only ten minutes ago.

CHAPTER 10

Johnny started to reach for the Twins residing in their holsters with coiled shell belt, but stayed the motion. He recognized the big man on the beefy clay-bank gelding as his second deputy, the appropriately named Silent Thursday.

Glyneen must have recognized him at the same time Johnny did. She crawled quickly behind the cover of Johnny's large body, lamenting, "Oh God, we're going to be all over town, Johnny!"

She meant of course that news of their, um, afternoon adventure was going to be all over town.

Kneeling, having only started to pull on his long-handles, Johnny regarded the big man incredulously. Silent sat the horse sideways to the trail, and he and the horse were staring off to the southeast, as though they both saw something of particular interest out that way.

"Silent, what in God's name are you doing up there?" Johnny asked as Glyneen, cowering behind him, quickly dressed.

"Wasn't sure what to do," Silent said in his deep

voice that some folks in Hallelujah Junction had likely never heard. Silent was that tight-lipped.

"What do you mean you weren't sure what to do?"

In his heavy, rumbling, flat voice, almost totally un-inflected, Silent said, "Miss Bonner said I'd find you at the creek. Didn't say nothin' about the two of you. I rode over and, well, I saw the two of you there and wasn't sure if I should say anything or not. I was fig-urin' on how to proceed."

"So, you were just going to sit there . . . ?" Johnny said with exasperation. The former bare-knuckle fighter could be an exasperating man.

"Figurin' on how to proceed, yessir." Silent Thursday kept his eyes on a faraway mountain. The horse seemed to be looking at the same formation, giving its light brown tail a few anxious shakes now and then, as though in acknowledgment of the awkwardness of the situation.

Johnny gave a churlish chuff. "Hold on." He glanced behind to see that Glyneen had pulled on her calico dress with a satin collar and was working on her stock-ings. Her feet were the only part of her exposed now, so Johnny thought it was safe for him to move.

He dressed quickly, his body having been dried in the cool autumn breeze after his swim. He had to slow down, because the pain in his upper-right chest flared up at the commotion, but he finally stepped into his boots and buckled the Twins around his waist.

He waited for Glyneen to pull on her shoes and secure the bone buttons on the side. Her cheeks were flushed with embarrassment as she looked up at Johnny guiltily, tossing her still-damp hair back behind her shoulders.

Johnny smiled and kissed her cheek. "Don't worry,

Silent won't say a thing." He winked. "For obvious reasons."

She smiled, then, too. He knew she was still thinking about Sheila, so he said, "She won't, either. It's not her way. This is still our secret and not one other person will know until you're ready to tell 'em."

"Does that mean you'll be ready sometime, Johnny?"

There was the question. Would he?

He thought he would, but he wasn't sure. The question perplexed him a little, but he tried to not let his eyes betray his confusion. He quickly smiled again and kissed her cheek. "Of course I will, darlin'."

That seemed to appease her, and she returned his smile with a genuine one of her own.

He took his young lover's hand and led her up the hill, remonstrating himself silently with: *You do right by this girl, you loco fool. She's better than you are and you know it, just like Sheila was better. But she's not Sheila. Sheila wouldn't have you, and she's likely better off without you. Glyneen's her own woman, and a good woman, and you need to rise to the occasion for once in your cursed life . . .*

"Silent," Johnny said as he approached the horse and rider at the top of the hill, "we'd appreciate your keeping what you saw here today under your hat."

Keeping his eyes on that faraway mountain, as though Johnny and Glyneen weren't standing beside him, Silent merely grunted and sort of hunched up his shoulders and ducked his head, like a big turtle not sure if he needed to retreat into his shell or not.

"I'll take that as a yes," Johnny said with a bemused chuff. "Now, what brings you out my way today? I know your shift in town isn't over yet." All three men—Johnny, Mean Mike, and Silent Thursday lived together out here in Bear Musgrave's old cabin. One or two of them was in town at all times, however, since they all wore badges and Hallelujah Junction, a rollicking boomtown, needed looking after around the clock.

"Lonesome's in town."

"What's that?" Johnny said with another bemused chuff. He'd swear he spent a good part of his day trying to decipher Silent Thursday's grunts and mumblings.

"Lonesome Stanley."

"Lonesome Stanley's in town."

"Yep."

"Who's Lonesome Stanley?" Glyneen asked Johnny.

"Gunfighter. Wanted as of last year for killing a Wells Fargo detective over in Elko."

"Mean Mike sent me to fetch you," Silent said, keeping his eyes on that mountain, as if he so much as glanced at Johnny and Glyneen, he'd turn to salt. "Federal warrant on him, Mike says. Told me to ride out here, find out how to proceed."

He turned his head slowly. His head was twice the size of most men's heads, shaggy with a cinnamon beard and thick, curly brows set over hazel, deep-socketed eyes. He was several inches taller than Johnny's own six foot four—a hulking, brooding giant of a man whose very presence frightened ladies and children and set babies to crying.

He was somewhere in his early forties , and it was generally believed that all the fighting he'd done across the frontier and even along the Mississippi, with Mike as his manager, had done damage to his thinker box. Johnny suspected that wasn't true. He suspected that Silent Thursday was far more insightful than he let on. Johnny had seen signs that the man had an enormous heart, though Silent tried hard to conceal that fact. Johnny had decided that Silent was silent mainly due to shyness.

Now he focused his eyes, reflecting the lemon hues of the west-angling sun, on Glyneen and said as though around a mouthful of rocks, "Miss MacFarland, I didn't, uh . . . uh, I didn't see nothin'."

"What?" Glyneen said, puzzled.

"I didn't see nothin'. Not much, leastways." Silent flinched a little, as though he thought he might have dug his hole a little deeper, and looked away again.

"Oh!" Understanding, Glyneen glanced at Johnny, her cheeks flushing again. Returning her gaze to the big man on the horse, she favored him with a tender smile. "Thank you for your discretion, Silent."

"Mmmm-hmmm."

Johnny couldn't help chuckling at the big man's obvious unease. Then he said, "Where was Lonesome Stanley when you left town, Silent?"

"Hotel bar." Silent touched his thumb to his lower lip and tipped his head back, implying that the gunfighter turned road agent appeared to have been getting a load on.

"All right—you can head back to town, Silent. Don't approach Lonesome but keep an eye on him. I'll be back to town shortly."

"Mmmm-hmmm."

When Silent had ridden off, Glyneen looked up at Johnny with concern. "I don't think you're ready to get back to work yet, Johnny. The doc thinks you should avoid physical strain for at least another week."

"Then he shouldn't have sent you out here." Johnny smiled.

Glyneen blushed and gave a lopsided grin.

"Come on." Johnny took her hand again and started leading her down the path toward the cabin. "I'll hitch your buggy then follow you back to town." She gave him a troubled look, so he added, "Don't worry, I'll make sure you're well ahead of me. No one will know."

She smiled then frowned again. "Are you sure you're ready, Johnny?"

"That swim and a tussle with you didn't do me any harm, so"—he raised her hand to his lips and kissed it—"yeah, I think I'm ready."

Glyneen laughed.

An hour later, the outlying shacks of Hallelujah Junction slid up around Johnny and his horse—a fine cream stallion he called Ghost—among the boulders and pines. A block ahead, Glyneen glanced over her shoulder at Johnny, gave a furtive wave, then swung her horse and buggy down a side street to the north and clomped onto one of the bridges that spanned the several tributaries of the Paiute River that threaded this canyon-dwelling boomtown.

Johnny followed the main street, which curved along the same route as the Paiute River, along whose banks the town had been built, west toward his jail-house office and the heart of the business district. The Sierra Nevada Hotel sat in the center of town, in a southward curve of the river as well as of the main street, or Paiute Street.

The street was crowded with wagons and buggies of all shapes and sizes and men and women of all shapes, sizes, and colors, as well. There were whites and blacks and brown-skinned men as well as a few Chinese who'd drifted to the mountain mining camps after they'd finished their work building the transcontinental railroad.

The sons and sisters of Han ran meat markets and grocery and clothing stores as well as laundries, bathhouses, and opium parlors. A Chinese woman who called herself Pearl ran the largest brothel in town. She commanded a tight ship, brooked no trouble, and had three sizable bouncers at her beck and call. Johnny, Mean Mike, and Silent Thursday were rarely summoned to the large, Victorian-like house on Virginia City Street to quell an argument or haul away a belligerent drunk.

Men knew to behave in Pearl's place or get tossed into the street and face a lifetime ban from the premises. No one wanted that, for Pearl served up some of the most beautiful and talented doxies in northern California, western Nevada.

Now as Johnny rounded another bend in the street, a gun blasted from somewhere ahead. A couple of blocks beyond, the Sierra Nevada Hotel raised its purple-painted, white-trimmed three stories high and proud above its log-framed first story and the surrounding other business establishments. On the street fronting the hotel was a notable lack of activity.

In fact, that part of the street was deserted. Then Johnny saw several men and a few women crouching behind rain barrels, water troughs, and wagons on the boardwalk across the street from the hulking purple building. Several more men were standing to each side of the hotel, peering cautiously around the front corners toward the street-facing windows and double front doors.

The gun belched again. And again.

A man shouted, and Johnny realized that the gunfire and the shouting were coming from inside the Sierra Nevada. He also realized that the two men standing on the hotel's near side, bellied up to the side of the hotel, their backs to Johnny and peering around the building's corner to the front, were his two deputies—the diminutive Mean Mike and the hulking giant, Silent Thursday.

Johnny spurred Ghost into a hard gallop, angling the horse to the street's left side. As he approached the Sierra Nevada's front corner, Mean Mike and Silent Thursday jerked their heads and anxious gazes toward him. Johnny brought Ghost to a sliding halt then swung down from the saddle and dropped his reins to ground-tie the well-trained mount.

Johnny ran up to where Mean Mike and Silent Thursday stood pressed up against the hotel's east wall just as two more gunshots cracked inside the place and a man shouted, "Damn devils is everywhere! What the hell kinda place you runnin', Brennan?"

Another gunshot. A girl screamed.

Johnny glanced at Mean Mike. "Lonesome?"

Mike dipped his chin in the affirmative. "Crazy polecat's goin' crazy! Just plumb loco, shootin' the place up! Just started a couple minutes ago! Me an' Silent was standin' out here, keepin' an eye on the place in case Lonesome left. We was keepin' tabs on Lonesome, like you said. Then suddenly there's a damn gunshot and folks yell and scream and come boilin' out of the hotel and into the street!"

"Anyone been hit?" Johnny asked.

"No. Just snakes." Mike pointed at his own temple. "The ones in Lonesome's head. But he's put a couple bullets through the front window and came close to pinkin' Windy Farmer!"

"Who's the girl inside?"

"One of the serving girls tripped on her way out of the place and rolled behind the piano. I seen her through the window. When Lonesome puts a bullet into the piano, she screams."

"Understandable."

"Yeah, I ain't faultin' her fer it."

Johnny slid both Twins from their holsters. "All right."

"You goin' in?" Mean Mike asked in exasperation.

"Yep."

As Johnny started around the hotel's front corner, heading for the front door, Mike said, "Hold on, Johnny! We'll go in the back. Johnny, wait!"

When Johnny was out of sight, his boots clomping on the boardwalk fronting the hotel, spurs chinging, Mike turned to Silent Thursday and said, *"See how he is?"*

Mike ran crouching down the side of the hotel toward the back. Silent slouched heavily along behind the little man, rifle on his shoulder.

Meanwhile, Johnny strode along the boardwalk, passing the windows of the hotel dining room on his left and then the heavy-timbered front doors. Just beyond the doors, he stopped at the first of two windows behind which was the saloon part of the hotel.

CHAPTER 11

The saloon was tony for this neck of the woods—elaborate mahogany bar at the rear, with a backbar outfitted with a leaded mirror. A brass footrail ran along the base of the bar. Brass spittoons were laid out here and there to keep as much of the chaw and as many cigarette and cigar butts off the uncarpeted wooden floor as possible.

There were over a dozen tables between the bar and the front wall. A baby grand piano sat against the wall to the right, under a large Confederate flag over which the head of a snarling grizzly had been mounted.

The serving girl, whom Johnny recognized as Norma Jean Whaley, cowered behind the black piano. He could see her peeking out from behind it now toward the window through which Johnny was peering. She gazed at him with beseeching in her wide, brown eyes.

Johnny returned his gaze to the only man in the room.

Lonesome Stanley danced oddly atop one of the dozen or so tables, almost in the room's center. He waved two pistols around. He wore an opera hat, a corduroy vest, and a black silk shirt with red sleeve gaiters, and corduroy trousers.

A red bandanna was knotted around his long leathery neck. He was tall and bearded, in his early forties. Oval steel spectacles were perched on his nose that was nearly as long and raptorial as Johnny's own Basque beak.

But Stanley was no Basque. He was a gunfighter and gambler originally from England but more recently from Missouri. His natural drunken truculence had made him a natural fit with those warmongering, moonshine-swilling hillbillies, and he'd joined the war not so much to keep the blacks enslaved but because he loved a good fight.

He'd come west after the war with a notorious appetite for rotgut whiskey, women, and five-card stud. It was said he'd been part of a gang that had robbed trains and stagecoaches, but no charges had ever stuck to the slippery English ex-Confederate.

The lout and drunkard had brashly prowled the West, gambling and killing "in self-defense" until someone had identified him two years ago robbing a mail train with two other road agents whom two express guards had sent to their rewards filled with buckshot. The U.S. Marshal for the Western Region had ordered up wanted dodgers bearing Stanley's pie-eyed mug.

Stanley had been known to see a "lady" around Reno, so Johnny had warned Mean Mike and Silent Thursday to keep their eyes skinned for him, as Stanley never could stay in one place long and seemed to enjoy rollicking mountain boomtowns and would more than likely sooner or later wear out his welcome in Virginia City.

His reputation as a violent drunk preceded him everywhere he went. Hallelujah Junction's near proximity to that hale settlement, with its many famous as well as infamous parlor houses, gambling dens, and drinking establishments, was a natural second choice for a man like Lonesome.

Now as Lonesome triggered the nickel-plated Schofield revolver in his right hand, aiming at something on the floor near the window through which Johnny peered, Johnny saw that the drunkard was not dancing. He was pivoting around, picking out targets wriggling around on the floor.

Imaginary snakes.

"Damn things are everywhere! Place is plumb crawlin' with 'em!" Lonesome aimed both big Schofields now at an imagined serpent slithering around near the piano, and blasted one gun and then the other, poking the tip of his tongue against the right side of his mouth in deep concentration. "Ain't there a law against keepin' snakes in this perdition, Brennan?"

"You're crazy, Lonesome!" boomed a man's voice from behind the bar at the rear of the room. "There are no snakes in here, ya blasted fool!" That would be Dave Brennan, the fellow who managed the Sierra Nevada Hotel's saloon for the hotel's owners in Sacramento. Wisely, he was keeping his head down.

"There's another 'un!" Lonesome cried, and triggered another shot, this one slightly right of the last round he'd fired.

Johnny cursed, swung around, and walked back to the double doors. He pulled the right door open and stepped into the hotel lobby, vacated now for obvious reasons. As he walked forward past a potted palm and a cabinet clock, toward where the doorways to the saloon and the dining room opened on opposite sides of the lobby from each other, Johnny glanced into the dining room on his left.

He could see three men in there, all crouched under a table. All three wore three-piece suits. They'd likely been enjoying a late-afternoon business lunch when Lonesome had started seeing snakes in the saloon and all hell had broken loose. The businessmen hadn't dared vacate the dining room and flee through the lobby and outside at the risk of being mistaken for a snake.

One of the men—round-faced, mustached, and with bushy side whiskers—looked at Johnny from beneath the table and made a circular motion near his left ear with the cigar he held in his right hand.

Johnny raised the barrel of his left shotgun, advising the three men to keep their heads down. He walked through the saloon's arched doorway on his right and extended both shotguns at the man standing on the table about ten feet away from him.

Lonesome was crouched as before, waving his six-shooters around, looking for another serpent. His face was flushed with fear and anger, his eyes wide and white-ringed. A third pistol lay on the table beneath his spread, black boots. He must have been carrying three; he'd emptied one but he still had two more Schofields in his fists. Johnny didn't know how many rounds he'd fired so far, but he had to assume the crazy old outlaw still had a few pills left in both wheels.

Out of the corner of his left eye, Lonesome spied

the newcomer in the doorway and jerked toward Johnny, swinging both Schofields around, as well.

"If you aim those hoglegs at me, you crazy old devil," Johnny warned, clicking all four of the Twins' hammers back to full cock, "I'll turn you into red paste and be done with your caterwauling, you drunken fool!"

Lonesome lowered the Schofields' barrels slightly and studied Johnny closely. "Who in thunder are you?"

"Johnny Greenway, marshal of Hallelujah Junction. Also, deputy United States marshal. You're under arrest on federal charges, though, under the present circumstances, I think we can find some local ones, too!"

Lonesome made a face as though he'd just taken a whiff of three-day-old rotten meat. "The hell I am!"

"The hell you're not! Set those hoglegs down nice and slow and come down off that table, you demented old drunkard!"

"I ain't no demented old drunkard!" Lonesome retorted with deep indignance. "I'm a bullion guard is what I am. I'm here on business. Righteous business! I'm a respectable man! I got a job!" He spat the words out like he was coughing up half-swallowed sour candy. "And this place is full of snakes! They're all over the damn saloon! Can't you see 'em?"

"Bullion guard?" Johnny said, beetling his brows with incredulity.

"That's right—I sure as hell am! Miss Bonner over to the bank just signed my employment contract not an hour ago. I came here to celebrate though little did I know the place was crawlin' with serpents of the devil!" He jerked his head as well as both pistols to the left, and triggered the left-hand one.

The blast thundered around the saloon, evoking

another muted shriek from the girl cowering behind the piano. The bullet tore into an ashtray on a table ahead and to the man's left. The ashtray flew up, emptying its contents of ashes and cigarette butts, and slammed against the front window before dropping to the floor with a clang.

"One more shot," Johnny warned, "and I'm gonna blow you to kingdom come!" Silently, he was chewing up the information Lonesome had just passed along—that Sheila Bonner had hired the man as a bullion guard. He wouldn't have believed it if he didn't think Lonesome Stanley was too crazy-drunk to make something like that up.

Johnny had run bullion for her until he'd taken the lawdogging jobs. He hadn't realized she'd been having such a hard time replacing him. Obviously, however, since she'd hired the likes of a notorious lout of a gunfighting drunkard in Lonesome Stanley, she was. Or maybe, sober, Lonesome could present himself a little more professionally, not to mention sanely, than he was doing here this afternoon . . .

Lonesome swung his head but not his guns back toward Johnny. Smoke curled from the barrel of his left-hand Schofield. His dark eyes flashed with deep suspicion and paranoia.

He smiled crookedly and said, "Oh, you'd like that, wouldn't you?"

"Yes, I sure would. You would, too, Lonesome, if you weren't so damn crazy-drunk. Now, lower the hoglegs to the table and climb down from there. If you try to take another shot, I'm going to blast you in little bitty pieces to your reward!"

"Someone's gotta kill these snakes. If I climb down, one's liable to bite me . . . drag me to hell." Lonesome grimaced, showing his teeth. "But you'd like that! Oho! I know you would." His insane smile grew, lunatic eyes flashing knowingly. "Because they're yours, aren't they?"

Johnny didn't say anything. He scowled at Lonesome skeptically, not sure how one dealt with a man this crazed.

"You're the snake wrangler. Oh, sure—I can see it now. Why . . . you're the serpent-wranglin' devil himself. Sure enough, I can see your green horns and serpent's forked tail. Oh, Lordy, it's you!" Tears glistening like liquid gold dribbled down the insane man's long, sallow cheeks. "Sure enough, it is—you're the devil himself! I'm right, ain't I? It's true!"

He still hadn't swung the Schofields toward Johnny but was aiming them generally toward the front of the saloon. His lunatic eyes were on Johnny, and Johnny knew the man was going to swing those damn guns on him again in seconds. He was on the verge.

When he did . . .

"I'm not the devil, Lonesome," Johnny said, shaking his head slowly. "And there are no serpents in here. You're just imagining . . . hallucinating. You've pickled your brain. I know it's not your fault, but if you so much as start to turn those Schofields on me, I'm going to kill you. I don't want to have to do that, Lonesome. You're a sick man and you need help. But so help me . . ."

The crazy man's eyes grew vaguely apprehensive, hesitant. His eyes rolled around, darting this way and that, as he considered Johnny's words.

Was he starting to believe what Johnny had just told him? Hard to tell. But he was chewing it over.

So far, so good.

Johnny took some of the steel out of his voice, hoping to calm the man down. "Set the guns down, Lonesome. Set 'em down nice an' slow."

Lonesome stared at Johnny, deeply confounded. The skin above the bridge of his nose crinkled deeply. His eyes danced with anxious thought.

"Now, Lonesome," Johnny prodded the man but kept his voice soft, almost gentle.

"All right." Lonesome depressed his Schofields' hammers. "All right . . . I'll . . . set 'em down . . ."

Slowly, he bent his knees and leaned forward, lowering the Schofields toward the table.

"That's right," Johnny said. "Nice an' eas—"

He stopped when he spied movement behind Lonesome and to the right. The girl, a brunette clad in the silks and satins of a serving girl, had lifted her head above the piano and was moving slowly out from behind it. Her wide, brown eyes were riveted on Lonesome.

No, Johnny thought, heart quickening. *Stay there! Stay down!*

The image of the terrified eyes of the whore at the road ranch passed across Johnny's retinas as Lonesome, having seen the girl's movements in the periphery of his own vision, jerked his head toward her.

"Oh!" the crazy man cried, snapping both Schofields back up again. *"A trap, is it?"*

"No!" Johnny shouted as Lonesome clicked both his pistols' hammers back and swung the guns toward the girl.

He leveled the revolvers on the brunette, who froze in place and screamed shrilly when she saw Lonesome swing the Schofields toward her. Johnny cursed as he squeezed the Twins' triggers. The sawed-offs roared, the buckshot slamming into Lonesome and hurling the man up off the table and clear across the room to slam against the wall maybe six feet up from the floor.

The man groaned, stretching his bloody lips back from his teeth, as he dropped straight down to the floor, leaving a long streak of fresh blood on the wall above him. What was left of him sat against the wall, legs spread wide, empty hands at his sides. His head hung to his chest.

Nearly every inch of his head and torso was tomato-red.

Chapter 12

Dixie Wade lifted another shovelful of dirt and gravel and tossed it up and out of the hole she was standing in. She kicked the spade into the ground once more, dug up another bladeful of sand and gravel, and tossed it out of the hole.

Exhaustion made her woozy. She leaned back against the side of the hole to catch her breath. She tossed her long, sweat-damp blond hair back over her head, heaved a heavy sigh, ran the sleeve of her wool coat across her sweaty forehead, and inspected the hole.

The grave, rather.

She stood shoulder-deep in the ground. That meant the grave was four feet deep or thereabouts.

She turned to where Henrietta sat on the ground, leaning back against a ponderosa pine, one plump knee drawn up to her chest. She was smoking a cigarette. A leather-covered flask sat against the tree beside her, her left hand wrapped around it. Henrietta's pale, fleshy face was pink from windburn, flushed from exhaustion. Her lusterless brown hair was damp with sweat. Some of it was pasted to her cheeks.

Henrietta had been helping Dixie dig the grave for Jake Teale for the past two hours. It had not been an easy task. Dixie hadn't asked Henrietta to help. This had been Dixie's job, for Jake had been Dixie's man. But Henrietta was a bighearted girl. She'd said that if Dixie insisted on giving her beau a proper burial, well, then, she couldn't just sit back and watch her toil alone up here from the porch of the Grizzly Ridge Inn.

She'd helped Dixie drag Jake's coffin up here, using Jake's horse and the rope he'd carried on his saddle. Dixie had purchased the coffin from a neighboring prospector who also built coffins for a second and often more lucrative living. If one thing was certain in these mountains when damned little else was, folks were going to die. They did it all the time, and now Dixie had found herself admiring the coffin-builder's practicality as well as his business acumen.

Why hadn't she thought of it? Building coffins couldn't be that hard. Leastways, it must have been a whole lot easier than spending the bulk of most of her days flat on her back staring at that robin's nest in her rafters.

Henrietta had helped Dixie drag the coffin up here a little after noon. It sat near the grave, the lid on but not nailed down yet. Jake's horse stood where Dixie had tied it to another tree some distance away, the cool mountain breeze jostling its mane and tail.

Dixie looked at the coffin. Again, her heart swelled.

He'd come all this way, with all that money, only to be shot within a few miles.

Within a few miles of him and Dixie spending the rest of their lives together, high on the hog, as Jake had liked to say. Dixie felt her lower lip swell and tremble at the confounding and infuriating unfairness of life. Quickly returning her mind to more practical matters, she shifted her gaze to Henrietta, who, just then taking another puff from the cigarette, blew the smoke into the breeze as she stared off toward a distant mountain, her eyes glazed with weariness.

"Henrietta, do you think four feet is deep enough?" Dixie asked.

Henrietta slowly turned her head to Dixie and frowned. She hiked a shoulder under her own wool coat. "I don't see why not."

"How deep are graves usually dug?"

"You're askin' the wrong gal, Dixie. I don't recollect ever bein' to a funeral before. This is my first one, if you can call it a funeral."

"I should have asked the coffin maker."

"Maybe he'll stop by later. He said he might pay us a visit tonight."

"I don't want to wait." Dixie hoisted herself up out of the hole. "Jake's been dead two days. It's time to get him in the ground proper and say a few words over him."

"All right." Henrietta set her cigarette stub on the ground beside her and mashed it out with a stone.

"Hold on," Dixie said.

Henrietta had started to rise but now she sank back against the tree again as Dixie walked over and picked up the flask. She unscrewed the cap and held the whiskey out to Henrietta.

"Snort?"

Henrietta shook her head. "Just had some."

Dixie took a couple of pulls from the flask. The whiskey burned but it filed the sharpest edges off her bereavement. She had the money, but it would have been a whole lot more fun spending it with the man she loved. Instead, she'd have to spend it by herself. It wouldn't be that bad. At least, she'd be away from here. She could live high on the hog alone.

Still.

He loved me. He really did love me. The only man who ever had. The only person in the whole world . . .

Holding the flask, Dixie turned to the coffin again. She took another drink of the whiskey, returned the cap, set the flask down, and walked over to the coffin. She dropped to a knee beside the wooden overcoat and removed the lid, letting it drop down over the side to the ground, where it landed with a hollow thud.

Jake's handsome face was turned slightly toward her, as if he were looking at her through eyes that were partway open. Far enough open that she could see the bottoms of his irises.

The loss of this wild man, the loss of his love, was a burning wound inside her. It was not so much in her heart as in her belly. It felt like a cancerous growth, burning and bleeding.

How odd for her to react this way, for she hadn't known him long. Only a handful of nights spread across a year. Still, she'd tumbled for him. And she knew he'd tumbled for her, for the hardness and rawness and young recklessness that she'd first seen in his eyes had softened and matured so that when she thought of him now, she saw a handsome man with kind eyes and lips curled in a tender smile.

She'd done that to him. She'd changed him. Softened his heart. And she'd like to think that he'd done that to her, as well. She couldn't be sure. All she knew was that she'd been pining for him, hoping for his return. He'd returned to her, filling her with joy. But soon after, he'd died, turning that joy to ashes.

It was a cruel trick. Like having a bucket of cold water poured over your head or having a rug pulled out from under your feet. At your most joyful moment in life. There could be no purpose in it but to injure as severely as possible. To mock and scorn.

And it had wounded her. Her feelings now for Jake Teale were a strange, toxic hybrid of grief and anger. Tempering it a little was the money he'd left her.

She lowered her mouth to his pale cheek and pressed her lips to it tenderly. "Thank you, Jake," she whispered in his ear. "I wish you'd been able to spend it with me."

A tear dribbled down her cheek. She brushed it away and hardened herself against the pangs of sorrow that threatened to pummel her from within. She had no time to cry. She had to bury Jake, retrieve the loot from where she'd hid it in an abandoned cellar behind the Grizzly Ridge Inn, and find a way out of these godforsaken mountains before the first snows rendered her escape impossible.

She could not stand another winter up here. Especially now, knowing she no longer had to endure those long, dark, snowy months . . . one gloomy, painfully cold day after another. For now she had the means of escape. At least, she had the loot. A way out of the mountains was another matter, for she knew none of the routes and was not certain she could survive on her own.

She'd tackle that problem later.

Dixie rose, walked around to the other side of the

coffin, and put the lid back in place. She turned to Henrietta, who sat regarding her with a vague sadness, maybe even a little envy for the love Dixie had felt for the outlaw Jake Teale. As far as Dixie knew, Henrietta had never been in love, and she was not in love now. Likely, she never would be. She'd never had anyone, just as Dixie had never had anyone before Jake, and Henrietta likely would never have anyone.

Just as Dixie likely would never have anyone again.

That thought formed a knot in her throat. She cleared it, swallowed it, brushed her hand across her cheek again, and said, "Help me get him in the grave?"

Henrietta heaved herself to her feet. "How're we gonna do that?"

"I don't know. I guess I'll get into the grave and then you . . ."

She stopped when a man's voice came to her ears on the crisp breeze. It was followed by a woman's voice.

"What is it?" Henrietta said, looking at Dixie curiously.

"Did you hear that?"

"Hear what?"

Dixie turned and walked over to the hill's northwest side. She stared down into the yard of the Grizzly Ridge Inn. A man sat on a horse in the yard, facing the porch. Clementine stood at the top of the porch steps, talking to the newcomer. Dixie could hear her cold, crisp tone but could not make out her words. Clementine had her hands on her hips, but just then she lifted her left hand and pointed up the hill toward where Dixie and Henrietta had dug the grave.

The man on the horse turned his head to stare in

the direction Clementine had indicated. He was a bearded, thickset man in a blue wool coat and high-crowned, black felt hat. It was hard to tell from this distance of a hundred yards how old he was. He didn't look young.

The man turned back to Clementine, dipped his chin, and pinched his hat brim to her. Clementine swung coldly around, walked back inside the building, and slammed the door behind her. The man turned his horse—no, mule, rather, Dixie saw now as the beast faced her with its pronounced ears—and batted his heels against its flanks.

He and the mule started toward Dixie and Henrietta.

"Uh-oh," Dixie said, fear gripping her.

"What is it?"

"Don't know. Not for sure."

Dixie watched the man cross the yard and start up the hill. Her heart shuddered, blood quickening through her veins. She looked for a badge on the man's chest but couldn't see one. He might be wearing it under his coat.

He could be a lawman. Maybe a bounty hunter.

Whoever he was, he was most likely on Jake's trail. If so, he'd want the loot. But Dixie would be damned if he'd get it.

She swung around and walked over to Jake's horse. She slid Jake's carbine from the saddle boot and pumped a round into the action. Holding the heavy rifle in both hands, she walked back over to the side of the hill and gazed down at the man riding toward her.

She could feel Henrietta's skeptical gaze on her. She ignored the girl.

As the man approached, Dixie could make out more details. He was old. Maybe sixty. Maybe even older than that. He had a high forehead and a long, broad nose that was almost purple with broken veins.

His thick beard was mostly brown but threaded with a good deal of gray. His face was very craggy, like the old, worn leather of a sofa inside the inn. It was very dark, giving him the look of a miner. The darkness appeared to be from dirt ground into his skin.

His eyes were sunk deep in bony sockets. They were large and as dark as the rest of his face as they studied Dixie closely, man and mule now drawing to within fifteen feet of her, the rider holding the reins in both his gloved hands, swaying from side to side with the mount's movements.

"That's far enough," Dixie said.

The man drew back on the mule's reins and said, "Whoa." He looked from Dixie's eyes to the carbine in her hands, which was aimed generally in his direction but without direct threat. The threat was so far a general one.

He returned his cautious gaze to Dixie's eyes, glanced at Henrietta, back to Dixie again, and said, "You have my boy up here?"

CHAPTER 13

Dixie frowned at the bearded stranger. "Boy?"

"My boy—Jake Teale."

Dixie heard Henrietta gasp behind her. It could have been an expression of Dixie's own shock. Dixie could only stare at the man.

"I heard at the mine that Jake Teale had ridden in here with a couple bullets in his belly. I heard he wasn't gonna make it."

Dixie studied the stone-faced man curiously. She was also annoyed. The news about Jake had probably come from Maud Horton. Maud lived up close to the mine and tended the miners' injuries.

Why couldn't the fat old bat keep her mouth shut? Dixie should have admonished her to stay silent, but Dixie had been too distracted by Jake's condition that night to think of it. Not that Maud would have kept her mouth shut, anyway. She had a habit of spreading rumors especially when she drank, which was often.

Dixie was still trying to comprehend what the bearded stranger had told her. That he was Jake's father. She'd never given any thought to the possibility of Jake having a family. She'd assumed that he'd been alone in the world as Dixie herself was. He'd never talked about a family.

Dixie dropped the rifle a little lower and scowled incredulously at the man. "I didn't know . . ."

"That he had a father?" the man said. "No, you likely wouldn't. I'm sure he didn't talk about me much. We had a, uh"—he glanced at the sky as though judging the time by the angle of the sun—"a *fallin'-out*, I guess you could say. A long time ago."

"You live around here, Mr. Teale?"

"I work at the mine. Have a little ranch down near Hallelujah Junction, but it never amounted to much so I came up here to prospect. That didn't amount to much, neither, so I signed up for work at the Reverend's Temptation. I heard about my boy, an' . . . well, I thought I'd ride over and have a look at him."

He cast his gaze beyond Dixie and Henrietta, to the crude pine box in which Jake lay. "That him up there?"

Dixie nodded. "We were set to plant him. Say a few words over him."

"You were, were you?" Teale winced as he put his weight on his left stirrup and swung his right leg over the mule's rear end, stepping heavily to the ground with another wince, as though all movement grieved him. "Why were you gonna do that?"

He didn't wait for an answer. He walked past Dixie and Henrietta and over to the coffin. He stood staring down at the dead outlaw, stretching his lips back from his teeth but otherwise giving little expression.

Dixie walked over to stand on the opposite side of the coffin from Mr. Teale. Henrietta stood where she'd been standing a moment before, behind where Teale was now, hugging herself as though chilled.

"That's him, all right," Teale said.

He drew a deep breath. With a grunt, he dropped to one knee. He removed his hat as an afterthought and held it down near the ground, staring into the coffin at the pale, swelling face of Jake Teale. He shook his head and winced again then spat to one side.

Returning his solemn gaze to the man in the coffin, he said, "I'll be damned."

Teale looked up at Dixie. "Who shot him?"

"Bounty hunter." She waited nearly a minute then, as Teale stared down gravely at his dead son, she blurted out on a wave of congested emotion, "I loved him. I loved your son, Mr. Teale." She brushed a tear from her cheek and cleared her throat, trying to steel herself again.

Teale looked up at her, frowning as though perplexed. "You did?"

"Yes."

He shaped the word with his mouth first without making any sound, then tried again and with more success, asked, "Why?"

"I don't know." Dixie shrugged and wiped another damn tear from her other cheek. She was on the verge of crying and she didn't know why. She hadn't cried since the night Jake had died, and she didn't want to now. Not in front of this stranger. "Why do people love other people? I just did, that's all."

"Did he treat you right?"

"Yes, he did. He loved me. I know he did."

That seemed to baffle the old man even more. He just looked at her as though wondering if she was crazy or maybe just a female with too soft of a heart that might have caused her to be taken advantage of by his outlaw son.

"He changed, Mr. Teale," Dixie said, wishing he'd stop looking at her like that. "I changed him."

"You did, did you?"

Again, the skepticism in his voice chafed Dixie. "Yes. I'm going to bury him right there. We dug his grave and were fixin' to plant him and say a few words over him."

"That's what you said," Teale said, still on one knee, looking up at her, the breeze stirring the thin brown hair at the nearly bald crown of his skull. "But I'd like to take him home. I'd like to bury him to home, next to my wife and my other boy."

It was Dixie's turn to be puzzled. "You would?"

"Yes, ma'am."

Dixie just stared at him, not quite understanding.

"I was too hard on him," Teale confessed with a tone of genuine regret. "I was too hard on him and Dale both. Dale turned out bad, too. Even worse than Jake. Both left home early. They got tired of the strap, I reckon. I couldn't do a thing with 'em. Their mother died when they were twelve an' thirteen, an' they just went to hell after that."

He paused, then repeated as though at a loss for other words, "I couldn't do a thing with 'em. But, you know, I always regretted the way I raised 'em. I always hoped that after Dale died—he was hung by a vigilance committee in Montana—I'd get the chance to make it up to Jake. Even if just a little bit. Well, now, Miss . . ."

"Dixie."

"Now, Miss Dixie, I'd like to try to make it up to him, if only just a little, by takin' him home and givin' him a proper burial. So we can all be together. My own time is short." He bunched his lips and pressed the end of his fist against his chest. "Bad ticker. We'll be a family again soon."

Teale returned his gaze to his son. His face grew long and the color washed out of it, leaving the nubs of his cheeks pale. He shook his head and winced again, and a sheen of tears closed down over his eyes. He dug a handkerchief out of his back pocket, raised it to his nose, and honked loudly.

"Damn," he said. "Both boys dead. Hilda, too. I'm all alone." He drew a breath and said with heart-breaking forlornness, "All alone in this godforsaken world."

Dixie had been thinking it through.

"You can take Jake home, Mr. Teale, on one condition," she said as though, having dug Teale's son a grave, having loved him, she had established a claim on Jake Teale's body.

"What condition is that, Miss Dixie?"

"That you take me with you."

Later that night, Dixie stared down at the two carpetbags on her bed and took a deep drag off her cigarette.

A storm had come up just after dark. Rain splattered against her window, and thunder rumbled distantly. A coal fire burned in the corner, filling the room with a pleasant heat against the mountain chill.

The brunt of the storm had passed, but Dixie was glad for the nasty turn the weather had taken. As far as she was concerned, she was done whoring for Heck

Torrance. The bad weather had kept most prospective customers away from the Grizzly Ridge Inn, so she hadn't had to explain why she wasn't working. Two prospectors, flush and giddy with fresh dust, had come in before the weather change; Clementine and Henrietta had serviced them both when Dixie, complaining of a headache, had shut herself in her room.

The bags on the bed were swollen with clothes and supplies she thought she'd need on the trail. She wasn't sure if the bags were too heavy to carry on a horse. If so, she could throw out some of the less necessary articles on her journey down the mountains with Mr. Teale.

Her main concern was the saddlebags. The bags were too obvious. Walt Teale—Dixie had learned that Teale's first name was Walt—would suspect the bags were stuffed with money. He'd likely want a cut of it. Dixie had no intention of sharing the money with anyone. That money was hers and Jake's. It was their love money. That's how Dixie had chosen to view it— as a symbol of her and Jake's love and what their lives could have been if they'd been able to be together.

No, she wouldn't share the money with anyone. Not even Jake's father. She had to find an inconspicuous way to get the money down out of the mountains.

First things first. She had to retrieve the bags from their hiding place.

She took a final drag from her cigarette, mashed the butt out in an ashtray on her dresser, and moved to the window. She opened the window and stuck her hand out. The rain had tapered off to a fine mist. Rainwater dribbled off the inn's eaves to patter onto the muddy ground below.

Dixie closed the window, stepped into a pair of fur-lined moccasins, and grabbed a hooded cape off the peg on her door, and shrugged into it, pulling the hood up over her head. She opened her door and poked her head into the hall.

Looking both ways, she saw no one. Heck Torrance's door was partway open. She could see a shadow moving beyond the crack, hear the tinkle of water in a basin. That would be the hardworking Henrietta giving Torrance a sponge bath. Dixie didn't know why she doted on the old man so. The old pimp had never treated any of his girls as anything more than property. Henrietta was a little simple in that way—the way of feeling overly tender for those who didn't return the favor.

The other doors along the hall, four on each side, were closed. Clementine was likely in her room by now, getting ready for bed. Possibly, she was still at work in the kitchen downstairs. Dixie would have to keep an eye out for her. Clementine was the one she was worried about, for she was the only other person who knew about the loot.

Dixie stepped into the hall, closed the door quietly behind her, and, turning right, walked quietly on the balls of her feet down the hall toward the stairs. As she passed the room she'd given to Walt Teale, she heard the low rumble of the man's snoring.

Dead asleep.

Good. Dixie wouldn't have to worry about him. Only Clementine . . .

She tiptoed down the stairs, running her right hand lightly along the banister. When she was halfway to the parlor on the first floor, she stopped and looked up the stairs behind her, frowning. She thought she'd heard something—possibly the squawk of a floorboard under a stealthy foot.

There were no lamps lit in the parlor, as everyone including Clementine appeared to have turned in for the rainy night. Dixie couldn't see much as she stared up toward the top of the stairs. No shadows moved, and there were no more squawks, which might have merely been the old lodge settling its moldering timbers as it did from time to time.

Dixie continued down the stairs. At the bottom, she stopped and placed her hand atop the newel post as she stood gazing back up the stairs, listening, watching, waiting to see if anyone was following her. She waited a minute and then a little longer.

Nothing moved. There were no more sounds except Jake's father's muffled snores and the creaks in the ceiling over where Heck Torrance's room was, and which could be attributed to the ever-laboring Henrietta.

Dixie stepped away from the stairs and crossed the parlor to the rear. There was a door back there with a curtained window. It was usually only used at nights for visits to the privy. Dixie unlocked the door, turned the knob, wincing against the soft click of the locking bolt withdrawing into the door. She glanced behind her quickly then slid her gaze to the stairs.

Still no movement. Everyone except Henrietta and the hollow shell that remained of Torrance after his stroke was still asleep or at least snugged away in their rooms. Clementine was either asleep or drinking rotgut whiskey and reading the dime novels she favored. She'd taught herself to read, which Dixie found impressive since she herself could barely sign her name.

Dixie went out and eased the door closed behind her.

She looked around, ever furtive, then strode straight out away from the lodge. She followed the trail toward the privy, the trail having been used so often it was nearly a trench sheathed in mountain sage and the short blond grass that grew at this altitude.

She swung around the privy and strode past the large log woodshed on her left. She skirted some wild berry bushes then turned right, stopping near the stone foundation of the Torrances' original cabin. The cabin had burned to the ground, leaving only the foundation and a root cellar a few feet out from the foundation, on the cabin's north side.

The cellar was well concealed by bushes that had grown up over the years. It wasn't used anymore but Dixie had stumbled onto it one afternoon when she'd been picking wild berries for syrup and jam and had silently opined even then, when she had nothing to hide, that the cellar would be a good place to squirrel something private away.

She certainly had something to hide now. She'd been anxious about the money ever since Jake had brought it, worried that someone would try to take it from her. She couldn't wait to strike out on the trail tomorrow with the loot. She wouldn't be safe even then—she'd have to make sure Walt Teale didn't discover it—but she'd be safer than she was here. Sooner or later, Clementine would blab to one of her lonely Lyles about the money, and the two would try to steal it. Dixie was a little surprised that Clementine hadn't already made an attempt.

She knelt beside the rotting, scorched wood door. When she grabbed the steel ring and pulled, the door squawked and groaned and wobbled on its ancient leather hinges. Several slats were missing from the door, making it so rickety that it felt to Dixie that it was about to disintegrate. Even with the rotten door, the cellar was still the safest place around here to hide the loot. She was sure none of the others knew about it. At least, no one besides Heck Torrance, and the old pimp was no longer a threat.

Dixie set the door aside, then, using the wooden ladder running down the front wall, climbed down into the hole. The ladder hadn't been damaged in the fire, and it was still relatively sturdy. Spiderwebs caught in Dixie's hair and clung to her face and arms. Her skin crawled. She hadn't wanted to come down here in the dark, but she'd had no choice. She hadn't wanted to use a lamp out of fear the light would give her away to anyone watching from the lodge.

At the bottom of the hole, she felt around for the bags. Fear built in her as she waved her hands blindly, searching for the leather saddlebags in the stygian darkness that smelled like scorched wood and moldy root vegetables. Several times, her flailing hands brushed the hole's earthen wall, coming up with nothing. Finally, her fingers brushed leather, and a second later, she pulled the bags up over her right shoulder and climbed back out of the hole.

As she gained her feet outside the cellar, a little breathless from the climb as well as anxiousness, a shadow moved before her.

Clementine stepped up close to Dixie. Dixie could see only her outline, but it was Clementine, all right. Ambient light shone in those amber eyes; it glistened in that kinky black hair tumbling wildly about her shoulders. Clementine made a grunting sound, and then there was a whir of displaced air a half second before the tall, black whore smashed a rock against Dixie's left temple.

CHAPTER 14

The day after he'd sent Lonesome Stanley flying across the Sierra Nevada Hotel in itty-bitty pieces, Johnny rode Ghost back into Hallelujah Junction. He stopped at a livery barn to rent a spare horse, then rode Ghost and led the spare roan over to the bank.

He tied the horses at the hitchrack and went inside. As he closed the door behind him, he saw Sheila Bonner talking to one of her two loan officers, an egg-shaped, gray-haired old gent with round steel spectacles and a rumpled suit. Sheila's gaze drifted casually to Johnny. Not recognizing him at first, for she was a good twenty feet away and he was likely silhouetted by the glass door behind him, she glanced just as casually away from him.

Instantly, she shuttled her gaze back to him, sudden recognition widening her eyes. For a few seconds, Johnny thought she would faint. Her lower jaw dropped slightly. A flush rose from her fine pale neck to her lovely face, like the mercury in a thermometer taken out of an icehouse on a hot summer day. Keeping her stricken eyes on Johnny, she said a few more words to the loan officer then touched the man's arm affectionately, shaping a wooden smile. She turned away, removing her gaze from Johnny, as though if she didn't see him he would no longer be there, and stepped into her office.

She closed the door behind her.

"You can run," Johnny said under his breath as he strode toward the swinging door in the low wooden rail that separated the bank's lobby from its clerical area and rear offices. "But you can't hide."

Sheila's secretary, a young fancy Dan named Harvey Wilson rose from his desk outside Sheila's office, clearing his throat self-consciously and saying, "Ex-excuse me, Marshal Greenway, but . . . um . . . do you have an appointment with Miss Bonner?"

"Nope." Johnny stopped at Sheila's door, knocked once, then opened the door and stepped inside. "Got a minute?"

She was sitting at her desk ahead and to the right, her head bowed over an open manila folder resting atop several other folders, behind a green-shaded Tiffany lamp. A cabinet clock ticked woodenly from the wall above a line of heavy wooden filing cabinets. The office still smelled, not unpleasantly, of her now-deceased father's Cuban cigars and Spanish brandy. They mixed, not unpleasantly, with her own pleasant smell including the subtle perfume she wore and which, when they were in bed together, he used to enjoy sniffing behind her ears for a particularly satisfying whiff of it . . . and of her.

"Actually, I don't," Sheila said, looking up with the previous flush in place. "I have a meeting with mine speculators from Reno this afternoon, and I have pages of—"

"Don't worry, I'm not here about the other afternoon. You remember the one—when you were ogling me and Glyneen MacFarland down by the creek . . . ?"

Sheila's flush of embarrassment turned to a bloom of rage. "I was doing no such thing!"

"Like I said, I'm not here about that."

"I rode out there only to—"

Again, he interrupted her with, "Your bullion guard isn't going to show today."

Her full lips were still shaped with the words of her previous sentence, but now she frowned and said, "Why not?"

"He saddled a golden cloud. Dead as a doornail. Lonesome Stanley, who had a federal warrant on his head, by the way, got drunk yesterday and shot up the Sierra Nevada Hotel's saloon and would have shot up a serving girl if I hadn't sent him to the pearly gates."

"Lonesome Stanley?" Sheila scowled in exasperation. "I know no Lonesome Stanley. The man who I hired to haul bullion is Herman Stanley."

"That's Lonesome's real name. Lonesome is Herman Stanley, and both Lonesome and Herman aren't going to show here today, because they're dead." Johnny gave a wry chuckle, shaking his head. "I swear, Sheila—don't you check these fellas out?"

Sheila tossed down her pen, bounded indignantly to her feet, and glared at Johnny from across her cluttered desk. "I did check him out! I think you're wrong! He showed me a whole sheaf of references including a letter from a prominent mine owner in Utah!"

"Yeah, well, they were forged. Had to be. Your bullion guard is . . . *was* . . . Lonesome Stanley. Notorious scalawag. Robber, too, though he wasn't much good at it. Oh, I don't doubt he was going to haul bullion for you, but whether or not he hauled it down here to the bank and not to Mexico is anyone's guess. Mine is that it would have ended up in Mexico."

Sheila just stared at him in shock. He almost felt sorry for her. She'd been duped. She was a proud young woman doing her best to fill her father's shoes here at the bank, and she was taking this Lonesome Stanley business hard. Of course she was. He should have known she would. He should have been a little gentler, but it was too late to backwater now.

"Anyway," he said, softening his tone. "I'm gonna haul it for you. Scribble me out a note to the mine manager up at the Reverend's Temptation, and I'll be on my way. Already have a pack mount. I'm ready to go."

"Why?"

"I need to get out of town for a while."

"Why?"

"Clear my head. I'm going back to work next week, but until then, I need a ride. A ride in the mountains always clears my head. You know that."

Sheila sat slowly back down in her gold-embroidered leather chair. Slumping back a little, letting her hands hang down over the chair arms, she probed Johnny closely with her warm brown eyes, and said, "I'm just wondering what it needs to be cleared of."

Now he was becoming annoyed. "Look, I didn't come here to talk about anything but business. I came here to get a note so I could—"

"Miss MacFarland?"

Johnny scowled. "Huh?"

"Is that what . . . or *who* . . . it needs to be cleared of, Johnny? Of Glyneen MacFarland?"

Johnny felt his jaws harden in anger. Catching himself, putting his wolf back on its leash, he chuckled drolly and shook his head. "Nah, nah, you're not gonna drag me into that. We're not gonna talk about Glyneen. We're not gonna talk about you showing up at my cabin the other day. Not about anything personal. We're back to where we started. I'm your hired hand. You're my employer. The rest didn't happen. Nada. Kaput!"

She frowned, puzzled, maybe a little hurt. "Why should you deny that the rest happened? It was wonderful . . . beautiful . . . for a time. For a very short time."

"Because it didn't work out." Johnny's wolf was straining at its leash again. He placed his fists on the edge of her desk and leaned toward her, feeling the heat of anger burn again in his cheeks. "Your idea of a husband and my idea of a husband were two different things. What you really wanted was a pet. You should get yourself a dog, Sheila. You'll be really good at training him."

She laughed at that, throwing her head back against the chair. Then the laugh turned into a sob, and tears washed over her eyes.

"Thank you for that, Johnny," she said, blinking the tears away and manufacturing a cold expression. Tears rolling down her cheeks and clinging like gold dust to her long, dark lashes, she said, "I might still love you, but I'll get over it. It'll be easier now . . . thank you very much . . . now that you've shown me what a cold, hard man you really are. A man who chose a job—a job of violence—over the woman he loved. If you're capable of love . . . of anything more than *rutting*. Here . . ."

Flushed and breathless with anger, she grabbed a lined pad of paper, picked up her pen, dipped it in a gold inkpot, and scribbled out a single-sentence note, scratching her signature beneath it with a flourish. "Here you go."

She tore the leaf from the tablet, blew on the ink, then folded the note twice and tossed it across the desk to Johnny. "Here's my note to the mine superintendent. Enjoy the ride. Enjoy the danger. Enjoy the violence. It's all part of your nature. I know that now. You're much more at home up there . . . with desperate men . . . than you ever were down here."

"Thanks." Johnny plucked the note off the desk. His heart fluttered, and he felt a little sick to his stomach, but he kept his eyes cold, his jaws hard. He wouldn't let her get to him. He walked to the door. "I'll be back in a few days."

"She doesn't deserve you, Johnny."

Johnny stopped with one hand on the doorknob and turned back to Sheila. She sat back in her chair, a bitter smile twisting her mouth. "Miss MacFarland deserves better than you. You're going to hurt her. You know you will. You've hurt every woman who's ever come into your life and made the mistake of loving you!"

A curtain of tears dropped down over her eyes again. As if to compensate, she increased the bitterness of her glare, flaring her nostrils and grinding her teeth.

The words of her parting volley were a rusty bayonet blade to his heart. A volley of rage swept through

Johnny. He turned to the door, drew his right hand back, making a fist, and thrust it forward, smashing his knuckles against the wood with the full force of his strength.

Behind him, Sheila gasped.

Johnny looked at the door. A crooked crack ran down the middle of it, above and below the impression his knuckles had left in the wood. He did not look at Sheila. He stared at the door for several seconds in horror, repelled by what he'd done.

He drew a breath and lowered his head in shame, humiliation. "Take it out of my pay."

He fumbled the door open, ramming it against his right boot. He stumbled through the door, nearly falling, and drew it closed behind him with a *bang!*

All eyes in the bank were on him as he strode heavily toward the outside door. The door seemed to be a long way away, and it took him a long time to traverse that twenty feet. It was like walking a mile in the wind and cold rain. When he was finally through the door and on the boardwalk fronting the bank, his head swirled, the street and boardwalk rising and falling around him.

Passersby stopped to regard him skeptically.

He realized he'd been holding his breath. He gulped air, steadied himself against the hitchrack, then stuffed Sheila's note into the pocket of his broadcloth coat and untied both sets of reins from the hitchrack.

He swung up onto Ghost's back and galloped north out of town, weaving carelessly through the traffic, men and women swiveling their heads toward him to stare.

He couldn't get out of town fast enough.

* * *

Sheila leaned forward over her desk, her face in her hands, trying not to cry but crying anyway, uncontrollably. She'd be damned if she didn't love the brute. The coldhearted brute!

Despite what he'd just said. Despite what she'd seen the other afternoon.

Fool!

She was trying hard to pull herself together when another knock sounded against her door. She looked up, ashamed and angry to find herself hoping that Johnny had returned to apologize and—what?

To drop to his knees and tell her that he loved her? Would always love her? Only her? Forever?

Whoever it was out there was far politer than Johnny had been. This visitor was waiting for her to invite him in.

"Yes?" Sheila called. "Who is it?"

"Doc Albright, Miss Bonner."

Disappointment settled heavily on her heart. She sniffed.

Seven kinds of a fool is what I am. I try so hard to portray myself as a professional woman who can compete in this man's world when, really, on the inside I'm just a silly, foolish girl . . .

"Come in, Doctor," she said, her voice quavering.

The door opened. Tall, lean, balding Dr. Kenneth Albright stepped tentatively into her office. He wore a long black frock coat, ribbon tie, and he was carrying his customary black gladstone bag.

Sheila pulled a handkerchief from a desk drawer and scrubbed at the tears that stubbornly refused to stop overflowing her eyes and dribbling down her cheeks like a persistent rain tumbling down a window.

The doctor closed the door. He studied her with a sympathetic downturn of his mouth corners beneath his scraggly, red-blond mustache to which a few breakfast crumbs still clung. Sheila cleared her throat and dabbed at the tears more energetically, wanting to compose herself. Humiliated by this excess of emotion.

"Go ahead," Albright said. "Have a good cry. Sometimes that's the best medicine of all."

She looked at him, curious.

"I saw him ride out of town like a bat out of hell." Albright glanced at the crack in the door. "Did he do that?"

Continuing to dab at the tears, which she'd finally gotten stopped, Sheila nodded.

Albright sighed. "Well . . . I can't help you with him. But . . ." The doctor set his kit on the edge of Sheila's desk and reached inside. He pulled out a small glass bottle containing a fine, pink powder. "I can help you with the morning sickness. Take a half teaspoon of this with tea twice a day."

CHAPTER 15

The stone had dealt Dixie a glancing blow.

On the ground, she looked up through a sheen of pain-induced tears to see the tall, slender silhouette of Clementine tower over her, glaring down at her, the stone still in her right hand. It was about the size of Dixie's clenched fist.

Clementine didn't say anything. She just glared down at Dixie for several seconds, tucking her lower lip under her upper one. Her eyes were large and black, as flat as a bear's eyes.

"No." Dixie winced against the burning pain in her left temple, felt blood well from the obvious cut, and shook her head. "You won't get it. It's mine . . . an' Jake's."

With a savage grunt, Clementine rammed her bare left foot into Dixie's belly.

Dixie shrieked and fell back against the ground, the wind momentarily knocked out of her. Clementine stepped forward, straddling Dixie, then dropped to her knees, the thin, pale wrap that hung on her shoulders, secured with a single button at her throat, buffeted out in the chill breeze, like the gossamer wings of some angry black angel. Dixie smelled the sour odor of whiskey on the doxie's breath.

"Clementine!" Dixie screeched as her opponent lifted the hand that held the stone, cocking her arm for another blow.

As Clementine started to swing the stone down toward Dixie's head, Dixie flung both her open hands up. The stone glanced off the heel of her left hand, which deflected the stone in Clementine's hand. Clementine grunted a curse as her own momentum drove her right shoulder down toward Dixie's side, the stone smacking the ground beside Dixie's head with a dull thud.

Clementine was taller than Dixie, but she was thinner and didn't weigh as much as Dixie. Before Clementine could right herself and raise the stone again, Dixie thrust her own body up, twisting to her right. She threw Clementine partially off her and then grabbed Clementine's right hand—the hand with the stone in it—with both of her own.

Fighting for the rock, Dixie rolled onto her side, shoving Clementine off her. Clementine groaned and cursed as Dixie rolled her onto her back, using both her hands to pry the stone out of Clementine's hand. Clementine writhed beneath Dixie, kicking her legs up, flailing with her free hand to fight Dixie off and to regain her advantage.

But Dixie had both of her hands around Clementine's hand, which she'd pinned against the ground. A moment later, she'd pried the rock out of Clementine's long-fingered grip.

"No!" Clementine screamed, bucking up off the ground with her hips.

Dixie straddled her as only a minute ago she'd

been straddled. She raised the rock with an animal-like wail, stretching her lips back from her teeth. Rage was a furious wildcat inside her.

She raised the stone behind her right shoulder. Clementine gazed up at her, black eyes bright with terror, her own lips stretched back from her teeth as she watched Dixie bring the stone down toward Clementine's head with one savage, arcing thrust. Clementine raised both her hands but at the same time she took her eyes off the stone to turn her head to one side, recoiling from the horrific blow she knew was coming.

Neither of Clementine's waving hands touched the stone, which Dixie slammed unimpeded toward her target.

Plunk!

"Oh," Clementine said as the stone smashed against her right cheek.

Clementine lowered her hands. Her body began to relax beneath Dixie. Clementine turned her face toward Dixie's, looking up again at Dixie in stunned horror. Her eyes widened again when Dixie smashed the rock down again with another resolute smack against Clementine's face.

As Dixie raised the stone again, sucking a sharp breath through gritted teeth, Clementine blinked up at her, slowly, heavy-lidded, and croaked, "No, Dixie . . ."

Smack!

"Thought you were going to take our money—did you?" *Smack!* "Kill me and skin out with Jake's money? The money he stole for *me*?" *Smack!* "For *us*?"

Dixie delivered two more savage blows then stared down at Clementine. The black doxie's head was turned to one side. It was too dark for Dixie to see the blood, but she knew it was there, for she felt it on her own hand that held the rock. Clementine's head looked misshapen. Her eyes were open. Dim candles seemed to burn in them. But they no longer saw anything.

Clementine was not stirring, not breathing.

Dizzy with rage and exhaustion, Dixie slumped to one side and rolled onto her back beside the dead whore. She stared at the sky. Stars appeared and reappeared, flickering, as gauzy, ragged-edged clouds passed over them.

She sucked in several deep drafts of air, catching her breath. She fingered the cut on her left temple, felt the blood oozing from the torn, swollen flesh.

She cursed then rolled onto her right shoulder to gaze back over at Clementine, who still wasn't moving. She was just a twisted dark shape over there beside Dixie. The saddlebags lay just beyond her.

Dixie rose onto her knees and crawled over Clementine's legs to the bags. She ran her trembling hands over the swollen, lumpy pouches. She had them. The money was hers. Clementine did not nor ever would get them. Since Clementine was the only person who knew about the bags, unless she'd told someone in the past two days, which Dixie didn't think she had, because she'd have known by now, Dixie and the loot were likely in the clear.

Now she just had to get the money down out of the mountains and to San Francisco or to Mexico or wherever she was going. She had no idea. She just knew she would leave here.

But first, Clementine . . .

Dixie rose and walked over to the dead whore. She reached down, grabbed her by the wrists, and dragged the girl's long, slender body to the yawning, black cellar. She lay the body out parallel with the cellar then dropped to her knees and rolled Clementine over the cellar's stone lip. The darkness consumed the dead whore, like the jaws of a giant, black hound.

Dixie heard the body strike the cellar's earthen floor with a heavy thud.

No less than what she deserves, Dixie silently told herself, to assuage a guilt pang. She'd never taken a life before. She'd never even butchered a chicken. She felt weak and sick to her stomach. She'd only been defending herself, after all.

She rose then bent forward, hands on her thighs, to catch her breath. Her heart fluttered. Her knees felt like mud.

What a night. What a crazy damn night. But maybe it worked out for the best.

The only other person who knew about the loot was dead.

Dixie picked up the saddlebags and draped them over her shoulder, staggering a little with the weight. She smiled at the prospect of the money snugged inside each pouch. That, too, added to her dizziness. My God, she was rich!

She raised the dark hood of her cape and looked around carefully, making sure no one was around. She doubted anyone in the inn—there were only Henrietta and Walt Teale, for Heck Torrance didn't count anymore—had heard the foofaraw between her and Clementine. The two fighting doxies hadn't made all that much noise, and they were a good distance from the lodge. The surrounding shrubs had likely absorbed most of the noise, as well.

Dixie stood pondering what to do with the money.

Should she take it up to her room and transfer it from the saddlebag pouches to her carpetbags?

No. Too risky. Teale or Henrietta might see her carry the bags inside. She wanted no one else to know about the money. Besides, she needed the carpetbags for clothes and supplies. Teale would become suspicious if he never saw her take anything out of the bags. And if and when it became apparent that she had no spare clothes or trail supplies he'd wonder what she was carrying in the bags.

Damn! How am I going to get the loot down the mountain without being conspicuous? I certainly can't take it down in the saddlebags.

At least, she couldn't carry the saddlebags in plain sight. Both pouches bulged with the money, and it would soon be obvious to Teale that she'd packed no supplies in either pouch.

Wait.

No.

Should she? *Could* she?

Jake's coffin.

Heart quickening, feeling both appalled at the notion that had struck but also somewhat thrilled at the ingeniousness of it, she hurried back the way she'd come. When she was halfway to the main lodge, she swung right and followed a footpath to the stable and the corral flanking it.

She stuck to the yard's deepest shadows as she made her way along the corral to the stable's front and only door. At the door, she stopped, looked around carefully, making sure no one was out and about, then quietly tripped the door's steel latch and slipped inside.

She emerged from the barn fifteen minutes later, a

little breathless from her grisly endeavor, and quietly latched the door behind her. The night's chill breeze tossed her hair that hung down from the hood of her cape; it dried and chilled the sweat that bathed her. Looking around again, feeling herself growing suspicious to the point of paranoia, she drew a deep, calming breath. Pressing her back against the stable, in the safety of the deep shadows that lay over this side of the yard, she raised the small sheaf of money she held in her right hand.

There were ten one-hundred-dollar bills. Not much relative to the rest in the saddlebags now stowed away in Jake's coffin, but enough to take the edge off Dixie's guilt over Clementine's death and leaving the simple, tenderhearted Henrietta to fend for herself.

She looked around again, listening and probing every shadowy nook and cranny at the yard's perimeter, then hurried back across the yard, past the woodshed and the privy. Twenty feet from the lodge's back door, her eagerness to finish her night's chores compelled her to break into a jog.

She'd taken only three jogging strides when a wooden scrape sounded behind her.

A man loudly hacked phlegm and spat. There was the squawk of rusty hinges.

Dixie stopped dead in her tracks, freezing in place and staring in wide-eyed horror at the lodge door before her, several strides away.

"Who's there?" Walt Teale's voice said behind her. "Who is that?"

The privy's fetor blew up around Dixie on the cold breeze that blew dead leaves about her moccasin-clad feet.

"Who's there?" Teale said again.

"It's me, Mr. Teale." Dixie turned, heart racing even faster than before, holding the thousand dollars down against her right leg, hoping the man didn't see it. "It's . . . it's Dixie."

"Oh." Teale sounded befuddled. He stood in front of the privy's partway open door, staring at her in the darkness. She could see only the man's thick, bulky outline. He appeared to be wearing only his long-handles, boots, and hat. "What're you doin' out here, Miss Dixie?" he asked above the wind. He rubbed his hands together briskly. "A mite chilly out here."

Dixie didn't have to pretend to shiver. "I know! That's why I'm going back up to bed."

Dixie started to turn away but stopped when Teale said, "What were you doing out here, Miss Wade?"

Dixie turned back to him. He'd sounded suspicious. What would there be for him to be suspicious about? If he didn't know about the loot, that was . . .

Maybe he did know about it.

"Couldn't sleep," Dixie said, trying to sound casual. "Just took a turn around the yard." She paused then, canting her head to one side, and said, "What about you, Mr. Teale? What were you doing out here?"

Teale strode forward. He wasn't much taller than Dixie, but he was a thick, lumbering figure with a large belly. In the darkness especially, he seemed threatening. And there was something threatening in his gaze and the menacing way he walked up to her to stand six feet away. He stared at her stonily for several seconds. She grew self-conscious about the cut on her swollen temple, about the crusted blood, but didn't think he could see it, certain that the cape's hood as well as her hair obscured it.

Teale smiled suddenly, glanced over his shoulder at

the privy, then turned back to her and said, "What's it look like?"

"Ah."

Dixie wrinkled her nose against the outhouse's stench. Was that all he was doing out here? Maybe he'd been snooping around the yard and the barn, looking for the loot . . .

"Better close the privy door, Mr. Teale," Dixie said, glancing at the door swinging back and forth in the wind and shepherding the stench this way and that. "We wouldn't want to lose the door. Besides, it's stinking up the yard."

Teale studied her. She couldn't see his eyes clearly in the darkness, but they seemed menacing again. He stretched his lips in a wan smile, nodded, and said, "Right."

"Good night, Mr. Teale."

"Good night, Miss Wade."

"Please, Mr. Teale. We'll be sharing the trail out of these mountains. Might as well start calling me Dixie."

"All right. Dixie it is." Teale turned and walked back toward the privy.

Dixie stared at his stooped, heavily striding figure, wondering . . .

As he grabbed the door and started to close it, Dixie swung around and retreated up the stairs to her room.

CHAPTER 16

*"Miss MacFarland deserves better than you. You're going
to hurt her. You know you will. You've hurt every woman
who's ever come into your life and made the mistake of
loving you!"*

Sheila's damning words echoed around inside
Johnny's head as he rode out of Hallelujah Junction
and started the climb into the mountains. He had
to force himself to hold the horses back on the
steeper inclinations, to keep from blowing them out
prematurely, or laming them, but he couldn't put
the settlement behind him fast enough.

He'd wanted to leave town to clear his head, but at
the moment his mind was louder than ever. His trans-
gression against his wife, Lisa, played out just behind
his eyes, nearly as real and raw as the night the men
led by Sonny Davis had broken into his cabin and
bucked out Lisa and David in a hail of gunfire.
Johnny had been wounded, left for dead . . .

He'd let that happen. If he hadn't been distracted,
half-drunk and arguing with Lisa about his dalliance
with another woman, he would have been ready for
the killers. But Lisa wasn't the first woman he'd injured. After Lisa, there was the drunk whore Lenore,

who'd killed herself with whiskey when Johnny had left her alone in her fetid crib when she'd needed him the most. He'd betrayed Lenore by falling in love with Sheila.

He'd betrayed Sheila with Glyneen. Early on in mind if not in body.

Maybe Glyneen was the real reason he hadn't married Sheila. Maybe his love for Sheila had frightened him, as committing himself to another person always had. Unconsciously, he'd feared losing his freedom and independence.

If Sheila was right, he'd eventually betray Glyneen, as well, leaving a trail of broken hearts behind him. He saw a sad and lonely old man in his future, stewing over a life of one misstep after another.

One betrayal after another.

Johnny might have given up drinking, but he was still a wretched drunk in his soul. Just a dry one. Sheila was right. Glyneen didn't deserve him. What's more, he didn't deserve her. He'd only hurt her again, anyway. Because that's what he did. He hurt those foolish enough to love him.

As he rode through the windy mountains, pines towered over him, striping the narrow trail with sunlight and shade. Rivers roared in rocky canyons. Crows cawed. Hunting eagles screeched in the vaulting cobalt sky. Stony crags jutted like dinosaur teeth.

Distant alpine slopes streaked with the dingy ermine of last winter's snows shouldered above, between, and beyond the crags, in the farthest distance, above cloud tendrils, beckoning him with their gray and windy remoteness, making him feel ever smaller, ever more insignificant, his transgressions just the usual ones of a mortal man and not so much like those of some black, demented god who'd been old and angry long before the earth's first shimmer of life.

Lord, how he loved the high country!

He'd been born here, to Joseba and Yolanda Beristain. He'd been raised herding sheep among these moody crags with his older brother, Arnauld, "Arnie" for short. His roots and his soul were still here. He belonged here with the solitary cedars and spruces and tamaracks growing from mere cracks in the stony slabs, twisted by the wind, brutalized by summer hail and winter snows, scorched by lightning, succored by the cold snow runoffs of spring.

He'd die here one day, alone, maybe the sooner, the better.

The aspens were bright gold up here. As he rode along a canyon, a fierce wind and cold rain descended, stripping nearly every leaf from the aspens near the stone overhang beneath which he took cover with his horses. The rain turned to snow then back to rain, and then it blew itself out, drifting on down the canyon. Johnny watched it go, the cloud vapor slithering among the wet, slush-rimed rocks. The clouds rose, parted, and the sun streamed down, seeming even brighter than before, flashing like liquid gold off the wet aspen and cottonwood leaves, like quicksilver in the dark green firs and pines. The sky was the icy blue of a Viking warrior's eyes.

On he rode, for it was still early in the day.

Gradually, his mind cleared. He felt his body relax in the saddle. Guilt still chewed at him, as it should, but not to the mad distraction it had before.

If he could only stay up here. Never return to town

where, against his own will, he would continue to wreak his havoc.

"A dark and brooding Basque," his foster father, Joe Greenway, had called him. His friend Bear Musgrave had said the same thing, adding, "The Basque folks are contrary, independent—loners, mostly, and unpredictable as the weather in the mountains most of 'em hail from. Quick to love, just as quick to get drunk and turn a saloon to little more than matchsticks!"

Johnny could hear his old friend's raucous laughter.

He camped that first night beside Roaring Creek, tending his horses then building a fire over which he cooked coffee, beans, and bacon. His mind was at rest when he fell asleep in his soogan, curled against the descending, high-country chill, but the same old dreams pestered him—the cutthroats breaking into his house.

Only this time, it was Glyneen screaming as they descended upon her and drove her to the floor. There was a child, as well, only one much younger than David. A baby, in fact.

Johnny woke before dawn, panting, bathed in sweat despite the white furry down of frost covering his blankets.

He camped the next night in Winter's Canyon, named after an old fur trapper who'd built and once occupied the ancient log, brush-roofed shack that stood at the edge of the beaver meadow running through the grassy chasm, with a tall, pine-clad mountain rising behind it. A waterfall lay a hundred yards to the west. Johnny found its soft drumming and chugging restful, as he had back when he was a boy running sheep through this meadow with his family, and Old Man Winter—Dalvin Winter—had shared his elk with the Beristains, as they'd shared their berries, fish, and mutton with him.

So many memories here. Nearly every gulch and hollow was choked with them. Some as painful as a thrust from a razor-edged blade, some as warm as a mug of chocolate on a bitter night by a popping fire.

The next day around noon, Johnny rode out of the timber at the bottom of a ridge and down into a narrow valley bisected down its middle by a slender stream.

A wooden bridge spanned the stream. On the other side of the stream, a long log cabin sat, smoke unfurling from its broad brick chimney to send a blue haze out over the stream and the jade beaver meadow enshrouding it. A broad wooden sign stretched across the cabin's second story, just up from the roof over its front porch.

The words: RILEY DUKE'S SALOON had been hand-painted in bold red lettering across the sign, which was a good six feet high and twenty feet long. A half-dozen saddled horses were tied to the two hitchracks fronting the place. A beaten-up old buggy with one red wheel sat near the horses, a beefy mule in the traces. Straw stuffing was bleeding out of cracks in the single, butterscotch cowhide seat. The frame of the sorry contraption was held together with bailing wire. The stout, gray-snouted mule wore a straw hat with holes cut for the ears.

Johnny put Ghost and the spare horse up to a hitchrack near the buggy and swung down from the saddle. He tied both horses to the rack then loosened

Ghost's saddle cinch, so the horse could rest easy. He brushed the trail dust off his frock coat and hat then walked up the porch steps, letting his thumbs rake across the butts of the Twins, whose holsters were thonged on his thighs.

You never knew who you were going to run into in these parts. Johnny had made a lot of enemies over the years he'd been a lawdog in this country. And he'd made more after he'd started hauling bullion for Sheila, for several men had made a play for the gold, and he'd sent each to his reward.

That tended to make the friends and families of those men a mite on the colicky side. He suspected he'd one day end up with a bullet in his back. But what was he going to do? Sheila had said he belonged up here with the desperate men who haunted these high reaches, and she'd been right on that score, too.

Johnny never stopped here at Riley Duke's when he was packing bullion. That would have been taking an unnecessary risk. Mostly, it was desperate men, men on the dodge from the law lower down, who patronized Riley Duke's place. But when he was headed up toward the Reverend's Temptation, before he'd picked up the gold, he usually stopped here for a rib-sticking meal, which always tasted good after two nights of trail food.

Riley Duke was known for pan-frying a mean elk steak or bear loin. His bighorn sheep's liver fried in butter with wild onions was a rare delicacy.

Johnny pushed through the batwing doors and looked around.

The bar lay to the back of the crudely appointed shack. A dozen or so plank tables lay between the door and the bar. Three of the tables were occupied, and two men stood at the bar at the room's rear. There was one decoration, and that was a stuffed crow, wings spread, nailed over the bar. That had been Duke's pet crow, Clancy, which Duke had apparently had trouble parting with.

There was sawdust on the floor, as there was in most places in gold country. The sawdust swallowed up the dust the drunk prospectors spilled so Duke could separate the gold from the wood shavings later on. He likely made more of a killing on spilled gold dust than on his drinks and grub.

There was one woman in the place though you wouldn't know right off she was a woman and not a big, fat, ugly man in wash-worn, bib-front overalls. Maud Horton had seen Johnny step through the doors. She turned her fat face with doughy nose and two little dark eyes set deep in suety sockets to the newcomer now and beckoned broadly with one fat arm, bellowing hardily, "Johnny! Shotgun Johnny! Get over here an' drink with ole Maud!"

Three sheets to the wind, she'd badly slurred the words.

Four men in range gear sat with Maud. They sat around her, facing her, one sitting on a chair back, his feet on the chair's seat, one arm resting on his knee. One sat with his hip hiked on the table. The two others sat in chairs. They'd seemed to be having a serious discussion when Johnny had walked into the room.

Now all eyes were on Johnny, Maud's eyes glinting drunkenly, the men studying him and his two holstered shotguns skeptically.

Johnny strode to a table on his right and tossed his

hat on it, running a hand through his long, thick brown hair. "Now, Maud, you know I gave up the bottle."

"Ah, don't be a wet blanket!"

Johnny grinned. "Sorry, darlin'. If I were to drink with any woman, I'd drink with you." He winked at her.

Maud flushed as red as a Nevada sunset and said, "Oh, you charmer." She slapped the table with a fat hand and leaned so far forward her chin nearly touched the table. "I'll be damned if you ain't a handsome devil. Look at him, boys—ain't he a handsome devil? Even with that big eagle's beak of his. As handsome a devil as I ever known"—she made a sad expression—"an' he won't drink with ole Maud!"

"You don't need him, Maud," said the man sitting on the chair back, glaring at Johnny from beneath the curled brim of his battered cream Stetson. "You got us. We're all you need." He glanced over his shoulder toward the bar. "Hey, Riley—bring Maud another bottle, will ya?"

Riley Duke had just appeared through a bear-hide curtain flanking the bar. He was holding a tray with a steaming wooden bowl and a plate of nut-brown bread, also steaming. "You don't think she's had enough?" Duke asked the man who'd asked for the bottle. "As it is, it looks like a half dozen of us are gonna have to carry her out and roll her into her buggy, and here it's just after noon!"

As Duke grabbed an unlabeled bottle off a shelf flanking the bar, his gaze switched to Johnny. The big, roly-poly man, every bit as fat as Maud if not fatter, and nearly as bald as an egg, a loosely rolled quirley dangling from between his lips, grinned and said in a raspy, breathless voice, "Hi, Johnny. You come for the bear or the elk?"

"I'll take the elk, Riley," Johnny said, lounging back in his chair and digging his makings out of his shirt pocket.

"Just coffee?" Duke asked as he stepped out from behind the bar, heading for Maud's table.

"Just coffee."

"What kind of man comes into Riley Duke's and only orders coffee?" This from the man—a small, blond-haired man in a brown vest under an open elk-hide coat—sitting nearest Maud. He was the smallest of the four. Johnny knew Willie Slater to be meanest of the bunch, too. Meaner than a lot of men.

Johnny knew all four men. Like most of Duke's clientele, they were bottom-of-the-barrel scum. Drifters who often took to wayward means—cattle rustling, claim jumping among them—for their livings though Johnny had never been able to pin anything hard on them. Maybe someday . . . if they lived that long.

The way all four were looking at him now, they each had one foot in the grave, only they didn't know it yet. Johnny wasn't in the frame of mind to put up with any prodding. He might belong up here with these desperadoes, but that didn't mean he couldn't cull his own desperate numbers from time to time.

Besides, he wasn't wearing his moon-and-star today. He'd left it at home. Today, he was just another desperado. Not that he'd ever been much of a fan of due process. Some men . . . even some women . . . didn't deserve it. He'd realized that when he'd snuffed the wicks of Sonny Davis and the other men who'd butchered his family, though the satisfying deed had gotten his badge taken away from him.

Hell, he'd known it back when a wealthy cattle-man had hired out to have Johnny's own family murdered. Joe Greenway had had the honors of ex-acting revenge for Johnny and his family. Johnny would have preferred to have had that privilege himself though he'd still been a teenager at the time.

And he was a long way from the overseeing eyes of the chief U.S. marshal in Carson City.

Johnny casually considered Slater, who sat near Maud, grinning at Johnny mockingly.

Chapter 17

"Huh?" Slater said, rising, stumbling a little from drink then giving his chair an angry kick. "What the hell kinda man comes into Riley Duke's Saloon and orders coffee?"

He spat the words out angrily though he was still showing his teeth through that arrogant, jubilant grin. He might have been a good-looking young man, maybe twenty-five, if his lower jaw hadn't been so overly square and his eyes so cold and mean despite the smile dimpling his suntanned cheeks.

"Come on, Johnny—out with it," Slater persisted. "What kinda man?"

"One o' them crazy Basque men who can't hold his liquor," said the man sitting on his chair back, feet on the seat. Stretch Wilkins turned slowly toward Johnny while remaining seated, and slid the flaps of his wool coat back behind the grips of the Remington on his left hip. The long-faced, unshaven man widened his own smile. "That's who."

The other two stared at Johnny, as well. Maud was, too. She had a faint smile on her own lips, in her own drink-glassy eyes, as though she was enjoying the entertainment. Riley Duke had made it halfway back

to the bar when Slater had thrown the challenge—
for that's what it really was—to Johnny. Big, round-
gutted, egg-headed Duke stood switching his anxious
gaze from the four men at Maud's table to Johnny
and back again. He held his large red hands out in a
silent appeal for peace.

"Easy, now, fellas," Duke said cautiously, quietly.
"Easy . . . easy . . ."

"Shut up, Duke," Slater said without taking his eyes
from Johnny. "I ain't talkin' to you. I'm just tryin' to
find out what Johnny has against your tangleleg—
that's all."

"It's all right," Duke said, nervously switching his
gaze between the two factions. "I don't care that he
don't drink it. In fact, the way that he gets when he im-
bibes, I'd just as soon he stuck to coffee." He raised his
voice affably, as though trying to defuse the building
tension. "I'll get that coffee and steak for you pronto,
Johnny! You fellas enjoy that bottle I set on your table
there. On the house!"

"Shut up, Duke!" Slater repeated. "It ain't you I'm
talkin' to."

He kept his eyes on Johnny. Johnny returned his
gaze. As he did, he slowly, deftly built his quirley without even looking at the paper as he dribbled tobacco
onto the crease between the first two fingers of his
right hand. He was leaning forward, arms on his table.
Without expression he stared back at Slater.

"Dammit," Slater bit out through gritted teeth. "I'm
talkin' to you, Johnny. Clean the grease outta your
damn ears an' answer my question! What kind of a
man comes into Riley Duke's place and don't order
whiskey?"

Slowly, Johnny rolled the quirley closed. It was so

quiet in the room just then that everyone could hear the soft crackling sound of the tissue-thin paper being rolled closed around the chopped tobacco. Still, Johnny kept his dark, expressionless gaze on Slater. Maud Horton flanked the blond toughnut. She was smiling deviously, expectantly, as she looked up at Slater and then at Johnny, her eyes dancing with rarefied delight.

The other three men at the table, all sitting, Slater being the only one on his feet, matched Maud's grin with eager ones of their own. Stretch Wilkins had his hand up close to the worn walnut grips of his holstered Remington.

Riley Duke backed up cautiously against his bar, stretching his arms out to both sides and placing his hands on the bar's edge.

"Dammit!" Slater bellowed in frustration, his face now beet-red, eyes pinched to slits. "Why don't you answer my question? Show a little respect for your betters, you greasy damn sheepdip-stinkin' Basque! Answer my damn question, or I'm gonna pull my Colt and give you the bullet you been deservin' for a long time, you smug sidewinder!"

Johnny stuck the quirley between his lips. He dug a lucifer out of his shirt pocket, dragged the sulfur head across the table in front of him. The sulfur exploded into flame. Johnny raised the flame to the quirley dangling from between his lips.

When the cigarette caught fire, Johnny sucked the smoke into his lungs and blew it out of his mouth around the quirley, and out of his nose, as well. A thick wreath of smoke swirled around in front of him.

He considered the angry young drunk across the room from him. Slater was so mad his eyes were nearly crossed. His face was as red as a velvet curtain drawn across a stage in some frontier opera house. Forked veins in his forehead bulged and throbbed.

The man sitting to Maud's left, on the opposite side of the table from Slater—Jate Durnberg was his name—cleared his throat and said, "You do realize he's carrying his twin sawed-offs—right, Willie?"

"Oh hell, I know that. He don't go nowhere without *the Twins.* Everybody knows that. But I don't think he can get those big poppers out faster'n I can skin my Colt." Slater curled his upper lip at Johnny. "Huh? Can ya, Johnny? Nah, I think if he tried, Shotgun Johnny's trail would end here today. Right here!"

"Easy, now, Willie . . ."

"I told you to shut up, Duke!"

Maud stared dreamily at Slater and then looked at Johnny. She widened her eyes a little, gave a little mewling cry of anxious delight, for hell appeared about to pop. Good-bye, boring afternoon! She grabbed the seat of her chair and sort of skipped it to her left a foot, so she wouldn't catch any double-ought buck intended for Slater.

Stretch Wilkins chuckled at that.

"What do you think, Johnny? Huh, Johnny? Cat got your tongue?" Slater paused, holding his right hand above the walnut grips of his .44. "Do you think you can haul out those barn blasters before I can skin my Colt?"

Johnny took another deep drag off his cigarette. He blew out the smoke and stared mildly through the billowing cloud at Slater. "I don't know," he said finally, his voice as mild as his expression. "Why don't you skin the Colt an' let's see what happens?"

Slater glared back at him, his mocking smile in

place. Then he frowned a little, as though he hadn't quite understood his opponent's response. "Huh?"

"Skin it," Johnny said, taking another casual drag off the quirley, blowing the smoke into a plume over his table, toward Slater.

Slater just stared at him. Very slowly, so slow so as to be nearly unnoticeable, the smile faded from the blond toughnut's lips.

The other men and Maud looked at him excitedly.

"Skin it," Johnny said, again mildly. "Let's see what happens."

Maud gave another thrilling cry and bounced her chair several inches farther to her left, so that she was snugged up so close to Jate Durnberg that she was practically in the man's lap.

Slater glanced at her then returned his gaze to Johnny. The smile had vanished. Now his brows were beetled. Long, jagged lines stretched across his forehead.

"Skin it." Johnny slid his chair back. He did it so fast that the move startled Slater, who jerked a little, nearly took a step backward before he caught himself. Rising slowly, leisurely, Johnny said, "Let's see what happens."

Slater didn't say anything. He just watched Johnny uncoil like a big cat from his chair. Slater's face was still as red as molten iron, but two white dots had formed on the nub of each cheek. They grew as slowly as the smile had faded from his mouth.

Johnny stepped out away from his table. He shifted the quirley to his left hand, hooked both thumbs in the pockets of his pants, near the butts of his ten-gauges, and walked casually toward where his opponent stood to the left of Maud's table. He kept his dark-eyed gaze on Slater. Slater's jaws had loosened so that the lower one hung slack though the man's mouth was closed.

The closer Johnny came to him, the wider Slater's eyes grew.

"Go ahead," Johnny said as he drew within six feet of his opponent. "Let's see what happens."

He stopped. Slater looked up at him. Johnny was half a head taller than the blond man, so that Slater had to look up at him. Still, he said nothing.

The others looked at him.

The room had again fallen so quiet that a hawk could be heard giving its ratcheting cry as it hunted rabbits out in the meadow surrounding the road ranch.

Johnny stared down at Slater staring up at him. The bulging vein in the blond man's forehead had disappeared. Nearly all the blood had left his face. His chest rose and fell quickly. A single sweat bead popped out on his left brow and dribbled down into that eye. Slater flinched, tried to blink the salt sting away.

"If you're gonna skin the damn thing, skin it!" Johnny shouted. His voice sounded nearly as loud as the detonation of both Twins at the same time.

Everyone in the room jumped. Slater leaped backward, getting his left boot caught on a nearby chair. Giving a mewling cry, he dropped to the floor on his ass. He cursed shrilly and pulled his Colt from its holster. He was so nervous, it took him a good three or four seconds, fumbling with the keeper thong over the hammer.

When he finally got it out, Johnny stepped forward and kicked the gun out of Slater's hand. The Colt flew high and bounced off the wall behind Slater to land on the floor with a hard thud.

Slater stared up at him, lower jaw hanging nearly to his chest, his mouth as wide and dark as a rabbit hole. Johnny stood over him, glaring down at him, thumbs still hooked in the pockets of his pants but not touching either Twin. Slater's expression was a mix of rage, terror, and exasperation. "Why . . . you . . . !" His head swelled until it looked like it would explode.

"Get out," Johnny said quietly but forcefully. "You're banned from the premises, Willie."

Slater looked at his friends, as though expecting help. They all sat staring incredulously, numbly, between Willie and Shotgun Johnny. So did Maud. So did Riley Duke.

Slater gurgled and chortled, giving an animal's expression of convoluted emotion, the primary one now being humiliation. He scrambled to his feet and ran, pinwheeling his arms and stumbling over chairs, wailing, to the front of the room and out through the batwings. There was a squawk of saddle leather. Hooves pounded, dwindling quickly.

Johnny turned to Slater's four friends. They all sat as still as statues, staring at him dubiously. Stretch Wilkins had closed his right hand over the grips of his Remington. His long face owned a pinched look of pained concentration, hesitation.

"You, too, Stretch?" Johnny said, arching one brow.

Stretch quickly removed his hand from the revolver and let his coat flap slide up over the gun and holster.

Riley Duke lowered his hands from the bar. "I'll, uh . . . I'll fetch that coffee for you now, Johnny." With a heavy sigh, he turned to walk back around behind the bar.

"Thanks," Johnny said as he strode back to his table, taking another drag from his quirley. "I'd appreciate that, Riley."

As he slacked into his chair, the men at Maud's table turned to one another, muttering and casting cautious glances toward Johnny.

"I'll be hanged," Maud intoned suddenly, shaking her head as though coming out of a trance, "if that didn't sober me right up!" Giving a warbling, anxious laugh, she picked up the fresh bottle Duke had brought and splashed liquor into her stone coffee mug.

"I never seen the like of that," muttered the fourth man at the table, Earl Crabb sheepishly brushing a fist across his nose and clearing his throat. "Never seen Willie get his horns twisted like that."

"Nope," Stretch Wilkins said, coming down off his chair back to sit in the chair, which creaked precariously beneath his weight. He glanced over his shoulder again at Johnny. "He ain't gonna take it well, neither."

"Willie?" said Jate Durnberg, chuckling ominously. "Hell, no!"

Riley Duke brought Johnny's mug of coffee then headed back to the bar, "I'll fetch that steak for you now, Johnny. Taters with it? Onions?"

"How 'bout a couple eggs and some flapjacks while you're at it?"

"Comin' right up!" Duke said, obviously still a little shaken, breathing hard, voice quavering.

When he'd disappeared through the doorway behind the bar, where he kept his living quarters and a rudimentary kitchen, the four men at Maud's table stopped casting furtive looks at Johnny and gave their full attention to Maud, who was already deep into her fresh mug of whiskey.

"Now, then, Maud," Stretch Wilkins said, keeping his voice low though not low enough that Johnny couldn't hear him, "where did you say we could find Jake Teale?"

"Yeah," muttered Durnberg, "and the big bounty on his head?"

CHAPTER 18

Dixie indulged in a long, hot bath in her room, washing Clementine's blood off her hands and out of her hair. She toweled off, slipped into a satin chemise, a pair of pantaloons, and a light cream wrap, then plucked the thousand dollars off her dresser and went to the door.

She opened it quietly and poked her head into the hall.

Snores resonated from Teale's room, several doors down the hall from Dixie's.

Dixie went out, closed her own door, and, clutching the hundred-dollar bills in her right hand, strode down the hall in the opposite direction from Teale's room. She stopped at Henrietta's door, tapped very lightly on the upper panel.

No response.

Dixie twisted the knob, not surprised to find the door unlocked. She went inside. The room was as dark as the bottom of a well save what little weak candle-light angled in through the now-open door. Dixie lit a lamp on Henrietta's dresser, closed the hall door, then turned up the lamp's wick, revealing the room and the thickset doxie slumbering in her bed, under several sheets and ragged quilts.

The room was a mess, clothing strewn everywhere. Henrietta kept Heck Torrance's room and the rest of the inn as tidy as an old maid's parlor, but her own room looked as though a cyclone had blown through it. Henrietta expended too much energy everywhere else to have much left over for her own quarters.

Careful not to trip, Dixie moved to the bed and sat on the edge of it.

Henrietta stirred but did not come instantly awake. The poor girl was always so tired that she was likely asleep before her head hit the pillow. Dixie felt guilty about waking her up, but it was for a good reason.

Dixie placed her hand on the girl's thick shoulder and gave her a gentle shake. "Henrietta, wake up."

The girl just grunted into her pillow, unwilling to leave the sanctuary of sleep.

"Henrietta," Dixie said softly, giving her another shake. "Please, wake up. I have to—"

"What is it?" Henrietta rolled onto her back and lay squinting sleepily up at Dixie. "Fire?"

"No, no. No fire."

"Is it Mr. Torrance?" Henrietta sat up, eyes widening with worry. "Did he fall out of bed again?"

"No, no." Dixie smiled tenderly at the unattractive girl and caressed her cheek with the backs of her fingers, soothingly. "Henrietta, nothing's wrong. I just need to talk to you."

"What time is it?"

"Well after midnight. I'm sorry, but it can't be helped. I have something for you."

Henrietta scowled dumbly. "Huh?"

"Henrietta, pay very close attention to what I have

to say, all right? Clementine is gone. I am going to leave in the morning with Mr. Teale. I think you should leave, too. As soon as you can."

"What? Clementine is . . ." She shook her head uncomprehendingly.

"She left earlier. Some man came for her. They rode off together. They looked quite happy."

"A man came for . . . What man? I never knew Clementine to have any man except the customers."

"Well, apparently there was one. Maybe they exchanged letters or some such." Dixie shook her head. "Anyway, it doesn't matter. She's gone. She's not coming back. I'm leaving in the morning with Mr. Teale."

"I know," Henrietta said. "I know that, Dixie. I wish you wouldn't . . . especially if Clementine is gone now, too. Are you sure she's gone, Dixie? Seems she woulda told me . . ."

"She said she didn't have the heart to tell you. She asked me to tell you. So, now I have, and she's gone, and now you must forget about her. I have something for you, Henrietta. A very special present."

"Present?"

Dixie smiled as she held up the thousand dollars.

Henrietta focused her sleepy eyes on the money. She looked at Dixie then back at the money then at Dixie again. "What's that?"

"Money." Dixie kept her voice low, in case Mr. Teale was prowling around out in the hall, maybe trying to listen through the door. "It's a thousand dollars, Henrietta. It's a stake for you, so you can leave here and make a fresh start for yourself."

"A thousand dollars?" Henrietta didn't seem all

that impressed. A thousand dollars to her—to one who'd had so little all her life and been treated so shabbily by everyone who had come into it—was probably as hard-pressed to conceive of a hundred dollars as a million. She'd never had any reason to ponder on how much money that was because in her small world that much didn't exist.

She'd been a whore since she was thirteen, which meant most of her money went to room and board. She'd likely never saved more than a dollar or two. Before she'd started whoring, she'd been cared for by her father, albeit poorly. The man had been a worthless alcoholic.

"It's a lot of money, Henrietta. And it's all yours."

"Where did it come from?"

"Jake had it on him when he died."

Henrietta widened her eyes and opened her mouth in shock. *"Ohh!"*

Dixie frowned. "What?"

Henrietta placed her hand over her mouth and stared down at the money in Dixie's hand. Judging by the horrified expression on Henrietta's face, you might have thought Dixie was threatening her with a poisonous snake.

Henrietta raised her stricken gaze back to Dixie. "That money's *stolen* money, Dixie!"

"No, no, no, no!" Dixie paused, frowned again curiously, and shrugged a shoulder. "I mean, so what if it is? It's yours now, Henrietta. No one will know. You'll use it to build a good life for yourself."

"No! It's stolen!"

"Henrietta, keep your voice down." Dixie cast an anxious look at the door.

"It's stolen money, Dixie. Clementine said Jake had a whole saddlebag full of the stuff, and you hid it somewhere!"

Dixie leaned forward and clamped a hand over Henrietta's mouth. "Keep your voice down, Henrietta! You mustn't wake up Mr. Teale! All right?" Dixie shook the girl's head to impress upon her the gravity of the situation. "Do you understand? I'm not going to take my hands away until you promise to pipe down!"

Henrietta just stared up at her, eyes bright with terror.

"Understand?" Dixie said again, keeping her voice hard but low.

Henrietta gave a feeble nod.

Dixie removed her hands. Suddenly, she regretted having come to Henrietta's room. Her heart had been in the right place. She'd wanted to give Henrietta enough money for a fresh start, so guilt wouldn't follow her around like a starving dog.

This was the thanks she got. If she wasn't careful, Henrietta was going to spill the beans on Jake's loot!

Henrietta continued to stare up at Dixie, her gaze now filled with recrimination, suspicion . . .

"Dixie," she whispered, narrowing her eyes, her own voice hard and shrewd now, "Clementine didn't leave with a man like you said, did she?"

"Of course she did. Henrietta, you have to—"

"No, she didn't!"

"She did, Henrietta. And you can leave now, too."

"Where would I go?" Henrietta was close to tears. "What about Mr. Torrance? Leave here? I like it here!"

"You can find someone else to take care of Torrance.

Or wait for him to die. He's damn near dead the way it is."

Dixie rose from the bed, anger and frustration burning inside her. She clenched the thousand dollars tightly in her fist and had trouble keeping her voice down. "Oh, what the hell do I care what you do, anyway? Forget it! I was trying to be good to you, you simpleton! Go ahead and toil away here, scrubbing that old man's ass . . . his sheets . . . spooning porridge into his miserable mouth! Laying with every filthy . . ."

Henrietta scrunched up her face and jutted her dull chin toward Dixie, fire in her eyes. "What did you do with Clementine?" she hissed.

"What?"

"You heard me." Henrietta shoved her face even farther over the edge of the bed and up, pointing it like a gun at Dixie. "What did you do to her? She knew about the money. Did you fight over it? Dixie . . . *Did you kill Clementine?*"

Dixie stared down at her. Her heart raced. Her hands turned clammy.

"You *did*, didn't you?" Henrietta hissed again, her voice sounding like the voice of some lunatic crone. "You killed . . . *oh!*" Again, she clamped her hand over her mouth in horror.

A keg of dynamite exploded inside of Dixie. Before she knew what she was doing, she'd pulled the thick down pillow out from beneath Henrietta's head. She placed her right knee on the edge of the bed and, leaning forward, shoved the pillow over Henrietta's face, forcing her head back down to the bed.

Henrietta screamed into the pillow. The muffled cry likely didn't penetrate much farther than the room.

Dixie placed her other knee on the bed and then, holding the pillow down over Henrietta's head, she straddled the fat girl, pinning her fast to the mattress. Henrietta flailed at Dixie with her fists and kicked with her legs. The bed rocked like a rowboat on a choppy lake. The covers went flying to the floor.

Gritting her teeth and hardening her jaws, Dixie threw all her weight forward and down, pressing the pillow hard against Henrietta's face, preventing the girl from taking another breath.

Killing her took a long time, much longer than Dixie had thought it would take to kill a person, with brief lulls in Henrietta's fighting before the girl's resistance resumed with renewed vigor.

Odd, Dixie vaguely thought, how stubbornly the fat girl clung to a life that had given her little but hard toil and grief.

Finally, another lull came in Henrietta's resistance. Only, this time the fighting did not resume. The soft, lumpy body beneath Dixie lay still and slack, arms flung straight out to both sides. After a minute of anxious waiting for the resistance to continue, Dixie slowly, cautiously removed the pillow, ready to clamp it back down on Henrietta's face again at the first sign of renewed fighting.

But the face that stared up at Dixie was a dead one.

Dead despite the wide-open eyes and mouth, the lingering terror in Henrietta's sagging lower jaw and lips stretched back from her small, white teeth.

Breathless, Dixie stared down at the fat, pale, dead face gazing up at her, unseeing. "Fool," she said, climbing slowly down from the bed. "You simple fool."

Quickly, heart still racing, Dixie picked the bed-covers off the floor and flung them back onto the bed. She drew them up and over Henrietta's motionless body. She picked up the banknotes she'd dropped then hurried to the door. She pulled the door open, looked out.

No one was in the hall.

Good.

She stepped out, drew Henrietta's door closed behind her, and began making her way back along the hall toward her own room. As she approached her door, she slowed her pace and turned toward Heck Torrance's door. As she stared at the old pimp's door, her brows beetled.

She pondered. She kneaded her lower lip between her thumb and index finger.

Her heart had slowed after she'd climbed off Henrietta's bed. Now it was picking up speed again.

Finally, she crouched low and slid the banknotes beneath her door. She straightened then walked over to Torrance's door. She twisted the knob and stepped inside, closing the door again behind her.

Henrietta had left a lamp lit, the wick low, on Torrance's dresser, cluttered with medicine bottles and salve tins for his bedsores. She always left a lamp burning to make it easier for her to check on the pimp during the night, which she always did, two or three times. That's how conscientious she was.

Had been.

Dixie knew that if she allowed herself to think about what she'd done, she'd feel bad about smothering Henrietta. Despite her having had no choice in the matter. Besides, hadn't she really only ended the poor wretch's suffering?

It was time now to end Torrance's suffering, as well. He no longer had Henrietta around to care for him.

Leaving him here alive, alone, would be worse than what Dixie was about to do. The way she saw it, it was the least she could do for the man.

She moved to the bed. Torrance lay on his back, covers pulled up to his chin. He was sleeping though breathing shallowly, making low, raking sounds in his throat. His face was pale and bony. His eyelids fluttered as he snored. Dixie could see his eyeballs darting around behind the paper-thin lids as he dreamed.

Dixie reached over and grabbed the pillow on the other side of the bed. She placed it over Torrance's face then leaned forward to press it down hard with both hands.

The old pimp hardly put up any struggle at all.

When he was dead, Dixie covered his slack face with the bedcovers and returned to her own room. There were still a few hours of night left. She needed to get some sleep. Odd, how calm she felt. She thought she really would be able to sleep, which was good.

She had a big day ahead. She was starting life all over again.

CHAPTER 19

The next morning, Dixie stood staring out the Grizzly Ridge Inn's front window at the yard beyond. She wore her wool coat and a scarf around her head. Knit mittens jutted from the pockets of the coat.

She was ready to go. She was ready to start life over again.

Snow had fallen during the night—just a light coating that resembled a heavy frost. It wasn't much of a snow, but it reminded Dixie that winter was on the way, and that she was lucky to be getting out of these mountains soon. The aspens fringing the edge of the yard had nearly entirely lost their leaves.

One more winter would kill her, she was sure.

She stretched her gaze to the right and saw Walt Teale drive Torrance's old buckboard out from between the stable's open doors and into the bright sunlight of the snowy morning. Teale wore his high-crowned black hat. His wool coat was buttoned up to his throat, and a ragged red muffler was loosely knotted around his unshaven neck. His frosty breath plumed in the golden morning sunshine.

As he drew the wagon up in front of the lodge, the

tailgate suddenly flopped open with a wooden bang, frightening the mule that Teale had tied behind the wagon. The mule jerked its head up and brayed. Dixie gasped when Jake's coffin slid back over the open tailgate.

She was sure it was going to tumble out of the wagon box and onto the ground. The lid was not nailed down so there was a chance it would tumble out and reveal the box's contents.

All of its contents, that was. Not only Jake.

The coffin slid two feet over the end of wagon and stopped. The bulk of the box remained in the wagon.

"Thank God!" Dixie muttered beneath her breath.

She hadn't nailed the lid down on the coffin because she'd worried she wouldn't be able to get it off again. Or that it would take her too much time to remove it. Likely, when she needed to remove the loot from the box, Walt Teale would be near and Dixie's time would be limited.

Besides, she hadn't thought he'd want to look in the coffin again. He'd already seen Jake's body. He'd have had no reason to view it again.

Now Dixie realized her mistake. She should have nailed down the lid. The wagon was old, and the tailgate was not secure.

Her heart slowing, Dixie watched Teale climb heavily down from the wagon seat. He moved slowly, wincing with every movement, like a man not only worn out but in pain. Probably arthritis. Teale ambled to the rear of the wagon and scowled down at the coffin almost angrily. Stretching his lips back from his teeth, he turned to thrust his left shoulder against the coffin, and driving his upper body slowly forward, he slid the coffin back into the wagon box.

His face turning red from the cold and the effort of his maneuvers, he lifted the tailgate back into place and secured the chains holding it closed. The job finished, he started toward the lodge. He swayed a little on his feet, as though light-headed, and swung his body quickly back toward the wagon, closing his hands over the top of the side panels to steady himself.

He lowered his head, giving his back to the lodge. He appeared to be trying to catch his breath.

Dixie stepped out onto the porch and moved to the front rail, drawing her coat closed at her throat, against the morning's late-autumn chill.

"Is everything all right, Mr. Teale?" she asked with genuine concern.

Teale took another couple of deep breaths. He grunted, lifted his head, brushed a gloved hand across his nose, then half turned to Dixie.

He nodded, gave a wan smile. "I'm all right." He waved a hand. "It's this . . . thin air up here."

"Are you sure you're all right?" His face was red and splotchy, pasty.

"I said I'm fine," Teale said a little indignantly. "Are the others up yet?"

"No. They likely won't be up for hours. No one stirs around here until at least noon."

She picked up the carpetbags she'd placed atop the porch steps earlier, clamping one under an arm, leaving one free hand to grab the neck of a burlap sack she'd set beside the carpetbags. She moved quickly but awkwardly down off the steps and over to the wagon. Teale still stood grasping the top of a side panel with one hand, as though afraid he'd fall if he released it. He had his nose tipped to the wind, sniffing it like a dog.

"Bad weather comin'," he said.

"We'd better get a move on, then." Dixie stepped up to the wagon and set the carpetbags in the box, between the driver's seat and the coffin. Teale's tack and war bag were in there, as well as feed sacks for the horse hitched to the wagon, and his mule.

"It's comin' from the north," Teale said. He'd turned himself around to stare in that direction, toward several massive granite peaks whose tips were hidden by dark, brooding clouds. He clung to the side panel now with his left hand. "When they come from the north, they're bad."

"Well, like I said," Dixie said, climbing up over the wheel, using the hub as a step, and onto the hard wooden seat, "we'd best get moving."

She studied the man critically. He kept his nose raised to the northern wind, but he'd closed his eyes. It was almost as though he was meditating or praying. "Are you sure you're all right, Mr. Teale?"

Teale opened his eyes and swiveled his head toward her. "Yeah. I'm fine. Just thinkin' on things, is all. When a man loses his last son . . . the last of his family . . . and is pushin' sixty . . . he starts thinkin' about things."

"What kind of things?" Dixie asked. She really wasn't interested in the conversation, though. She really just wanted to get as far away from the Grizzly Ridge Inn as possible.

"Regrets, maybe," Teale said. He hiked a shoulder. "You know—things you might've done different . . . to make things turn out . . . different."

"Well, you'll have plenty of time to do that on the

trail, Mr. Teale." Dixie gave a cold smile and patted the seat beside her. "Come along now."

Teale frowned, puzzled. "What about breakfast? And . . . I don't know . . . don't you wanna say good-bye?" He glanced at the lodge to indicate the people he believed still lived there.

"I said my good-byes last night. As for breakfast . . ." Dixie reached behind her and pulled the burlap bag up out of the box and set it on her lap. "I've made us ham-and-egg breakfast sandwiches, and I prepared a jug of coffee, as well. It's not going to stay hot in this weather, however, so let's get on the trail and I'll pour you a cup. We'll eat as we ride."

Teale turned his perplexed gaze to the lodge again. "I don't know. Seems odd. It's gettin' on late in the mornin', an'"—he turned back to Dixie—"no one's even *stirrin*'?"

Dixie had to check her anger though she couldn't help the crispness in her tone. "I told you they won't stir until noon. This is a whorehouse, Mr. Teale. Not a hotel. And since we had no stay-over customers, there is no reason for Clementine or Henrietta not to sleep in. They always do when they get the chance, which would be understandable if you knew how hard we all worked."

Teale studied her with his washed-out, dark brown eyes, his black, gray-flecked brows beetled suspiciously. "What's your hurry, Miss Dixie? What with the bad weather comin', why not lay over another day? It's cold enough. My boy will keep out in the barn. It got down well below freezin' last night."

"Mr. Teale, if you'd had to work in a place like this for as long as I have, doing what I did here, you'd want to get out as quickly as possible, as well. Now, would you please come up here and get this wagon moving? I'm sorry to lose my patience, but I'm afraid I've lost it!"

All she needed was for Teale to walk back into the lodge and discover the bodies of Henrietta and Heck Torrance. That might very well put an end to her plans.

Teale turned back to the lodge, scowling at the upper-story windows.

Dixie's heart thudded. She was growing more and more anxious. She felt as though ants were crawling around in her undergarments.

"All right," Teale said finally. He walked to the front of the wagon and grunted and groaned his way up onto the seat, losing his breath again as he did. Fairly panting, and flushed, he said, "We'll get movin', Miss Dixie. Maybe get ahead o' the storm . . ."

Dixie heaved a long, silent sigh of relief as the man uncoiled the ribbons from around the brake handle, released the brake, and clucked to the dun gelding in the traces.

Dixie could tell, even before they were a mile away from the Grizzly Ridge Inn, that it was going to be a long, perilous journey out of the mountains.

They made their way through an aspen forest to which only a few autumn-gold leaves still clung while the rest danced down around them, like giant gold raindrops. As they reached the edge of the clearing, a vast vista opened before them—one of deep canyons, conical spires, and steep mountain slopes the furry green of pine forest. At the bottom of a distant valley was the twisted white line of what Dixie figured was a raging river.

As they started down into the vast canyon, the trail became perilously rocky and very steep in places, dangerously narrow in others. Sometimes the drop was so steep that Dixie had to cling for dear life to the wagon seat. Even then, she thought several times that gravity was going to pitch her headfirst out of the wagon seat and onto the double-tree hitch below.

Teale slowed the horse into a mincing, halting walk, saying, "Hoah, now—hoah, now—hoah, now . . ." in a low, pinched voice, as though worried the horse would take a single stride too long, slip, fall, and pull the wagon down on top of it.

At another point on their journey down the canyon, the trail turned a sharp bend around a high, stone belly. The side of the trail nearest the belly of granite—or whatever kind of rock it was—was a good six or seven feet higher than the trail's other side. The hazard likely could have been negotiated more handily by a narrower, stouter prospector's wagon drawn by a sure-footed mule or burro.

But Heck Torrance's wagon, large and lumbering, one of its wheels turning crookedly and screeching like an angry blackbird, was just barely up to the task. Before they rounded the bend and the rocky trail leveled somewhat, Dixie was certain the crooked wheel was going to fall off the axle, or the wagon's strained frame was going to rip apart and cast her and Teale onto the rocks below.

On a couple of steep rises, the double-tree groaned, as did the splintered gray wagon tongue, as though it were about to break into pieces. Dixie glanced anxiously over her shoulder at Jake's coffin, which had slid back against the tailgate, threatening to burst through it. If that happened, Dixie was sure the cover would fly off and out would bounce Jake and the fifty thousand dollars in cold hard cash residing inside with Jake's body.

Dixie and Teale made their way down to the bottom of the canyon and rode for a time along the thundering San Joaquin River. Dixie was relieved to have made it down that gnarly stretch from the higher reaches in one piece. She hadn't traveled through this country in the four years she'd practically been imprisoned by old Heck Torrance in the Grizzly Ridge Inn—she'd been brought up here as part of a wagonload of girls from the streets of Reno—so little looked familiar out here. But she knew that she and Teale had just started their journey and that there was more rough country ahead.

What aggravated her and Teale's situation was the rain that had started before they'd reached the river. It had begun gently enough, the sky clouding over, the pale clouds descending without thunder or lightning. But the air turned abruptly cooler. The wind blew. Dark clouds were rolling in—purple clouds splotched with white.

Snow clouds.

The wind picked up, howling like banshees along the high crags looming over the canyon.

Teale looked up, stretching his lips back from his teeth. He shook his head. "Yep, shoulda laid over another day," he muttered as though to himself. He clucked and shook his head again.

Dixie huddled inside her coat, shivering against the building chill. As cold as she was, and as fearful of the dangerous journey she had ahead of her, she was glad they'd left the lodge. If they hadn't Teale would have eventually gone looking for Henrietta. He would have discovered Heck Torrance, then, too.

Dixie was glad they were far enough away from the lodge, if only a couple of miles as the crow flies, to make turning back impossible. Now, whatever happened, they'd have to keep heading down out of the mountains toward Hallelujah Junction, toward freedom.

A great roar filled her ears. The gentle rain became almost instantly a hammering deluge, battering Dixie about her head and shoulders. There was a thunderous roar, evoking a scream from the young woman's throat. She turned her head to look over the river's white froth toward the ridge on the opposite side of the canyon.

A witch's finger of blue lightning had just struck a boulder leaning out from the ridge wall maybe three quarters of the way up from the bottom. The boulder exploded, shattering, chunks of rock flying out from the belly of the ridge wall and tumbling down the wall toward the canyon floor. Dixie could feel the reverberations of all that falling rock through the seat of the wagon beneath her.

Teale cursed and shook the ribbons violently against the horse's back, yelling, "Time to take cover!"

CHAPTER 20

Shotgun Johnny galloped into the yard of the Grizzly Ridge Inn as a freezing rain lashed him, hammering down at nearly a forty-five-degree angle from a plum-colored sky.

The wind threatened to tear his hat from his head. It nibbled at his yellow rain slicker and tugged at the long tails of his red, neck-knotted bandanna. Thunder rumbled and lightning stitched sizzling designs across the stormy firmament.

Leading the packhorse by a lead rope, Johnny galloped Ghost up to the inn's log stable. Rain poured down over the building's overhang to carve a trench into the dirt six feet out from the wall. Johnny leaped down from the cream's back, pushed through the fall of water, opened the stable doors quickly, and led both mounts inside.

He unsaddled Ghost and led the cream into an empty stall. Doing so, he noticed that all of the stalls except one were empty. Only a single mount, a dapple-gray with a black mane and tail, was stabled here though the smells of more horses lingered in the humid air. The dapple-gray kicked its stall and whickered in a greeting of sorts.

Johnny fed the cream stallion a bait of oats. While the horse greedily munched the oats from its wooden bucket, Johnny gave him a quick rubdown with scraps of burlap then set a wooden bucket under the stable's overhang, filling the bucket from the falls in less than a minute.

He set the bucket of fresh rainwater in Ghost's stall.

With Ghost tended, he removed the packhorse's canvas panniers and pack frame and gave the horse the same treatment he'd given Ghost, finishing the tending by setting a bucket of rainwater in the horse's stall. He turned to the cream canvas panniers bulging with the bullion he'd picked up from the Reverend's Temptation.

Sixty-four thousand dollars' worth of high-grade gold ready for the U.S. Mint in San Francisco. Johnny knew the gold buoyed Sheila's bank as well as propped up her deceased father's less-than-profitable business interests, many of which he'd ventured into in his later years when his willingness to take financial risks had started to outweigh his good business sense.

Without the gold hammered out of the Reverend's Temptation by a team of seventeen men led by a crusty old superintendent, Sheila would lose her proverbial shirt. She and Johnny might have severed the knot, but he felt every bit as responsible for the gold as he had when they'd been planning to get married.

He could not deny that he carried a chip on his shoulder over what she'd done to him—pulling out of their marriage as though it had been a lousy business proposition merely because he'd chosen to wear a badge—but he'd never stop wanting to protect her . . . wanting nothing but the best for her, including financial security and personal happiness.

He pondered the question of what he should do with the gold while he sheltered here from the storm. He had to keep it safe at all costs.

Maybe he should squirrel it away out here in the stable . . .

He nixed the idea. He wanted the gold as close to him as possible.

He pulled the panniers up over his shoulder, grunting with the heavy burden. The bags weighed as much as a full-grown man—one packing some extra weight, as well.

Slouched a little under the dead weight, Johnny stepped back out into the lashing rain and closed and secured the stable doors. He hurried through the waterfall cascading off the roof and crossed the yard to the main lodge. He climbed the steps, crossed the porch, and knocked on the door built from three vertical halved logs.

He pounded three times with his left fist. Waiting for a response, he turned and stared off across the yard to a distant ridge cloaked by the heavy, roiling storm clouds and the pouring rain.

A lightning bolt slashed nearly straight down maybe a hundred yards out from the lodge, turning a cedar into sparks and flames. Johnny could smell the brimstone and the burning cedar carried to him on the swirling wind.

He turned back to the door, pounded again.

When no response was forthcoming, he tried the latch. The door opened, jerking a little in its frame. Johnny poked his head into the lodge.

"Hello?"

He hadn't stopped here in years. He usually took another route from the mine to Hallelujah Junction,

but he'd chosen this route because he'd sensed that
bad weather was on the way. The route near the San
Joaquin River was usually the best route in bad
weather, as the trail dropped faster to the lower elevations, and it wasn't as exposed to the lightning, which
was always a formidable and deadly hazard. Especially
this time of the year.

The last time he'd been through here, the place
had been run by a couple named Torrance. The inn
was mostly just a whorehouse but the couple had
lodged overnighters here, as well. Now Johnny hoped
they also took in sodden, trail-weary pilgrims seeking
shelter from storms.

He could see no one in the cabin before him—a
parlor area furnished in the Victorian style, with whitewashed log walls and badly worn, brocade-upholstered
armchairs and a fainting couch or two. A brick hearth
lay to the left. A piano abutted the wall to the right,
beyond which Johnny remembered lay a kitchen.

"Hello?" he called again, louder.

Still, no response. He could hear no one moving
about.

Johnny stepped in and closed the door. He set the
bullion on the floor, removed his hat, and looked
around again.

"Anybody here?"

Holding his hat in his hands, he crossed the parlor
to the kitchen door, and again he looked around, calling. Here, too, he neither saw nor heard anyone.

He walked back through the parlor to the bottom
of the stairs.

"Hello?" he called. "Anybody here? I stabled my
horse outside, just looking for shelter from the storm,

is all. A bit of grub might be nice." He paused. "I got money to pay!"

Growing frustrated, he climbed the stairs and yelled down the second-floor hall: "Hello? Anybody here? Name's Greenway. Johnny Greenway." He paused. "Torrance, you . . . anyone here?"

Apparently not. Anyone in the building would have heard him by now. Even if they were asleep. Unless they were very heavy sleepers, he silently opined.

Obviously, the place was still occupied. It hadn't been abandoned. Someone had cleaned and dusted recently. There were no cobwebs or mice or rats running around. No broken windows—at least as far as he could see. Someone had laid in a good supply of wood downstairs by the fireplace.

"Well, hell," he said aloud. "First things first, I reckon."

Torrance or whoever lived here would likely be back soon. Maybe he or they had gotten caught in the storm and were waiting it out somewhere, just as Johnny figured to do here.

He went back downstairs, pegged his hat on the wall by the door, and shrugged out of his slicker beaded with rainwater. The slicker had protected him for the most part from the rain, but the cold had penetrated his bones. He hung the slicker on a peg beside his hat and set to work building a fire with the split wood in the corrugated-tin box beside the hearth.

When he had several fledgling flames going, licking at the dry wood and perfuming the parlor with the smell of pine and cedar, he went into the kitchen for food. There was half a cured ham on the oilcloth-covered dining table. There was also a basket of eggs and a cutting board with several slices of bread on it.

It looked as though someone had made sandwiches and then abandoned their mess.

Peculiar.

Anyway, Johnny was hungry, so he built a fire in the black range and started a pot of coffee. He rummaged until he found some lard. He smeared a dollop of lard around in a cast-iron skillet, watching it melt, its whiteness turning clear, the smell of pork fat rising. He broke a half-dozen eggs into the skillet, cubed a big chunk of the ham, tossed the ham into the skillet, and scrambled the eggs with the ham.

His eggs and ham were done about the same time as the coffeepot was sending a thick rush of fragrant steam from its spout. He poured a stone mug of coffee, slathered some butter on two slices of bread, and set the buttered bread in the skillet. Using a thick leather swatch to insulate his hand, he lifted the skillet off the range and carried it and his mug of coffee into the parlor.

He set both down on the hearth then added more wood to the fire, shifting it around with the poker, mixing the burning wood up nicely, building up the flames and sending a sweet-smelling warmth throughout the room.

With the fire going nicely, he picked up the skillet and the coffee and sank into a chair near the bottom of the stairs. From this position, he had a good view of the yard through the two front windows, one on each side of the door. If and when the lodge's inhabitants returned, he'd know about it in time to do something with the gold that still lay on the floor near the door.

He wasn't sure what he was going to do with it, but it would spend the night here in the lodge with him. It was already getting late in the day, and even if the storm cleared out, the trails would be slick and dangerous. He wouldn't head out again till morning.

Rain drummed against the walls and streaked down the windows.

Lightning flashed frequently and the thunder was doing a good imitation of a kettledrum played by an overeager drummer.

The ham and eggs, which he scooped up with the buttered bread, was good. Damned good. Even better with the strong coffee he'd brewed. The fire popped and crackled, the flames listing this way and that depending on how fiercely the cold, damp wind blew down the chimney or sucked at the blaze, drawing straight up the smoke and cinders from the dancing orange flames.

When he'd finished the food and the coffee, he set the skillet and the cup aside, rose, and walked over to the gold. It couldn't lie there forever. He stood considering it, then glanced at the ceiling.

He'd claim a room up there for the night. Might as well stow the gold up there now.

He picked up the panniers and ascended the stairs. He considered the five doors on each side of the hall dimly lighted by a bracketed oil lamp on the wall. Since no one else was here to challenge him, he supposed he could have his pick of the litter. Since the third door on the left was open a crack, he chose that room, shoving the door open wider and peering inside.

This room, too, was partially lit by an oil lamp, its wick turned halfway up. The feeble flame spread a shuddering, watery light around the room. Female clothing lay everywhere, spilling from a chest of drawers and strewn about the floor. It looked like someone had moved out in a hurry, riffling through clothing, choosing what and what not to take, then lighting a shuck.

Hmm.

Anyway, the bed had sheets and quilts on it and looked comfortable enough, and there was water in the pitcher mounted on the washstand, so the room would do. If the doxie who'd put her brand on the room returned and took umbrage with Johnny's having moved in, he'd choose another room.

Until then, home sweet home.

He looked around for a place to stow the gold. One place was as good as another. He carried it over to the open armoire, set it inside, and closed the doors. The cabinet was no safe, but he'd likely not find a safe here. The armoire would be a makeshift safe. The lock would be the Twins. Anyone trying to squirrel the gold out of there would have to do so with a bellyful of double-ought buck.

He left the room. Drawing the door closed behind him, he saw that the door of the room directly across the hall wasn't latched. He considered the door, curious. Maybe he should take a gander into the room. Maybe he should take a gander into *all* of the rooms. He wasn't sure why, but . . . something just didn't seem right.

Where in hell were the inn's inhabitants?

He headed for the unlatched door. He'd just placed his hand on the knob and started to push the door open when a great cawing and squawking rose from outside. He stopped, turned his head to look behind him. The din came from the rear of the building.

He pulled back on the knob of the door he'd

started to open, closing that door, and reopening the door of his own room. He went in and crossed to the curtained window in the far wall. He slid the lacy, moth-nibbled curtain aside with the back of his right hand and gazed into the inn's backyard.

The rain appeared to have stopped. It had been replaced by a fine, granular snow swirling on the wind. The still-stormy sky had lightened somewhat, offering a fairly good view of the privy flanking the lodge, and what appeared to be a woodshed flanking the privy on Johnny's right. A patch of brush lay behind the woodshed—stunted cedars and shrubs forming a roughly rectangular shape, which was likely the sight of a now-defunct building.

What appeared to be turkey buzzards and large ravens were flapping around that patch of brush, rising and falling as though descending on carrion.

Carrion?

"What the hell are they feeding on back there?"

CHAPTER 21

Johnny studied the birds for a time, hearing their frantic caterwauling as they fought over what they'd found over that way. He raked a thumb down his jawline then turned away from the window, left the room, and closed the door. He headed down the stairs and then outside, walking along the lodge's southeast side, heading toward the rear.

He strode past the woodshed, the wind still blowing though not as hard as before. The shin-high grass was wet, and the falling snow was forming an icy crust on it. More purple clouds were moving in, which likely meant this was just the beginning of the snow.

He cursed. The snow on top of the rain, which would freeze overnight, would make travel even more hazardous. That was the trouble about mountain travel this time of the year. Winter came early to these elevations well above seven thousand feet.

The angry squawking and chortling grew louder as Johnny approached the brush. Several of the birds saw him, increased their tooth-gnashing cries, and flapped heavily away, their wings making windy, sinewy sounds before they lighted on a nearby cedar or dropped to the ground maybe fifty feet away, mewling and sort of growling, reluctant to leave whatever meal they'd found.

Johnny figured it was maybe a dead dog or cat. Possibly some farm animal or a deer.

As he pushed through the brush, he stopped suddenly, shocked to find two young, lean, charcoal-colored wolves scuffling over something lying half in and half out of a root cellar. They saw Johnny at the same time Johnny saw them. One turned tail immediately and ran away, tail down, glancing cautiously back over its shoulder.

The other studied Johnny coldly, narrowing its eyes and working its black-tipped nose. Johnny placed his right hand on the Twin holstered on that hip. He did not have to slide the weapon from its holster, however. The second wolf was reluctant to give up its meal, but it sensed that if it pressed the matter it would die.

It growled, showed its teeth, and raised its hackles. Then it gave a frustrating yip, wheeled, and headed off after the first wolf.

Johnny removed his hand from the shotgun's stock and walked forward, the scowl on his face turning more severe when he realized that what he was staring at was a dead person. One that lay half in and half out of the root cellar.

He stopped and dropped to a knee beside the body. "My God," he raked out.

A dead woman. A dead black woman. She lay twisted, partly on one side, her one remaining black eye open and staring. The other eye had likely been plucked out by one of the carrion-eaters. Her head had been severely bashed in, exposing her brain.

Her extremities had been chewed on. Especially

her private parts. That's where the animals went to work first, for the privates were the easiest way inside the body.

But the animals had not bashed in her left temple. That was likely what had killed her. A person had done that. They'd killed her and dumped her in the cellar. The animals had found her—the wolves likely summoned by the quarreling birds. The wolves had dragged her partway out of the cellar, and then the birds had converged, and the free-for-all for supremacy over the carrion was what had summoned Johnny.

Johnny shook his head. "Christ almighty."

He picked up the girl's hands and dragged her back to the cellar. The wolves would likely drag her out again but he didn't know what else to do with her. The ground was too sodden to try digging a grave. Besides, the snow was coming down harder.

Let the carrion-eaters have her. The ground was really no protection, anyway. The way Johnny saw it, either the wolves and buzzards would get her, or the worms would get her. Didn't make much difference.

He dropped her back into the cellar and closed what was left of the door, which wasn't much. The wolves appeared to have chewed away several slats.

He brushed his hands on his pants and turned and walked back out of the brush. When he saw the lodge, he paused to study it from a fresh vantage, seeing it in a whole new light.

Where were the others?

He strode with more purpose back around to the front of the lodge, up the porch steps, and back inside. He paused, looking around as though he might have missed something before, before he knew that a young woman had been murdered here. He didn't know what that might have been, though, so he headed upstairs, unconsciously now caressing the butt of his right Twin with the palm of that hand.

He paused outside the door of the first room on his left. He turned the knob, shoved open the door. The room was empty. He turned to the room on his right, opened the door, and poked his head in.

Nothing there, either.

He checked the next two doors, then, avoiding the door to his own room, he twisted the knob of the door directly across from his. He poked his head inside, looked around, and froze.

A man lay on the bed to Johnny's left. Even before Johnny had walked slowly up to the bed, he knew the man was dead. The man wasn't moving even a little. Not breathing. His eyes were open a little, his face slack, mouth halfway open. A pillow lay at an angle beside his shoulder.

Heck Torrance. A much older and more wizened Heck Torrance than Johnny remembered, but Heck Torrance just the same.

Johnny went out and tried two more doors before opening the last door on the hall's left side and stopping just as he'd done when he'd opened Torrance's door. He went in, walked slowly up to the bed.

A chubby young woman stared up at him, features frozen in an expression of raw horror. Her eyes were badly bloodshot. Her arms were stretched straight out to both sides, and her legs were spread, one bent inward at the knee. A rumpled pillow lay beside her.

She, too, had been suffocated with a pillow.

Johnny stared down at her, tapping his fingers on the holstered Twins, pondering.

Finally, he left the room and checked out the rest of the house, every nook and cranny. He found no more bodies. Torrance and the girl were the only two. Three, including the black girl lying out in the cellar, of course.

Three people murdered.

With one missing. Another girl had resided in the room Johnny had taken. She was gone. No sign of her.

Damn puzzling.

He turned to the kitchen window. The snow was coming down harder than before, and it was lying, not melting. The wind moaned under the eaves, made the ceiling beams creak above Johnny's head. Darkness was falling, only a little pale light remaining in the blue-black dark clouds that were settling over the sky once more in earnest.

He was in for more of this nasty mountain squall. A taste of the long winter to come. Oh well, he might as well have another cup of coffee.

He retrieved his cup from the parlor and refilled it from the pot he'd set on the range's warming rack. He returned the pot to the rack, returned to the parlor, and sagged into the brocade-upholstered armchair he'd sat in before, near the bottom of the stairs, his back to the rear wall. From here, he had a good view of the windows though, with darkness closing down over the canyon, there was no longer much to see out there.

He'd drunk a third of his cup of coffee when he heard something beneath the moaning wind and the ticking of the snow against the walls and windows. What he'd heard was the drumming of hooves. Several riders coming fast.

Johnny's blood quickened, but he remained where he was.

The drumming grew louder until he saw the silhouettes of what he thought were three or four riders entering the yard, checking their horses down to trots as they turned them toward the stable. The men were talking, yelling above the wind, though Johnny couldn't make out what they were saying. By their tones, they were eager to get out of the weather.

They were seeking shelter here, just as Johnny was.

Nothing to get his blood up about, he told himself. Just the same, he took his coffee in his left hand and unsheathed his right-side Twin with his right hand. He rested it atop his thigh, generally aimed at the door.

He sat sipping his coffee. For a while, he heard nothing from the stable. The newcomers were inside, tending their mounts. About fifteen minutes after he'd heard them ride up, there was a wooden thud as someone shut the stable doors and dropped the locking bar into place.

Voices rose again. Boots thumped and spurs chinged.

The three men appeared beyond the window to the right of the door. They filed onto the porch, boots hammering the damp wood. One of them pounded on the door then opened it and poked his hatted head into the lodge.

He was bearded and square-jawed. Snow rimed the broad brim of his black hat.

"Anybody home?" he called, looking around. He held his right hand out of sight behind the door.

"Just me," Johnny returned. "Come on in and take

a load off, friend." He put a little steel in his voice as he added, "But first, holster the hogleg."

Johnny sipped his coffee.

The man turned his head to Johnny. He studied Johnny for a moment. The other two studied Johnny from the windows on each side of the door, each holding up a hand against the light of the two lamps Johnny had burning in the parlor. They each held a revolver down low against their right legs.

"Who're you?" the bearded man asked Johnny. He glanced at the double-bore ten-gauge resting on Johnny's leg.

"You first."

"Blackie MacGregor." He tipped his head to his right, then his left, announcing, "That's Cimarron. That's Chester Northrup."

"Johnny Greenway," Johnny said, again steeling his voice a little as he said, "No need for the iron."

"What about you?" Blackie said.

"You first."

"Teale here?"

"Nope."

Blackie flinched, as though not approving of the response, then glanced at Cimarron and Chester Northrup. He gave each a little nod then pushed the door open wider and stepped inside, holstering his Remington New Model conversion revolver.

The other two men moved from the windows to the door. They stepped into the lodge, also holstering their revolvers but doing so reluctantly, frowning at the shotgun on Johnny's leg.

When they all had their guns sheathed, Johnny sheathed the Twin and took another sip of his coffee.

"That's a helluva pair of shotguns, mister," Blackie said. He was square-faced, dark-eyed, with a nasty scar cutting down through the beard on his left cheek.

"Shotgun Johnny," said the man called Cimarron, standing now to Blackie's left. He was the shortest of the three, with pale yellow hair, and a matching mustache. He gave a knowing, coyote-like half grin. "Has to be. No one but Shotgun Johnny wears a pair of gut-shredders like most men wear six-shooters. An' shoots 'em the same."

Johnny took another sip of his coffee.

"Where's Teale?" asked the man to Blackie's right. Chester Northrup was thickset, large-gutted, nasty-eyed. He wore a plaid wool shirt under a buckskin coat stained by the soot of many cook fires.

"I have no idea."

The men looked at one another owly-like, like they weren't sure whether they believed him. They returned their dark gazes to Johnny, and Blackie said, "You after him, too?"

"Nope. He's all yours. I'm not one bit interested in Jake Teale. Not this time around, anyways."

"What are you interested in?" asked Northrup, flaring a nostril.

"A good night's sleep."

"Not Teale?" asked Blackie, disbelievingly. "Ain't you a marshal now? That's what I heard. I heard they was crazy enough to give you your badge back."

Northrup chuckled dryly at that, keeping his mean eyes on Johnny. Johnny was neither surprised nor offended by the comment. He was well aware of his reputation as the hot-blooded Basque lawman who'd hunted down and murdered his family's killers without first giving them the benefit of a judge and jury. And as the drunk he'd become when he'd been stripped of his moon-and-star.

"I'm on vacation."

"No, no." Cimarron grinned shrewdly as he turned to Blackie and Northrup. "He's on a bullion run. He runs the bullion from the Reverend's Temptation to the bank in Hallelujah Junction." His grin broadened, turned lusty. "For that purty banker gal, Sheila Bonner."

The other two looked at Cimarron then returned their gazes to Johnny with renewed interest. Johnny gazed back at them and took another sip of his coffee.

Blackie glanced around then said, "Where's Torrance? Where's the girls?"

"Torrance and two girls are dead," Johnny said. "Coffee on the range. The one who takes the last of it has to make a fresh pot. Them's the rules." He smiled.

Blackie frowned, studying Johnny closely. The other two did, as well.

"What'd he say?" Blackie asked Northrup before turning to Johnny again. "What'd you say?"

"Coffee on the range. The one who takes . . ."

"No, no—I mean about Torrance and the girls, dammit!"

"Oh. They're dead. Two upstairs, one out in the cellar. Looks like someone suffocated Torrance and the girl upstairs with pillows. The one out in the cellar had her head bashed in."

The three newcomers stared at him as though he'd spoken in a foreign tongue. The short, yellow-haired Cimarron shaped a crooked smile, as though he thought Johnny was joking. Northrup said, "Pshaw!"

"Sure enough," Johnny said. "Two dead inside. One dead outside."

The three looked at one another again. Cimarron removed his coat, shook the excess water off it, and hung it on a peg on the left side of the door. Turning to Blackie, he said, "Teale done it. Sure enough."

Blackie kept his scowling gaze on Johnny but said to Cimarron, "We heard Jake took a coupla pills he couldn't digest."

"Still, though . . ." Cimarron turned to Johnny. "Was it Jake?"

Johnny remembered hearing Teale's name bandied about in Riley Duke's Saloon. He'd heard the name before then. Teale was a slippery outlaw who worked mostly alone, holding up stagecoaches and robbing prospectors and the banks of small mining towns. Johnny had seen wanted dodgers for him, but he'd never seen the man himself. Some called Teale "The Phantom" because few had ever seen him twice.

"Your guess is as good as mine on that one, friend."

Blackie said, "Jake Teale. He was here, wasn't he?"

"If so, he's not now."

"Where's Dixie?"

"Who's Dixie?"

"Pretty blonde." Blackie raised his hands and touched his shoulders to suggest that Dixie's blond hair was shoulder-length. "She'd taken a shine to Teale. That's what he'd come here for. Her. They was gonna run off together."

"So we heard tell," Northrup explained.

"With a boatload of loot he'd taken from several banks in California," Cimarron said.

"Off a few stagecoaches, too," Northrup added.

It was Johnny's turn to scrutinize the newcomers suspiciously. Doing so, he canted his head to one side and narrowed one eye. "What's your interest in Teale? The bounty on his head or the loot he's carrying?" He crooked a wry smile. "Or both?"

Chapter 22

Another lightning bolt slashed the air, dangerously close to where Walt Teale had just then stopped the wagon and set the brake. Dixie screamed at the fiery flicker that seemed to explode behind her retinas, and was followed not a full second later by an ear-numbing crash of thunder.

Dixie felt her hair stand on end.

"Jeepers, that was close!" Teale proclaimed.

The mule and the horse agreed, one braying, the other pitching in its harness and loosing a shrill whinny.

"Easy," Teale said, holding on to the reins despite having set the brake. "Easy, now, easy!"

The wagon rocked forward as the horse threatened to bolt. The mule pulled on the rope tying it to the back of the wagon.

Teale had pulled the rickety contraption through some trees roughly a hundred yards north of the San Joaquin River. He'd remembered that there was an old prospector's shack back here—one that he'd used at one time when he'd been panning for gold on his own, before joining the mine—and he'd been right.

The cabin sat hunched, dark, and bleak amongst tall lodgepole pines, at the base of the steep granite ridge washed slick and shiny as a knife blade by the pouring rain.

"Doesn't look like anyone's here," Teale yelled above the roaring deluge. "You go on in and start a fire. Should be dry wood. It's the custom of the country to leave fuel!"

"All right!" Dixie started to climb down out of the wagon, then stopped.

She glanced at the coffin in the wagon's bed, behind Teale, who turned to her scowling. "What is it?"

"N-nothin'. You sure you don't need any help, Mr. Teale?"

"No, I can handle it. Hurry, now, girl—we ain't gettin' no drier chinnin' out here in the rain!"

Dixie climbed down, grabbed her two carpetbags out of the wagon box, glanced at the coffin once more, then ran around behind the wagon to the shack, which she could smell moldering out here under the dripping pines. The smell of mold was heavy in her nose. As she broke into a jog, Teale hoorawed the horse around the side of the cabin and, apparently, toward a small barn or stable behind it. The mule's terrified, angry brays dwindled as Teale and the wagon disappeared from sight.

Dixie stepped through the fall of water tumbling off the cabin roof's overhang. Someone had propped a board against the door, apparently to hold it closed against such weather as this, or possibly against curious bears or other such critters. Dixie had to kick several times at the board, for the bottom end had sunk into the ground and some grass had grown up around it, making it hard to dislodge.

The board finally gave after her fourth, hard kick, and dropped to the mud.

Dixie tripped the door's steel-and-string latch. The door slackened in its frame, and Dixie drew it open, poking her head into the musty darkness. "Hello?" she couldn't help calling despite being fairly sure the cabin was not occupied.

She was relieved when no one answered, including no animals that might have taken over the premises and not have felt too kindly about being challenged for their sanctuary. She suddenly wished she had a gun.

What if she was challenged for her and Jake's grub-stake?

Again, her mind returned to the coffin. She felt a little guilty that she no longer thought as much about Jake as she did about the money sharing the wooden overcoat with him. Thinking about that money, about how vulnerable it was out there in that coffin, made her heart hiccup and race.

She kept wondering, obsessively, if Walt Teale knew about the loot. She also kept wondering if he suspected she'd stowed it in the coffin with his son . . .

She left the door open as she moved around in the cabin, trying to get her eyes to adjust enough that she could find a lamp, if the place had a lamp. Even a candle would do.

As images started to clarify a little, while remaining dark, she saw a table against the wall to her right. She could see the black stove ahead and slightly to the left, as well as the chimney pipe running straight up through the ceiling.

She moved to the table and looked and felt around with her hands for a lamp. She didn't find a lamp but she did find an open airtight tin with a candle inside it.

So far, so good.

She rummaged around for another couple of minutes until her hands found a box of lucifer matches on a shelf above the table. She was pretty sure the shelf was littered with a good many mouse turds, as well. That was the only thing those little, ricelike things she'd felt beneath her hands could be . . .

She gave a shudder of revulsion. It was a small price to pay, though, she supposed—enduring a few mouse droppings on her journey to a life of luxury.

She lit the candle and then, using the dry wood she found in a couple of wooden fruit crates beside the stove, got a fire going in the stove. As the flames grew, they offered enough light now that she could better see the cabin around her.

The place was shabby as hell and caked in dust and cobwebs to which dead flies clung. But there was the stove, enough wood to last the night, some canned goods on a shelf, and even a bottle of what appeared to be whiskey. There was one small cot against the wall opposite the table. If Teale was a gentleman, he'd likely let her have the cot and sleep on the floor. Dixie had seen a bedroll among his gear.

She found a couple of airtight tins of pinto beans and a cast-iron skillet. When the stove had warmed sufficiently, she set the beans on the stove. She was starving. Teale probably was, too. Neither one had eaten much all day. She'd made the sandwiches, but the trail was so perilous that they hadn't been able to eat much. They hadn't stopped because they'd been trying to stay ahead of the bad weather.

While the beans cooked, she peeled her sodden coat off her shoulders and draped it over a chair near the stove. She hung her wet hat on a wall peg. She wanted to peel out of her wet dress and underclothes and bathe her chilled body in the growing heat from the fire, but Teale would be here soon.

Her clothes would have to dry on her body.

When the beans had cooked, Dixie scrubbed a tin bowl clean with the hem of her skirt, poured a portion of the beans into the bowl, then sat close to the fire, hungrily eating. She'd taken only a few bites, however, before she looked up suddenly, frowning.

Where was Teale? He should have finished his chores by now.

Suspicion grew in her. It nibbled at her consciousness the way some varmint—a mouse or a chipmunk—was nibbling at something beneath the floor.

Dixie envisioned the money in the coffin. She envisioned the lid, which was not nailed down.

Teale had found the money!

Quickly, she put herself through the torturous process of pulling on her wet coat, which weighed a good three times its normal weight and felt even colder than before. She hurried outside then traced Teale's route around the cabin to the rear. She saw the stable hunched in the rain, the fading light and the downpour touching its shake-shingled roof with silver. A ponderosa had grown up against its left wall.

The stable was only a little larger than the cabin. A dilapidated corral sagged off its right side, several of the rails having crumbled away from the upright posts and fallen to the ground overgrown with brush and small trees. The stable's two doors were open, pulled back against the stable's front wall.

Dixie hurried through the doors, blinking in the dim light, peering into the shadows. The wagon lay before her. To each side, the horse and the mule stood, wearing hackamores and tied to a post from which ancient tack hung.

A bucket of water and one of feed sat on the ground near each. Both mounts were munching oats. The mule did so while turning its head to gaze curiously into the wagon's bed. The beast twitched each ear in turn, grains of half-chewed oats sifting down from its leathery lips.

Dixie followed the mule's eyes to the wagon bed, blinking, squinting into the heavy shadows relieved only by the intermittent flashes of lightning, the bright light of which could be seen between the logs where the chinking had worn away. Walt Teale was down on one knee beside the coffin. He had one arm draped over the wooden coffin in which his son resided. His head was lowered so that his hat hid his face. His head moved.

Dixie frowned, not sure what was happening. Then beneath the rain and between thunderclaps, she heard him sobbing, a strangled mewling sound issuing from deep within his chest

Hesitantly, Dixie stepped forward. "Mr. Teale . . ." she said loudly enough to be heard above the weather. "What's . . . what's wrong, Mr. Teale . . . ?"

Teale looked up at her suddenly, as though startled. His eyes were filled with tears and redness. Tears streaked his bearded face. He regarded Dixie as though with great beseeching, and then he wailed above another clap of furious thunder, "I wasn't a good father to him! I wasn't a good father to either of 'em! Ya understand? I wasn't a good father, an' now here he lies, an' it's all because of me! Both went by the gun an' it was all . . . my . . . *fault*!"

He lowered his head again, so that again the crown

of his hat hid his face, and he bawled loudly, head bobbing even more violently than before. "It's all my fault," he wailed, bobbing and shaking his head. "All my fault!"

Dixie felt a little guilty at her relief to not find the coffin open and Teale going through the loot. At the same time, she was taken aback by the man's untethered display of sorrow. She hadn't expected such a spectacle from such a previously stoic man. He'd said fewer than a dozen words to her all day, but here he was on his hands and knees, spewing his guts out about how he'd raised his sons.

Crying like a child.

Suddenly, Dixie felt sorry for him. Worried about him, too. He did not look well. He looked pale, his eyes sunken.

"Come on, Mr. Teale," Dixie said, moving closer to the wagon and reaching out with her right hand. "Let's get you inside. You must be chilled to the bone. I know I am."

Teale just knelt there, sobbing.

"Please, Mr. Teale," Dixie said, bending forward and wrapping her right hand around his left wrist, over the sleeve of his rain-soaked coat, "let's get you inside. I have a fire going. I boiled coffee and beans . . ."

"No." Teale pinched the bridge of his nose between his thumb and index finger and shook his head. "No, I'm gonna . . . I'm gonna stay out here. I don't deserve no comforts."

"No, no, no, Mr. Teale. You'll die out here!"

"Let me die! It's better'n I deserve! You don't know the half of it, ya see!"

"It's not, Mr. Teale! It's really not! We've all made

mistakes!" Dixie tugged on the man's wrist. She didn't want to leave him alone out here with the money. Also, she was genuinely worried he'd die out here and leave her to make the trek down out of the mountains by herself. Her motives were selfish, of course, but there you had it. It was a dog-eat-dog world. She could forgive herself, because she felt genuine sympathy, as well. "Please, Mr. Teale. Come inside. I'm not going in until you do!"

"Go on an' leave me!"

"I will not!" Dixie tugged harder. "Please, Mr. Teale!"

Teale looked up at her again. His eyes were round and stricken, like those of a man staring out through the bars of an insane asylum. Gradually, the insanity . . . the storm of unbridled grief . . . flickered and gave way to rationality. It was like frost being scraped from a window if only to make a small ring of moderate clarity. Tears continued to roll down the man's craggy face.

He looked away. Swallowed. Nodded. Drew a phlegmy breath. "All right."

Dixie helped him down from the wagon. When he had both feet on the ground, he grimaced and pressed his fist against his chest.

"What is it?"

"I'll be all right," he said, though most of the words were drowned by another thunderclap.

"What is it? You're feeling poorly, I can tell. Are you sick?"

Teale made another face. "My ticker. It started actin' up when I was in the mine."

Dixie glanced at the coffin, reluctant to leave it out here unguarded. She had no choice. She'd close the doors. No one would be skulking around out here tonight. Not in this weather.

She helped Teale out of the stable. While he leaned against the stable's front wall, head down, drawing air in and out of his lungs as though trying to catch his breath, Dixie closed the doors and secured them with the steel latching bar.

"Lean on me," she said, wrapping one arm around the man's waist.

She and Teale started back toward the cabin, through the slashing rain that appeared to be part snow now. Like raining slush. The temperature was dropping.

Dixie didn't like the rasping sounds she heard grating in Teale's chest. He was having trouble breathing, and he stumbled as he walked. He was very weak. So weak that his knees almost buckled several times. A couple of those times he would have fallen if Dixie hadn't caught him.

"Here we go," she said as they finally made it to the cabin's front door.

She held Teale with one arm while using the other hand to trip the latch and shove the door wide. She helped Teale inside by the light of the flickering orange flames. She led him over to the cot, sat him down on the edge of it, and helped him out of his coat and hat. She tossed both onto the chair by the fire, then shoved the old man back onto the cot. She picked up each foot and set it on the cot. He didn't seem able to make the maneuver without assistance.

"I'll get you some coffee and beans."

Dixie started toward the stove but stopped when Teale said, "Don't want any. Ain't hungry."

Dixie turned back to him. She stared down at him, fear gripping her. The panic was as cold and wet as her coat and her clothes and her body beneath the sodden attire. She feared that she was staring down at a dying old man.

She feared there was a very good chance that by morning, Walt Teale would be dead.

And she'd be alone.

CHAPTER 23

Teale looked up at Dixie as she stared down at him. The old man read her mind.

"Don't worry, Miss Dixie," Teale said, giving a wan smile. "I ain't gonna die on ya."

"No, you're not." Dixie swung around and walked over to the stove. She shoveled beans into a bowl, poured a cup of coffee, and brought both over to Teale. She shoved the bowl at him, set the coffee cup on the windowsill on the other side of the cot. "You're going to eat those beans and drink that coffee. You need the sustenance. You need to keep your strength up."

Teale took the bowl in his gloved hands. He looked down at it without delight, even winced a little. "All right, Miss Dixie. You're the boss. I'll eat the beans, but . . ."

He glanced around, blinking his eyes as if to clear them. His chest was still rising and falling heavily.

"But what?"

"There wouldn't happen to be a bottle of whiskey around here, would there?"

Remembering the whiskey bottle—at least, she'd

thought it was whiskey—she hurried over to the shelf and pulled the bottle down and dusted it off with her hands. She found another, fire-scorched tin cup, cleaned it out with her skirt hem, and splashed a couple of healthy fingers of whiskey into it.

She brought the cup over to Teale, who was nibbling at the beans though it was obvious from his sour expression that the food brought him no pleasure. He set the bowl on his chest and accepted the whiskey. He sipped it, took another sip, then another, draining the cup.

He waved for more.

Dixie poured more whiskey into the cup.

He took another sip, smacked his lips, and sighed. "Good stuff."

"You look better."

"The whiskey helps."

"You need more than whiskey, Mr. Teale. Finish those beans. The coffee, too."

Teale grimaced down at the beans. "I will, Miss Dixie. I'll eat the beans." He raised the cup then smiled and winked at her. "But, first . . . to soothe my ticker."

Dixie gave a wan smile then walked over to the table. She shrugged out of her coat, draped it over the chair by the fire, then took up her own bowl of beans and sat in the chair so close to the fire that it almost burned her. But it felt good, too, chasing the brutal cold out of her bones.

"It's my fault Jake is where he is." There'd been such a long silence, the only sounds the popping of the fire in the stove, that Teale's voice startled Dixie. She turned to him. He lay on the cot, staring at the ceiling, the bean bowl and the cup of whiskey resting on his chest, rising and falling to the rhythm of his breathing, which was less harried now.

"That's not true, Mr. Teale," Dixie said, impaling the last few beans in her bowl with her fork. "We all make our own choices."

"I hardened him. His brother, too. I didn't know how to handle 'em, so I left it to their mother. But they was wild . . . sorta like myself, I reckon. I didn't know how to settle 'em down so I whipped 'em. Lordy, how I whipped those boys."

Teale shook his head in disgust at himself.

"It wasn't that I didn't love 'em, Miss Dixie. Truly, it wasn't." Teale turned to her. His eyes were glassy now from the whiskey. Dixie had set the bottle on the floor by the cot, and he'd obviously poured more into the cup. "It's just that . . ." He scrunched up his face with the effort of finding the best words to express what was on his tortured mind. ". . . I didn't know how to show 'em. I was proud of my boys. I really was. They both turned out strappin' an' handsome, but . . . they had that wild streak. Didn't wanna work . . ."

He paused, turned his head, and resumed staring at the ceiling. "I didn't know how to handle 'em. Lordy, how I worked. A ranch takes work. Sometimes around the clock, especially during roundup and calving season. But Dale an' Jake—they always seemed to disappear just when I needed 'em most. So . . . I cut 'em loose. Told 'em if they didn't work, they wouldn't eat. Not there. Not at home. So they left . . . went their separate ways."

Teale sobbed, sleeved a tear from his cheek. "That broke their mother's heart. She took ill soon afterward.

I didn't know how to care for her. So . . . she died. Now both my boys are dead, too. They're all dead."

Dixie stared at the haggard man. She was having trouble not crying now herself. Her heart felt swollen and tender. Teale looked so grieved, so sad . . . so lonely. Not unlike herself.

Lost and alone in a world neither could understand.

"I'm so sorry, Mr. Teale," Dixie said after she'd cleared an obstruction from her throat. She rose and dragged her chair over to Teale's cot. She poured some of the whiskey into her empty coffee cup, sipped it—not bad at all—and leaned forward, offering the bereaved old man a reassuring smile.

"Jake was a good man, Mr. Teale. I mean, I know he robbed stagecoaches an' such . . . but he turned out to have a big heart. I mean . . ." Dixie sipped her whiskey again and, staring down at it, tapping her thumb against the rim, said, "I mean . . . he loved me, Jake did. He really did, Mr. Teale. We were going to run away together . . . to be married."

Teale scrutinized her through his drink-bleary eyes, appearing befuddled. After a time, he said, "You really loved Jake? You found somethin' to love in that boy?"

"I really did, Mr. Teale. He was a good man, Jake was. Deep down in his heart."

"Or," Teale said, shaping a crooked, wolfish smile, "maybe it was them saddlebags full of stolen loot you loved."

Dixie felt as though she'd been slapped across her face. She wasn't sure what she'd heard.

She sat back in her chair, staring at the man, aghast. "What?"

Teale kept the sly grin. "You heard me."

"How . . . how . . . did . . . ?"

"When I heard someone had seen him ride up to the Grizzly Ridge Inn, I also heard he was packing a lumpy set of saddle pouches, Jake was."

Dixie felt her heart throbbing in her temple. She didn't know what to say. Panic began building in her again.

"Ah hell, don't worry." Teale sipped his whiskey, scrubbed his mouth with his hand. "I ain't after that money."

"You're not?"

"Hell, no. I don't care about nothin' but gettin' my boy home, so's I can bury him good an' proper." He paused then shaped that coyote grin again, one eye narrowed. "It's in the coffin, ain't it?"

Dixie's mouth was dry but she swallowed anyway. "Did you check?"

"Nah. Didn't need to. Where else would it be? I seen what you got in your carpetbags—clothes an' such."

Dixie's heart was beating fast again. She wrung her hands as she said in a trembling voice, "He . . . he brought it to me. I mean . . . it's for us. So we could start a new life . . ."

"He stole it for you?"

"Yes. Those were the last jobs he was going to pull. It was for us . . . him an' me . . . so we could start over . . . make a decent life for ourselves." Dixie saw skepticism creep into the man's gaze. It riled her, annoyed her. "He loved me, Mr. Teale. He came back with that money . . . he came all that way . . . to the Grizzly Ridge Inn . . . with two bullets in his belly. He didn't have to come back. He could have gone to Frisco . . . Mexico . . . by himself. He didn't have to come back, Mr. Teale. He came back because he loved me!"

"I'll be damned," Teale said. He suddenly seemed puzzled. But also convinced. He nodded slowly. "He really did, didn't he?"

"He did." Dixie brushed a tear from her cheek. "And I loved him. I saw the good in him. I changed him. He changed me. He made me want a better life . . . for both of us."

Teale continued to stare at her, still befuddled, as though he was still having trouble making sense of what she'd told him. Of joining his cold-blooded, un-compromising outlaw son to the notion of love.

"I'll be damned," he said finally. "You must be a special person, Miss Dixie . . . to have melted that boy's cold heart."

"Thank you, Mr. Teale." Dixie looked down at her clenched hands then regarded the man again. "About the money . . ."

"I told you I don't want no part of it. That's yours. You take it."

"You don't want *any* of it?"

"Nope. He stole it for you. You take it. I done some bad things in my life. I raised him wrong, treated his mother bad. I don't have long left. I reckon one good thing I can do is help you get him and that money down to Hallelujah Junction and on the stage to Frisco or wherever you wanna go." Teale smiled. "I reckon you'd be my daughter-in-law, iffen Jake had lived. I like the sound of that. Daughter. Sure enough, I'll help you down out of these mountains and send you off on that new life you was supposed to start with Jake."

It was Teale's turn to brush a tear from his cheek.

Dixie sobbed, then, too, suddenly overcome with emotion. "Thank you, Mr. Teale." She leaned forward and pressed her lips to his bearded cheek.

"Thank you," Teale said when she pulled her face away from his. He fondly fingered the place on his cheek where she'd kissed him. "That felt nice. I ain't never felt nothin' so nice in a long time."

Dixie smiled and shoved his bowl of half-eaten beans into his hands. "Here, finish the beans. And the coffee. You've had enough whiskey." Dixie took his whiskey cup and poured the whiskey into her own. "Finish your supper and go to sleep. We have a big day ahead of us."

"All right." Teale beamed up at her as though he'd fallen under the pretty woman's spell. He took a bite of the beans and then, chewing, he frowned again as he stared up at her. "You know, though, Miss Dixie . . ."

"Just Dixie, Walt."

"All right, Dixie it is. You know, Dixie, if I found out about that loot, others have, too. Nothin' attracts men like moths to a burnin' lamp like money. Others will follow. They might be on our trail right now, in fact."

Holding her whiskey cup in both hands against her breasts, Dixie scowled at the black window above Teale. "I suppose you're right. Damn, I hadn't thought about that. I wish I had a gun."

"I have one." Teale reached down and with his right hand slid an old-model Colt from the leather holster on his right hip. "I've had this trusty old conversion pistol for many years. Used to be right good with it. We just have to keep an eye out, that's all. Anyone gets close, I'll discourage 'em with this."

"Have you ever shot anybody before, Mr. Teale?"

"Not since the war. But I cleaned up right well during the War of Southern Rebellion. Once took out a supply wagon guarded by four graybacks all by myself. Er . . . well . . . I reckon me an' Lymon Henry did it. He got two but only killed one. I killed the other three. They never knew what hit 'em."

Dixie feigned a smile and nodded. "Right impressive."

"I can kill a man—don't you worry. Leastways, if they get in close, and if they're after the loot, they'll get in close, all right. Don't you worry, Miss . . . er, I mean Dixie. Don't you worry your purty head. I'll take care of you. And first thing I'm gonna do in the mornin', before we leave here, is hammer a couple of nails through that coffin lid."

"Good thinking, Walt," Dixie said, patting his forearm.

Teale holstered his pistol with a grunt then glanced at the window in the wall to his right. Furry snowflakes were splatting against it. He made a face.

"The bad weather should work in our favor—shouldn't it, Walt?" Dixie asked hopefully, staring at the melting snow running in slushy chunks down the window. "I mean, it'll hold back anyone who might be after us."

"Could be," Teale said without conviction. "On the other hand . . ."

"What?" Dixie prodded when the old man seemed reluctant to continue.

Teale sighed and scooped a few more beans into his mouth. "On the other hand, the snow might make us easier to track."

Dixie glowered at the window.

"Here," Teale said, raising his left hand to her. "Help me up."

"What are you doing?"

"Going to spread my bedroll on the floor. There's only one bed. The lady gets the—"

Dixie rose from the chair and placed her hand against the old man's shoulder. "Don't be ridiculous. You need the bed worse than I do."

"Nonsense."

"You stay right there. I'll be fine on the floor."

"Nope." Teale dropped one foot to the floor.

"Don't make me mad now, Walt! You listen to your daughter-in-law. Your son was about to marry a very headstrong woman, one who is accustomed to getting her way." She crouched to lift the old man's foot back onto the bed. "You will regret raising this lady's ire!"

Teale chuckled as he lay his head back down on the pillow. "All right, all right. I reckon you are strong in your ways." He looked up at her, smiling again. "Wish things had worked out different. I wish you an' Jake coulda hitched up. Wish I coulda known you both, together an' happy. I reckon if things was different, you might could've come to live with me at the ranch. It ain't much, and it's probably even less now, since I ain't been back in a year and I'm sure the buildings and corrals have gone to seed. Still, it's a nice place . . . with a good view of the mountains."

Again, Dixie squeezed his forearm. "That would have been real nice, Walt."

"So many things I wanted to do different. Even when I was doin' 'em." Walt turned to her, beetling his brows. "Know what I mean?"

Dixie turned down her mouth corners, nodding. "Indeed, I do."

"And now it's too late."

"Maybe not."

"No, it's too late, all right. Leastways, for me. I'm old, worn out. But you . . . you're a rich young lady." He smiled broadly. "Oh, what a fine life you'll have. You'll find another man and the whole world will open before you."

"I hope so, Walt." Dixie smiled again as she turned to the window. More snow was sticking to the glass. "Truly, I do."

CHAPTER 24

"Why, we're after both, for sure!" said the short, yellow-haired Cimarron in response to Johnny's question. "We're after both the bounty on Teale's head as well as the loot he's carryin'."

"Uh . . . but, of course," added the black-bearded Blackie quickly, "we're only after the loot to turn it in. You know, we want to make sure it gets back to its rightful owners."

"Sure, sure," chimed in Chester Northrup, the big-gutted, mean-eyed bounty hunter. "That money was likely stolen from hardworkin' folks just like ourselves. We'd want it returned to us if it was ourn!"

"Oh, sure—that's what I meant," Cimarron said as all three stood in front of the Grizzly Ridge Inn's closed front door. "There's likely a sizable reward on the loot, too."

"But even if there wasn't," Johnny said, seated in the brocade-upholstered chair at the back of the parlor, near the stairs, "you'd go ahead and turn it in. Since it was likely taken from hardworkin' folks . . . just like yourselves."

Blackie's bushy black brows beetled over his dark-brown eyes. Anger glinted in those eyes, and his prominent jaws hardened. "Ain't that what we just said?"

"Just makin' sure," Johnny said. "I'd hate like hell for you fellas to turn from bein' the hunted to bein' the prey. My prey." He grinned affably. At least his lips did. His brown eyes bore home the warning underlying his words. "Since I'm the deputy U.S. marshal in these parts, I reckon that job would be up to me."

"I thought you was on vacation," said Northrup, crisply.

"I done told ya, Chester," Cimarron said. "He's on a bullion run." He looked at Johnny. "Ain't that right?"

Johnny didn't respond. He just sat there gazing blandly back at the three obvious cutthroats, absently running his left thumb around the coffee mug in his hand.

"Just out of idle curiosity," Blackie said, grinning like a donkey with a mouthful of cockleburs, "how much you carryin'?"

"Yeah," Northrup said. "Just out of idle curiosity."

"Here's another question . . . out of idle curiosity," Cimarron added, also grinning, his eyes glinting greedily. "Where you got it hid?"

"Just out of idle curiosity?" Johnny asked.

"Yeah," Blackie said, still grinning and casting his two accomplices quick glances. "Just out of idle curiosity. Just for harmless chinnin' on a cold mountain night."

"It's upstairs," Johnny said, evenly, his face expressionless. "Second door on the left. It's in the armoire."

The dung-eating smile very slowly faded from Blackie's lips. The other men's smiles faded, as well, until they were staring at him skeptically, half-disbelieving. Maybe going over it in their heads.

Was he telling the truth?

Is that where the bullion really was?

Johnny could see the rocks rolling around in their heads, just behind their eyes. All three stared at him searchingly, their speculative gazes flicking at least once to the two ten-gauge, sawed-off shotguns holstered on his thighs.

"So there you have it," Johnny said quickly, so abruptly that all three jumped, hands jerking toward their six-shooters. He feigned a sigh, throwing his head back, then tapping his fingers against his open mouth. "Well, fellas," he said, rolling his shoulders as though to relieve the stiffness in them, "I do believe I've got a date with the old mattress sack. You help yourselves to whatever food you can find. Like I said, there's coffee on the warming rack in yonder."

He rose slowly, fluidly, like a cat emerging from its lair at sundown, ready for the long hunt ahead. He threw back the last of his coffee then said, "Here!" and tossed the empty mug to Blackie, who gave a surprised yelp as he caught the mug against his chest. "Save me a trip and set that in the kitchen for me, will you?" Johnny smiled winningly. "Good night, fellas. Maybe see you in the morrow. Have a good night's sleep!"

He yawned again, gently slapping his lips, as he climbed the stairs. A quick, furtive glance over his shoulder showed him the three cutthroats still standing in front of the door, cunning casts to their gazes as they watched him ascend the stairs.

Johnny went into his room and closed the door.

"Hmmm," he said, pressing his back to the door, pondering the situation.

Some might have thought he'd been downright foolhardy, telling Blackie, Cimarron, and Chester Northrup where he'd hidden the bullion. The way he saw it, he was only saving himself time and preventing himself from having to keep watching his back.

There was no way that men like those three would not, could not, come after the bullion. They knew Johnny was hauling it. Now that they'd run into him, they'd have to make a play for it. If they didn't, their dreams would haunt them.

Now Johnny knew *where* to expect them if not exactly *when*.

They could make a play tonight or possibly early in the morning, before dawn. There was no telling what men like that would do. The smart thing to do would be to wait and try to catch him off guard. But that wasn't their style. They were impatient men. They wouldn't want to risk letting Johnny and the bullion slip out from under them.

Johnny poured a glass of water, drank it down, then kicked out of his boots. He built a fire in the coal brazier in the room's corner then crawled into bed. He kept the lamp burning on the dresser, the wick turned low.

He'd get some sleep. He could sleep with one eye open, so to speak. That was no problem. He'd done that for most of his life, including when he was with his family, herding sheep in the mountains, where predators were always on the lurk—sometimes the animal kind, sometimes the human kind.

He listened for a time to the wind moaning and

howling, making the timbers creak. The wet snow pelted the walls and windows.

Beneath the sounds of the storm, he could hear the three cutthroats talking in hushed tones. The storm prevented him from hearing what they were saying.

He knew. He may not have known *exactly* what they were talking about, but he knew what they were *generally* talking about.

The bullion.

Johnny drew a couple of deep, slow breaths. Sleep wrapped its gauzy shroud around him. It was not a peaceful sleep, however. Dream images assaulted him—the door of his home in Carson City kicked open, the shotgun exploding, throwing David onto the table.

Lisa made love to him. But she turned into a slathering ogre who became Sheila who became Glyneen who said, "You'll love me forever—won't you, Johnny?" in the grating voice of the ogre, whose small eyes glowed red.

At one point the ogre grew the head, but still with the glowing eyes, of the saloon girl Johnny had cheated on Lisa with . . .

Somewhere in the midst of those dreams, a baby cried. Johnny couldn't see the child. It was as though it was hidden from Johnny. He didn't think it was David, but he wasn't sure why he thought that.

At the tail end of the night, Glyneen's voice came to him again, in her own clear, chiming voice pitched with heartbreaking pleading: "You don't love her anymore—do you, Johnny? You wouldn't hurt me—would you, Johnny? You wouldn't hurt a woman who loved you as much as I do . . . would you, Johnny?"

He was almost grateful when a sound tugged at the one-quarter conscious part of his brain and pulled him up out of his restive slumber. Instantly, both Twins were in his hands, and he was ratcheting all four hammers back with a single sweep of his thumbs.

He sat straight up in the bed. Pearl light angled through the room's single window to his left. The room around him was all shadows with blurred edges.

He pricked his ears, listening, his heart thudding heavily, his index fingers drawn taut against a trigger of each Twin.

Around him was only silence . . . until he heard it again—what he'd heard the first time.

A floorboard chirping softly under a stealthy tread.

A man's shout exploded in the lodge below Johnny: *"Get him, Blackie!"*

The shout was followed by the thundering crash of a .45 revolver.

The bullet tore through the floor and into the ceiling just off the left side of Johnny's bed. At the same time, the door ahead of him and to his right was smashed open to slam against the wall with another thundering crash.

A man stepped into the room, swinging a rifle toward Johnny.

Johnny's left-hand Twin bucked and blossomed.

Blackie screamed as he flew back and triggered his rifle into the ceiling.

Below, the .45 thundered again, the bullet making an eerie sound as it tore up through the bed mattress, pluming goose feathers and missing Johnny's left calf by the width of a cat's whisker before it thudded into the ceiling above the bed.

A short, thick, yellow-haired man bounded into

the room behind Blackie, wailing incoherently as he extended two long-barreled revolvers straight out before him, looking around quickly then swinging both hoglegs toward the bed.

Johnny dispatched Cimarron a half second after his first wad of double-ought buck had thrown Blackie onto the dresser, knocking the lamp to the floor, spilling kerosene, which the lamp's wick promptly ignited. Blackie tumbled to the floor with his coat on fire but, already shaking hands with the devil, he sounded no complaints.

Cimarron flew back through the open door and into the hall. He slammed up against the wall then rolled along it, in the opposite direction from the stairway, and unseated the wall lamp from its bracket. The coal oil must have splashed on the yellow-haired cutthroat, as well. Not dead yet, he gave a screeching wail as the oil ignited, setting his head and bloody torso on fire, adding insult to his injury, as it were.

Meanwhile, Chester Northrup continued hammering .45 slugs up through the floor, two more ripping through the bed and into the ceiling. As soon as Johnny had sent Cimarron to a fiery perdition, he flung himself forward, rolling off his right shoulder. He struck the floor and rolled again as another .45 slug chewed a hole through the moldy, lime green rug and into the ceiling.

Johnny rose quickly, aimed both Twins at the floor, near the hole in the rug, and triggered both of his last two barrels into the floor on each side of the hole.

The hammering blasts were followed closely by bellowing wails from below. Boots pounded the first-story floor as Northrup ran around screaming, "Help!

Ah, Jesus, help me—I'm *blind*! Oh God—oh God—help *meeee*!"

Not in the mood to help, Johnny holstered the Twins and stepped into his boots. He grabbed his hat, pulled the panniers out of the armoire, and started for the door.

Flames licked up around him, smoke roiling, the cloying smell of coal oil hanging heavy in the smoky air.

Johnny stepped through the door and into the hall. Flames were licking up the walls on both sides of Cimarron, who was crawling off down the hall toward the opposite end. He looked like a big dog in flames. He was yipping and howling like a dog, too.

Johnny headed slowly for the stairs, taking the time to dig his makings sack out of his coat pocket and to roll a quirley. The fire wasn't too large just yet though it was heading that way fast. Johnny saw no reason to try to put it out. There was no one else to work the place, anyway. Maybe, just maybe, the Grizzly Ridge Inn had run the course of its life.

Now it was a funeral pyre.

Descending the stairs, the panniers draped over his left shoulder, Johnny slowly rolled his quirley closed. Smoke billowed down around him as it bled out of the second-floor hall. Below, Northrup was still running around screaming, *"I'm blind! I'm blind! Oh, sweet Jesus, help me—I'm blind!"*

The fat man was stumbling around as he held both hands to his bloody face. Loony from pain and fear, he ran around the room, bouncing off the walls, knocking over chairs and tables and wailing at the top of his lungs. He'd fallen and was crawling up the piano when Johnny reached the bottom of the stairs.

"Help me!" Northrup sobbed as he knocked over

the piano bench and followed it down to the floor. "Oh God—*help me!*"

Johnny stopped. He plucked a lucifer from his coat pocket then scraped the sulfur tip to life on his thumbnail. He lit the quirley, cast away the match, and let the cigarette dangle from between his lips as he casually reloaded both Twins, taking his time.

When he had them both loaded, he dropped the left one into its holster and secured it. He took the right one in both hands. Northrup was just then gaining his feet, crawling up the front of the piano, banging raucously on the ivory keys. He turned toward Johnny— a bloody, faceless specter—and opened his bloody mouth to scream, *"Help me!"*

"All right," Johnny said around the quirley in his mouth. "But you sure as hell don't deserve it."

He blasted the man up off his feet and back over the piano to slam against the wall. Northrup bounced off the wall and slumped belly-down atop the piano, one leg and one arm hanging down the piano's opposite side, both limbs swinging as he died.

Johnny replaced the single spent wad with fresh, snapped the shotgun closed, holstered it, and left the smoky premises.

CHAPTER 25

Glyneen MacFarland pulled the sorrel hitched to her single-seat surrey up to the hitchrack fronting Sheila Bonner's house in Hallelujah Junction, and pulled back on the reins. The sorrel stopped. The buggy rocked to a stop behind it.

Glyneen glanced at the neat brick dwelling with gingerbread trim and a single, small turret—a miniature Victorian and one of the finest houses in town, with a well-tended yard encircled by a white picket fence always kept in the best repair, including a fresh coat of paint. Glyneen was humbled by the house, so much grander and stylish, although not all that much larger, than the stone-and-log one she shared with her elderly parents by Crow Creek.

She'd felt the burden of self-consciousness build as she'd pulled the buggy up to the house. While boasting high red wheels, the single-seater surrey with a black canvas canopy had seen better days. As had the tall sorrel gelding in the traces. Her father had traded a load of firewood for the horse, which had belonged to a now-deceased army doctor, several years ago.

The horse had been getting up in years even then. While Smoky, as Glyneen called the horse, had been as dependable a puller as any horse you'd find, these days he was gray around the muzzle, his withers growing more and more prominent, his fetlocks drooping, and his eyesight so diminished that Glyneen hardly dared take him out at night.

Glyneen knew that Sheila Bonner rode around in a handsome phaeton drawn by a sleek black Morgan and outfitted with a fringed leather canopy and two red seats of overstuffed cowhide.

Studying the stately, tidy manor before her, shaded by majestic cottonwoods and ponderosa pines, Glyneen reached into a pocket of her checked wool coat and withdrew a powder blue envelope. She felt compelled to read the note one more time, just to make sure that she hadn't imagined the invitation. She couldn't think of one good reason why Sheila Bonner would want to see her.

Glyneen removed the note from the envelope, opened the single leaf of tissue paper bearing Miss Bonner's own personal, gold-leaf letterhead, and frowned down at the breeze-ruffled page on which two sentences had been beautifully scripted in an elegant, educated feminine hand in indigo ink:

Dear Miss MacFarland,

I know this invitation will come as a surprise to you, but I would very much like to visit with you. Would you mind calling on me at my house on Saturday afternoon, say, around teatime? Please be assured I have no quarrel with you, feel no animosity whatever. I do, however, have a serious matter I feel the need to discuss.

Truly yours in friendship,
Sheila A. Bonner

"*A serious matter I feel the need to discuss,*" Glyneen read aloud to herself, under her breath. Folding the note and returning it to the powder blue envelope, Glyneen frowned at the house again and said, "Hmm."

She returned the note to her pocket, set the wagon's brake, tied the reins around it, then climbed down from the seat. She patted the sorrel's left withers and said, "I won't be long, Smoky."

At least, she hoped she wouldn't. She felt awkward enough visiting her beau's former lady friend. What made it worse was knowing that she and Miss Bonner resided very firmly in two separate classes of society and that hers was well below Miss Bonner's. She hoped the conversation would be short and sweet, and that she would take her leave in a half hour at the most.

She not only felt outclassed as she stepped through the gate in the picket fence and strode along the brick-paved path toward the well-kept porch with white wooden pillars holding up the shake-shingled awning, but she began wondering what Johnny saw in her, Glyneen. Especially after having been with such a moneyed and classy lady as Sheila Bonner . . .

Glyneen hated the way she was feeling suddenly. Small and inadequate. She was a simple girl from the rural South who'd followed her illiterate, gold-feverish prospector father west only to live a life of near-squalor. At least, compared to Miss Bonner's life it was squalor. The only thing saving her from wretchedness was her job as Dr. Albright's medical assistant and midwife. The pay wasn't great, but it helped her and her parents get by.

Glyneen had just mounted the porch steps when a voice said, "Oh, hello. I thought I heard a wagon pull up but I couldn't be sure."

Off the end of the porch, to Glyneen's right and partially concealed by a plum tree, Miss Bonner rose from her knees. She held a hand towel in her garden-gloved right hand. Dirt smudged her right cheek. She smiled beneath the broad brim of her straw hat and said, "I'm so glad you came. I was afraid you wouldn't."

"Your note sounded . . ." Glyneen halted, feeling awkward and self-conscious in front of this beautiful, cultivated woman. "Well, it sounded urgent."

"Urgent?" Miss Bonner smiled more broadly, the cheeks of her lovely, brown-eyed, heart-shaped face dimpling. "No, it wasn't urgent. I mean, it's nothing so dire as that."

"Oh," Glyneen said, feeling outdone in the conversation so far, and she'd only just got here! "Well, I . . . came."

"I'm glad." Sheila gestured toward the front door. "Shall we?"

She seemed to wait for Glyneen to climb the steps ahead of her, so Glyneen did just that, then, having gained the porch, stepped to one side. Sheila strode confidently past her, setting her trowel and garden gloves on a wicker table, then opened the house's heavy oak front door. She walked inside, removing her straw sunhat and shaking out her chestnut hair, which tumbled thickly, prettily, about her slender shoulders clad in a loosely woven, spruce green cape.

Her hair smelled subtly of orange blossoms and just as subtly of burning autumn leaves. Glyneen had detected the scent of burning leaves when she'd pulled up to the hitchrack. Miss Bonner had apparently been burning leaves, probably in the house's backyard. Imagine having the leisure time, even on a Saturday, to do something as superfluous as burn leaves . . .

Glyneen moved in behind the pretty banker, a little surprised to see that Sheila was a couple of inches taller than she. Well, no, not surprised. Just further *humbled*, Glyneen supposed would be the right word, if she was as good at finding the right words as Miss Bonner was.

But, then, Glyneen hadn't had the advantage of an advanced education, as Miss Bonner obviously had.

Unbuttoning her cape, Sheila said, "My housekeeper, Mrs. Godfrey, made a coffee cake this morning before she left. I'll bring us each a piece, and do you drink tea, Miss MacFarland?"

Miss Bonner had paused in the kitchen door from which rich, sweet aromas of cinnamon and sugar wafted, and she was eyeing Glyneen speculatively, as though ready to judge her on the basis of whether or not she drank tea. That was probably just in Glyneen's paranoid imagination.

"Of course, of course, I drink tea."

Miss Bonner smiled. She was beautifully flushed from exertion and the cool autumn air. Why did she have to look so damned ravishing? Glyneen had been working for the doctor most of the morning, traipsing about the countryside looking in on the doctor's patients—two prospectors with broken bones, one with syphilis, and a young Chinese doxie dying from consumption.

Miss Bonner had been gardening and burning leaves.

Miss Bonner nodded at the parlor that opened off the other side of the foyer from the kitchen. "Please, hang your hat on the tree there by the door and make yourself comfortable. I'll be back in a minute."

While Miss Bonner disappeared into the kitchen, Glyneen removed her coat and felt hat, hung both on the wooden tree by the door, then stepped into the parlor. It was a medium-sized room, at least by Glyneen's standards, and furnished with the heavy leather furniture and game trophies that bespoke a male as opposed to a female presence. Glyneen attributed the style to Miss Bonner's father, Martin Bonner, who'd lived here alone for several years before Miss Bonner had come to Hallelujah Junction to tend him and the bank in his final days. Even the smell of the man's pipes and cigars remained. There was a cabinet stocked with several stout bottles of dark-colored liquor, none of which Glyneen would know anything about. Her parents didn't drink.

She walked over to the hearth and sank into a short leather sofa sitting perpendicular to the fireplace. Before her was a coffee table on which a potted plant grew—a small parlor palm, she believed. She did know about some plants, as she'd once tended an elderly lady, a former housekeeper for a wealthy mine owner, who'd had a collection of various, exotically named houseplants. Miss Bonner likely knew them all.

Opposite the table was another leather sofa, a twin to the one Glyneen sat in. Miss Bonner made her fidget only a minute or two before the woman herself entered the room with a silver tray on which a china teapot and two matching teacups and saucers sat. Two slices of coffee cake had been set on two china dessert plates. The delicate china had been painted, probably by hand, with small pink flowers blossoming around a serene little garden cottage composed of five or six deftly drawn pink lines.

"Here we are," the pretty banking lady said as she set the tray on the table. "I hope you don't mind cinnamon. Lots and lots of cinnamon," she said, setting first the teacups on the table and then the plates of coffee cake. "Mrs. Godfrey adds more cinnamon than the recipe calls for then adds a little more for good measure."

She chuckled then sat down on the sofa opposite Glyneen. It was then, when Miss Bonner had laughed, that Glyneen realized that she, too, was nervous. Glyneen hadn't noticed it before. Miss Bonner was good at hiding her emotions. Probably a by-product of the banking trade. Glyneen, who didn't know her very well, and mostly just by reputation, thought of her as professionally taciturn, aloof, downright inscrutable.

She couldn't have been more Johnny's opposite. Johnny wore his passions on his sleeve. His bitter hatreds, as well. Maybe that's what Glyneen loved about him. He was a big, handsome, passionate man. If the truth be known, his violent explosions—or the constant possibility of same—excited her in ways she'd never experienced excitement before. They did so even in bed, though she wouldn't have admitted that to anyone. She only halfway admitted it to herself, having been raised that it wasn't ladylike to think about such things.

Yes, Miss Bonner was nervous. Glyneen saw it in the flush in her cheeks, which could no longer be solely attributed to the weather. That knowledge made Glyneen feel a little better, maybe not quite so intimidated. It put them on slightly more even ground. At least, right here, right now, in this neat and elegant house.

"Tea?" Miss Bonner asked perfunctorily as she lifted the pot and, holding the tip of her right index finger on the lid, poured the ginger-colored tea into Glyneen's cup. The steam wafting from the cup smelled vaguely of orange rinds and mysterious Oriental spices, not all that different from Miss Bonner herself.

"Now, then," Miss Bonner said, picking up her own teacup and sipping, glancing at Glyneen through the rising steam, "I suppose you're wondering why I invited you here."

Glyneen did not sip her tea. She left the cup in its saucer on the table. Neither did she touch her dessert. She felt a little more in control, not quite as nervous, than she'd felt when she'd first ridden up to the Bonner house. "You said you had something you wanted to speak to me about."

"Yes . . ." Miss Bonner, fumbling a little with the delicate silver fork, cut into her wedge of coffee cake, staring down at it, the rose in her cheeks growing a little brighter.

"If it's about the other day, Miss Bonner," Glyneen said, her own growing confidence affording her grace enough to assist the nervous young lady across from her, "please, don't think another thing about it. I know you didn't expect to find us there . . . like that. I mean, it was embarrassing for all of us. I mean, I'm sure he took you there, and I'm certain you never expected to . . . well, you know . . ."

"Be discovered by a former lover, however accidentally?" Miss Bonner forked a piece of the dessert into her mouth and chewed, gazing directly, frankly, across the table at Glyneen. A little incriminatingly, as well.

"No," Glyneen said, frowning uncertainly. "I meant by anyone. It's a private place. You know that . . ." She paused. "Don't you?"

"Of course."

Glyneen recognized that as a lie. It was in the smug defensiveness of the woman's tone. As well as the too-quick response.

"Did you mean, since I knew it was a private place, I shouldn't have intruded on you?" Miss Bonner asked quickly on the heels of her previous response, as though to overshadow the lie, her tone growing nasty.

"No!" Glyneen said, disappointed to find that she was the one again on the defensive. "That's not what I meant at all. I just meant that . . . we were trying to be discreet, but . . ."

"But a *former lover* came calling."

Glyneen lurched to her feet. She strained under the burden of her indignation, feeling her lower lip tremble, trying not to wail.

She drew a breath, channeling her emotion into the anger that was her right to feel, as well as to express, and hardened her jaws. "Don't take that tone with me, Miss Bonner. I know you're an important and well-educated person, a woman of *power and means*. But you turned Johnny away when he was ready to marry you. Besides, you're the one who—"

"I'm pregnant."

Glyneen stared down at the woman staring up at her. Miss Bonner's brown eyes were wide and crystal clear. She held her hands in her lap.

Surely, Glyneen had misheard.

"What?"

"You heard right, Miss MacFarland. I'm pregnant." Miss Bonner looked down as though in shame.

Glyneen continued to stare down at her. A full minute must have passed before she found the words with which to express her next question. A question so unfathomable and horrific that she really didn't want to hear the response. She felt like a chained prisoner awaiting her death sentence.

"Is it Johnny's?"

Miss Bonner looked up at her again. Glyneen thought that the woman's upper lip trembled, however slightly, briefly. Her wide brown eyes were softly luminous with emotion. "Yes."

Glyneen closed her eyes.

She swayed dizzily and half fell, half sat on the sofa, leaning back against the overstuffed leather cushions. She opened her eyes and looked at Sheila Bonner regarding her with what appeared to be genuine concern, lips parted as though about to speak though she didn't say anything.

"Why did you tell me?" Glyneen asked, her voice tart with anger.

"I didn't tell you to torture you, I assure you. You were going to find out sooner or later, and I wanted you to hear it from me."

"Does Johnny know?"

"No. I didn't even know until a week ago. I thought I was just feeling the strain of overwork."

"Did you try to . . . you know . . . get pregnant?"

"No!" Miss Bonner cried, offended now herself. "Of course not!"

"All right. What are you going to do about it?" Glyneen herself was astounded by the sternness of her tone, the rage building within her.

"What do you mean?"

"Are you going to keep it?"

"Of course! I would no sooner abort a child than I would saw my own hand off!"

Glyneen sat staring across the table bearing her untouched tea and untouched cake at Miss Bonner, who sat gazing back at her, the rose in her cheeks now there due to anger. Glyneen's heart was racing. It raced as it broke.

The room spun around her.

"All right, then," she said finally, when she could find words again. "All right, then . . . I do hope the best for you . . . Johnny . . . and your—"

"No!" Miss Bonner cried. "The reason I invited you here was to assure you—"

"I know very well why you invited me over here, Miss Bonner." Glyneen heaved herself to her feet then had to reach down immediately to steady herself on the low table lest she should fall. "You invited me over here to gloat . . . to assure me . . ."

"Glyneen, please stop!"

Glyneen swung around, as tipsy as though she were drunk, and made her unsteady way toward the foyer. "You wanted me to see how much more you have than I have . . . how much more *educated* you are than I am . . . and to prove to me what a much *better catch* you are for Johnny!"

She laughed caustically as she spun around at the

door to the foyer, facing Miss Bonner once more. The woman had risen and started to follow Glyneen, but she'd stopped when Glyneen had stopped, her own eyes looking stricken.

Stricken by the sudden self-knowledge of what a slattern she was, no doubt!

"Informing me of the baby was the bow on the package, wasn't it?" Glyneen had barely cried those last two words out before a series of chortling sobs racked her. She raised her right hand and placed the top of her wrist against her open mouth, trying in vain to stifle the wails that exploded out of her. "I love him, damn you to hell! And he loves me! I knew that when you saw us together the other day—I could tell by the look in your eyes—the devious, jealous look in your eyes—that you were going to find a way to take him *back*!"

Wailing, she swung around, ran through the foyer, and stumbled her way out of the house.

Sheila stood frozen in place behind the sobbing young woman.

She stood staring into the parlor where the girl had left in a storm of raging emotions. Sheila wanted to go after her, but what was the point? Glyneen was in no state to listen to reason. Even if Sheila told her now, as she'd tried to do a minute ago, that she had no intention of taking Johnny away from her . . . that she had not in any way, shape, or form changed her mind about not marrying Johnny . . . even now after having learned that she was pregnant with his child, Glyneen wouldn't believe her.

What Sheila had wanted to say would have been nothing more than words to the poor girl. Flat, empty words. Lies.

"Oh, for pity's sake!" Sheila said when she started to recover from her shock of the girl's unexpectedly irrational, emotional response. "I have to stop her. She can't leave here in the state she's in."

She rushed through the foyer and outside. She stood atop the porch and gazed toward the street beyond. Glyneen was gone. Only dust sifted in the air behind her vanished buggy. To the north came the clatter of the girl's surrey and the thuds of her horse's galloping hooves.

Concern touched Sheila.

Glyneen was heading north rather too fast for that trail. The trail curved then dropped abruptly as it swerved very close to the edge of Dark Water Canyon just a hundred or so yards . . .

Sheila stiffened when a horse's cries and a young woman's sudden scream cut shrilly through the cool autumn breeze. The screams were followed by a great clattering and thudding.

The din was followed quickly, all too quickly, by deafening silence save for the soughing of the wind.

CHAPTER 26

"I don't mean to worry you, Dixie, but . . . uh . . . I think someone's followin' us."

"What? Who? *Where . . .* ?" Dixie turned her head to stare back along the trail behind the wagon, beyond Teale's mule that was tied to the tailgate.

The mule appeared nervous, giving soft brays and twitching its big ears.

"I don't know, but I can tell the way ole Wilbur's actin', he senses somethin' . . . or some*one*." Teale sat on the driver's seat, to Dixie's left. Again, he glanced back over his left shoulder to inspect their back trail.

"Maybe it's just his imagination," Dixie said. "I've been keeping watch and I haven't seen anyone. He's kind of old, isn't he—Wilbur?"

"He's old, all right. But his senses are still good. Their sniffers is usually the last thing to go on a mule." Teale glanced at Dixie. "Like I said, I don't mean to worry you. I just thought you should know we might have a shadow. Now, it could be anybody. Doesn't necessarily have to be someone—"

A loud whoop cut Teale off.

Dixie gasped and grabbed the edge of the seat with both hands, stiffening. "What was that?"

Teale looked around. So did Dixie. Enough snow had fallen the previous night to cover the ground. It was too cold for it to melt. The sky was low and gray, the brooding clouds portending more snow in the hours ahead.

Dixie and Teale were traversing a deep valley with high, rocky ridges. Somewhere to their right was a river. Dixie couldn't see it but she could hear its low roar.

Large piles of gray granite were piled up along both sides of the trail. The rocks had closely abutted the trail for the past half mile or so, ever since the trace had dipped down onto the canyon's relatively flat bottom. Dixie guessed the rocks and boulders, among which pines, cedars, tamaracks, and spruces grew, had tumbled from the valley's high ridges a long time ago. Those rocks were mantled with the ermine of the freshly fallen snow.

Crows cawed and the breeze blew, feathering the fresh powder. The crows and the breeze and the hidden river were the only sounds. Sometimes the mule gave an occasional, speculative bray. Dixie had thought it was only being a mule, but now she knew the mule had indeed sensed another presence.

"What do you think that was, Walt?" Dixie asked.

"I don't know," Teale said quietly, looking around with renewed fear furling his gray-brown brows. "Coyote. Wolf, maybe . . . ?"

It came again, sounding much closer now. It had originated on the trail's left side, from somewhere in that jumble of snow-covered rocks. It echoed threateningly, further setting Dixie's nerves on edge.

"No," Dixie said, shaking her head and staring at the passing rocks and boulders to the left of the trail. "That was no animal. That was a man."

"I think you're right," Teale said, taking the reins in his left hand. With his right hand, he lifted the right flap of his coat, exposing his gun and holster. He slid the old Colt from the holster then let the coat flap drop back into place.

Keeping the reins in his left hand, he clicked the Colt's hammer back, raising the barrel and staring into the rocks.

"Right you are, miss!" a man's voice yelled to the left of the trail.

Again, Dixie gasped, her heart racing. Atop a large boulder to the left of the wagon, a man-shaped shadow appeared, running across the top of the rock. He gave another loud whoop and laughed.

"There he is!" Teale said, and aimed the Colt.

The revolver bucked and roared. The bullet crashed into the top of the boulder just as the running man, throwing his arms out to both sides for balance, leaped down out of sight in some cranny among the rocks.

"Damn!" Teale said, pulling the Colt back down to his shoulder and ratcheting back the hammer again. "Missed the son of a buck!"

"Oh my God!" Terrified, Dixie grabbed Teale's right arm with both her hands.

"Let go, Dixie! Let go! That's my shootin' hand!"

Dixie released the man's arm and returned her hands to the wagon seat. The horse kept pulling the wagon forward though its muscles rippled anxiously along its back and it looked around fearfully.

As the wagon approached a foot-wide crack in the nearly solid wall of rock to the left of the trail, a man's face suddenly appeared in it, grinning.

"Boo!" the man yelled.

Dixie screamed.

"Ah, you devil!" Teale snapped off another shot too quickly. The bullet slammed into the face of the rock a good foot to the right of where the man's face had been, though the face wasn't there any longer. The man had retreated back into the rocks again.

"Walt—there!" Dixie cried, having spied a man standing atop another rock, this one on the right side of the trail and maybe thirty feet up. The man was tall and bearded, clad in a ragged buffalo coat, and he was rising up and down on his fur boots, waving and laughing.

Teale turned. The man swung around and disappeared a whole second before Teale fired.

As the wagon rolled forward, haltingly behind the jittery horse, another man appeared along the trail's left side. There was a gap in the rock wall, and the man was leaping over small rocks as, laughing, he ran through the gap.

"Damn!" Teale snapped off two more shots, both bullets merely plunking into the rocks far wide of the leaping man's figure.

That man, too, disappeared into larger rocks, and the wagon rolled on past the gap, another high wall of ancient granite rising to form another formidable rampart on that side of the trail.

The trail traced a sharp bend to the right. As the wagon followed the bend, Dixie drew another sharp breath, for another man appeared, standing on a low rock along the trail, on the trail's left side. His butterscotch-colored hide coat was open, exposing a red flannel shirt and suspenders. He wore a bullet-crowned, badly weathered hat. He held a Winchester in his hands.

He grinned, his unshaven cheeks broadening, at Dixie and Teale now as he raised the Winchester, aiming down the barrel toward the wagon.

Dixie screamed and leaned forward, covering her head with her arms, as the rifle belched loudly, echoing.

"Oh, you dog!" Teale cried, and triggered his pistol at the rifle-wielding devil.

Dixie looked up to find the rifleman gone, just like the others. Teale held the Colt straight out before him, gray smoke curling from the maw.

Dixie spied movement in the corner of her left eye. She jerked her head in that direction to see a man's gloved hand slide up from the wagon bed between Dixie and Teale, and tap Teale on the shoulder. At the same time, a man's mocking voice said, "Guess what, old man? You're out of bullets."

Teale and Dixie both screamed.

Dixie turned her head to stare up at a very tall, rail-thin man with a hatchet face grinning down at her and Teale. The man stood atop Jake's coffin. He looked at Dixie and winked and slammed the barrel of the nickel-plated revolver in his hand against Teale's head. The old man grunted and flew out of the wagon, striking the snowy trail below with a wailing moan.

"No!" Dixie cried, looking down at Teale sprawled on the trail but falling behind now as the wagon kept moving. She saw three more men standing in the trail ahead of the horse. One of them, the big man in the buffalo coat whom Dixie had seen earlier on the rocks, stepped forward and grabbed the horse's cheek strap, halting the frightened beast.

Dixie recognized him now that she had a better look at him. He was Vernon Draeger. The other two on the trail with him were Huey Melbourne and Scrunge Pitt. Dixie didn't know if Scrunge was his real name or not, but that was the only name she'd heard him called. The one standing atop Jake's coffin was Pete Driscoll.

All four had visited the Grizzly Ridge Inn more than a few times, so Dixie knew them better than she wanted to. They were human scum. Bottom-feeding carp. Dixie didn't even know what they did for a living but they occasionally had enough gold dust to buy a tussle or two.

"What the hell do you think you're doing, Driscoll? You have no right to terrorize us this way!" She cast her gaze back to where Teale lay about twenty feet back along the trail, writhing and groaning on his back. "Are you all right, Walt?"

"Oh, he'll be all right," Driscoll said, glancing back at Teale and then turning his long, ugly face back to Dixie. He had a crooked eagle's beak with two dark eyes set way too close together. One was slightly crossed so that it appeared to be staring at the end of the ugly, pitted nose. "I just gave him a little love tap." He chuckled and glanced at Teale once more. "Sure did fall hard, though. Ouch—that tumble had to hurt. Especially a man so old."

"Why'd you do it?" Dixie wanted to know.

She started to get up to climb down off the wagon to check on Walt Teale. Driscoll gave her a hard shove back down to the seat. "You know why we did it, Miss Dixie."

"We heard all about Jake Teale headin' for the Grizzly Ridge Inn with a couple of lead slugs in his belly." This had come from the bearlike Vernon Draeger. He'd walked up to stand by the wagon's left wheel, one boot propped on the hub. He leaned forward against his raised right knee, smiling up at Dixie, narrowing one eye shrewdly. "We heard tell how he came a little heavy"—he winked conspiratorially— "if you know what I'm sayin'."

"No, I don't know what you're saying," Dixie shot back. "I have no idea what you're talking about. That is Jake in the coffin there, and that . . . whom you so brutally abused," she fired at Driscoll, "is Jake's father. We're taking Jake to his home ranch to bury him with the rest of his family."

Scrunge Pitt, the man in the butterscotch coat and flannel shirt and suspenders, walked up to the opposite side of the wagon from Draeger. He grabbed Dixie's wrist and gave it a hard squeeze. "Where is it? Where's the loot, lady, or so help me . . ." He'd pulled a pistol and now he shoved it up, clicking the hammer back to press the barrel against Dixie's head, just behind her right ear. ". . . I'll send you to where Jake's done lit out fer!"

"Now, now, Scrunge," said Driscoll, still standing on Jake's coffin. "That ain't gonna be necessary. There's only a few places it could be." He smiled at Dixie. "Ain't that right, Miss Dixie?"

Dixie glared up at him. She was trying hard to keep

her eyes off the coffin. She didn't want to give them any clue about where the loot was. On the other hand, they would likely find it sooner or later.

Fear rippled through her. Fear and desperation.

If these men took the money, she would have nothing. She would be worse off than she'd been before Jake Teale had showed up at the inn with the money. She had no home. All that she owned was in the two carpetbags—maybe five dollars' worth of clothes and toiletries.

She manufactured her best puzzled smile. "Fellas, please," she said, chuckling and sliding a stray lock of hair back from her left eye, tucking it behind her ear. "I really think you've been sold a bill of goods here. Jake wasn't carrying any loot when he came to the inn. He had about seven dollars and fifty cents in coins, and that's all. If he had any loot, he must have buried it somewhere along the trail. I assure you! I don't have it! I wish I did, but I don't! Now, please, let me go over and help Mr. Teale back to his feet so we can continue our journey. Judging by those clouds, we're in for more bad weather very soon."

Pete Driscoll stood atop the coffin, his ugly face stretching a lewd smile. "Miss Dixie, you sure are a terrible liar. Even for a whore. Why, I could see through that lie from a mile away." His crossed eyes roamed across her body. "But you sure are purty."

He stepped from the coffin to the wagon seat. He dropped from the seat to the floor of the driver's box and placed his hand on Dixie's arm. "What do you say you an' me go off by ourselves for a spell . . . just like old times?"

Before Dixie could respond, Driscoll said to the

others, "Boys, go through all the gear in the wagon. Check the coffin, too. Find somethin' to pry up that lid. If that money ain't nowhere else, it's likely in the wooden overcoat, sure enough."

He returned his goatish gaze to Dixie. "In the meantime, me an' Miss Dixie are gonna have us a little private fun. This cold weather always makes me randy!"

He hopped down off the wagon then turned around, grabbed Dixie around the waist, and pulled her down. "Be back in a minute, boys!" he called, and headed off toward a break in the rock wall, jerking Dixie along behind him.

He pulled her so quickly back behind the wagon and then into a little alcove in the rock wall that Dixie didn't even have time to resist. She had all she could do just keeping her feet.

"Save some fer us!" yelled Scrunge.

Driscoll stopped inside the alcove and pulled Dixie up close to him. "Now, then . . . alone at last, my lady!" He chuckled, blowing his sour breath at Dixie's face. He wrapped his arms around her and slid his face up close to hers, about to kiss her.

A howl rose from somewhere behind Dixie, in the canyon around where the wagon and the other three men were. Dixie gasped. Driscoll gave a sharp grunt and frowned, looking into the canyon over Dixie's head.

"What the hell was that?" asked one of the men rummaging around in the wagon.

Driscoll shoved Dixie aside so hard that she almost fell. He strode back out into the canyon. Another howl arose. It became a series of demonic yips and yowls.

They were loud and they sounded close, echoing up off the canyon floor to the rocky crags jutting skyward.

Dixie walked tentatively back into the canyon, looking around warily, hoping she hadn't been saved by wolves only to be eaten by those same wolves. She saw that Walt Teale was sitting up now, leaning back against the rock wall on the opposite side of the trail from her, looking worn out, washed out, beaten down. His hat was off, and his thin hair slid in the breeze across the top of his nearly bald head.

Again, came the howl, swirling.

"Wolf!" yelled the bearlike Vernon Draeger in his thundering voice.

He and Huey Melbourne were in the wagon, going through Dixie and Teale's gear. Scrunge Pitt stood near the wagon's open tailgate. He'd been leaning forward on Jake's coffin, but now he swung around, drawing a pistol from a holster under his butterscotch coat.

Draeger, standing in the wagon to the left of the coffin, drew both of his own revolvers and clicked the hammers back. He turned to stare up at the rocks on the trail's left side. "I think it's comin' from up there!"

"I think it's behind us!" yelled Pete Driscoll, standing near Dixie but facing down-canyon. He'd also drawn two revolvers and was holding them up near his shoulders, barrels angled up, hammers cocked.

Dixie found herself stepping slowly backward, instinctively seeking the shelter of the niche Driscoll had pulled her into. Just as she'd started to back into the notch, she spied movement to her right, where a large, black bird winged straight down from the rocks over the canyon to land with a loud, wooden thump atop the coffin in the wagon bed.

"Nope," the bird said. "It's right here."

Facing down-canyon toward Dixie and Driscoll as well as Walt Teale, the "bird" held two stubby guns—sawed-off shotguns—in his black-gloved hands. He swung one of the savage-looking weapons to his right, slamming the stout barrels into Vernon Draeger's bearded face.

Draeger bellowed as his two-hundred-plus, buffalo coat–clad pounds flipped straight back over the side of the wagon to the ground. The "birdman," who was really just a man, albeit one dressed nearly entirely in black and with a birdlike beak, whipped his left-hand gun to his left, slamming the stout barrels of that gun into the shocked face of Huey Melbourne.

Melbourne went the way of Draeger but on the opposite side of the wagon.

Scrunge Pitt had whipped around, having heard the commotion behind him. He raised both his pistols and took a chestful of buckshot for his trouble. He was hurled straight back and into Driscoll, who had just started to turn toward the wagon, as well. Driscoll went down hard, with an anguished yell. What was left of Scrunge Pitt, his chest bright red with fresh blood, landed on top of him.

Dixie stared down in shock and horror. Driscoll and Scrunge Pitt lay six feet in front of her, Pitt's body shaking atop Driscoll as though he were very cold. He wasn't cold, however. He was dead. His brain just hadn't been told the full story yet. It would in a few seconds.

Driscoll stared up over Pitt's shaking left shoulder, glowering in shock and dismay as well as revulsion as he realized that the man on top of him had been nearly torn in half, and that he was dead.

"Christ!" Driscoll complained, sliding Pitt's body off his own.

He, as well as Dixie, turned to the big, black-clad, shotgun-wielding man standing atop Jake Teale's wooden overcoat, both sawed-offs extended straight out before him. Smoke curled from both barrels of the right-hand one.

The man himself was tall and handsome, his olive skin, dark brown eyes, dark brown hair, which was down over his collar, as well as his hawklike nose, marked him as Basque. They were a common breed in these parts though they were often mistaken for and treated as half-breed Indians.

This one wore black whipcord trousers, a black vest, and a black broadcloth coat over a white shirt. He wore a black slouch hat and a long, red bandanna knotted around his neck, the tails of which hung down his chest, buffeting in the chill breeze.

Outlaw, Dixie thought. Had to be. She could see the hardness, the deviltry in the man's eyes. Sure. Another outlaw, all right. Another handsome damn outlaw who likely knew just how much money was stowed away in the coffin beneath his polished black boots.

CHAPTER 27

Shotgun Johnny stared over his shotguns toward the girl, a lithe blonde in a shabby coat and wool muffler, gazing back at him, fear and something else in her gaze. He wasn't sure what that other thing was. She almost looked unhappy to see him, despite the fate these four likely had planned for her.

He'd get back to her later.

He looked at Pete Driscoll. Yeah, he knew Driscoll. He knew the others, as well—Driscoll, Vernon Draeger, Huey Melbourne. The now-dead man was/had been Scrunge Pitt. Pitt had needed to die a long time ago, after he'd killed those Basque settlers in the Marmot Valley, stealing their gold and kidnapping and raping their only daughter. Johnny had been a marshal at the time, but there hadn't been enough solid evidence to get the charges to stick.

Well, Pitt was dead now. Justice delayed, maybe, but justice just the same.

"Shotgun Johnny Greenway!" Vernon Draeger spat out bloodily as he clung to the side of the wagon to Johnny's right. His nose was smashed flat. Blood oozed from it and his smashed lips. Through his snarl,

Johnny could see that his two front teeth were broken. Bits of the teeth clung to his bloody lips.

Driscoll climbed heavily to his feet, wincing against the pain that his run-in with the dead Scrunge Pitt had caused him, and angrily picked up his hat. "Damn you, Greenway! We was in the middle of somethin'!"

"I know what you were in the middle of," Johnny said, glancing at the girl. "Now get your horses and get out of here. Head back up the trail, not down. If I see you again—I mean if I *ever* see any of your ugly faces again—I'll kill you."

He glanced to his left in time to see Huey Melbourne, who'd just gained his feet unsteadily, reach for the Schofield tied low on his right thigh. The man's face was ruined, as bloody as Draeger's, and rage blazed in his blue eyes. He jerked the Schofield up, his eyes widening, lips stretching back from his own broken teeth.

Johnny turned his left-hand Twin on him, dropping the barrel slightly and squeezing the left barrel.

What smacked against the rocks on that side of the trail was hardly enough for anyone to go to the trouble of burying, since it was missing its head an' all.

"Jesus!" wailed Driscoll.

Johnny switched his gaze to the tall, hatchet-faced outlaw, keeping the bearlike Vernon Draeger in the corner of his right eye. "Seems I'm making the carrion-eaters happy here today. You two wanna give 'em another helping?"

"Nope." Draeger backed away from the wagon, wagging his head from side to side, holding both hands shoulder-high, palms out. "Nope, nope. We sure don't. We was just leavin', Johnny!"

"Now, that was what I was hoping you were *not* going

to say, Vernon," Johnny said, grinning coldly and keeping his eyes on Driscoll, whom Johnny knew to be unpredictable. "I'd like nothing better than to kill the remaining vermin of you an' Pete right here and right now. If the lady wasn't here, I'd do just that. Who'd know? But since she is here, I wouldn't want her to get the wrong idea about me. Wouldn't want her to think I was anything less than civilized."

"Oh no—we wouldn't want anyone to think you wasn't civilized, Johnny!" Driscoll said, not without some irony though Johnny had thought irony beyond the man's brain capacity.

"If I were you two gut wagon dogs," Johnny said, "I'd pull my picket pin right fast before I change my mind and make the world a better place."

Driscoll grinned with challenge. "You only got one wad left, Johnny."

"That's right." Johnny turned his right-hand Twin toward Draeger and then back to Driscoll. "Which one of you wants it?"

"No, no, no, no, no!" Draeger said, wagging his head again. "I don't want no part o' this. I'm done, Johnny. You can blow Pete's head off for all I care!" As he strode down the trail, back in the direction from which the wagon had come, the big man brushed past Driscoll. "It couldn't hurt his appearance none— that's for sure!"

Driscoll glared at Johnny for a few more seconds then turned and crouched to retrieve the pistol he'd dropped when Scrunge Pitt had knocked him off his feet.

"Leave it," Johnny said.

Driscoll glared at him again, flaring his nostrils.

He cursed and walked off down the trail behind Draeger, heading back to where they'd tied their horses.

Johnny looked at the girl. She stood with her back against the rock wall to his left, twenty feet away from the wagon. She gazed back at him, her pretty blue eyes cast with a vague skepticism. He looked at the older man leaning against the rocks on the other side of the trail from the girl. The man, too, gazed back at him, his expression hard to read. His face was pale behind his patchy gray-and-brown beard.

Johnny looked down. Only then did he realize that he was standing atop a coffin. It made him feel a little funny. He didn't know why. He was no stranger to death. He'd killed enough men to fill a small cemetery.

Make that an average-sized cemetery.

Johnny looked at the girl again. "Jake Teale, I presume?" He glanced at the coffin again.

The girl didn't say anything.

"You're Dixie," Johnny said. He didn't need to make it a question. He knew who she was.

He stepped down off the coffin then leaped out of the wagon bed. He looked at the cold, gray sky from which a fine snow was falling. He walked over to the old man, who stared at Johnny dully, and dropped to one knee beside him.

"How bad you hurt?" Johnny asked.

"I'll make it," the old man said, his voice hoarse, a little pinched.

"Can I help you to your feet?"

"If you want." The old man halfheartedly raised his arm.

Johnny straightened and, crouching, grabbed the

man's arm and helped him rise. The man was heavy and obviously weak. Johnny didn't like his coloring, either. It took nearly a full minute to get the oldster upright.

"Who're you?" Johnny asked the man, who was breathing heavily from the effort of standing.

The old man studied him closely. "You're Greenway. The former marshal who hauls bullion for the Reverend's Temptation." He gave a one-quarter, crooked smile. "Shotgun Johnny."

"Your turn."

"I worked at the mine."

Johnny nodded before repeating, "Your turn."

"Walt Teale." Dixie had answered for the old man. "Jake's father."

"Where you taking your son, Mr. Teale?" Johnny asked the old man.

"To his ranch near Hallelujah Junction," Dixie answered for him again. She'd walked up to stand beside Teale. "He wants to bury him with the rest of his family."

Johnny kept his eyes on Teale, who gazed back at him, one eye squinted. "That right, Mr. Teale?"

"That's right," Teale said. "You got a problem with that? With a man wanting to give his boy a proper burial?"

"Not at all. Right honorable, in fact." Johnny turned to Dixie. "If it's just you two, you're gonna need help."

"We can manage." Dixie took Teale's arm. "Are you ready to get back into the wagon, Walt?"

Teale winced as he rubbed the back of his head then worked his left shoulder, which he must have injured when he'd been smacked out of the wagon. "Yeah . . . I'm ready. We'd best get a move on, I reckon."

Johnny watched the girl, whose head came up only to Teale's shoulder, help the old man to the wagon.

"You sure you don't want my help?" Johnny asked. "Bad weather comin'. And bad men haunting the trail. *Your* trail. There's more toughnuts where these four came from. Word gets around fast about bounties . . . and stolen loot."

Dixie and Teale stopped and looked back at Johnny. They looked at each other, silently conferring.

Dixie turned back to Johnny and said, "We can manage."

She and Teale continued toward the wagon.

Johnny walked back into the rocks where he'd left his horse and the packhorse. They were well concealed; he wasn't worried anyone had found the bullion strapped to the packhorse's back. Besides, if anyone would have gotten close, Ghost would have given a warning neigh, as the horse was trained to do.

Johnny mounted up and continued down the trail. He checked his pace down to a slow walk, staying well behind the girl and the old man's wagon. He'd ridden for maybe an hour like that, with the wagon just out of sight ahead of him, keeping a close eye on his back trail, when the girl's scream cut through the cold, gray air.

"Hy-yahh, Ghost!"

He nudged the horse with his heels and shot up the trail. He released the packhorse's lead rope, knowing the mount would stay close on its own.

He and Ghost galloped up a low rise through heavy forest. As they crested the ridge and started down the opposite side, Johnny saw the wagon stopped at the bottom of the rise a hundred yards away. The buckboard appeared stalled in the middle of the San Joaquin River, at a relatively narrow, shallow, gravelly area called Lucky's Ford.

It wasn't so lucky for the old man and the girl at the moment, however. They hadn't made it across. The old man was standing, yelling, and whipping his reins against the back of the horse in the traces. The horse lunged forward. The wagon jerked and swayed. Its right-rear wheel appeared to be stuck.

The girl wasn't in the wagon.

As Johnny galloped down the rise, approaching the river and the wagon, he looked around for Dixie but didn't see her. He galloped Ghost into the river, which was flowing faster than it normally did this time of the year, likely due to the previous rain and snow tumbling down out of the high country. The black water, laced with the white of rapids around half-submerged rocks, frothed around the cream's fetlocks.

"Where's the girl?" Johnny called as he rode up along the wagon's left side.

He startled Teale, who jerked a frightened look at him then canted his head to the right and said, "She fell out. We hit a rock and tipped, and she fell into the river. She's downstream!"

Johnny booted Ghost into another lunging gallop, quickly traversing the stream and bounding up the opposite bank. Johnny swung the horse sharply right and galloped along the shoreline, following the river's curving course. There was a hundred-foot gap between the river's grassy bank and the pine forest, so he and the horse had relatively easy going as well as an unobstructed view of the river.

As he followed a sharp left curve, he gave the river a close scan. He didn't see the girl until Ghost had taken several more lunging strides. Then he saw her out in the middle of the stream, which was roughly fifty yards across at this point. The main current had taken her into its powerful embrace and was tugging her along at a good clip, just then pulling her down a low falls.

Only her head was showing as she slapped at the water around her, fighting to keep her head above the river, the current turning her this way and that. Even from this distance, Johnny could see the fear in her eyes. Occasionally, the strong currents pulled her under and she fought her way back to the surface.

He galloped ahead and removed his rope from his saddle, under his right thigh. When he was roughly a hundred feet ahead of the girl, he checked Ghost down sharply and leaped out of the saddle. He ran out onto some large rocks jutting into the stream's cold, dark water, and yelled, "I'm gonna throw a rope!"

He couldn't tell if the girl had heard him or not above the stream's low roar. Beneath the roar, he heard her sobbing.

Johnny swung the rope above his head, paying out a large loop, and tossed it. The end fell short of where it needed to be. He drew it back, paid out another loop, and threw it harder this time. It landed only fifteen feet in front of her, and she was just then turned to face upriver, away from the rope.

Johnny gritted his teeth. She wouldn't see it in time to grab it.

But then the current spun her around so that she was facing the rope. Hope grew in him, and just as quickly died. The rope was moving downstream even faster than she was and angling toward the bank. She was going to miss it.

The rope wasn't going to work.

Cursing, throwing down the rope coil, Johnny hop-scotched the rocks back to shore. He mounted Ghost and galloped downstream. Dixie was ahead of him now, but he quickly overtook her. When he was a good fifty yards ahead of her, he leaped off Ghost's back and shrugged out of his coat while kicking off his boots. He removed the shotguns from around his waist then ran onto more rocks fingering out into the stream. He ran out to the very last rock—a small boulder about two inches beneath the river's surface—and threw his arms up and forward and followed them into the river.

The cold was almost paralyzing.

He surfaced, saw Dixie's bobbing form ahead and slightly to his right, still upstream. He kicked and thrust his arms back behind him, thrusting himself ahead, directly into the powerful main current. Dixie was maybe thirty feet away from him now but she was on a course that would take her past him if he didn't pick up more speed and get farther out into the river.

Johnny pulled his head under, kicked fiercely, and pulled the water back behind him with his arms and cupped hands. Through the murky blue-green water ahead and to his right, he saw her floating skirts and kicking, pantaloon-clad legs. He angled toward her, hearing himself grunt beneath the water as he fought against the current, trying to reach Dixie before she passed him. If he didn't get her this time, he never would.

He gave one more furious thrust and reached forward with both open hands. He felt one of her own hands, grabbed for it, missed, grabbed for it with his other hand, and managed to close his fingers around her forearm. As the current tried to pull her past him to his left, while sailing them both downstream, Johnny pulled the girl toward him. He wrapped his arm around her.

She was groaning, sobbing, crying, shivering.

"I got you!" Johnny yelled, his face just inches above the river's fast-moving surface. "Hold on to me and don't fight me!"

"Oh God! Oh God!" she cried, clinging to him desperately.

Holding her with an arm wrapped around her waist, he fought desperately with his free arm and his legs, trying to get them to shore. He didn't feel that he was making much progress, however, for the current was just too strong to parry it with only one arm, until the current slowed and the river widened.

Now he made some progress until, after what seemed half a lifetime later, he pulled himself and the girl up the rocks piled along the shoreline. He climbed onto a dry boulder then pulled her up behind him. Her body was nearly slack, soaked hair matted to her head and shoulders. She was spent. Only half-conscious, she was moaning, shivering, her blue lips trembling.

CHAPTER 28

Johnny pulled her up onto the rocks then crouched to draw her up over his shoulder.

He knew she didn't weigh much even dripping wet, but to him, spent now himself, and shivering, she felt like an anvil on his shoulder. He made his way off the rocks, careful not to stumble and fall. He was glad to see that Ghost remained where Johnny had dropped the reins. The packhorse had followed and was roughly fifty or so yards back upstream, idly grazing.

Johnny set the groaning girl onto Ghost's back.

"Grab the horn," he told her. He was so cold that it was hard to get the words out. Making a bad situation worse, more snow was coming down, liberally threading the ice-cold breeze.

The girl sat shivering, her hands in her lap. She was in shock.

Louder, Johnny said, "You have to grab the horse . . . I mean, h-horn . . . until I climb up behind you."

Numbly, slowly, as though she were still in the water, she slid her hands forward and wrapped them around the horn. They were mottled blue. Johnny toed a stirrup and swung himself back onto the saddle. But then he remembered that he'd dropped the Twins near the rocks. His coat, hat, and boots, too.

"Keep hold of the horn," he told the girl, who sat stiffly, shivering, both hands wrapped around the apple.

Johnny climbed down, untied his heavy winter coat from around his rain slicker and bedroll, and reached up to wrap it around the girl's trembling shoulders. He set his hat on his head then wrapped the Twins around his waist and secured the buckle. He sat to pull his boots on. Even that took twice or three times longer than usual. He felt half-frozen solid, which probably wasn't too far from the truth.

When he'd finally gotten himself seated on the saddle behind Dixie, he booted Ghost forward. He did not bother with the packhorse's rope. The horse would trail him. Especially in this weather, it wouldn't want to be left alone. Johnny meant hay, oats, and freshwater to the gelding.

"Where we going?" Dixie asked after several still-born attempts to form the words.

"Town ahead," Johnny said. "N-not . . . not too far. L-lucky's Ford."

"G-good . . . name . . ." she said, teeth clattering.

Johnny couldn't help chuckling at that.

He put the horse into a trot and was glad to hear the packhorse following, occasionally stepping on its lead rope. He was also glad to see that Teale had gotten the wagon out of the river. The man sat on the driver's seat, reins in his hands, regarding Johnny and the girl dubiously.

"Christ almighty, I thought for sure she was a goner!"

She might still be, Johnny did not say.

"Lucky Ford's ahead,'"Teale said. "Only a mile or so. They got 'em a hotel there. Hotel an' saloon!"

Johnny did not bother telling the man he knew about the place. He had no energy to waste. As it was, he and Dixie might not make it to the town. It might be wise to build a fire here, but they'd likely have a devil of a time finding dry wood. No, their best bet was Lucky's Ford.

He put the horse into a hard gallop. As he rode, he wrapped the girl in his arms, so they could share body warmth despite his doubting either of them had any to share. After about five minutes, he slowed the horse to a trot. The wind was too cold for galloping right into it, and, sitting in front of Johnny, the girl was getting the brunt of it.

He knew she was still alive by the time they reached the town only because he could feel her trembling between his arms. Or maybe he was trembling enough for both of them.

Dully, he watched what was left of the town, once a prosperous mining town, push up along the trail, at the base of a high northern ridge. The twenty or so business buildings had been boarded up long ago, when the mine on the ridge had plundered the last of the gold from the mountain. There was still a hotel kept open for passing pilgrims.

That was the Lucky Inn.

Rather than ride on toward the hotel, however, Johnny swerved to the left well before reaching it. He climbed the ridge, following an old, well-worn wagon path up the gradual incline. The mine, unimaginatively called the Lucky Strike, was no longer in operation, but Johnny had sheltered in the superintendent's old quarters on previous bullion runs, when the weather had dictated that he use the route through Lucky's Ford. He'd never stayed in the inn, because, like most places in these remote mountains, it was often haunted by desperadoes.

Those types knew that Johnny hauled bullion for the bank, and he hadn't wanted taking a chance on one of those Sierra Nevada desperadoes making a play for it. It would have been like teasing a child with chocolate. Enough other outlaws had made plays on the bullion even when Johnny hadn't taken unnecessary chances. To avoid trouble, he'd always cached the bullion in an old mine shaft, sheltered his horses in the stable flanking the old bunkhouse once used by the miners, and made himself comfortable in the not-uncomfortable superintendent's shack.

That's where he was headed now.

The ridge had been cleared of forest. Now old mine tailings bulged out from the slope at the base of the black mouths of abandoned mine portals. Various mining implements, including old tipples and rusty railcars and rails lay here and there among the wild raspberry shrubs and junipers that had grown up once the miners had pulled out.

Johnny rode past the old mine offices—board-and-batten structures slowly being reclaimed by the mountain—as well as a stamping mill and a well for ore processing. An abandoned general store lay to the right of the trail, just beyond the mine offices, its second floor and false facade having been consumed by fire probably started by a lightning strike.

Johnny passed the long, L-shaped board-and-batten bunkhouse and pulled up in front of the superintendent's cottage—merely a single-room log shack with a shake-shingled roof. Johnny had left split stove wood inside after his last run through here, as well as food. He couldn't wait to get his hands on that wood now, and to get a fire going in the shack's little monkey stove.

Walt Teale pulled the wagon up beside Johnny, on his right, and scowled incredulously as he drew the rig to a stop. "What the hell we doin' up here? The hotel's below. Ingram Haskell has whiskey down there . . . soft beds . . . fire in the hearth . . ."

Johnny shook his head as he half dropped from Ghost's back. "Too risky. You an' me will stay in the bunkhouse. I'm gonna get the girl in the shack here, get a fire going for her. There's only one bed in here."

Shivering violently, he untied the panniers from the packhorse's frame, hauled them over to the wagon, and dropped them inside with a heavy thud. The cold wind whipped the ends of his bandanna around his neck. The snow was coming down harder, building a fresh layer upon what had fallen previously.

Breathless, Johnny turned back to Teale still regarding him skeptically. "Listen close, Teale. There's a stable for the horses behind the bunkhouse. There's an old mine portal behind the bunkhouse, just up the slope. You'll see it. It's got two old wooden doors on it. They aren't locked. Stow the wagon in the portal. Safest place."

Johnny walked over to Ghost. He tossed his reins up to Teale and pulled the girl down from the horse's back. Holding Dixie in his quavering arms. She was unconscious, maybe even dead by now, for all he knew.

He turned back to the old man. "Can you manage it?"

Teale looked at him, still dubious, and nodded. "I can manage."

"You sure?"

"I said I could, didn't I?" the old man snarled, indignant. "I'll tend the horses and the mule, stow the wagon, but I ain't stayin' in no rat-infested bunkhouse when there's a hotel only spittin' distance away!"

He whipped the reins over his horse's back and pulled the wagon around behind the superintendent's shack. Johnny watched him go. He didn't want the man to go to the hotel. He was liable to get drunk and blab about whom he was traveling with.

But there was nothing Johnny could do short of shooting him. Not in his condition. Besides, he felt he could trust the man with the bullion. At least temporarily. Even if the weather would have made running off with it possible, Teale was in no condition to abscond with the gold. Johnny wouldn't worry about him. He had to get himself and the girl in front of a hot fire. He hoped to hell the wood he'd left was still waiting for him inside.

He tripped the door's hook latch and drew it open with his foot. He looked around quickly, glad to find the place not under current occupation though he hadn't thought it would be. He'd never seen any evidence that anyone except himself had ever overnighted in the old shack.

He hurried inside, crossed to the left, where a cot lay against the wall at the west end of the cabin. The cabin's little sheet-iron stove was near the cot. Johnny lay Dixie on the cot, which was covered with a motheaten bearskin. She was pale blue and she wasn't moving. He couldn't tell if she was dead though she appeared to be breathing albeit shallowly. He'd have felt for a pulse but his numb, shivering fingers wouldn't have been able to detect one.

First thing, build a fire, he had to remind himself. He was so cold that his thinker box had gone dull. His joints ached. Hell, his bones ached clear down to the marrow. His blood felt as though it had turned to ice.

The wood was still in the corrugated tin washtub where he'd left it on a previous trip.

He opened the stove's flue and, first using pine-cones and needles and then adding kindling to the tinder, he got a fire going in the little stove. It made a wheezing, rasping sound and then a crackling sound as the kindling took. The smell of pine perfumed the cabin.

Letting the fire grow gradually, afraid to hurry it at the risk of smothering it, he rose from his knees and turned to the cot. Next . . . he had to get Dixie out of those wet clothes.

He moved stiffly, hung his heavy coat over a chair then dropped to a knee beside the cot.

"Don't take this wrong or nothin'," he told the unconscious young woman, "but we gotta . . . gotta . . . get you outta your duds." He'd pitched his voice with irony, trying to lighten his mood. The situation was dire. She might be dead, and, if so, he might not be far behind her. He had to get them both out of their soaked, frigid clothes and bathed in the heat of a hot fire.

It took him a long time to get her out of her clothes—sodden wool coat, high-button leather shoes, stockings, skirt, pantaloons, pink bloomers, then came the fitted shirtwaist, camisole, and chemise. "I just want you to know, girl," he said, stuttering like an imbecile, "I've never had less fun undressing a woman before in my life. I purely haven't, no need to worry." He chuckled.

As he undressed her she started shivering again, so at least he knew she was alive, if even only just barely so. Her body temperature was likely perilously low. Possibly too low for her ever to recover.

That had been one cold bath they'd both taken.

"You ladies need to think of somethin' else for you to wear—a dozen articles of clothing don't seem near enough to me." Again, he chuckled.

When he had her lying naked on the bearskin, he drew two striped trade blankets up to her chin. He added two small logs to the fire, continuing to build the flames, then got to work skinning out of his own clothes, which felt like a heavy layer of ice clinging to him like a second skin. One hell of an uncomfortable second skin.

Naked, his cold, damp body feeling rubbery, and still shaking so violently that every movement was painfully awkward, he tossed yet another, slightly larger log on the fire. Then he closed the stove's single door and latched it, enjoying the creaking sound as the iron heated, filling the shabby cabin with sweet warmth.

"Oh, baby . . . yeah . . . I like the sound of that!"

The warmth wasn't penetrating his own frozen body yet, but he could detect it on his skin, and it would penetrate soon. Eventually, the marrow in his bones would thaw. He just needed to keep the fire burning.

He moved to the cot again, got down on his knees, peeled the blankets down the girl's body, exposing her. She had a nice body, well filled out exactly where a man preferred it to be, but he felt not so much as a single tingle of excitement. He wasn't sure he'd ever be able to feel that tingle of male excitement ever again even if he lived another hundred years.

"Don't take this wrong, neither, sweetheart, but I'm gonna try to get your blood flowin'."

He took a corner of one of the blankets and kneaded her flesh with it. He started with her head, drying her hair and rubbing her cheeks. He moved to her arms, rubbing hard, then her breasts and belly and thighs and calves and shins. By the time he'd gotten down to her feet, caressing each with his bare hands, which he'd finally worked some feeling back into, she squirmed around and opened her eyes.

"Oh God," she said, shivering more violently again, "where . . . are . . . we . . . ?"

"Don't matter," Johnny said. "You're safe."

He caressed her feet a little longer. She crossed her arms on her breasts but not out of modesty. She was hugging herself against the cold still weighing heavy on her despite the heat building in the stove.

Johnny rose. He climbed onto the cot with her. She slid over a little, not objecting, knowing exactly what he was up to and it had nothing to do with her former occupation. He pulled both blankets over them and then turned to her and wrapped his arms and legs around her. She did the same to him, burying her face in the hollow between his well-defined chest muscles.

They shivered together for a long time, entangled in each other's arms.

Johnny rose to feed more wood to the fire, stoking it with a poker, then closed the door again and returned to the cot. He and the girl cuddled together again. He could feel her shivering abate as his own did, as well.

Finally, they slept.

When Johnny woke, he saw that the window above the cot had gone black with night. He also discovered that he had been wrong about never feeling the male tingle again. He looked at Dixie, whose face was just inches from his own. She arched a brow.

"Sorry." Johnny tossed the covers back, and rose.

The cabin was warm but it could be warmer. He was warm now, as well. But he could be warmer and he was sure Dixie could be, as well. It took a long time to completely rid the bones of a chill like the one they'd taken out of the river.

"I'll take that as a compliment," Dixie said, propping her cheek on the heel of her hand and drawing the blankets up over her again, her eyes on him. "After what you've been through—fetching my worthless hide from that river. Don't ask me how I managed to tumble out of that wagon."

Johnny opened the stove doors. "Accidents happen."

"I feel like a fool. We both could have died."

"Like I said . . ." Johnny shifted the wood around in the stove, exposing the wood to more oxygen, building up the flames.

"I've never met you before, but I've heard of you . . . Shotgun Johnny."

Johnny set the poker over the corrugated tub containing the firewood, then added a couple of large logs to the fire. He closed the doors then sat back, resting his arm on an upraised knee, and glanced at the girl. "I've heard of you, too, Miss Dixie. You see, I came from the Grizzly Ridge Inn."

She gave a slow, tired blink. "I had a feeling you had, since there's only one trail down from there."

"I met some friends of yours up thataway. We all spent the night together, at the inn. They're weren't all that friendly, and they're dead now—burned up in the inn. Quite a few bodies in that pyre, turned out. A chubby girl and an old man I know to be Heck Torrance."

Dixie studied him, expressionless. She sucked in a corner of her lower lip, chewing on it.

"Found a black girl out in a root cellar. Carrion-eaters were fighting over her. Making an awful mess of things." Johnny gazed back at her.

She gazed back at him.

"Awful doin's up there," he said after a while. "Desperate doin's, I would think."

"Desperate times call for desperate measures."

"A lot of desperate folks in these mountains, Miss Dixie."

Her eyes turned bleak, her voice droll. "Hangin's too good for me."

"I'm not a judge."

"The loot's in the coffin."

"I know." Johnny nodded, then added, "Leastways, I sort of figured that."

"Were you after him, too? Jake?"

"Nope." Johnny turned his head to stare at the stove. He could see the orange conflagration through a narrow gap around the door. "I left my badge down below. I'm just on a bullion run."

"He loved me."

Johnny turned to her. Her eyes were wider now, sorrowful . . . desperate. A sheen of emotion shone in them. "Jake Teale. He loved me. The only one who ever did." She brushed a single tear from her cheek.

He stared back at her. He sensed the darkness in her. It tugged at him . . . at his own dark soul. He didn't like that it did. He'd come up here to get away from that darkness . . . his weaknesses . . . but here they were.

What had he expected, really? Sheila had been right. Maybe he really did belong up here . . . at home with his own desperate people.

"He really did love me," she insisted.

Johnny smiled. "I don't doubt it a bit."

"He never loved anybody before he met me. He told me, and I believe him. But he *loved me*. I never loved anybody before I met Jake. But I *loved him*."

"Like I said," Johnny said, smiling again tenderly. "I don't doubt it a bit."

They sat studying each other for a long time. Finally, Dixie brushed another tear from her cheek, sniffed, and said, "How 'bout you—you got a woman?"

"Yes."

"Do you love her?"

"Not like you and Jake," Johnny said with a sigh, turning to the stove again but not seeing the stove as much as the dark corners of his own dark soul. "Not like you and Jake."

"Come here." Dixie smiled and patted the cot. "Come back to bed. We got us a long night to get through . . . you an' me. Might as well keep each other warm through it."

Johnny looked at her, smiled again. He stood with

a sigh. "All right, Miss Dixie," he said, and folded his long, husky body back onto the cot and drew the blankets up over them both.

"Miss MacFarland deserves better than you. You're going to hurt her. You know you will. You've hurt every woman who's ever come into your life and made the mistake of loving you!"

CHAPTER 29

In the Lucky Inn a hundred yards below the old mine buildings, Willie Slater said, "I'll be hanged if it ain't gonna be a long, stormy night. I'll be whompoorooed if I might just get it started off on the right foot by takin' Miss Jubilee upstairs for a tussle!"

The scruffy little blond devil threw back the last of his whiskey and slammed the shot glass down on the table. He wolfishly eyed one of the two girls sitting at a table near the building's right wall, near the quietly ticking potbelly stove.

The girl Willie was eyeing was a plump, sandy-haired girl with a nice, full-hipped and full-busted figure with usually a saucy expression though she was looking a little bored at the moment. So was the other girl, Cora, a skinny brunette. The storm had kept away most of the business that ran through the Lucky Inn of an evening, not that business on even an average evening these days was all that much—just a few drifters and prospectors, for the most part. Occasionally a team of mule skinners hauling freight to the Reverend's Temptation farther up the mountain for whiskey and all the trimmings.

The only customers to have shown so far were Willie Slater and his pals Stretch Wilkins, Jate Durnberg, and Earl Crabb.

"You sure you're up for it, Willie?" Stretch Wilkins was playing solitaire while the two others, Durnberg and Crabb, were just sitting in their chairs, eyeing the two whores in much the same way that Willie Slater was. They hadn't made plays on the women, however, because they'd spent the last of their jingle on the single bottle of whiskey that sat half-empty on the table before them, and on a single room for all four men for the evening.

Willie turned to Stretch sitting to his right. "What do you mean—am I up for it?"

Durnberg and Crabb looked at each other, grinning. They turned to Stretch, still grinning, then turned back to the girls staring back at them blandly, shaking their crossed legs.

Stretch squeezed the deck of cards in his hands and hooked a crooked, slant-eyed smile at Willie. "Never mind."

He pretended to return his attention to the cards laid out before him, giving a single, soft snicker.

Willie stared at him. He stared at the backs of the heads of Durnberg and Crabb, who were staring at the girls again like two boys looking longingly through a glass display case at candy they couldn't afford. Willie could tell by the wrinkled skin behind their ears that they were still grinning.

Mocking him.

Willie stood quickly, fairly leaping out of his chair. He whipped his bowie knife out of his belt sheath and with one sweeping motion with his right hand and arm, slammed it into the table before Stretch Wilkins. The

blade was embedded in the middle of the queen of
hearts. He'd missed Stretch's hands, still closed
around the deck of cards, by about three inches.

"Chew it up and spit it out a little finer, Stretch!"
Willie yelled, his voice rocketing around the otherwise silent room.

The storm moaned outside, the wet snow splatter-
ing against the windows and then running down them
in slushy streaks. That and the ticking of the wood-
stove were the only sounds.

The barman, Henry Snyder—a big, fat, long-haired,
apron-clad man—stood behind the bar at the back of
the room, over an open dime novel he'd been reading until Willie had gotten his neck in a hump. Now
he regarded Willie and Stretch dully. He was accustomed to such dustups. He'd scrubbed enough blood
out of the floor over the years to fill a couple of fifty-
gallon beer kegs.

That didn't mean he enjoyed doing so.

"Say it, Stretch!" Willie bellowed, glaring red-faced
down at Wilkins.

Stretch looked at the knife embedded in the table
before him. Slowly, he turned his head to his left and
lifted his chin until his gaze held on Willie's. "Oh well,
Willie," he said, feigning a concerned expression, "I
just thought you might be too much on edge. You
know . . . after Shotgun Johnny caused you to crap
your pants the other day in Riley Duke's Saloon!"

Stretch and the other two men shared snickering,
devilish laughs. Willie glared at them, his anger building. He looked at the girls. They were looking at him
now, the light of mockery flashing in their eyes as they
continued shaking their crossed legs. Jubilee was

smoking a cigarette and she laughed as she exhaled a smoke plume.

Willie turned back to Stretch. He started to slide his right hand toward his new Colt—a spare he'd fished out of his saddlebags, since Shotgun Johnny had made him leave his other one on the floor of Riley Duke's Saloon. He froze when he saw that Stretch had removed his own right hand from his deck of cards. He now held that hand under the table, near his right hip.

Stretch's brown eyes blazed like sunlight off gold as he stared up at Willie. "Don't do it, Willie. You see, your bluff's done been called."

Willie stared down at him, lips compressed until a white line formed above his mouth. His cheeks were crimson, swollen with blood. A vein bulged above his right brow. His eyes were as wide as silver dollars, and as dark as the sky at midnight.

The snickering had stopped. Silence like that inside a dead man's casket had returned to the room. All eyes were on Willie. The girls were looking at him, too . . . expectant . . . waiting . . .

"Your bluff's done been called, Willie," Stretch repeated, his voice flat and hard.

Willie glanced around once more—at his other two pards, at the girls, at Henry Snyder. Returning his gaze to Stretch, he said, "All hell—I was just funnin' with you, Stretch!" He slapped Stretch on the back, hard. "Don't get your bloomers in such a twist. It ain't good for your health, if you know what I'm sayin'." He winked at the tall, unshaven, long-faced man. "Good thing we're here for a reason and I need all hands on deck or I'd have to slap you down for your back talk!"

Willie laughed again though there was no humor in it. Smiling like a kid on Christmas morning knowing he has a special gift waiting under the tree, he turned to the girls. "I hope you fellas can hold down the fort. Let me know iffen you see . . . um, well, you know who I'm talkin' about. Me? I'm gonna take me this lovely li'l Jubilee upstairs and bleed off a little sap!"

Willie stopped at the girls' table, grabbed Jubilee's left arm, crouched, and pulled her up over his shoulder. Jubilee screamed in shock and dropped her cigarette onto the floor, sparks flying. "Put me down! Put me down, dammit!"

"Willie, you know the rules!" Snyder barked from behind the bar. "You gotta pay first!"

"Put it on my account!"

"You don't got no account!"

"I do now!"

Willie laughed as he carried the girl across the room and over to the stairs that rose to the left of the bar. "Willie!" Jubilee cried, gritting her teeth as she hung down the young firebrand's back. "Dammit, Willie, you ain't gettin' no free one!"

Willie only laughed again. He was already halfway up the stairs, the girl swatting her hands against his back. To no avail. Willie topped the stairs then disappeared into the Lucky Inn's second story, where the doxies plied their trade and where Snyder rented rooms to overnight travelers.

Stretch Wilkins listened to Willie's boots thunder in the ceiling over his head. He heard the hinges as a door was shoved open then the squawk of the girl dropping onto a bed.

"Willie, damn you!" Jubilee cried.

Willie gave a victorious whoop. There was the resolute thud of the door closing.

Silence save for the storm and the fire in the stove.

Snyder gave an angry chuff then returned his attention to the book laid open on the bar before him. The other doxie, Cora, dragged Jubilee's makings pouch over to her side of the table and began rolling a smoke.

Stretch turned to Durnberg and Crabb and said through a cagey smile, "I'll bet you each a dollar, when we're all flush again, that Willie's back down here inside of ten minutes."

Crabb chuckled through his crooked front teeth.

Durnberg threw his bushy-haired head back on his shoulders and laughed.

All three men sat in hushed silence, glancing at one another and casting occasional looks at the ceiling around where they'd heard the door close. Cora smoked with a desultory air, bobbing her foot. Snyder read his book, occasionally opening his mouth to yawn loudly.

No sounds came from the second story.

At least, not until maybe six minutes after Willie had hauled the girl upstairs. Then there was an anguished wailing cry of, "Dammit! Damn you, Jubilee!"

Her high-pitched voice returned with, "You can't blame me, Willie! That ain't my fault!"

Willie gave a groan that sounded part grizzly wail and said, *"Ahh, hell—damn you!"*

"Willie!" she screamed just before there came the crack of an angry hand against flesh.

"Damn his blackhearted hide!" Snyder said, casting his angry gaze at the ceiling.

Boots thudded on the second floor. A latch clicked. Hinges groaned. More thuds made their way across the ceiling. Willie appeared at the top of the stairs. He started down the steps, his face flushed even redder than before.

Jubilee's muffled sobs could be heard in the ceiling.

Grinning, Durnberg and Crabb turned to Stretch.

Stretch gave his head a brief shake in the negative, and, wiping his own smile from his face with a brush of his hand, returned his attention to his game of solitaire. Durnberg and Crabb cast their own sober gazes at the floor, Crabb humming quietly and toeing an old bloodstain half-covered with sawdust.

Snyder turned to Willie, who was halfway down the stairs, and said, "You better not have marked that girl, Willie!"

"Shut up and pour me a whiskey!"

"You're broke!"

"Pour me the damn whiskey!" Willie said, bellying up to the bar in front of the apron. He slapped his hand down sharply on the badly scarred wood. "Pour me the damn whiskey, Henry, before I start shootin' up the place!"

"Ah hell!"

Snyder reached under the bar. He pulled up an unlabeled bottle, produced a shot glass from a pyramid near a gallon jar of pickled goose eggs, set the glass in front of Willie, and filled it.

Willie had just wrapped his thumb and index finger around the glass when the saloon's front door opened. Instantly, Willie's Colt was in his right hand.

He swung toward the door, extending the revolver as he clicked the hammer back.

The other three were on their feet then, too, slapping leather and clutching steel. They cocked their own hoglegs and aimed them at the door through which a stoop-shouldered, thickset old man entered on a gust of wind laced with wet snow.

CHAPTER 30

The old newcomer wore a blue wool coat, the shoulders mantled with snow. So was the man's high-crowned black felt hat. It clung to the man's salt-and-pepper beard, as well, and to the red scarf hanging loosely around his neck.

As he turned from the door, which he'd just closed behind him, his gaze fell on Willie and the other three, Wilkins, Durnberg, and Crabb, all of whom were aiming six-guns at him.

The old man blinked his deep-sunk eyes, which turned a shade darker with apprehension. "Hold on now," he said slowly, in a deep, phlegmy voice. "I don't want no trouble."

The whore Cora stubbed out her cigarette and, rising, turned to Snyder and said, "I think I'll go up and look in on Jubilee." She glanced once more, darkly, at the four men with their guns drawn on the old man. Then she headed for the stairs.

"I'll call ya if I need ya," Snyder assured her in a bossy tone. He turned toward the old man still standing by the door and added with a shrewd grin, "The old man might need a little lovin' on such a stormy night."

Cora didn't look back as she continued climbing the stairs.

"How 'bout it, old-timer," Willie said from where he stood with his back to the bar. "That what you're here for—a little lovin'?"

"Nah, I ain't here for none o' that."

Durnberg and Crabb snickered a little, glancing at each other.

"What are you here for, then?" Willie asked.

"Whiskey. It's damn cold out there, an' I came a far piece."

"What's your name?"

"Teale. Walt Tea—" The old-timer stopped abruptly, apparently realizing his mistake. He narrowed his eyes at Willie and then at the other two.

The other two glanced at Willie standing behind them, their brows arched speculatively.

Willie raised his own blond brows as he strode slowly forward, keeping his cocked Colt aimed out before him, about halfway out from his right side. "Well, now . . . Walt Teale." He stopped about ten feet in front of the old man, whose face appeared washed-out and pale behind his wet beard. "You wouldn't happen to be any relation to *Jake*, now, would you?"

Teale glowered at the little, blond, anvil-jawed toughnut before him.

A good ten seconds passed before Jate Durnberg said, "Where's the wagon, Teale? Where's the girl?"

"Best of all," said Stretch Wilkins, "where's the *loot*?"

Willie just stood smiling up at the old man, his Colt

aimed at the old man's belly bulging out the front of his coat shiny with melted snow.

Teale just stared back at them, his eyes as dark as coals beneath his shaggy salt-and-pepper brows.

"See, we know two people left the Grizzly Ridge Inn," Willie said. "We seen the tracks."

"Judging by the size of one of the sets of footprints," Stretch put in, "one was a girl. Likely, Teale's lady friend—Dixie Wade."

"Shut up, Stretch!" Willie barked out of habit. "I'll handle this, just like I always do!"

Stretch cut a sidelong glance at him. Willie didn't like the look at all. He wasn't used to it from Stretch— that look of stubborn defiance. As though he didn't see Willie as the pack leader anymore.

Quickly, Willie returned his attention to Teale and tempered his tone. "Stretch had it right, though. We seen the tracks. You must've been the one who left the inn in a wagon. We took a shortcut to get here ahead of you. There ain't been no one else through here . . . till you showed up."

He paused.

"Where's the loot, old man?" Quickly, Willie turned to look behind him at Henry Snyder taking it all in. "You got your ears plugged back there, Henry?"

Snyder returned his attention to his book.

"Cough it up, old man," Stretch said to Teale. "We know Jake was carryin' loot. Takin' it up to the inn. He was gonna fetch Dixie. We heard it from Maud Horton. What me an' the boys is thinkin' is Dixie found herself another fella to help her outta the mountains with it . . . in a wagon."

"We checked out the inn," Durnberg said, narrowing his eyes, coyote-like. "Torrance was dead in his bed. Same with one o' the girls. Two o' the girls was missin'. One went in the wagon . . . judgin' by the tracks around the yard." He glanced at Willie. "Oh, sorry, Willie—I hope I wasn't steppin' on your toes."

He flared a nostril. He, too, had gotten awfully brave after Shotgun Johnny had pulled that low-down dirty stunt on Willie at Riley Duke's place. Willie's heart thudded heavily, humiliation weighing heavy in him. Of course it hadn't helped matters that he'd made such a show of hauling the whore upstairs a few minutes ago only to be unable to complete the mission, so to speak.

Or to even get it started, damn his tangled nerves, anyway.

Willie's worm was turning, however. Soon, he'd be one wealthy fella. As soon as he got his hands on the loot and shot the three miserable skunks he'd once called his friends.

Until they'd laughed at him, he'd called them his friends. Here they were, still laughin' at him. But Willie Slater would have the last laugh, and he'd make water on their bloody carcasses.

Willie slid his gaze back to Teale, raised the gun, extending it straight out from his shoulder, and gritted his teeth. "Where is it, old man? Where's the loot? You got three seconds. One . . . two . . ."

Teale threw up his hands. "Hold on, hold on. Don't shoot me, for chrissakes!"

"Why not?" Willie said.

Teale stared back at him then slowly shaped a cagey

smile of his own, furling his heavy brows over his dark eyes. "'Cause you don't know the half of it."

Willie and the other three looked at one another, curious.

Willie turned back to Teale. "What're you talkin' about? I think you're stallin'."

"Nah, nah. I ain't stallin'. I'm sayin' there's more loot than you boys thought there was. Plenty more. Some of it's gold."

Again, they shared dubious glances.

"I need a drink," Teale said.

Smiling confidently, he reached up and shoved Willie's gun aside then brushed past the blond firebrand as he lumbered toward the bar under the weight of his wet coat. Willie stared at him, incredulous. It burned him that he was getting so little respect these days. The only reason he didn't shoot the old man in the back was because he seemed so pleased with himself, not to mention that he'd said the magic word:

Gold.

Teale bellied up to the bar, set his red muffler on the bar to his right, looked at Snyder, and said, "Whiskey. Leave the bottle."

"You got money?"

Teale removed his hat, tossed it down onto his muffler, and scrubbed a hand through his thin hair. "I ain't askin' for a handout, mister."

Snyder regarded the old man skeptically as he poured a drink out of the same unlabeled bottle Willie's drink had come from. Teale reached into a pocket of his dark canvas trousers and tossed a dime onto the counter.

"Imagine that," Snyder said. "A flush man appears out of the wind and the snow."

"Don't you got somewhere you'd rather be, Henry?" Willie asked him, pointedly, as he bellied up to the bar beside Teale. "By the way, that wasn't a question."

Snyder regarded him darkly, pinching up one side of his fleshy, unattractive face. He pulled the bottle off the bar but stopped when Teale said, "You can leave that."

Snyder turned back to him. "You got a buck?"

Teale tossed a couple of coins equaling a dollar onto the bar. Regarding Teale and Willie dubiously, Snyder swept the coins off the bar and into his hand then dropped the money into a bucket. Picking up the bucket by its bail, he swung his unwieldy body heavily around and pushed through a curtained doorway flanking the bar, and he and the bucket were gone.

As Durnberg, Crabb, and Stretch Wilkins approached the bar, canting their heads skeptically to one side, Willie turned his own untouched whiskey glass between his index finger and thumb, and scrutinized the old man beside him. "Gold?"

"Yep," Teale said self-importantly, leaning forward against the bar, looking at the amber liquid in his glass then tossing a half of the shot straight back.

He sighed and smacked his lips.

Durnberg and Wilkins moved up on Teale's left. Crabb—the tallest of the bunch, and wearing a fox fur coat—bellied up to the bar to Willie's right.

Willie leaned up very close to Teale, glowering menacingly at the old man, and said with his lips about four inches from the man's bearded right cheek, "Spill it."

Teale threw the rest of his whiskey back then re-filled his glass. He turned to face Willie, ignoring Wilkins and Durnberg now standing behind him, and said, "Bullion from the Reverend's Temptation."

Willie felt his cheeks warm. To his right, Earl Crabb said, "You talkin' 'bout the bullion Johnny's carryin' down to Hallelujah Junction?"

"*Shotgun Johnny*," Jate Durnberg said for emphasis, moving around so he could get in on the conversation more directly. So did Wilkins.

"*Willie's* Shotgun Johnny?" Wilkins asked with a jeering glance at Willie.

"Shut up and listen to the man, Stretch!" Willie said, checking his rage.

"I don't know what you mean by *Willie's* Shotgun Johnny," Teale said, "But iffen you mean *Shotgun Johnny Greenway*, then . . . yep."

"He headed this way, is he?" Willie asked, not liking the way his heartbeat was picking up and his hands were getting warm.

"Oh, he's here." Teale smiled with self-satisfaction and took another sip of his whiskey.

Willie's heart hiccupped. Fury burned through him as the incident at Riley Duke's Saloon flared through his mind once more, making him want to grind his molars to fine powder. At the same time, he had to repress the involuntary impulse to squirt down his leg.

"Where?" Crabb asked.

"First, we gotta get somethin' straight."

"What?" Durnberg said.

Teale kept his gaze on Willie, rightfully assuming that Willie was the leader of this bunch, Riley Duke's Saloon notwithstanding. That made Willie feel better about himself.

"We split everything right down the middle."

"What *everything* are we talking about?" Willie asked. "Just to be clear, I mean."

Teale sipped his whiskey again. A little glassy-eyed, he looked from Willie to each of the other three men in turn. He looked at Willie again and said, "The loot Jake rode to the Grizzly Ridge Inn with is in the coffin."

"What coffin?" Willie and Stretch asked at the same time.

"Jake's coffin."

"What's Jake doin' in a coffin?" Willie asked, squinting curiously at the old man.

"He's dead," Teale said, frowning. He pulled a rolled-up, folded-up piece of paper out of his pocket. He unfolded it, unrolled it, and held it up for the others to see. It was a wanted dodger that included a photograph of Jake Teale along with WANTED DEAD OR ALIVE and 1,000 DOLLARS.

"And he's got a thousand dollars on his head."

Willie and the others studied Teale in silence for a time, brows beetled skeptically. Finally, Earl Crabb laughed and Stretch Wilkins said, "You mean to tell me you fetched your son's body so you could claim the reward on his head?"

Teale flushed. He tossed the whiskey back as though to cover his chagrin then brushed his fist across his nose. "I was gonna bury him, too. Give him a proper burial . . . somewhere. But, hell, why not cash in? Jake woulda done the same to me if the tables were turned."

Willie found himself grinning at the old devil.

Teale scowled at him, indignant, and said, "Listen, that boy was bad. Bad clean through. Both him an' his brother. There wasn't nothin' I could do with either one of 'em. Their ma coddled 'em somethin' awful and came down on me like a wagonload of burnin' coal every time I took the strap to 'em!"

He paused, scrutinizing each man before him staring at him, grinning coyote grins.

"I loved Jake," he said defiantly. "Of course I did . . . but he was bad. And I'm old. I got a bad ticker. I can't work up at the mine no more. It was killin' me. Why not cash in and take that money . . . and the loot . . . and the bullion in them panniers headed for the bank . . . and head to Arizona? Lay on a white sand beach for a few years or however long I got left. Probably only a few months, judgin' by how logy I feel right now."

The others howled.

"A white sandy beach in Arizona, eh?" said Crabb.

Teale winced as he pressed his fist against his chest then clumsily splashed more liquor into his glass.

"Sure, sure," Willie said, still grinning up at the old devil. "Why the hell not cash in on your dead son? Hell, he'd do the same to you."

He glanced at Stretch Wilkins and winked.

"Where's the loot?" Willie asked the old man.

"Where Johnny told me to hide it. He's with the girl."

"What girl?" Durnberg asked with renewed interest.

"Dixie?" Willie glanced at the door, as though she might be standing there. "Is she with you?"

"She's with him—Johnny. Went for a swim. Both of 'em."

"Where are they now?" Willie asked, his voice rising with anger, impatience.

"First—we got a deal?" Teale wanted to know. "We split everything even-like. The reward money, the loot . . ." He grinned with one half of his beard-shrouded mouth, and his drink-bright eyes flashed as he said, ". . . the bullion."

"Sure, sure," Willie said, waving a dismissive hand in the air. He grinned. "Even the girl." He did not like the way his heart quickened once more, anxiously, as he said, "Where's Shotgun Johnny?"

CHAPTER 31

Dixie's bladder woke her.

Dreams of the raging river that had tried to swallow her like a giant predator fish hadn't helped placate the urge. She rose slowly, trying not to awaken the big man lying beside her. That was impossible, however. His muscular arms were wrapped around her like a thick cocoon.

As soon as she stirred, he sat up and reached for the shotguns he'd hung from a peg beside the cot.

"No, no, no!" Dixie said, placing a soothing hand on his chest. "It's just me—Dixie. I need to use the chamber pot, is all. Go back to sleep."

The big man relaxed some. He'd risen a while ago to stoke the stove again, and in the light of the fire showing through the cracks around the door, she saw him squint up at her through the dark shadows and flickering red light. The shadows and light slid across the severely handsome planes of his face bisected by a long, resolute nose. "You sure?"

"Everything's fine."

He filled his lungs and sank back against the pillow, closing his eyes, falling back asleep.

Dixie climbed over him. Standing, she appreciated the fine figure of a naked man he was, one who'd satisfied her most thoroughly, then drew the blankets up over him again. She scoured the cabin for a chamber pot but didn't find one. Growing desperate, she decided she'd have to use the privy. At least, she hoped there was a privy. There had to be one around here somewhere.

She'd check behind the shack. That was the most obvious place. If there wasn't one, she'd make water in the open. Who was around to see her, after all?

The important thing was—she had to evacuate her bladder before it burst!

She slipped into her dress and her coat. She pulled on her stockings and shoes. It was warm in the cabin, but she could feel the chill breeze pushing through the cracks between the unchinked logs. She was tired of being cold. She'd throw on a few things to keep the brunt of the cold out and make as quick a trip as possible.

She buttoned her coat then moved to the door. Wincing, she flipped the latch and glanced toward the bed, hoping she didn't wake the big man again. He needed his sleep. He'd risked his life to save hers in the river. And then he'd done his damnedest to "comfort" her. He was understandably exhausted.

He grunted a little at the tinny click of the latch and muttered something, but otherwise remained asleep. Dixie opened the door just enough to slip through it then drew it closed behind her, gently latching it.

She looked around. The night was murky. Several inches of fresh snow had fallen. The storm had moved on, however. The black sky was awash in vibrant star glitter. The air was so cold it burned her lungs, and the swirling breeze tried to suck her breath away.

She swung to her left and hurried around behind the shack, keeping a close eye on the snowy ground to keep from tripping over anything. She held her coat closed at her throat.

She was glad to see a privy right where she'd expected to find it—directly behind the shack. She headed toward it, then, after taking three strides from the shack's rear corner, stopped suddenly. She whipped her head to her right.

She'd heard something over that way. It had sounded like a whisper. A man's voice.

All she could see was a very small tumbledown shack—or was it a stock pen of some kind? Perhaps a chicken coop? It was an irregular shadow hunched against the snow and the star-filled sky that arched over the far side of the ruined structure, dwarfing it, humbling it.

Dixie stood, ears pricked, heart quickening.

No, she decided when she did not hear the sound again and saw no movement around her. It had just been the breeze lifting some of the fresh powder, whisking it across the snowy ground.

Continuing to look around warily, she strode to the privy. She opened the door, stepped inside, and drew the door closed, securing the nail in the ring. She shivered as she did her business, the cold wood pressing against the undersides of her legs and rump, feeling like a block of ice, numbing her flesh. Finishing, she rose and dropped her skirt. She reached for the nail in the door then stopped.

A shadow moved outside the privy. She could see it through the cracks between the planks forming the front wall, just right of the door. Again, she heard the whisper. It had come from behind her, behind the privy.

Her heart lurched almost painfully.

Someone was out there. She was sure of it.

"Johnny?" she said. She'd spoken too softly to have been heard above the wind. She cleared her throat and called his name a little louder.

"Yeah, it's me," he said. "Just checkin' on ya."

"Oh, thank God!" she said, slapping her hand to her chest in relief.

She flipped the nail from the ring and started to open the door. As she did, it dawned on her that the voice that had answered her call hadn't sounded like his—Johnny's. She'd been too quick to believe that it had been.

Her mistake became even more apparent when she stepped out of the privy and found a short, wiry man standing in front of her, grinning diabolically beneath the brim of his pale Stetson.

"Hi, there, Miss Dixie," Willie Slater said.

Dixie opened her mouth to yell for Johnny but before she could even start to call out, a big, stinky hand was clamped over her mouth from behind, and a thick male arm wrenched her violently up off her feet.

Johnny was slow to rise up out of his slumber.

He slept so deeply that it was only by sheer will and strenuous effort that he forced himself to swim up through the heavy, clinging quicksand of sleep. His unconscious mind told him that it was dawn or later and that he needed to rise. It also told him that something was wrong.

When he rolled onto his back and forced his eyes

open, he saw immediately that his unconscious had not been old-womaning him into either waking prematurely or believing that something was amiss, because he saw the gray light of dawn pushing through the cabin's three windows. He also saw that the bed to his left was empty.

Dixie was gone.

He sat up instantly, looking around, raking a hand down his face. "Dixie?" The call had come out on a phlegmy croak. He cleared his throat and repeated, "Dixie . . . where are you?"

She was not in the cabin. He had a vague memory of her rising in the night and saying that she needed to use the thunder mug. That was his last memory of the girl. He did not remember being aware of her returning to bed.

Quickly, he rose, sucking a sharp breath through gritted teeth. The fire had gone out, and the cabin was as cold as an icehouse. The worn puncheons beneath his bare feet felt like the surface of a frozen lake. He hurried to the front window, slid a dirty floursack curtain aside, and peered out.

No sign of her.

He checked the other two windows, cupping his hands and blowing on them, his breath frosting in the air around his head. Still, no sign of her.

Maybe she'd just gone out to use the privy again or to fetch more wood. Possible. He might have been so dead asleep he hadn't heard her though that wasn't likely. He might not have slept last night with one eye open, but he'd have heard the door open and shut.

Wouldn't he have?

Quickly, he dressed. His clothes were cold, making him shiver.

He stepped into his boots, strapped the Twins around his waist, pulled on his striped winter coat, set his hat on his head, and stepped outside. He looked at the ground revealed by the smoky gray light of dawn. Here and there he could see the faint outline of Dixie's footprints, but just barely. The wind had done a good job of filling them in.

She'd left the cabin a couple of hours ago.

Johnny looked down the slope and to his left, where the Lucky Inn's two-story, wood-frame building jutted up from the main street at the base of the hill. The inn faced the main street, so Johnny could see only part of the side facing him as well as the back of the place.

Had she gone down there?

He looked around in front of him and didn't see any sign that she'd headed down the slope. He did see faint prints leading off to his left, however. He followed the intermittent sign around shack's front corner and down the side toward the rear. He stopped at the shack's rear corner.

The faint prints of her shoes trailed away toward the privy.

Johnny started to head that way then stopped and hurled himself straight back around the corner of the cabin, striking the ground hard on his back just as two bullets chewed into the shack's logs, spitting slivers across the newly fallen snow. At the same time, the screeching reports of two rifles shattered the breezy morning silence and chased their own echoes skyward.

"Damn!" a man snarled.

Two men had poked their hatted heads and Winchester rifles around opposite sides of the privy as Johnny had taken that first step away from the shack.

He'd recognized both bushwhackers despite their heavy coats, pulled-down Stetsons, and the mufflers wrapped around their necks.

One was the long-faced Stretch Wilkins.

The other was Jate Durnberg.

Now as he rolled to his left, up against the shack's wall, there was the metallic rasp of both rifles being cocked quickly, and the crunch of running footsteps. Johnny reached under the flaps of his striped coat and ripped both Twins free of their holsters.

Still on his butt, half sitting up, Johnny leaned right to peer around the cabin's corner.

Wilkins and Durnberg were running toward him, extending their rifles out from their shoulders. They were aiming above where Johnny lay on the ground, because they'd guessed he'd gained his feet by now.

They'd guessed wrong. It cost Durnberg his life, for as the bucktoothed man spied Johnny, he fired his Winchester high—at least three feet over Johnny's head. Johnny tripped both of his right-hand Twin's triggers, the buckshot tearing into Durnberg's coat and face and peppering his hat, picking him up with a shrill scream and throwing him straight back through the privy door and inside, slumped back over the hole, jerking as he died.

Wilkins fired high, as well, knowing his mistake even as he made it and cursing loudly, realizing that he was only a heartbeat away from ending up like Durnberg.

Johnny leaned a little farther to his right, extended his left-hand Twin toward Stretch. Both barrels belched smoke and flames. Stretch screamed as he flew backward to land in the snow ten feet from where he'd been shot. He lay spread-eagle, moving his arms and legs as though making an angel while the snow beneath him turned red.

"Oh! Oh! Oh!" he cried, and then fell suddenly still.

Johnny rose. He pressed his back against the shack's log wall and reloaded the Twins quickly, awaiting another attack. When no more rifles belched or bullets screeched toward him, he edged a look around the shack's rear corner.

What in hell was going on here . . . ?

CHAPTER 32

As Johnny gazed into the yard behind the shack, the gray dawn light intensifying as the sun inched up in the east, Dixie's voice came to him suddenly, screaming, *"Johnny!"*

The scream was strangely muffled, as though she was either far away or inside a building.

Johnny frowned, trying to follow the plea back to its source.

The trouble was the wind was blowing the fresh snow around. It blew the scream around, too, making the pinpointing of its source a difficult chore.

The blowing snow obscured his vision, as well. The clouds hunkered low, a solid mass allowing no sunlight to peek down between them. The landscape he gazed into was a bleak gray-and-white one. There was the gray of the privy and the near-blackness of the rocky slope where the breeze swept it clear of snow. There was also the cold, grim granite wall of the ridge rising nearly straight up from seventy yards farther up the slope.

A mine portal lay straight up the slope, bored into the base of the high granite ridge. Johnny usually stored the bullion in that tunnel mouth. That's where he assumed that Walt Tcale had stored it yesterday, as per Johnny's instructions.

It was up from there, along the base of the cold, bleak mass of granite, that the scream seemed to have come.

Johnny swept the terrain around him again closely, wary of a trap. When he spied no movements, sensed no would-be ambushers near, he stepped out away from the shack and crossed the twenty-foot gap between the shack and the privy. He moved slowly around behind the latrine. When he was sure no one was waiting back there with the intention of drilling a bullet in his back, he paused to look around again.

"Johnny!" Dixie's scream again caromed through the wind and drifting snow.

He peered up the ridge, not able to see anything for a moment but a shifting curtain of white. When the breeze abated and the snow cleared, the jutting wall of rock appeared again at the top of the slope. He could see no movement—only snow and rock and the occasional abandoned tram car, or *tub*, as the miners called them—humping up here or there. A rusted pick with a rotten handle, swept clear of snow by the wind, lay against the side of a large slag pile on the rim of a processing pit ahead of Johnny.

He walked ahead, moving around the edge of the deep pit, and continued up the slope. He held the Twins in his hands, extended halfway out in front of him, ready for the next ambush, which he knew would come. They—whoever "they" were—were using the girl to lure him up here. They knew he'd have no choice but to take the bait.

For one thing, they had the girl and he couldn't

very well leave her in such a predicament. For another thing, they'd likely taken her to exchange her for the bullion. Of course, they knew he was hauling the bullion. Most folks in this part of the mountains knew Johnny Greenway hauled bullion down from the Reverend's Temptation.

Willie Slater and Earl Crabb were the other two men in Wilkins's and Durnberg's bunch. They knew very well about Johnny and the bullion. And Willie Slater was likely carrying around a fairly large chip on his shoulder after his slap-down at Riley Duke's Saloon.

"Johnny!" Dixie screamed again. Her voice sounded ghostly and grief-stricken as another wind gust ripped it, flung it to and fro before and around him.

He was certain, however, that she was somewhere at the base of the granite ridge, possibly inside the mine shaft. Her screams had been more and more hollow-sounding.

Johnny continued climbing the ridge, pulling his hat down tight so the cold wind didn't rip it off his head. The wind whipped at the muffler he'd wrapped around his neck. His gloved index fingers caressed the Twins' triggers inside the steel guard housing.

At the top of the slope, near the base of the massive ridge, whose crest jutted two hundred feet above him, Johnny stopped. He looked to his left, then his right. Nothing around but abandoned mine debris and some rusted rails left over from the ore transport systems. He turned to look back down the slope, scrutinizing the rocks and other debris bulging up along the long declivity that dropped to the abandoned town at its base.

Nowhere on the slope or in the canyon beyond did he spy any movement aside from the swirling snow.

"Johnny!"

He swung to his left and walked along the base of the ridge, moving around slag heaps and more abandoned tubs. He came to a mine portal in which he'd stored the bullion and assumed/hoped like hell that Teale had stored it there, too.

He approached the portal slowly, carefully, extending both Twins straight out in front of him. He swung his head to his left and right, making sure no one was coming up behind him. He stepped into the portal and was relieved to find Heck Torrance's wagon parked inside, several yards from the entrance, all but concealed from the outside.

Johnny walked up to the wagon. He was doubly relieved to see the bullion-stuffed panniers lying beside the coffin, right where he'd set them.

"Johnny!"

The girl's scream had come from straight ahead, from deeper inside the tunnel.

"Johnny, please . . . help me . . . ! They're going to kill me!" A racking sob followed.

Johnny moved around the wagon, stepped into the tunnel's deeper shadows. The tunnel walls were supported by heavy though aging wooden beams. The beams were cracked in places, buckling around the cracks, as the heavy granite mountain pushed down against them.

Iron tram rails ran along the tunnel floor, foreshortening into the distance until the deeper shadows swallowed them.

Johnny moved slowly into those heavy, musty

shadows. His heart thudded heavily. His hands sweated inside his gloves as he caressed the shotguns' eyelash triggers with his index fingers. A gun could flash ahead of him at any moment. He likely wouldn't even hear the bark before the bullets plowed into him.

He was walking into a trap.

He knew it, hated it, but there was nothing he could do about it. They, whoever they were—most likely, Willie Slater and Earl Crabb—had Dixie. Johnny couldn't just take the bullion and walk away. She was a killer. She didn't deserve his help. Still, he couldn't leave her.

"Willie?" Johnny called, his voice echoing loudly off the stone walls around him. "Earl . . . ?"

The only response was the girl's soft sobs. His boots crunched gravel as he moved slowly deeper into the chasm that smelled of earth, rodents, and moldy timbers.

"Release the girl!" Johnny called. "You can have the bullion. It's all yours."

Still, no reply.

He was in almost total darkness now as he walked twenty-five, thirty yards into the mountain. There was a little faded gray light here and there, bleeding down through either air vents that had been drilled through the rock from above or through natural flues and fissures. It was some light. Not much, but enough so that he could occasionally see the iron rails on the ground to his right, see one or both of the unevenly chipped, stone walls to his right and left.

He passed through an area that was as black as the inside of a glove. He walked carefully, occasionally tripping over the rails or rocks that had bulged out of the walls or fallen from the ceiling.

The girl's sobs grew gradually louder.

Gray light shone ahead of him. It glinted off something near the cave's floor. The glint flickered, and then, as he continued walking, he realized that the light was reflecting off eyes.

Dixie's eyes.

"Please help me," she begged through a choked sob as he came within six feet of her. She sucked in a breath, sniffed. "Get me out of here! I don't want to die in here—alone!" She lowered her head, crying.

Johnny swung around, expecting to find someone stealing up close behind him.

Nothing.

He looked into the shadows to each side of Dixie. Still, nothing. He peered at her more closely. She sat with her back against an overturned tram car. Her hands were pulled back behind her. Johnny leaned forward to gaze down between Dixie and the car. Her wrists were bound together and tied with a heavy rope to a steel handle at the right end of the car.

Dixie sobbed, her head bobbing. "Please, get me out of here, Johnny!"

"Where are they?"

Dixie lifted her head, glanced around. "I . . . I . . . don't know. I thought maybe they'd—"

"Behind you, Johnny!" a man's voice shouted.

Johnny wheeled, raising both shotguns. He stared back toward the ragged circle of gray light marking the mine's entrance. Two men stood inside the tunnel, shoulder to shoulder. They were stick figures from this distance of sixty yards. One stick was considerably smaller than the other.

The smaller stick would be Willie Slater. The larger one was Earl Crabb. They both held something in their hands. Johnny thought he saw another figure behind them but he couldn't be sure.

Were Slater and Crabb wielding rifles?

Johnny stood, extending both Twins straight out in front of him, his mind whirling. The trap was about to be sprung. In what fashion, he had yet to see.

But then he saw exactly how the two cowardly dogs were going to spring it. Slater and Crab stepped apart, each moving to an opposite side of the tunnel. Crouching, they swung the objects in their hands.

As Johnny heard the deep, wooden thuds of what he now realized were picks or sledgehammers, a cold stone dropped in his belly. He watched, rage burning in him, as Slater and Crabb smashed the heavy hammers against the sides of the moldering support frame fifty feet inside the mine.

They raised the hammers again, swinging them out to one side, then smashed the heavy iron heads down against each side of the support frame.

Johnny dropped to a knee beside Dixie, set the shotguns down, and quickly fished his barlow knife out of his pants pocket. He opened the blade and started going to work on the heavy ropes. He needed a bigger knife. The barlow's blade was too small to cut through the heavy ropes quickly.

"I'm sorry," Dixie cried. "I'm sorry!"

The heavy hammers thudded again almost in unison.

Breathless, Johnny said, "I'm gonna get you out of here!"

He sawed at the ropes angling up above the girl's bound wrists.

Again, the heavy hammers thumped loudly. Johnny could hear the rotten wood cracking, giving . . .

Johnny wasn't going to saw through the ropes in time. *"Dammit!"*

He dropped the knife, rose, picked up both Twins, and ran down the mine tunnel toward the entrance. He'd closed the gap between him and his targets enough to render the Twins effective.

As he ran, both men laughed as they smashed their hammers into the side of the frame—one after the other, putting the full force of their shoulders and arms into their work.

"There she goes!" howled Willie Slater, his diminutive silhouetted figure stepping back and toward the middle of the mine shaft, lowering the heavy hammer to his side.

All at once, the ceiling dropped straight down ahead of Johnny with a thundering roar that made the blasts of both Twins sound little louder than the crack of a derringer by comparison. Suddenly, the ragged sphere of gray light was gone. Before Johnny was now only black ink.

Johnny dropped as the ground shuddered beneath his boots.

He pressed himself flat against the ground, covering his head with his hands. Dust wafted over him, choking him, momentarily blinding him.

Behind him, Dixie screamed.

CHAPTER 33

The thunder of the cave-in was damn near deafening.

The ground beneath Johnny shook and pitched like a stone bear awakening from its slumbers. Johnny pressed his chest and forehead against the ground, gritting his teeth, waiting for the whole mountain to fall down on top of him, instantly crushing the life out of him.

At least, it would be fast. He'd be buried here forever in this mountain sarcophagus. He'd be buried here with Dixie, the killer whore. That was probably fitting. Two lost, desperate people who'd found each other for comfort for one stormy mountain night and ended up spending eternity together under several tones of granite.

Right fitting, indeed.

Suddenly, the roar stopped. A few more rocks thudded to the floor of the mine several feet ahead of Johnny. One more fell and then the ground stopped rumbling and vibrating, and silence descended.

Frowning, Johnny lifted his head and opened his eyes, gazing toward the mine entrance. Where it had been, that was. It was no longer there. He could see by several wan shafts of gray light slanting down through fissures in the arched ceiling that the mine mouth was sealed up tighter than a cork in a new whiskey bottle.

Dust peppered his eyes, his nose. He sneezed, sleeved grit from his face.

Dixie had gone quiet.

He turned to look back at her. A vagrant thread of gray light revealed one shoulder of the girl and a lock of dirty blond hair falling down over it.

"Dixie?"

She didn't answer right away. She sniffed, cleared her throat, and said thinly, "Here."

"You all right?"

She gave a droll chuckle. It was partly a sob, which made it more of a strangling sound. She cursed and said, "Are *you* all right?" Her voice was pitched with bitter sarcasm.

"Well, at least the whole mountain didn't come down on top of us." Johnny rose to his knees. He felt around for the Twins and returned them to their holsters on his thighs.

"Thank God for small favors."

Johnny heaved himself to his feet. "Yeah, it's a small one, but a favor nonetheless."

He walked over and knelt down beside her. He felt around for where he'd dropped his barlow knife, then went to work on her ropes again. He saw her face in the weak gray strand of watery light as she turned to him and said, "Aren't you mad at me?"

"For what?"

"For calling for you. I couldn't help it. But I didn't know it was a trap, I swear! I thought they'd take the bullion and leave, and leave me here. I didn't know I was bait. Oh God—I've always been deathly afraid of being underground . . . of being buried alive! I couldn't help but call for you, and . . . now here you are. Buried underground with me!"

Her voice had been growing more and more shrill with terror as she more thoroughly realized the severity of their predicament. She'd fairly screamed those last words. Now she hung her head, bawling.

Johnny finished cutting through the ropes. He pulled her arms around in front of her because she didn't seem to feel the need to. He removed the last of the cut ropes around her wrists then squeezed her hands in his own. "We'll get out."

"How?" she cried.

"We'll dig out. One rock at a time, if we have to."

Johnny started to turn away from the girl. She grabbed his arm, squeezed angrily. "Teale sold us out, Johnny. He sold us out for the bullion and the loot. He was even going to cash in his own son for the bounty on his head!"

Johnny gave a droll chuckle. "Don't doubt it a bit."

Johnny walked into the murky darkness. The dust was still sifting, irritating his eyes and his nose. Where the slender strands of weak gray light didn't penetrate, the darkness was nearly complete. He reached into a pocket for a lucifer and scraped it to life on his thumbnail.

He held the flickering flame up before him. The weak amber flame showed him the blockage before him. It appeared to be a solid mass of rubble. It extended for what he guessed was a good twenty, possibly thirty, yards into the mine from the front.

When the flame burned out, he lit another match, held it aloft, and again studied the mass of splintered timbers and rock. Hope bled out of him like the blood from a fatal wound. He could move some of that debris, but some of it was buried under several massive, anvil-shaped granite slabs. The way those slabs angled down out of the ceiling, there would be no crawling over or under them. There was likely more rock just as formidable behind what he was looking at here, at this end of the pile.

Tombstones.

Slater had gotten his revenge for the incident back at Riley Duke's Saloon. A sweet revenge it was, too. He hadn't even had to waste a bullet on Johnny. By caving in the mine, Johnny would die slow. Since there were a few, slender shafts letting in air, he and the girl likely wouldn't suffocate. They'd starve or die of thirst.

Slowly.

Very damned slowly . . .

"Oh God," Dixie said, the panic building in her voice. "Oh God . . . oh God . . ."

Johnny's own heartbeat quickened. Panic was beginning to dog him, too. He wasn't all that fond of being buried alive himself.

Still, he and the girl had to keep their wits about them. They weren't dead yet.

Johnny walked back over to where Dixie paced, dimly dappled by a couple of strands of weak gray light. She hugged herself and sobbed, muttering, "Oh God . . . oh God . . . I can't die like this. Not like this! Oh my *GOD*!"

Johnny placed his hands on her shoulders, squeezed. "Settle down. Take deep breaths. Slow, deep breaths!"

"What the hell good is that going to do?"

"It will calm you down. We have to stay calm, Dixie. We have to keep our heads and look for another way out of here!"

"What if there is no way outta here?"

"There's gotta be! We have to look for it!"

"Oh God . . . oh God . . . we're going to die! We're going to—!"

Johnny slapped her hard across the face.

She yelped as her head whipped to the side.

She turned her face back toward his. She stared up at him in shock, her chest rising and falling heavily but not as sharply as before.

"We're going to find a way out of here," Johnny told her, tightly, commandingly. "Both of us. Together." He formed a smile, one that was meant to lend a little levity to the situation. "What the hell else do we have to do—right?"

She drew a deep breath, gave a reluctant nod. "All right . . . if you say so."

"Thatta girl."

Johnny looked around. The mine continued back into the mountain. He knew that sometimes mine shafts connected with other shafts. If they could find a branching shaft, they might be able to follow the secondary shaft to another entrance. Also, there might be an air vent large enough to climb up through to the outside.

"Follow me," he said, moving slowly forward, digging another match out of his pocket.

Dixie hurried up beside him, breathless with agitation. "Let me take your hand."

Johnny closed his left hand around hers and led her deeper into the mountain. It was dark back here. He snapped the match to life. Ahead, the shaft turned to the right. He and the girl followed the bend, Johnny scouring the walls and the ceiling with his gaze, looking for another way out.

It didn't look good. All he saw was discarded rubble left by the miners who'd once chiseled and blasted the ore out of the mountain—airtight tins, bottles, cigarette stubs, old tin flasks, even old burlap candy and tobacco pouches. He stepped over an old boot missing half its sole, wondering idly and fleetingly what the circumstances of the discarded boot had been.

Maybe someone had lost his foot to a tram car. All sorts of grisly accidents occurred in mines like this one. If he and Dixie didn't find a way out of here, their ghosts would likely be dancing of a night with those of all of the miners who'd died here . . .

The thought gave him an added chill, and he quickly banished it.

He and Dixie continued following the shaft to the right, the rusted tram rails on their left. They walked mostly in darkness, for there were few fissures or air vents in this part of the shaft. Johnny didn't want to waste his lucifer matches. He had only a half dozen or so left.

After they'd walked what Johnny estimated to be another fifty or so yards, the futility of their situation weighed heavier on them both. At least, it weighed heavier on Johnny, and he thought he sensed Dixie's growing hopelessness, as well. She was gravely silent, and the hand he was clutching in his own was growing clammy.

As they walked a few more yards, a gray splotch of light shone ahead. The faint illumination angled down the shaft's left wall to glimmer in a small pool on a tram rail. The light was very faint but noticeable and allowed some lucidity to a small area immediately around the pool.

Johnny stopped and looked down at the gray splotch illuminating the tram rail. "What have we here?"

He followed the angling pillar of light up the wall and into the ceiling. The illumination came from a small hole in the ceiling on the shaft's far left side, where it curved down to form the wall.

"Another shaft?" Dixie asked.

"Too small unless it was only exploratory."

Johnny released Dixie's hand, stepped over to the cavity, and peered up into it. It appeared to be a narrow flue rising crookedly through the mountain above. It must open on to the outside or it wouldn't be lit with daylight.

Studying the hole more closely, he estimated that it was a little larger around than he was. In other words, he should be able to fit inside it—to crawl up through it. At least, it looked possible for the short stretch he could see from down here in the shaft.

He reached up with both hands. On his tiptoes, he could reach about a foot into the cavity. He felt around, searching for something solid to hold on to.

"What're you doing?" Dixie asked.

"I'm gonna see how far I can climb into this crack."

"Do you think it reaches the outside?"

"It must." Johnny spat dust lingering in his mouth from the cave-in. "Only one way to find out."

He grabbed two knobs of rock that felt stationary and pulled his head up into the cavity. As he did, he swung his feet forward against the cave wall. Pushing against the wall with his feet and pulling with his arms, he inched up inside the hole. He lifted his head to look for more handholds. There were damn few. The sides of the fissure were aggravatingly smooth. Probably polished by running water a long time ago.

He saw what looked like a possibility, wrapped his left hand around it, and continued to hoist himself upward. He made it only another inch before the knob of rock he clung to broke free of the wall.

Down he tumbled through the hole, losing his hat. He couldn't get his feet under him in time to break his fall, so he struck the floor of the shaft hard on his right shoulder and hip, giving that knee a good hammering, as well.

His ears rang and bloodred roses blossomed behind his retinas.

"Oh, Johnny!" Dixie cried.

She knelt beside him, placing a hand on his shoulder. "Are you all right? Please don't die on me!"

Johnny grunted, groaned. He pushed up onto an elbow. "Damn," he said, and spat some fresh grit from his mouth.

Dixie gazed at him hopelessly. "It's not going to work, is it?"

Johnny shook his head. "Don't think so. Nothing to hold on to. Steep climb, to boot." He spat again. "Damn, I thought I'd found a way."

Dixie sank to her butt, leaned back against the mine wall, and drew her knees up under her skirt. "Oh well."

"Oh well, what?"

"Oh well, I guess that seals it. Us, I mean. Our fate."

Johnny pushed himself up. He scuttled over against the wall and leaned back against it, beside Dixie. He raised a knee, rested an elbow atop it, fingered a pebble between his gloved thumb and index finger. "Maybe something will come to me."

Dixie gave a droll chuckle at that.

They sat in grim silence for a time. The only light was the watery sliver coming down from the fissure above their heads.

Dixie turned to him, looked up at him. "That young lady is going to miss you."

"She will but she shouldn't."

"Why not?"

"I don't deserve being missed. She'll be better off without me."

"Yeah, well, at least you have somebody."

"What about you? No one?"

Dixie shook her head. "There was only Jake. Not that I deserve more. This fate here—maybe this is the fate I deserve." She gave him a crooked smile. "No offense. I reckon I deserve worse than dying with the man who saved my worthless hide twice."

"No offense taken, but it looks like I might've saved it only once."

"Duly noted."

They sat in silence for another few minutes before Johnny turned to her and said, "Why'd you kill 'em—Torrance and the girls?"

"For the money, of course. Jake's stolen loot." Dixie drew a deep breath as she absently smoothed her skirt over her knees. "Clementine tried to take it from me. Henrietta *wouldn't* take it from me," she said with a wry laugh. "Leastways, she wouldn't take the thousand dollars I tried to give her for a stake. She said it was blood money. I was afraid she'd blab to Teale about the loot, but wouldn't you know it turned out he'd known about it all along?"

Dixie shook her head. An ironic smile faded slowly from her lips. "Maybe there's another reason I killed her. Maybe I killed her because I didn't like how she shamed me by being better than me. She wouldn't take stolen money. Me? I took that blood money without batting an eye."

"What about Torrance?"

Dixie shrugged a shoulder. "With Henrietta dead, who'd have looked after him?"

Johnny picked up another pebble and hurled it against the opposite wall.

"Wait," Dixie said.

Johnny turned to her. "What is it?"

She was staring off down the shaft to their left. "Something looks different over there."

"Over where?"

"Just down the shaft a ways. Not as . . . dark."

Johnny followed her gaze. She was right. Now with the benefit of the weak gray light from this vantage, something did look different only a few feet farther down the shaft.

Johnny rose and, limping a little on his bruised knee and hip, walked into the darkness beyond the pool of gray light.

CHAPTER 34

After he'd walked a few feet, Johnny saw that ahead of him was the end of the mine shaft. The tram rails pushed straight up against the shaft's rear wall, as though continuing right through it.

Only, was it really a wall?

He shoved his hand out. His fingers touched wood.

"What the hell . . . ?"

He dug another match out of his pants pocket. Igniting it, he held it up before him.

"I'll be damned," he said.

The flickering red flames cast a wavering circle of light over a pair of double doors. Stout wooden double doors constructed of long, narrow planks and iron bands. There was an iron locking bar, and the bar was in place over its heavy iron brackets.

Dixie had walked up to stand beside Johnny. "Could . . . it be . . . ?"

"A door to the outside?" Johnny said, a smile stretching his lips. "I don't see why not."

Of course, it could just be a door to another part of the shaft, or to a room in which supplies had been stored. In fact, that was most likely the case since the lock was on this side of the doors. Still, hope lightened his spirits.

With some effort, he lifted the locking bar from its brackets. The iron had rusted, and it was coated with dust, but after a couple of hard pulls, the bar rose from the brackets. Johnny dropped the bar, and it swung down to hang against the door. There were two iron handles. Johnny wrapped his hands around both, gave them a shove.

They didn't budge.

He shoved again. Still, no movement.

"Must be stuck," he said.

He threw his shoulder against the crack running vertically down between the doors. This time the doors wobbled a little and made cracking sounds but still did not open.

Johnny threw his shoulder against the doors once more, then again, again, and again.

"I think I'm loosening them up," Johnny said, stepping back and wincing as he rubbed his bruised shoulder.

"Let me give it a shot." Dixie rammed her right shoulder against the doors.

They creaked, groaned.

"Easy now," Johnny warned. "Better let me . . ."

Dixie stepped back, bunched her lips, hardened her jaws, and rammed her shoulder against the doors once more.

She screamed as the doors sprang open with a raspy bark. Dixie flung her hands out to both sides as her momentum sent her flying through the doors.

Shocked to feel a stiff wind blowing against him, and seeing a canyon yawning just beyond the open doors—a straight plunge for maybe a hundred feet—

Johnny flung his own right hand out. He wrapped it around Dixie's left wrist as she dropped through thin air into the roaring chasm at the bottom of which a churning white river pummeled rocks maybe a hundred feet below the mine.

Dixie became a dead weight in Johnny's hand as she dropped below the floor of the shaft and swung back toward the mountain to smack against the canyon's rock wall beneath Johnny's boots. She almost pulled Johnny into the canyon with her, onto the massive pile of mine tailings he saw rising below, on the raging river's near shore.

The doors had been used to dump ore out of the tram cars and into the canyon. He never would have suspected that.

Dropping to both knees at the lip of the chasm, he wrapped both his hands around Dixie's left wrist. She screamed and gazed up at him in horror as she dangled down against the side of the ridge, a stiff wind blowing her hair and her dress.

"Johnny!" she screamed. "Please, don't drop me!"

"I'm trying not to!" Johnny gritted his teeth as he tried to pull her up with both hands. "No offense, but you're not as light as you look, sweetheart!" He removed his left hand from her wrist and reached down. "Give me your other hand! Hurry!" He felt her wrist slipping from his grip.

She flung up her other hand. Johnny missed it.

She twisted out over the canyon and the river, buffeted like wash on a line, then turned her body back toward the ridge and flung her arm up desperately, sobbing. That time Johnny grabbed her hand, squeezed, and, rising slowly from his knees and scuttling farther back inside the shaft, dragged her up against the ridge wall.

Finally, he pulled her onto the floor of the shaft, where she rolled onto her back and lay gasping, her cheeks red from the wind, her windblown hair resembling a tumbleweed, sticking out around her head, her eyes still wide with horror.

"You all right?" he asked her, on one knee beside her.

"Oh God," she gasped, sitting up and pulling her feet toward her, away from what seemed like the canyon's slathering jaws, as though the canyon and the river roaring across its floor were a giant beast hungry for a feast. "I thought I was really a goner that time!"

"I gotta admit I did, too." Johnny chuckled, smiling down at her. "That's officially the third time now."

He rose and stepped up to the lip of the canyon, between the shaft's stout open doors. He looked around, getting his bearings. He turned his head to look up at the granite wall stretching up beyond the portal.

Dixie crawled tentatively up to the canyon's edge, edged a cautious look down at the raging river, which must have been the San Joaquin again, then up at Johnny. "Are we any better off? That's one hell of a deep canyon and I don't see an easy way into it."

"I don't think we can climb down." Johnny looked at Dixie then pointed to his left as he faced the mine shaft and the mountain's granite wall. "But I think we can climb out, head that way. That's south. I think we're roughly a hundred, maybe a hundred and twenty-five, yards back from the face of the mountain, from where we started. The wall looks craggy enough, with enough cracks and ledges, that we should be able to climb along it to the southern face. Then down."

"Ah hell, I don't like heights!" Dixie said, her face turning pale again.

"I don't, either, but it beats the hell out of being buried alive." Johnny nodded at the dark, open shaft before them.

Dixie looked at it, too. "Point well taken."

The main obstacles were the cold wind and the snow-covered ice that clung to some of the stone slabs, mounds, spurs, cornices, and pinnacles, and in the crenellated troughs between the features.

There were enough natural shelves, starting from within a few feet to the left of the shaft doors, and clefts and fissures and nooks and crannies in the face of the mountain, that the two climbers managed to inch their way up from the shaft, around the belly of the mountain, and forward to the south face without any real problems aside from windburn, skinned hands, noses, and knees, and muscle pain from the strain.

A few times they each slipped, but the wall was not so sheer that they were in danger of falling. If they had fallen, they wouldn't have fallen far before finding some ledge or thumb of rock to cling to. The biggest danger was slipping on the ice crusted beneath the powdery snow, falling into a gap, and braining themselves, or breaking a bone.

The descent of the southern face was the hardest part. When they climbed over to the face from the east side of the mountain, they were roughly a hundred feet off the ground. Johnny descended first, clinging to cracks and ledges and anything else he could wrap his hands around or wedge his boots against. Dixie followed his path, staying just above him. If she fell, he'd catch her. Or try to, anyway . . .

Johnny came to within the last six feet of the ground, took a breath, and stepped off the ledge he'd found himself on. He hit the ground bending his knees to distribute the impact. Dixie dropped after him, and he caught her, and they hugged, laughing their relief at making it not only *out* of the mountain in one piece, but *off* the mountain in one piece, as well.

Johnny's lightness of mood was short-lived.

The bullion.

He pulled away from Dixie, looked around to get his bearings. The town of Lucky's Ford was ahead and on his left, a hundred yards down the rocky slope crisscrossed with old ore wagon trails. He could see the Lucky Inn poking its two stories and high false facade at the cold, gray sky from the mostly abandoned town's heart.

The mine portal where Walt Teale had stowed the wagon containing the bullion was straight ahead, probably fifty yards west along the face of the mountain.

Johnny started toward the now caved-in entrance to the shaft. He soon found himself running, slipping on the freshly fallen snow and ice patches remaining after the storm's initial rain.

Johnny didn't know why he was running. Of course, the gold was gone. He had to see for himself . . . to get through the horror and rage of finding the bullion taken from him for the first time—Sheila's gold— then follow the thieves' trail. Slater would die for his sins. Earl Crabb, as well. Same with Teale. The man was a scourge.

They'd all die hard. Even if Johnny had been wearing his moon-and-star, they'd die hard. But he'd left the badge at home, so there was no question whatever of Slater and Crabb's fate.

Johnny would take the gold back to Hallelujah Junction. Just a little off schedule, was all. But better late than never.

He stopped running and stared straight ahead. He could see the portal now. The wagon marked it. Heck Torrance's wagon had been pulled partway out of the collapsed mine shaft. It sat at an angle, only its tongue out of sight inside the shaft. Jake Teale's coffin had been pulled out of the wagon bed and onto the ground. It lay on its side near the wagon's open tailgate.

A quick glance into the wagon told Johnny what he already knew about the bullion. Still, it made his heart kick.

Jake Teale lay belly-down beside the overturned coffin, his arms straight down at his sides. His legs lay stiff and straight upon the ground, boot toes slightly angled out away from each other. Teale lay with his forehead pressing into the gravel. There was no give in his neck.

They'd left him here, like this. Even the outlaw's own father hadn't seen fit to pay him any more respect. The three conspirators must have decided they had enough with the bullion and the loot. Hauling Jake in for the reward was too much trouble for the size of the additional payout.

Dixie's footsteps sounded behind Johnny. She'd broken into a run now, too.

Johnny turned to her, grabbed her, and pulled her back, blocking her view of Teale with his own body.

"No," Dixie said, squirming out of his grasp. "I want to see."

"No need. The loot's gone, Dixie."

"I don't care about the loot."

She pulled her arms fiercely out of Johnny's grip and stepped around him. She stood over Teale, looking down. She gasped and raised her hands to her mouth.

"Savages!" she cried.

She knelt beside the stiff body. She placed her hands on Teale's left arm and rolled him onto his back. Johnny stared down over Dixie's shoulder at the two heavy-lidded, half-open eyes staring up at her.

The dead man's face was at once ashen and blue. His hair slid around in the cold wind. The wind nipped at the collar of his shirt, which was buttoned up to his pale blue throat. His lips were drawn back taut against his teeth. There was a forlorn, vaguely puzzled aspect to his blind gaze.

Dixie bowed her head, sobbing. No doubt thinking about all that might have been.

Johnny would be damned if he didn't feel sorry for her—despite the thieving killer Jake Teale was. Despite the thieving killer Dixie herself was.

Johnny gave her a few minutes then stepped up behind her, placed his hand on her shoulder. "Come on, Dixie. I have to go. I have to get after those three vermin."

Dixie looked up at him quickly, tears brimming her blue eyes. "What about Jake?"

Johnny just stared down at her.

"Please. I have to bury him. I have to bury him proper."

"I don't have time. I have to get after the bullion. My job is to get that bullion back to Hallelujah Junction."

"Leave me here, then. I'll . . ." Dixie looked down at Jake. "I'll stay here . . . find a way to bury him. If I have to wait till next spring, I'll stay right here."

"Have it your way."

Johnny stepped around her and started walking down the slope. He headed for the stable flanking the Lucky Inn and was relieved to find his stallion inside. The packhorse was gone. He intended only to saddle Ghost and to get after Slater and Crabb, but when he reemerged from the stable fifteen minutes later, he sat astraddle Ghost and was leading by a rope hackamore the horse that had pulled Torrance's wagon.

He stopped and looked up the slope toward the mine portal.

Dixie remained where she'd been a few minutes ago, on her knees beside the body of the killer Jake Teale. Just staring down at him, the wind blowing her hair.

Johnny cursed and booted Ghost on up the slope to the wagon.

Chapter 35

Walt Teale watched the backs of the two men riding ahead of him along the deep-rutted, snow-crusted, two-track mountain trail.

Willie Slater and Earl Crabb rode side by side, stirrup to stirrup. Slater rode to the left of Crabb. They both wore heavy coats against the wintry chill. Crabb, the larger of the two by several inches and many pounds, wore a fox fur coat. The men's breath frosted in the air beneath their hat brims. Slater was leading the packhorse carrying the bullion—over fifty thousand dollars in gold, they'd estimated after they'd taken a gander inside the panniers once they'd gotten away from Lucky's Ford.

When you coupled that with Jake's loot, which resided in the saddlebags draped over the rear of Slater's dun, they had a hundred thousand dollars to split among the three of them. That was a little over thirty thousand dollars apiece.

That was all right. Teale could live with that.

He'd needed the young curly wolves' help to get any of it. He knew he couldn't have gone up against Shotgun Johnny Greenway alone. He'd wanted to take something down out of these mountains, by God. He hadn't cared about taking his son down, giving him a "proper burial." That had been a load of sheep dip he'd fed the girl to get his hands on the loot. He didn't really see Jake as his son, anyway. He hadn't for years.

Oh, he might have had a little come-to-Jesus meeting with himself over Jake's casket a few nights back at the Grizzly Ridge Inn, when the girl had walked into the stable, but he was over it now. What's done is done. Time to move on. Jake wasn't worth a single tear.

Jake Teale had been a cold-blooded outlaw to his father, Walt. Nothing less, nothing more. A stranger.

A stranger worth money.

Why not cash in? Any fool would. The outlaw Jake Teale sure as hell would have cashed in on Walt Teale, had the tables been turned.

He'd gotten lucky when Greenway had shown up with the bullion though Shotgun Johnny had complicated matters concerning the loot. But the gold he'd been carrying was an added bonus. A big one. Teale wouldn't have gotten any of it—not Jake's loot nor the gold—without the help of Slater and Crabb.

Yeah, thirty thousand was all right.

As long as Slater and Crabb thought it was all right.

He studied the backs of both men now, feeling a dark apprehension adding more strain to his already-straining ticker. They were talking between themselves in low tones, occasionally glancing over their shoulders at Teale. They were smiling shrewdly, as though they were planning something.

What?

Maybe shooting him and making their own pieces of the pie that much bigger?

He wouldn't put it past them. After all, they'd set up their own two men—Stretch Wilkins and Jate Durnberg—by sending them down the slope to ambush Johnny. Just as expected, the girl had called for him, luring him up the slope. Wilkins and Durnberg thought that Slater and Crabb would be backing them. But they hadn't backed them. Instead, they'd fed them to the proverbial wolf—Shotgun Johnny.

Cowards themselves, they'd lured Greenway into the mine shaft then caved it in on Johnny and Dixie. Teale himself had seen what Slater and Crabb were going to do, so he'd held back himself, allowing Wilkins and Durnberg to go out in a hail of buckshot. If they'd been able to take out Johnny, great. But as it had turned out, with Durnberg and Wilkins out of the game, the pie had been made larger by two fifths.

Again, Willie Slater glanced back over his shoulder at Teale. He was grinning like the cat that ate the canary. He turned his head forward, muttering and chuckling.

"What're you two talkin' about up there?" Teale called as they followed the trail through a narrow ravine peppered with now-leafless aspens and a few pines.

A creek chuckled over rocks on his right, between snow-dusted banks. It was getting late, and shadows were closing down over the canyon, adding an extra chill to the already-cold air.

Both men hipped around in their saddles, regarding him with those dung-eating grins on their faces. "What's that, old man?" asked Slater.

"The name's Teale," Teale said, his cold cheeks warming with anger. "*Mister* Teale to you two pups."

Slater and Crabb shared a smile then returned

their insolent gazes to the older man. "All right," Slater said, "*Mister* Teale it is. Now, could you repeat the question, *Mister* Teale?"

The warmth of anger lingered in Teale's cheeks. He was being mocked, and he didn't like it. "I asked what you two were talkin' about up there . . . all secret-like."

"What we were talkin' about?" asked Crabb. He was bigger than Slater though not any taller than Teale. He was bald under his hat, and his big ears stuck out. He wore a thick, cinnamon beard on his broad, savage face with dark, jeering eyes obscured by the shadow of his cream Stetson's broad brim.

"Yeah," Teale said. "What were you talkin' about up there?"

Again, Slater and Crabb shared a look. It was a snide one.

Slater cackled a girlish laugh and said, "We was only talkin' about how we was gonna spend our share of the loot. That's all we was talkin' about, *Mister* Teale."

Teale glowered at them. "You sure about that?"

"Hell, yeah," Crabb said. "What else would we be talkin' about . . . *Mister* Teale?"

Teale continued to glower at them. He knew what they'd been talking about. He didn't want to say it. He didn't want to detonate any bombs. Not here. Not until he was ready. As it was, his gun was tucked away under his coat, and he'd have one hell of a time fishing it out of its holster.

As they continued riding, Slater looked back at him again, that jeering, oily-eyed smile in place. "How 'bout you, *Mister* Teale? How're you gonna spend your share of the loot?"

Teale pressed the heel of his left hand against his

saddle horn and leaned forward on it. He looked off, pondering for a time. Then he said, "Me, I'm gonna go down to Arizona. Leastways, I'm gonna spend the winter down there."

"And lay on that white sand beach?" said Slater, laughing.

"You oughta go to Mexico, *Mister* Teale," Crabb said, staring straight ahead now but raising his voice loudly enough for the old man to hear behind him. "That's where you'll find the most and the finest senoritas. *That's* where you'll find the white sand beaches."

"Nah," Teale said, leaning out to one side to spat a wad of chew into the thin, crusty snow. "Too many Mexicans in Mexico." He brushed his gloved hand across his bearded mouth and sniffed.

Slater laughed. "The old man has a point, Earl," he said. "The old man has a point at that. Lots of bean-eaters in Mexico."

"Maybe," Crabb said. "Still, though, you'll find the purtiest young women you ever seen down in *Old Mexico* . . . lyin' on a white sand beach, no less!"

They soon stopped for the night on a low area flanked by a rocky ridge and sheathed in aspens. The site was well off the trail, and the three thieves figured the aspens would help screen their fire from passersby. Slater and Crabb didn't think anyone was behind them, and neither did Teale.

The gold would not have been missed yet by anybody except Shotgun Johnny Greenway, of course. Though even he probably wasn't thinking much about the gold. The bullion guard was likely just then dying

COLD DEAD CASH 325

a very slow, miserable, and terrifying death inside that granite grave.

"At least he has the girl to help distract him from his worries," Slater pointed out as the three men sat around their fire just after the sun went down, eating beans and drinking coffee laced with whiskey.

"I still think we should've kept her for ourselves," Crabb said, splashing a little more whiskey into his steaming coffee cup, which sat on the ground to his right. He was lounging back against his saddle as were Slater and Teale.

"Nah, she was more valuable as bait for Johnny. She wasn't all that much, anyways. Hell, with that fifty thousand we're each gonna . . . er, I mean with that *thirty thousand*, excuse me," Slater quickly corrected himself with a laugh, glancing nervously at the old man, "we can buy an' sell girls two, three times better-lookin' than that used-up doxie."

Both men had glanced quickly at Teale on the heels of Slater's misstatement.

Or had it been a misstatement?

Chewing his beans, holding his bowl in one hand, his spoon in the other hand, Teale studied both men sitting on the other side of the fire from him. Warning bells tolled in his ears. His logy old heart beat faster, chugging like a worn-out locomotive. He glanced down at his old conversion revolver, which he'd set on the ground to his right, near his knee.

Within an easy reach.

He looked at the other two men again. The fire's flickering orange flames cast light and shadows across their faces—across the cold, severe planes of Crabb's bearded face and across the soft, clean-shaven countenance of Slater's face. Both men still wore their hats; the brims cast their eyes in menacing shadows. Occasionally, Teale saw the whites of their eyes as they cut quick, furtive glances at him through the dancing flames.

They looked like specters over there, half-concealed in shadow. Evil phantoms plotting a devil's play against him.

Teale swallowed a mouthful of beans, set down his empty bowl, and picked up his coffee and whiskey. He held up the cup in front of his face and stared grimly through the steam at the conspirators. "I know what you done got planned."

Slater scooped up another mouthful of his own beans, frowned at Teale, then swallowed his food. "Huh?"

"I know what you two have in mind."

"Oh?" Crabb asked. He'd finished his own beans and was sitting back against his saddle, rolling a smoke. "What's that?"

"You intend to kill me and take my cut."

Crabb looked at him and chuckled. "Don't go gettin' nervy, old man. I mean, *Mister* Teale. We ain't got nothin' of the sort in mind. You did your part, we'll do our part. That means we split it all up—the gold and Jake's loot—three ways, just like we agreed."

Teale studied him suspiciously, narrowing his eyes. He sipped his coffee and whiskey and said, "It's him, then." He slid his gaze to Slater.

"What's that?" Slater said, smiling his patronizing smile.

"It's him," Teale told Crabb. "He's hatchin' a plan to kill us both. While we sleep, most like. On account of he's a coward. I can see it in his eyes—the yellow in him. He'll try to kill us while we're asleep—I know he will!"

"Hey, now, wait a minute!" Suddenly, Slater's eyes were pinched to slits. He lowered his chin, cheeks darkening from the blood rush in the flickering light and shadows across the fire. Keeping his irritated eyes on Teale, he slowly closed his right hand over the walnut handle of his holstered Colt.

Holding his freshly rolled but unlit quirley, Crabb turned to Willie. Crabb's own expression had turned from curiosity to suspicion. He wrinkled the skin above the bridge of his nose as he said, "We got a deal—don't we, Willie?"

"We got a deal, Earl." Slater ripped his gaze from Teale to Crabb. "I done told you that. I don't go back on my deals with my friends."

Teale wrinkled his nose as he said, "Just like you didn't go back on your deal with Wilkins and Durnberg?"

Crabb kept his head turned to Slater.

Slater said, "Shut up, old man. You're just tryin' to cause trouble!"

"He's got a point, Willie," Crabb said. "It was your idea to throw them to Johnny. You did it so natural-like, too. Like it was just a last-minute decision. Like it was a harmless joke you was gonna play on 'em. But you had it planned all along, didn't you? Not backin' them against Shotgun Johnny. Leastways, you had it planned as soon as we left the Lucky Inn with the old man here."

"So what if I did?" Slater said, indignant, keeping his right hand closed around his Colt's butt, whipping his gaze between Teale and Crabb. "It worked out purty damn well, did it not? Don't listen to this old scudder, Earl. He's just tryin' to drive a wedge between us. You know what I think?" Willie's mean little eyes narrowed again as he glared at Teale. "I think he's trying to hide the fact that that is exactly what *he's* got planned!"

"No, it ain't." Teale shook his head resolutely. "That ain't my way."

"Ha!" Willie laughed. "But it's your way to turn in your own son for the reward on his head. Leastways, it was before we got the bullion and Jake's loot. The reward's peanuts compared to that, an' not worth the trouble of toting a stinking carcass—even that of your son—down the mountains for the bounty money."

Rage flared in Teale, and he thrust an angry finger out over the fire at Slater. "Shut up about that! I haven't considered Jake my son for years! He left home early and took up a life of . . ."

"Of what?" Crabb said, casting a faint, knowing smile across the fire at Teale. "Of murder and thievery? As though that ain't just exactly what you've done yourself."

That caught Teale by surprise. He glared at the man, feeling supremely, undeservedly insulted. A sharp-edged clam closed around his heart, squeezing. Suddenly breathless, Teale said, "I haven't killed nobody!"

"Oh?" Slater said. "What about Johnny an' the girl?"

"I had nothin' to do with that. You two did that!"

"I didn't hear any objections," Crabb pointed out.

Teale stared aghast at them both.

Slater smiled at him. "Jake Teale's old man," he said, jeering. "The apple sure don't fall very far from the tree, does it?"

Teale's chest rose and fell sharply. That crab squeezed his old ticker even harder as rage boiled up in him, exploding. "Mangy dogs! Dirty, lyin' stinkers!"

Teale dropped his coffee cup and reached for the old conversion revolver beside him. He fumbled with the gun, getting it caught up in the leather somehow. Slater gave a screeching laugh and bolted to his feet, crouching like a cat about to pounce, and slapping leather.

He whipped up his Colt but just as he clicked the hammer back and extended the revolver across the fire at Teale, thunder clapped.

Only it wasn't thunder, both Teale and Crabb realized as Slater flew back screaming into the darkness, triggering his Colt skyward.

CHAPTER 36

"What the hell?" Crabb bellowed, grabbing his own revolver and rising.

The roar of the second shotgun blast blew up the night. It blew up Earl Crabb, as well.

He screamed as the buckshot picked him up and sat him down ten feet back from the fire, near where Willie Slater lay moaning. Crabb looked down at his wide-open belly, opened his mouth in astonishment, then crossed his arms over the gaping cavity, as though to cradle his intestines.

Seeing himself laid open, he screamed again, shuddered as though deeply chilled, then flopped back down against the ground, dead.

Shotgun Johnny stepped out from behind an aspen at the edge of the camp, his right-hand Twin unfurling gray smoke from both its barrels. Johnny looked down at Walt Teale. The old man seemed to be no threat. He lay on his left side, clutching his left arm with his right hand, gazing up at Johnny and stretching his lips back from his teeth.

His face was ashen, sweat-beaded, and several forked veins were throbbing in his forehead.

"Help!" he rasped. "Help me . . . my *ticker* . . . !"

Johnny glanced down in disgust at the old devil. He wanted to finish him but it looked like he wouldn't need to waste a wad.

Johnny walked over to where Willie Slater lay moaning on the other side of the fire, at the very edge of the firelight. He stopped and gazed down at the blond coward. Willie stared up at him, blinking his eyes as though to clear them of the ghost he must be seeing.

"Where . . . where the hell . . . did you . . . come from?" Willie wheezed out. His chest and belly a mass of oozing blood and torn coat and shirt cloth.

Johnny extended his left-hand Twin, angling the maw down at Willie's head. "Hell."

The ten-gauge thundered, sending Willie Slater's cowardly butt back to the damnation in which he'd been spawned.

Johnny turned as hooves clomped and a wooden rattling sounded. Dixie had driven Heck Torrance's old buckboard in which Jake Teale's wooden overcoat resided, up through the trees and into the edge of the firelight. As she pulled the brake handle back, Dixie cast her gaze at the ailing Walt Teale.

"You old bastard!" she scolded him, grabbing a canteen off the seat beside her.

Still clutching his stiff left arm, Teale wagged his head. "Ticker," he raked out. "Another . . . spell . . . !"

"Good!"

Johnny holstered one of the Twins and began reloading the other. He glanced around warily, in case the thunder of his gut-shredders had drawn unwanted visitors. Meanwhile, Dixie climbed down off the wagon, setting one foot on a wheel hub then dropping the last two feet to the ground. She walked slowly over toward Teale, who, Johnny just then noticed, had recovered enough from his spell to have pulled a gun up from somewhere.

The old man's eyes flashed cunningly as he cocked the old hogleg and thrust it toward Johnny, barking, "All mine, now, dammit. All mine!"

Johnny's heart hiccupped as Teale leveled the revolver at him.

"No!" Dixie cried, stepping in front of Teale.

The gun barked.

Johnny lurched forward, "Dixie, no!"

Johnny didn't see the flash. Dixie had blocked it from his view. He'd seen only her black silhouette against a brief redness. She jerked, stumbled backward a few shuffling steps, then dropped to her knees.

"Oh," she said quietly, bowing her head to look down at herself. "Oh boy . . ."

"Dammit!" Johnny ran forward, raising the Twin he'd just loaded, snapping it closed. He sent both wads into Walt Teale, who screamed as the double-ought buck shredded his shapeless body and sent his cowardly soul the way of his devious cohorts.

Johnny fell to a knee beside Dixie, who'd flopped back onto the ground. She lay looking up at him, shuddering, holding her hands over her belly.

"Dammit, Dixie," he said.

Her lips twitched. The firelight glinted in her mussed blond hair. Her eyes looked up at him, stricken. She managed to shape a sad smile as she said, "Just a little . . . payback . . . for all the times . . . you saved me . . . J-johnny . . ."

The light went out of her eyes. Her chest stopped

moving. Her hands slid away from her bloody belly to fall slack at her sides.

Johnny stared down at her in horror. He stared at her for a full minute, not quite believing that she was gone. This wild, desperate young woman.

Finally, he swiped his hat off his head, ran an angry hand through his thick brown hair, and lifted his face to shout at the stars: *"Dammit to hell!"*

Johnny built up the fire, brewed a fresh cup of coffee, then sat on a rock and sipped the coffee and smoked cigarettes as he waited for dawn.

When dawn came, he used a shovel from the wagon to dig two graves under a sprawling lodgepole pine. Only two—one for Jake and one for Dixie. The three outlaws could rot where they lay.

It took Johnny a long time to dig, for the ground was already freezing. He pried out rocks, cut through roots, chipped and gouged the hard soil and shoveled it out of the holes. He dug the graves side by side, six feet deep.

He laid Jake Teale in one. He gentled Dixie down into the grave close beside Jake's. He filled in the graves with dirt and covered them both with rocks to keep out predators.

He erected a single wooden cross that he'd fashioned from pine branches and rawhide from his saddlebags. He centered the cross in the ground ahead of the two graves.

He stood regarding the graves fronted by the single cross, removing his hat and holding it over his chest. The two lovers were together at last. They'd be together forever.

He didn't admire much about either one of them. But he did admire their love for each other.

Sheila's words echoed in his head: *"You've hurt every woman who's ever come into your life and made the mistake of loving you!"*

She'd been right. But maybe a man can change. Maybe *he* could change.

It was worth a try. After all, he had a good-hearted, beautiful young woman waiting for him in Hallelujah Junction. He'd be damned if he wasn't suddenly in a hurry to ride down and marry Glyneen MacFarland.

He'd turned loose the outlaws' horses and Teale's mule to make their own way. He'd also freed the horse that had pulled the wagon. He had no more use for the wagon. He'd secured the bullion and Teale's loot to the packhorse.

Now he mounted Ghost and set out on his last journey down the mountain, headed for a new life for himself. He was ready. If Dixie and Jake had taught him one thing, they'd taught him that life was short and that he was ready to live it.

In the late morning of that day, Sheila Bonner stood in the crisp autumn sunshine among the cedars growing around the cemetery flanking the First Lutheran Church in Hallelujah Junction. She wore a dark green dress with a matching felt hat and shawl. She held a bright spray of fresh autumn wildflowers in her gloved hands, down low in front of her.

The mourners were dispersing from the cemetery's newest grave, partly in the shade of one of those cedar trees. One of those mourners were Glyneen MacFarland's mother, who limped and shuffled down the hill toward where several buggies waited below, outside the wrought-iron fence encircling the cemetery. Glyneen's elderly father was too ill to attend the funeral. A stout neighbor lady, younger by only a few years, dressed all in funeral black, shepherded the bereaved mother around the tombstones and through the small crowd of sadly muttering mourners.

The Lutheran minister gave Sheila's shoulder a reassuring squeeze as, smiling at her tenderly from behind his round spectacles, he walked past her to join the others exiting the cemetery, his closed Bible in his hands.

Only Sheila, Mean Mike O'Sullivan, and the hulking Silent Thursday remained at Glyneen's grave. Johnny's two deputies stood to Sheila's right, both men holding their hats in their hands, both dressed in brushed black broadcloth pants, pin-striped poplin shirts, and shabby suit coats. Mean Mike was freshly shaven, and Silent had had his thick beard trimmed for the occasion. His suit coat was a couple of sizes too small for his large, rawboned body.

Both men were looking down at the coffin that they had helped ease down into the grave.

Now Mean Mike looked over at Sheila. A sad smile made his lips twitch. He cleared his throat and said with a pained expression, "It . . . it ain't your fault . . . Miss Bonner. It just ain't."

"Thank you," Sheila said tonelessly as she stared down at the simple pine box containing the pretty, young Southerner, Glyneen MacFarland.

Glyneen had died instantly when her buggy had struck the floor of Dark Water Canyon. The doctor, for whom Glyneen had worked so dutifully, had said her neck and back had been broken. The horse had lived through the fall though it, too, had incurred several broken bones, and one of the townsmen who'd heard the horrible din and come upon the scene had put it out of its misery with a single gunshot.

Sheila wished she could have been so lucky.

Mean Mike elbowed Silent Thursday, muttered something to the big man, and the two men shuffled away from the grave. Silent Thursday gave Sheila a little nod though he was too shy to meet her gaze. He slouched on past her to start down the hill. Mean Mike gave Sheila a warm smile, then, setting his hat on his head, followed Silent on down the hill toward their waiting horses.

Sheila stared down at the plain pine box. She wanted to cry, but she felt too hollow for tears. She hadn't cried once since the accident. She'd been unable to cry. She was still numb, deeply stricken and befuddled by her part in the young woman's death.

She stepped forward and dropped the flowers onto the coffin with a soft thump.

Placing her hands on her pregnant belly, she turned her gaze to the blue, snow-mantled peeks jutting in the northwest.

"Oh, Johnny," she whispered. "Oh, Johnny, can you ever forgive me?"

Almost overnight, Dead Broke turns into
a lawless hotbed of angry out-of-work miners
and out-for-blood merchants. In desperation,
Mayor Nugget considers a few hairbrained
schemes like bringing in mail-order brides,
building ice castles to attract tourists, even planting
other minerals in the mines to fool investors.
Dead Broke needs law and order,
so Nugget sends for top gun Mick MacMicking.
But a notorious gambler named Connor Boyle
has other plans—and with his band of hired
guns will blow Dead Broke off the map completely
to get what he wants.

For this town to survive, Nugget, Mick, a drunken
lawman and a woman gambler will have to
put the dead back in Dead Broke . . . and some
cool-hand killers in the ground.

National Bestselling Authors
William W. Johnstone
and J.A. Johnstone

DEAD BROKE, COLORADO

First in a New Western Series!

On sale now, wherever Pinnacle Books are sold.

JOHNSTONE COUNTRY.
WHERE DYING IS EASY AND LIVING IS HARD.

Live Free. Read Hard.
williamjohnstone.net

1885

PROLOGUE

Allane Auchinleck was drunk that morning.

But then, most wastrels on This Side Of The Slope would have pointed out that Allane Auchinleck was seldom sober any morning, any afternoon, any evening. Any day of the year. Since he had barely found enough gold in Colorado's towering Rocky Mountains to pay for good rye, he brewed his own whiskey. It wasn't fit to drink, other miners would agree, but it was whiskey. So they drank whatever Allane Auchinleck was willing to sell or, rarely, share.

Auchinleck charged a dollar a cup—Leadville prices, the other miners would protest, but they paid.

After all, it was whiskey.

And in these towering mountains, whiskey—like anything else a man could buy or steal in Denver, Durango, Silverton, or Colorado Springs—was hard to find.

Besides, Auchinleck usually was so far in his cups that he couldn't tell the difference between a nickel and a Morgan dollar. For most miners, one cup usually did the job. Actually, two sips fried the brains of many unaccustomed to a Scotsman's idea of what went into good liquor. Two cups, a few men had learned, could prove fatal. Auchinleck held the record, four cups in four hours—and was still alive to tell the story.

Although, it should be pointed out that those who had witnessed that historic drunken evening would swear on a stack of Bibles—not that a Good Book could be found this high up—that Auchinleck's hair, from topknot to the tip of his long beard, wasn't as white, but had been much thicker, before he passed out, not to awaken for three days. That had been back in '79.

But then, Auchinleck was accustomed to forty rod, and it was his recipe, his liquor, his cast-iron stomach, and his soul, the latter of which he said he had sold to the devil, then got back when Lucifer himself needed a shot of the Scotsman's brew.

On this particular glorious August evening, with the first snow falling at eleven thousand feet, Auchinleck was drinking with Sluagdach. Most of the miners had already started packing their mules and moving to lower, warmer—and much healthier—elevations. Some would head south to thaw out and blow whatever they had accumulated in their pokes. Many would drift east to Denver, where the heartiest would find jobs swamping saloons or moving horse apples out of livery stables. Others would just call it quits as a miner and find an easier way to make a living.

But not Allane Auchinleck. "Mining is my life," he told Sluagdach, and topped off his cup with more of his swill.

"Aye," Sluagdach said. "And a mighty poor life it has been, Nugget."

Nugget had become Auchinleck's handle. There are

some who say the Scotsman earned that moniker because of his determination, and not for his lack of profitable results. More than likely, the moniker had stuck to the miner like stains of tobacco juice because Nugget was a whole lot easier to remember or say than Auchinleck.

That was the year Sluagdach came in as Auchinleck's partner. It made sense, at the time (though Sluagdach was a touch more than just fairly inebriated) when such a partnership had been suggested in a tent near the headwaters of the Arkansas River.

They both came to America from Scotland, Auchinleck had pointed out. They could enter this deal as equals. Nugget still had his mule; Sluagdach had had to eat his. Sluagdach had a new pickax, while Nugget had been the first to discover that Finnian Kuznetsov, that half-Irish, half-Russian, had run into a she-bear with two cubs and had not been able to raise his Sharps carbine in time. The she-bear won that fight, and the cubs enjoyed a fine breakfast, but Nugget had given the Russian Irishman a burial and taken the shovel and pack, and a poke of silver, and Kuznetsov's boots and mink hat. Although he did not let his partner know, Nugget had also found the dead miner's mule (lucky critter, having fled while the she-bear and cubs enjoyed a breakfast of Kuznetsov), which is how come Nugget brought a mule into the partnership, his own having been stolen by some thief, or having wandered off to parts unknown while its master slept off a drunk.

"I said," Sluagdach said, raising his voice after getting no response from his drunkard partner, "that a mighty poor life it . . ." But the whiskey robbed his memory, as Nugget's whiskey often did.

"Who can be poor when he lives in this wild, fabulous country?" Nugget said, whose tolerance for his special malt had not fogged his memory or limited vocabulary. "Look at these mountains. Feel this snow. God's country this is."

"God," Sluagdach said, "is welcome to it."

That's when Nugget, against his better judgment, reached into the ripped-apart coat that he had also taken from the dearly departed dead miner and pulled out the poke. By the time he realized what he was doing, the poke had flown out of Nugget's hand and landed at Sluagdach's feet.

The muleless miner stared at the leather pouch, reached between his legs—he did not recall sitting down, but that Scotsman's liquor had a way of making men forget lots of things—and heard the grinding of rocks inside. It took him a few minutes for his eyes to focus and his brain to recall how to work the strings to open the little rawhide bag, and then he saw a few chunks fall into the grass, damp with snow that hadn't started to stick.

No matter how drunk a miner got, he was never too far gone not to recognize good ore.

"Silver," he whispered, and looked across the campsite at his partner.

"That's how Leadville got started," Nugget heard himself saying.

"Where was his camp?"

After a heavy sigh, Nugget shook his head.

"Best I could tell," he explained, "he was on his way down the slope when 'em cubs et him."

"To file a claim." Sluagdach sounded sober all of a sudden.

Nugget felt his head bob in agreement.

One of the nuggets came to Sluagdach's right eye. Then it was lowered to his mouth, and his tongue tasted it, then it went inside his mouth where his gold upper molar and his rotted lower molar tested it. After removing the bit of ore, he stared at his partner.

"This'll assay anywhere from twenty-two to twenty-five ounces per ton."

No miner on This Side Of The Slope and hardly any professional metallurgist from Arizona to Colorado would doubt anything Sluagdach said. No one knew how he did it. But he had never been more than an ounce off his predictions. Sluagdach had never made a fortune as a miner, but his good eye, teeth, and tongue knew what they saw, bit, and tasted.

Unable to think of anything to say, Nugget killed the bit of whiskey remaining in his cup, then belched.

"Where exactly did that ol' feller got et?" Sluagdach asked. His voice had an eerie quietness to it.

Nugget's head jerked in a vague northeasterly direction. Which he could blame on his drunkenness if Sluagdach remembered anything in the morning.

Finnian Kuznetsov had met his grisly end in a grizzly sow and her cubs about four miles southwest.

"Think this snow'll last?" Sluagdach asked.

"Nah." It was way too early, even at this altitude, and, well, twenty-two to twenty-five ounces per ton had to be worth the risk.

They set out early the next morning, finding the hole where Nugget had rolled Finnian Kuznetsov's remains and covered them with pine needles and some rocks, which had been removed by some critter that had scattered bones and such all over the area. Then they backtracked over rough country, and around twelve thousand feet they found Sluagdach's camp.

Two months later, they had discovered . . .

"Not a thing," Sluagdach announced, although he used practically every foul word that a good Scot knew to describe that particular thing.

By then, at that altitude, winter was coming in right quick-like, and their supplies were all but out. This morning's breakfast had been piñon nuts and Nugget's whiskey. Sleet had pelted them that morning; Sluagdach had slipped on an icy patch and almost broken his back, while Nugget's mule grew more cantankerous every minute.

"We'll have to come back next spring," Sluagdach said.

With a sad nod, Nugget went to his keg of whiskey, rocked the oak a bit, and decided there was just enough for a final night of celebration—or mourning—for the two of them.

It was a drunk to remember. Sluagdach broke Nugget's record. "Shattered it" would have been a more accurate description. Five cups. Five! While Nugget had to stop drinking—*his own whiskey*—after three.

It wasn't because he couldn't handle his wretched brew. It was because he now saw everything. He saw that Sluagdach would dissolve the partnership. Sluagdach would come back to these beasts of mountains and find the Russian mick's discovery. Sluagdach would go down in history. Allane "Nugget" Auchinleck would be forgotten.

Auchinleck. What a name. What a lie. He remembered way back when he was but a lad, living near the Firth of Clyde in the county of Ayrshire on Scotland's west coast and his grandfather, a fine man who had given Nugget his first taste of single malt when he was but four years old, had told him what the name "Auchinleck" meant.

"A piece of field with flat stones," the old man had said.

It had sounded glorious to a four-year-old pup of a boy, but now he scoffed at it all. *A piece of field with flat stones.* Oh, the stones were here all right, massive boulders of granite that held riches in them but would never let those riches go. And flat?

He laughed and tossed his empty cup toward the fire.

There was nothing flat on This Side Of The Slope.

That's when Allane Auchinleck decided it was time to kill himself.

He announced his intentions to Sluagdach, who laughed, agreeing that it was a fine, fine idea.

Sluagdach even laughed when Nugget withdrew a stick of dynamite in a box of dwindling supplies. *Laughing? That swine of a Russian mick.* No, no. Nugget had to correct his thinking. Sluagdach was a Scot. The Russian mick was Finnian Kuznetsov, dead and et by a Colorado she-grizzly's cubs.

"I'll speak lovingly of you at your funeral," Sluagdach said, and he cackled even harder when Nugget began to cap and fuse the explosive.

It wasn't until Nugget lit the fuse by holding the stick over the fire that Sluagdach acted soberly.

For a man who should, if the Lord was indeed merciful, be dead already, or at least passed out, Sluagdach moved like a man who really wanted not to be blown to bits.

He came charging like that she-bear must have charged the old Russian mick, and the next thing

Nugget recalled was his ears ringing and the entire ground shaking. Somehow, Sluagdach had knocked the dynamite away, and it must have rolled down the hill toward that massive rock of immovable stone.

Nugget could not recall the explosion, but his ears were ringing, and he felt stones and bits of wood and more stones raining down upon him. They would cover him in his grave. Peace of earth. God rest this merry gentleman.

"You ignorant, crazy, drunken fool."

That was not, Nugget figured out eventually, the voice of St. Peter. He sat up, brushing off the dust, the grime, the mud, the sand, and looked into the eyes of his equally intoxicated fellow miner. His partner.

He didn't think anyone would call him sober, but he realized just how drunk he was—and how close to death, real death, he had come.

However, "Oh . . ." was about all Nugget could muster at that moment.

"Oh." His partner wiped his bloody nose, then crawled out of the rubble and staggered toward the smoking ruins of part of the camp they had made.

"Mule!" Nugget remembered.

The brays gave him some relief, and as smoke and dust settled, he saw the animal through rocks and forests about three hundred yards away. It appeared that the tether had hooked like an anchor between some rocks and halted the beast's run for its life. Otherwise, the mule might be in Leadville by now.

Maybe even Omaha.

He started for the animal, but Sluagdach told him to stop. "Come up here!" his pard demanded.

Well, Nugget couldn't deny the man who had

stopped him from killing himself. He climbed up the ridge, where he looked down into the smokiness.

He could smell the rotten-egg stench of blown powder. And he could see what one stick of dynamite could do. It had created a chasm.

And unveiled a cave.

"Get us a light," Sluagdach said.

Somehow, the campfire still burned, and Nugget found a stick that would serve as a torch, so they walked, slipped, skidded, and slid down into the depression and toward the cave.

"Bear," Nugget remembered.

"If a silvertip was in there, it would be out by now," Sluagdach argued.

They stopped at the entrance, and Nugget held the torch into the opening.

The flame from the torch bounced off the left side of the cave. Slowly the two men staggered to that wall, and Nugget held the torch closer.

"The mother lode," Sluagdach said.

He didn't have to smell and taste the vein of silver to know that. What's more, when they moved fifty yards deeper into the cavern, the torch revealed something else. At first, Nugget thought it was an Egyptian mummy. He had seen an illustration in one of those newspapers he could not read.

But this wasn't a mummy. He held the torch higher, praying that it would not go out. At least there was no wind here to blow it out.

"It's . . ." Nugget could not find the words.

"The biggest . . . chunk . . . of silver . . . I ever . . . did . . . see."

I am dead, Nugget thought. *Or I'm dreaming.*

His partner stuck his dirty pointer finger in his

mouth, getting it good and wet, then touched the gleaming mummy that was a statue of precious metal.

The biggest nugget Allane Auchinleck had ever seen. The biggest one anybody had ever seen.

Maybe he was dead after all.

Sluagdach brought his pointer finger, sloppy with his slobber, and rubbed it on the giant nugget. It was shaped like a diamond. A diamond made of pure silver.

Sluagdach then put his finger back in his mouth.

His eyes widened.

"It . . . I . . . I . . . aye . . . aye . . . It . . ."

That's when the wind, or something—maybe Sluagdach's giant gasps at air—blew out the torch.

And Sluagdach collapsed in front of the silver diamond.

Nugget never knew how he did it, but he found his pard's shoulders and dragged him out into the fading light of the camp. The old man stared up. But his right hand gripped the coat above his breast, and the eyes did not blink.

"Your ticker," Nugget whispered.

Yes. The sight of that strike . . . it had been too much for a man, even a man who had downed five cups of that lethal brew.

That meant . . .

Nugget rose. "No partner." He ran back to the campfire, found a piece of timber, part of the suicidal destruction he had reaped, and stuck it in the coals till the end ignited. The wood must have been part pitch, because it blazed with a fury, and Nugget raced back down, past his dead pard, and into the cave, where he held the blazing torch again.

It was no dream. No drunken hallucination. It was . . . real . . . silver . . . the strike of a lifetime.

He ran back, ready to mark his claim and get his name onto a document that made this . . .

"All mine."

When he stepped outside, it was dark. He walked slowly, using the timber as his light, and stopped in front of the body of his poor, dead pard.

"I won't forget you," he whispered to the unseeing corpse. And in a moment of generosity, he proclaimed:

"You're dead, and I was broke, but Colorado will remember us forever, because I'm naming this mine and the town that'll grow up around it 'Dead Broke.' That's it." He felt relieved.

"Dead Broke, Colorado." He nodded. The flame seemed to reflect in the dead man's eyes, and maybe it was because of the light, but he thought Sluagdach nodded in agreement.

"Dead Broke, Colorado," he said again. "Because who would want to work and live in a place called Sluagdach Auchinleck?"

1886

CHAPTER 1

From *The New York Daily Comet*

"The town of Dead Broke, Colorado, high in the fabled Rocky Mountains, was burying two miners, a lady of the night, a gambler, and a city policeman when I exited the stagecoach on a crisp autumn day."

That's what I wrote in my tablet as soon as I learned from Slick Gene, the constable of this vibrant—and, as you readers likely have deduced, violent—town after stepping out of my conveyance, which the citizens in this remote town call a city.

Slick Gene went on to explain that the two miners got into a fight over who would buy the first drink for the lady of the night, the gambler decided to bet on the miner with the pearl-handled derringer, and the city policeman stepped inside, either to drink the special mixture of gunpowder, egg shells, one plug of chewing tobacco, and grain alcohol that was aged ten days in an oaken bucket and then sifted through a straw hat, or to collect his payment from the owner of the establishment, who happened to also be the betting gambler.

What happened next won't be positively known until we find the dearly departed in the afterlife—as the only persons inside the establishment at the time of the, perhaps, misunderstanding, were the gambler, one John Smith, owner of the appropriately named Smith's Place; the raven-haired sporting woman, known as "Raven"; Sweet's mine employee Sean "Irish" O'Rourke; Granite Mine Company employee Mac "Scot" O'Connor; and city policeman John Jones.

Slick Gene says that John Smith was shot four times, stabbed twice, and that his head was bashed in by a heavy spittoon. Raven was shot twice and stabbed four times. Irish was shot five times, and Scot the same; Jones was beheaded with an ax.

"This will be some funeral, and your gravedigger will be quite busy," I comment.

"Well . . ." Slick Gene offers me a cigar, which I accept, and he takes another for himself and lights both fine smokes. "It ain't the record. Seven got kilt last year, but that wasn't contained to one bucket of blood, as it spilt out onto the street and ended in Chin Lee's Bath House."

He stops to remove his hat as Raven's coffin passes, Slick Gene being a gentleman.

"As far as the gravedigger"—his hat is returned to his curly black hair—"Jenkins the undertaker owns the lot where we plant 'em, and he has graves dug six at a time. So they's ready. Kids like to play hide-and-seek all the time there."

He sees the perplexed look on my face.

"Orphans," he explains. "And come fall, we'll have about twenty graves dug. Can't dig graves after the hard freezes come. And hard freezes come early this high up on This Side Of The Slope."

The last coffin passes.

Well, it is not a coffin. The only coffin was Raven's. Wood is not scarce, though many trees have fallen to be turned into cabins and homes and businesses and privies, but most bodies are wrapped in bedrolls or sheets or the heavy winter coats of the deceased. Newer residents who have found rich veins of silver are now building frame homes, and bricks and stones are being freighted in from Greeley, Denver, Pueblo, and Colorado Springs. The mayor of Dead Broke paid for the lady's coffin, which was brought in from Denver. It was originally bought for a mine owner who died of natural causes, but the delivery was delayed.

"We had us a hot spell," the lawman says. "Rare for us. And Mr. Albany started to ripen up, so we just used the best quilt he had. Mr. Albany was a generous fellow. Just ask any of those on his payroll. So we figgered he would have donated his casket to that handsome woman. He sure did like the ladies."

A boy beats a drum as he follows the last of the dead and a handful of mourners.

Slick Gene and I smoke our cigars for a moment, then the lawman says, "You'll be wanting to see the mayor."

It is not a question. "That would be most helpful."

"I figgered," Slick Gene says. "That gal from Denver wanted to talk to him. So did the scribes from *Harper's*, *Frank Leslie's*, San Francisco, Tombstone, Colorado Springs, Boston, London, Paris, Omaha, Cheyenne, San Francisco—no, I already said San Francisco—Salt Lake City, Denver—but that Denver inkslinger was a man, not the woman who come first— New Orleans, and Kansas City. Well, Nugget ain't shy. He likes to talk. I'll take you over to his place."

Nugget is the duly elected mayor, and the miner whose strike led to this bustling, if somewhat rowdy, city two miles above sea level.

His name is Allane Auchinleck, but in this rapidly expanding boomtown, he is called Mayor "Nugget." The nickname comes from one of the geological wonders of our Western territories and, indeed, the world.

Roughly one year ago, Nugget found one of the richest silver veins—in a cave that was unearthed by a stray stick of dynamite. The mayor gladly allows me inside his home, a three-story masterpiece of wood, where his den houses the great miracle of silver— a nugget, shaped like a diamond, that weighs 1,776 pounds. On occasion, Nugget says, he used to chip some off when he was short on cash, but now that his mine is working shifts around the clock and his company has expanded into three other mines that aren't as productive as Dead Broke No. 1 but certainly bring envious looks from less fortunate operators, his credit is good across Dead Broke, Colorado, and, indeed, our entire United States.

"If I ever wanted to see England or Germany or Africa, I guess my credit would be good in them places, too," he says. Then grins. "And if it wasn't no good, I'd just buy the country for myself."

The gem is one of the wonders of the world. Four guards, each armed with four pistols, a shotgun, and a Winchester repeating rifle, are on duty every minute of every day. Six men have been killed trying to steal this fortune, three killed outright, and three more hanged after a speedy (three minutes is indeed speedy) trial on the front porch of the wonderful home of Mayor Nugget.

Dead Broke, dear readers, is far from broke.

As I sip fine bourbon on the covered and screened porch of Mayor Nugget's home, the peals of hammers, the whines of saws, the snorts of oxen, the squeaking of heavy wheels of wagons, the songs of workers, and the curses of mule skinners come from all directions. Dead Broke constantly grows. More and more people arrive, some to seek their fortune in the rugged mountains, others to take their fortunes from men and women who live and work here.

My first sight of a bloody and ghastly shootout is far from all one finds in this magnificent city. Although I stopped counting the number of saloons at 43 and the number of brothels and cribs after 69, I have found three theaters—*Othello* was being staged on my first evening by a troupe from London at the Camelot, while a reading of Milton was scheduled at the Paramount and a burlesque attracted a standing-room-only crowd at the Dead Broke Entertainment Hall. One can find the usual beef houses and cafés with checkered curtains, but there are six Chinese restaurants, three places serving spicy chow from south of the border, a French bistro, four German names, and Jake's Italian Q-Zeen. There are four doctors, two dentists, nine undertakers, three cobblers, sixteen livery stables. The population is 9,889, Mayor Nugget tells me.

One of the guards beside the Diamond Nugget clears his throat.

"Them five that got kilt yesterday," he points out.

Our fine, bearded, rail-thin mayor laughs, and he faces me. "How many folks was on that stagecoach you rode in on?"

"Twelve inside," I say, "three in the boot, six up top. Plus me."

Nugget looks back at the guard who had spoken.

"Take away five, that's ninety-eight eighty-four. Plus twenty-one . . . Hey, Nugget, we've topped ten thousand. Not even counting the inkslinger, since he'll be going back East."

"That's cause for a celebration," Nugget says, and he takes me to the Paramount for a performance—and no one cares to hear my argument that Dead Broke is still ninety-five living residents short of ten thousand.

But aged bourbon and a wonderful ballet make me forget about such picayune thoughts. The air is fresh when we depart the theater, the skies so close one can almost touch the stars, and even at ten in the evening, Dead Broke is alive and well. Banjos and tinny pianos play all across this city.

Slick Gene is killed the next day. Shot in the back.

"Dagnabbit!" Mayor Nugget roars. "Now we're below ten thousand. That's it. I'm bringin' real law to this city! I'm sendin' fer Syd Jones."

"Syd Jones!" I cry out.

Syd Jones, the lawman who tamed Denver. Who tamed Laramie. Who cleaned up Tucson and Dodge City. Who shot it out with the Jones Gang in Prescott, Arizona Territory, and buried all four of them. The hero of fifty-nine dime novels—of which I penned four of the liveliest and best-selling, and highly recommend *Slick Syd; or, The Silver Star's Chase After the Dirtiest Scoundrel in Arizona Territory*—and the man who could light a match in a woman's mouth from forty-four paces with a single shot, blindfolded, and fired over his left shoulder without peeping.

"That's right . . . we're bringin' law and order to

Dead Broke, so folks will stop writing that 'Dead' is what Dead Broke is all about."

Yes, Dear Readers, Dead Broke is changing. Dead Broke is losing its roughshod, violent ways. Syd Jones will tame this town. And as the silver keeps coming in by the ton and ton and tons more, Dead Broke is far from Dead. Dead Broke is rich, vibrant, and soon to be safe for all sexes, all ages, all citizens of our glorious United States.

Dead Broke will live forever.

Visit our website at
KensingtonBooks.com
to sign up for our newsletters, read
more from your favorite authors, see
books by series, view reading group
guides, and more!

BOOK CLUB
BETWEEN THE **CHAPTERS**

Become a Part of Our
Between the Chapters Book Club
Community and Join the Conversation

Betweenthechapters.net